UNBEKNOWNST

People of Oregon, 1845 - 1881

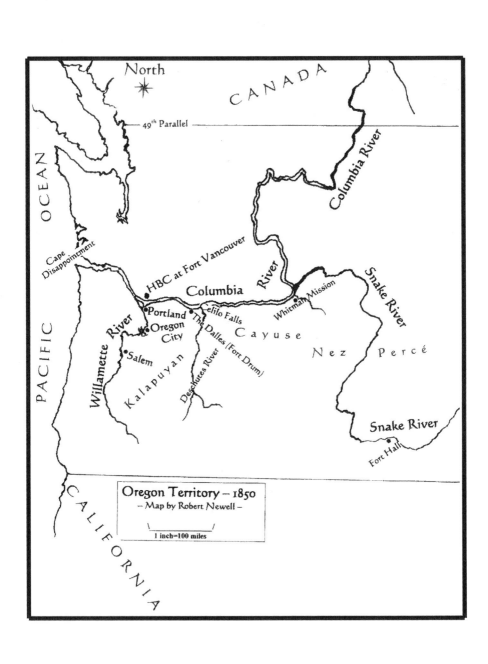

UNBEKNOWNST

People of Oregon, 1845 - 1881

A Novel by

RC Marlen

RC Marlen's books and eBooks may be ordered through booksellers,
various sites on the Internet,
and directly from the author at:
www.rcmarlen.com

This book is historical fiction and continues the story, some characters, and times that were presented in RC Marlen's book *GRIST*. The author devised the story with daily scenes and dialogue around actual historical events as the formation of Oregon Territory, Cayuse Wars, Whitman Mission Massacre, development of Oregon City and Champoeg, happenings at Hudson's Bay Company, et cetera. Many newspaper articles and letters are authentic; Joseph L. Meek's stories were found in several sources and believed to be true; descriptions of the homes of the Newells, Meeks, and Baileys are described from facts. As noted in the List of Characters, the author created the fictional family of the McAlisters. All other characters are historic figures.

Readers with an interest in the historical research are encouraged to consult the list of books at the end, although it is not a complete list of all books referenced.

To emphasize again, all the characters in this novel are authentic, except for the McAlister family, who were conceived in order to weave together a compelling storyline within the flow of actual history.

ISBN: 978-0-9906247-1-4

Sunbird Press
Salem, Oregon

Front Cover: Tools used by a blacksmith during the reenactment of old-time blacksmiths at Champoeg State Park on Living History: Blacksmith Day, July 2014.

Back Cover: Mount Hood and Trillium Lake

ALSO BY RC MARLEN

A TRILOGY:

—

Inside the Hatboxes, 2005
The Drugstore, 2006
Tangled Threads, 2008

AND THE PREQUEL:

—

Drop of Fire, 2009

HISTORICAL NOVELS ABOUT OREGON:

—

GRIST: A Story of Life in Oregon Country, 2012

Unbeknownst II: Time Travel to Mid-Nineteenth Century Oregon, 2014

LIST OF CHARACTERS:

MAIN HISTORICAL CHARACTERS (in order of appearance in story):

18?? -1851	James D. Saules (Black Saul)
1807-1869	Robert Newell (a.k.a. Doc or Bob)
1812-1882	Margaret Jewett Bailey, née Smith
1807-1876	Dr. William John Bailey
1810-1875	Joseph Lafayette Meek
1819-1907	Albert Bayless
1826-1910	George Luther Boone
1830-1917	Louis Southworth
1823-1907	Mary Ann Bayless

FICTIONAL CHARACTERS:
MacAlister Family

OTHER HISTORICAL CHARACTERS (in order of appearance in story):

Kitty Newell: married Robert Newell in 1834, member of Nez Percé tribe. She and Robert Newell had five children who are referred to as *Métis* at different times in this book.

Sarah and Eliza Flett: young sisters (9 and 10 years old) who lived with Margaret Jewett Bailey in 1845 for a few years.

Mary Jane Holmes: Black girl (1841-1925) living in Salem and other nearby areas.

Children of Robert Newell and Kitty (with birth dates): Francis (6/14/1835), William (3/30/1838), Marcus Whitman (4/17/1840), Robert, Jr. (2/28/1842, Thomas Jefferson (11/25/1843).

Oofaaf: elderly man from Kalapuyan tribe.

John McLoughlin: Chief Factor of The Hudson's Bay Company (often called the Fort).

George Winslow: Black man who, in 1834, came to Oregon from California with Ewing Young's party of eight men.

Cockstock: Indian from Wasco tribe.

Dr. Elijah White: physician for Methodist Mission, 1837-1840, sub-Indian agent in 1842.

Lieutenant William Peel: Member of the British Navy, son of Prime Minister of Great Britain.

Captain H.W. Parke: Member of the British Royal Marines.

Virginia Meek: third wife of Joseph Meek, daughter of Nez Percé Chief *Kowesote* and sister of Kitty Newell.

Holmes family – Robin and his wife, Polly: slaves who came in largest wagon train (fifty-four wagons) to Oregon in 1844 with three of their children – Harriet, Celi Ann, and Mary Jane.

Nathaniel Ford: White owner who kept the Holmes family in slavery and leader of the wagon train, which brought the Holmes family to Oregon.

Milton and William Sublette: fur trappers with Newell and Meek.

Mountain Lamb: (a.k.a. *Umentucken Tukutsey Undewatsey*) first wife of Joseph Meek and member of Snake Tribe.

Marguerite McLoughlin: wife of John McLoughlin.

Matthew P. Deady: Prominent lawyer of the times; handled the Baileys' divorce and had brief contact with Holmeses in custody case for their children.

Rebecca Newman Newell (1832-1867): second wife of Robert Newell, married in June of 1846, mother of eleven children.

George Abernethy: owner of a general store in Oregon City, Governor of Provisional Government of Oregon from 1845-1848, Treasurer of *The Oregon Printing Company*.

Peter Skene Ogden: employee of The Hudson's Bay Company.

Chief Joseph (1785-1871): (a.k.a. *Tuekakas*) eloquent and wise leader of the Nez Percé.

Reuben Boise: Attorney for the case *Holmes vs. Ford* that was resolved in 1853 in favor of a Negro.

George H. Williams: presiding Chief justice of Oregon's Territorial Supreme Court for *Holmes vs. Ford*, an unprecedented case of a Negro winning over a White.

Asahel Bush (1824-1913): original owner and editor of Salem's newspaper *The Statesman*, strong figure in Oregon's democratic party, and founder of the Ladd and Bush Bank.

Harvey Higley, owner of the third general store built in Champoeg; it was the tallest building in the town and was destroying in the 1861 flood.

PART I

Robert and Rebecca Newell in Oregon Country
1845 – 1848

Gravestone Honoring Black Pioneers (front and back)
Located in Salem Pioneer Cemetery on Commercial Street (between Rural and Hoyt Streets).

The Salem Pioneer Cemetery is cared for by:
City View Funeral Home
390 Hoyt Street S, Salem, Oregon
(Offices located across from the cemetery entrance.)
www.city-view.org

CHAPTER 1

FALL OF 1845

To her right, the eastern sky began to glow with a faint hint of light and the stars began to dim. She looked one last time at the North Star that had guided her through the night and whispered, "Good Night, Polaris. It's time for us to sleep." She thanked the bears – Ursa Major and Ursa Minor – who had kept her company, and then she scanned the woods for a safe place to bed down.

Soon the firmament began to dazzle; fuchsia and purple splashed above the horizon in vertical spires against a deep blue-gray background. She stared at the show and smiled, though only for a moment, for it faded fast and the world was becoming light; fear seeped back into her stomach. She needed to hide. After locating a cedar with low hanging boughs, she crawled under it and into the shadows. Years of accumulated needles were there; she pushed them into a pile for a bed as she had done on previous nights, carefully accumulating more and more for warmth and comfort. Finally, she pulled off her Grandpappy's coat and covered herself. After walking for more than eight hours, sleep came easily; she closed her eyes and asked the tree to stand guard, "Don't let them find me."

She dreamed of the times when her grandfather had taught her about the stars in the heavens. In his voice, the words came to her: "Mattie, remember, if you can't find Ursa Minor, it's because that little bear likes to hide sometimes. At those times, I look for Orion. He's easy to see and he always seems to be there. Look above his belt of three for the top, brightest star – it points to Polaris, the North Star. Remember this and you'll never be lost." And hours passed.

She woke from her dream with bittersweet emotions rippling down her skin in gooseflesh. Motionless and with eyes tightly closed, she relived the dream – her grandfather's words echoing in her ears. Through her closed eyes she saw daylight, so she would wait until dark to continue her journey. Finally, she crawled to the other side of the tree trunk and peed.

When she crept back to where she had bedded, it was no longer warm. Pulling the coat snugly around herself, she crouched against the trunk and thought. *Grandpappy.* A tear popped from one eye and slipped down her cheek. Only a week ago they had been together, laughing and talking. She took her grandfather's flask from the coat pocket and drank some water. From another pocket, she removed a strip of *charqui* and tore a bite of the dried mutton with her teeth. As she chewed on the meat, she thought about the happenings from the past month and gnawed at the memories until she had broken them down enough to swallow. *Grandpappy died peacefully in his sleep last Sunday and my life no longer had any peace. I guess my problems really started when Mama died last month.*

Living on the high plains in the Siskiyou Mountains, she grew up amid sounds of sheep and piles of wool. Her grandfather had brought Mattie and her mother as household slaves when he came from Kentucky with his son, daughter-in-law, and their two sons, Jed and Tom; but she only knew about coming from Kentucky because she had been told. Eleven-year-old Mattie could not remember how long she had lived in California. *Until last week, my life was wonderful.* She had chores, but everyone had chores. Her mother did all the cooking and serving as well as the washing. Mattie cleaned the house, fed the chickens, and helped with all her mother's work. Mattie's favorite job was polishing the shoes; there were so many shoes. She would sit on the floor in the pantry, polishing and trying them on, and then walking out into the kitchen in all the different shoes to show her mother. They would laugh at the oversized shoes on her feet. She liked that.

In fact, when she ran away last night, she knew exactly which shoes were best to take for this long journey – no girl shoes. Using Jed's shoes required two pair of wool socks for her feet not to slip. She was headed north to Oregon Country. As she ran from the house in the dark, she pulled a pair of boy's breeches and two shirts from the clotheslines in the back of the house. They had dried. When she was far enough from the house where no one could see her, she put on one shirt and the breeches, tucking her homespun dress deep into the pant legs for warmth and winding the other shirt around her neck against the wind. When leaving, she had grabbed all the possessions that her grandfather had given her before he had died as well as his hat and coat that she took from a hook near the back door. Because of her thick, curly hair, his leather hat with a wide brim fit fine on her head. While changing her clothes, she had knelt on the ground and untied the string from around the end of her pillowcase. She dumped it, looking for her Grandpappy's belt and knife. She fed the belt through the pant loops, buttoned the hunting knife case around the belt, and cinched the belt tightly around her waist to the hole she had hammered into the leather the day before. She had kept the nail, thinking it might come in handy, and dropped it into the tinderbox her Grandpappy had given her. A fishhook was in the tinderbox, as well; she was a good fisherman. After dressing, she quickly put everything back into her pillowcase before heading north. She had been planning to leave since the first night after Grandpappy died when they came and forced themselves on her.

Suddenly, her daydreaming ended as she realized the darkness had arrived. Hurriedly, she gathered her things and stood. She looked up to the heavens to find the Little Bear and the North Star before wending. She headed north, but her thoughts stayed in the south in the only house she had ever known. *Without Mama and Grandpappy, it was not the same place anymore.*

Problems had begun when her mother died. The problems started when additional jobs were distributed among the family as a result of the work that her mother had done, but work that a girl of eleven could not do. Everyone was crabby with added tasks, yet a larger reason for the irritability loomed over the adults. The death of Mattie's mother had been caused by the carelessness of Grandpappy's two grandsons, Jed and Tom McAlister.

Those two grown boys had been hoisting heavy sacks of grain into the upper loft of the barn, using the horse to pull the ropes. They stopped their work with a sack suspended over the door to the milk parlor. The rope was taut and held by the horse when they went behind the barn. They claimed they went to relieve themselves, but everyone thought otherwise – to have a drink or smoke.

Mattie's mother came from the house while they were gone. She was going to milk the cow and was singing like she always did. The rope snapped just as she passed below the sack of grain. Whether it was the impact of the heavy sack crushing and killing her or the rock where her head hit, no one knew for certain. She bled a lot from the head wound, but the bleeding didn't prove anything. What they did know was this: dead is dead. And she was dead when the boys came back and found her.

The abrupt end to her singing was heard in the shed where the boys' father worked, and he went out to see. He was furious and beat the boys with the horsewhip, "You're supposed to inspect the ropes before this kind of job. Damn it all! That rope is threadbare in more places than the snapped part. We have plenty of rope and it only takes a minute to change it. Shit! Tom," he screamed, "don't you run from me! Stand and take your medicine like a man." The coil of the whip reached and caught the eighteen-year-old by his ankles and the boy dropped. The father beat those two for ten minutes and then sat on a stump by the backdoor and cried. His wife stood at the door with a hint of a smile on her face.

At that very moment, Mattie and Grandpappy walked up from the creek with some fish on a string and came upon this scene. Mattie saw her mother on the ground and ran to her. Grandfather followed. He had to pull the hysterical child off her mother. Before he turned to walk to the house with the screaming and kicking Mattie, Grandpappy raised his voice to demand, "Are you all crazy? Have the four of you no decency? Tom and Jed, wrap her in a blanket and then dig a hole so we can put her to rest." He looked at his smiling daughter-in-law when he entered the house and cursed, "Damn it all. You're not going to smile for long. She was your workhorse and now you get to do it all." The realization of his words dissolved her grin. "Bring me a basin of water and a cloth. This child is distraught."

After her mother was gone, Tom and Jed taunted Mattie at every opportunity, "You're our slave. A black, ugly slave who needs to do whatever we say."

One day, just for meanness, they held her down and cut her long braid and scoffed, "And you can't run to Grandpappy for help. He's gone to the neighbors and ain't here to help ya." She put her hands to her head and felt her cropped hair. It didn't even come to the top of her dress.

And every day, they would repeat, "Did you understand me yesterday? He's our grandpappy, not yours. How can he be yours? You're black and he's white."

Mattie was holding two tin cups of water, which they had asked her to fetch, but when she came close, they picked up the downed acorns at their feet and threw them at her. Those words about Grandpappy confused her. All of them had the same last name; she was Mary Anne McAlister. Her Grandpappy was a McAlister, like Tom and Jed. She had never thought about the color of her skin and his. He always had been her Grandpappy.

"Come on, Girl, we want our water. We been working hard, splitting this firewood."

As fast as they could pick up acorns, they barraged her with the hard and often broken shells of the acorns. Jed was just a year younger than his brother, but twice as mean, "If you don't bring me my water, I'm going to whip you. Slaves get whipped for not obeying."

She took a step and they pitched more acorns as hard and fast as they could. Then, Jed noticed a small rock about the size of an acorn and sent it flying. It hit just above her eye and she screamed, dropping the cups.

The scream brought their mother outside. She walked out to Mattie and grabbed the girl by the ear, "Mattie, let them work. With you here, they ain't goin' to do nothin' but play with ya. Now git!" As Mattie ran to the house, crying, she added, "Git that ironing done quick. And I need help with supper."

When Grandpappy came home that night, he washed the gaping wound on her brow and consoled her about the cut braid, saying, "It'll grow long again. You just as pretty without it." As he tended to the cut, he began to sing *The Riddle*:

> I gave my love a cherry that has no stone
> I gave my love a chicken that has no bone
> I gave my love a ring that has no end
> I gave my love a baby with no cryin'

"Sing with me, Mattie. Let me hear your beautiful voice."

How can there be a cherry that has no stone?
How can there be a chicken that has no bone?
How can there be a ring that has no end?
How can there be a baby with no cryin'?

He stopped his singing and reached for his fiddle. "You sing the last verse while I play." In a soft voice, she sang:

A cherry when it's bloomin' it has no stone
A chicken in an eggshell it has no bone
A ring when it is rollin' it has no end
A baby when it's sleepin' has no cryin'

The song sparked a memory of the riddle of her color. Mattie asked, "How can you be my Grandpappy if you white skinned and me and my mama are Negroes?"

"Mattie," he hesitated, "I should call you Mary Anne. I named you when you were born. You were so little and the best thing that ever happened in my life."

"Grandpappy, that don't explain nothing."

"I know, I know. Give me time. I just ain't too sure that you're old enough to understand."

"Tell me."

He wiped his lips with his handkerchief, returned it to his pocket, and took a deep breath. "It all has to do with my son. You see ... he has always loved your mother. Because of that you were born."

Mattie gasped.

"He loved her from the first day when I came back from buying her at the slave auction. No, that ain't right. My son is mean and always has been. It took a few weeks for your ma to see that we were goin' to be good to her, and that's when she began to sing. He never loved anybody in his whole life until he heard your ma singing. She sang as clear as a mockingbird and as melodious as a meadowlark. Well, you know! And you sing as pretty as she did.

"Your ma was always happy and singing hymns. The songs went to his heart and that's when I saw somethin' I never thought possible. He loved her and what was more amazing was that she loved him. Yep, I never knew why she loved the mean and hard man that he was. Humph, and his sons are just like him – meaner than hell. We both know that."

"I do. They both are mean to me when you or my mama ain't here. But their pa was never mean to me." She stopped with a frown before saying, "He's really my pa, too?"

He pursed his lips and nodded. "But he wasn't nice like a pa should be. Ain't that right?" Mattie blinked as her mind absorbed who she was. Her Grandpappy just went on talking with a far-off look in his eyes. He peered out into nowhere and muttered, "I was so happy the day you were born. I remember your ma saying to him that he made her so happy to give her a little girl. 'Now, promise you be good to her always,' she said. And I heard him promise. But for him, to be good to you just meant to ignore you.

"Now you can understand why my daughter-in-law was smiling when your mother died. My son has always loved your mother more than her. So, it don't matter the color of my skin and yours. You are my granddaughter and he is your father." He took her hand and placed it next to his. He pointed at their hands, "Look, you ain't as dark as your ma was. See, you is honey brown. And your hair is softer, not kinky. Just curly! You're going to be a beautiful woman when you grown. I hope I git to see you."

Mattie threw her arms around him and buried her head into his shoulder, "I love you, Grandpappy."

"Okay, that's enough of explaining. Let's git my tinderbox and have another lesson on makin' a fire. I'm gittin' cold. Remember, when you can make a fire here in my room for me, the tinderbox is yours to keep."

Mattie looked to the sky to check her direction and started walking faster. She wondered how long she had been thinking because she had lost track of the time. *I need to stay alert and look for danger. I shouldn't let my mind wander like that.* It was getting colder and clouds were coming in. She pulled Grandpappy's hat down tighter on her head, tucking her hair under it to make a closer fit, and picked up her pace. Touching her hair reminded her of how she got the nickname of Mattie. Her mother had told her: when she was just a baby, one of the boys remarked that her hair was all matted and he started calling her Mattie. Soon the name became a term of endearment and everyone called her the same.

Traveling by the stars was not her only reference; a well-marked trail went through the Siskiyou Mountains. It was a trail made by the natives and used for centuries, but she avoided it. Walking directly on the trail would put her in plain sight if the family came looking for her, and Indians could see her as well. She kept moving away from the trail and closer to the trees. Soon she was going downhill at a good pace. Swallowing with a dry throat, she reached for the flask and then remembered it was empty. She mumbled, "Grandpappy's flask don't hold much water." She knew it was a flask for spirits, not water. Though she had no other container, she did not worry knowing that she would find water in the many streams at the bottom of hills.

Most eleven-year-old girls would not have attempted a journey such as this. Mattie was like her Grandpappy – resourceful and confident. After traveling three days, the way seemed easier, not more difficult. Though it was December, it was mild and fishing in the rivers was second nature to her. One day she found a hollow log and floated most the day down the Willamette River, sleeping while she floated until the river got rough. Then she paddled to shore with a thick, flat piece of the bark she had pulled from the red cedar. She rested until dark and started walking again.

And the days passed.

Only a few times did she smell smoke from someone's campfire or cabin. In the darkness, she did not know where they were, but she walked with caution until the smell faded. It didn't seem strange to her that she saw no people, because she walked at night. She worried more about animals – the cougars and bears.

Although she was not counting the days, she knew a couple of weeks had passed and realized it was only a matter of time before she would come upon people. She had no plan about what she would do or say. She was like the other animals roaming in Oregon, seeking food, finding shelter for sleep, and living life with nature. She took each day and enjoyed her freedom from her brothers and their mother.

* * *

One rainy evening as she awoke from her daytime sleep, she reached around the tree, which served as her bedroom, and grabbed what she thought was a knobby bump on the bark. It moved! Mattie whimpered in surprise.

"What's da matter wit you? Are ya hurt?"

Though he spoke in not much more than a whisper, Mattie jumped at the sound of a man's voice and turned her face toward the questioner. She had no time to respond before he was talking again.

"No! Don't talk," he uttered in a whispered whoop. "Jus' put your face back down. They a-goin' ta see us 'cuz of your face shinin' like the moon." He pulled on his hand. "An' let go of my hand. You squeezin' it so hard."

Puzzled, Mattie released his rough hand from hers.

The rain began to plummet like pebbles, but the cacophony of water pounding on the land didn't drown the sound of horses coming at a gallop. By this man's conduct, she knew danger was approaching so she yanked her hat farther down over her face. Huddled there, she wondered why she had not run away. She wondered why she was allowing him to tell her what to do. He was a stranger and could hurt her. But, when six horses stopped ten feet from the tree, those thoughts flowed away like the water streaming between her boots.

One of the riders complained, "It's too dark and ya can't see a thing in this damn rain. Did you see where he went?"

She heard a few negative grunts from the other horsemen.

In a smooth movement, Mattie crumpled to the ground into a ball beneath her dark coat and the man hiding with her eased down slowly like a bough bending in the breeze. In the darkness, they blended into the base of the tree, looking much like a burl on the trunk – just a knobby growth. They remained motionless. The woods had bushes and brush growing here and there, the Willamette River rolling quietly in a curve only fifty feet from them, and heavy tree growth covering the banks.

The same rider continued, "I don't hear any hoof beats, but he can't be that far ahead. Spread out and see if he stopped around here."

Soon she heard the clop of hooves, riding away. With muscles clenched, she strained not to move. Mattie feared that one of the riders might have remained behind as a lookout and would see them.

Minutes later the horses returned.

"That's the trouble with a darky; you can't see 'em in the dark." No one laughed. He cursed with a loud voice and then said, "Let's go home. At least we let him know that he needs to git out of Oregon. The law is the law." They trotted off to the north.

Silence, except for the falling rain and the hum of the rolling river, but still the two did not move. Minutes passed. While breathing deeply to relax, she wondered. *What law could they be talking about?* Huddled beneath her coat, she smelled the fear, which had oozed from her skin.

Finally, the man unfolded from his squat and, in a normal tone of voice, told her, "They gone. You can git up."

When Mattie peeked out, she saw only the silhouette of a man standing above her with droplets of water dripping off the brim of his leather hat and down his back. Instantly, remembering her half-brothers coming to her bed to abuse her, she feared being raped by this stranger. When she rose to his side, she was close enough to see that the brim on his hat was wide, well-worn, and discolored where, over the years, his fingertips had slipped up and down the edges to adjust the fit on his head. In fear, she thought about running.

His eyes darted to the left and right while he asked, "What you doin' out here alone? You ain't nothin' but a boy." He hesitated, "Since I don' know ya, are you a runaway?"

Mattie was as tall as this man and she had instant relief knowing that he thought she was a boy. For the first time, she was glad that her hair was short. Between the falling raindrops, she looked into his black eyes and saw his concern, yet she shook her head and said, "No, not me."

With a tilt of his head and a twinkle in his eye, he said, "Aw, I think ya is a runaway." And they grinned like old friends or partners in crime.

Mattie asked, "What was the law they talked about?"

Before answering, he cupped his hands around his mouth and imitated some kind of owl and then turned to her, "My name is James D. Saules. What's your name?"

"Glad to meet you, Mr. Saules. I'm Mat ... " and she hesitated only an instant before becoming, "Matthew."

"Oh, call me Black Saul like everyone does." He turned toward the sound of a horse approaching as Mattie dropped to the ground under her coat. "Git back up. It's Cricket, my horse. He comes when I make that owl call. Wish I could make an authen'ic sound like a cricket, but I can't." He grimaced and said, "I been thinkin' I need to leave. I can give you a ride if it ain't far to your place."

"I don't ...." This time she could not think fast enough to know how to answer.

"Like I said, I think you is a runaway with nowhere to go."

The rain started falling harder. In Oregon, the rain was always fluctuating – starting and stopping with soft drizzles, misty sprays, or thudding droplets. Sometimes it rained with sunshine. But in winter, most of the time the rain fell for days, and this was December.

Black Saul turned to Cricket, put his foot in the stirrup, and with a smooth motion pulled up into the saddle. "Give me your hand and come with me to a friend's cabin that's close by. I can't take the chance of jus' standing here; I needs to go. My friend might help ya out."

Mattie hesitated and looked over her shoulder at the woods, where she felt safe, before lifting her hand to his. He was skinny but strong and pulled her up to sit behind him before they started north.

"We'll follow the river; those men took the road. I goin' to Doc Newell's place. His real name is Robert Newell. Do ya know him?"

"No."

"Well, most folks just call him Doc or Bob. Everybody 'roun' here knows him. So you ain't from here. Is that right?"

Mattie didn't answer at first. She took a deep breath and frowned in the darkness before answering, "Maybe I met him." Changing the subject she repeated her question, "What law were they talking about?"

"They mean the Lash Law, I guess. You gotta know 'bout it."

Again she didn't respond and he began to explain, "Some of the newcomers from wagon trains don't want us niggers here in Oregon, so they whip us when they want and we's 'posed to leave."

The law about which he spoke was confusing, for one reason, because it never went into effect before it was repealed. People often called it the Lash Law of 1844. It was an act dealing with Slavery, Free Negroes, and

Mulattoes. Section 1 declared, 'Slavery and involuntary servitude shall be forever prohibited in Oregon.' Sections 2 and 3 stipulated that Negroes of slaveholders and free Negroes had three years to leave Oregon County. Negro children could stay until eighteen years old but then had to leave. The penalty for not abiding by this law was a whipping – a lashing. The law stated that the offender would receive upon his or her bare back not less than twenty nor more than thirty-nine stripes, to be inflicted by the constable of the proper county.' If the Negro did not leave, six months later the punishment could be repeated.

"I thought we were free here in Oregon. This is Oregon, isn't it?" She had a lump in her throat and a fear in her stomach. "I feel a little sick."

He chuckled, "Now I knows you a runaway. Yep, this is Oregon. We got less than ten miles to go. It won't be long. Doc can look at you if you is sick and you can rest wit' him."

They rode along the Willamette River, weaving around growing trees and downed ones. They passed only a few small log cabins, which looked deserted, and they frightened a couple of black-tailed deer out of the bushes.

At one point, Mattie reached into her pocket to clutch her Grandpappy's tinderbox. It brought her comfort.

Black Saul started talking again. "Ya asked me 'bout the law those men talked 'bout and I ain't good at explainin'. In Oregon they say slaves are free, but the law say we can't stay but for three years. After three years we's 'posed to leave. It don't make much sense. Why, I came by ship 'bout three years ago. So I been here since forty-one and ain't nobody bother me 'til last year when they made that new Lash Law."

Bewildered and worrying that she would never be free, she asked, "Why did you come to Oregon?"

"Remember, I tol' ya I came on a ship in eighteen forty-one. I was a cook on the ship and then decided to stay. Back then there weren't nobody ta bother me 'bout bein' here. I picked me a fine wife." He laughed, "Well, that weren't quite true. This Indian lady picked me and wanted me to stay. It was the ship called *Peacock* I came on, and it went aground at the mouth of the Columbia River. They call it Cape Disappointment 'cuz so many ships haves troubles there."

It was a well-known fact that many a captain sailing a ship had trouble at the mouth of the Columbia River; it forms a bay twenty-five miles long by six or so miles wide and has a multitude of points and promontories. There are two channels or entrances over this infamous bar, with middle sands holding the bones of many vessels.

"So I hads to wait for another ship called *The Porpoise*." He laughed again. "She tol' me to stay wit' her so I jumped ship and here I is still."

His deep voice, telling his stories, relaxed her a little and helped her not to think about her predicament. Even so, a subtle fear floated inside her chest. On the other hand, whenever she remembered she was going to meet a stranger – she felt panic. To distract herself, she asked, "What do you do here?"

"Why, when I came it don't take me but a short time to see that people need transportation up and down the Columbia River. So I got me a boat called a *bateau*. I been tol' that's a French word for this flat bottom boat. You know 'em 'cuz everybody's got 'em here in Oregon. With my *bateau* I can transport people and goods. I git to see lots of places, and I bought a farm last year near Oregon City. Oh, an' I do odd jobs at the Methodist Mission in Astoria from time to time. But what I like best to do is playin' my fiddle for people. I good at fiddlin' and can play all night if there's somethin' to whet my whistle. I play fine dancin' tunes."

James D. Saules just kept talking. Mattie shivered every now and then, though not from being wet, holding on to Black Saul warmed her; she shivered because she was scared. After a while, the rain abated and the overcast sky opened with a bright half moon drifting among the nimbus clouds, which lurked full of rain just waiting to perform again. However, even without rain, they still got wetter – riding below tree boughs, water often cascaded down on them.

"Why don't you tell ol' Black Saul 'bout your story? Where you from?"

Mattie didn't want to tell anything and changed the subject again, "Who were those men on horseback? Why were they after you?"

"Oh, I don't know 'em. I jus' know they newcomers. You know, some of those new people who come on wagons to live here. They is high-flown and ain't like the old-timers. I rode over from my place and was tryin' to deliver some papers that The Hudson's Bay Company asked me to give to Doc. Those men saw me, pulled me off Cricket, and tol' me they goin' to give me a lashin' right there. I got away and you saw what happened after that."

The land opened into a prairie as far as they could see in the moonlight, and they left the riverside. They traveled east of the river and it started to rain again.

"We's almost there. I hear'd that Doc put down a wood floor. His wife is Kitty. She's most likely real happy 'bout that floor 'cuz it was jus' clay b'fore." He talked until they came to a solitary cabin.

Before they dismounted, Robert Newell opened his door and came out with a barking dog, "Well, Black Saul! I wondered who was coming at this late hour. Who is that with you?" He stood under a short roof over a porch and waited for the riders to come out of the rain. He was tall and thin, wore a leather vest over his sun-faded flannel shirt, and had brown galluses, with leather buttonholes, holding up his pants.

After Black Saul slid down from his saddle and helped Mattie off the horse, he greeted his friend on the porch with wild backslapping and laughs. "Hell, I is on business." He fumbled with a button on his shirt pocket before slipping out a damp and crinkled envelope. "This here is from the Fort."

"I think I know what it's about." And Doc, with only a glance at his name on the outside of the folded paper, slipped it into his vest pocket.

As the introductions were made, a woman came out of the cabin and Doc Newell turned, "Margaret, here is Black Saul. He came with this boy who is cold, tired, and probably as hungry as he is. That pot of deer stew you brought me will fill them. Let's all go inside. Black Saul, you know where the barn is. Go give Cricket some feed. Hurry back to get warmed and filled with some good food."

When Black Saul headed to the barn, Mattie kept her head down and stayed in the same spot, shuffling her feet.

So, Margaret approached her. "I'm Margaret Bailey. I live not far from here. This is my dog Crow. I know he is as black as a crow, but that's not why I named him that. It's because he likes to chase crows."

Giving the dog a pat on the head, Mattie said, "My name's Mat ... Matthew McAlister. Glad to meet you." And her legs crumpled.

Doc Newell grabbed her with his arms around her dripping coat, "Let's get you inside to sit. Margaret, he's soaked. Will you see if we have some dry clothes for him?" Doc took her hat and dropped it onto the table as he walked her toward the hearth where a rocking chair stood; he lowered her into it and slipped her arms from her Grandpappy's wet, oversized coat. A trail of water had dripped across the new floor.

The house was located in the French Prairie and was a one-room log cabin similar to the others Mattie and Black Saul had passed that evening. It smelled of cooked meat, wood smoke, herbs and roots. As Mattie looked around, she saw that it was not made of lumber from a sawmill – the logs were hewn. Only the new floor was cut planks, like Black Saul had mentioned.

When Black Saul came back from the barn, he and Margaret started chatting like the old friends whom they were. That's when Mattie noticed that she had dripped water from the door to the rocker and she lifted her face to Newell. "I've soiled your new floor. I'm sorry."

He laughed and insisted, "It may be fairly new, but I've done worse to it with mud and horse manure."

She liked his face – rugged and strong, creased from sun and wind. The beard on his chin touched his chest and was graying, yet his mustache remained the color of his youth, a dark and rich brown. He was slender with hardened muscles from his trapping days. Mattie relaxed from his laugh and words.

Finally, Doc said, "You look to be the size of my older sons. I'll see if I can find some dry clothes for you."

Mattie clutched the shirt buttons near her small breasts before saying, "I just need to sit by the fire. I'll dry." She looked downward in embarrassment and saw the bricks around the hearth, forming a half-circle design; she concentrated on the pattern to calm herself.

Margaret started putting bowls on the table and noticed that something didn't seem right. She puzzled as to why the boy was clutching his shirt. The men noticed nothing. She thought that the boy was pretty enough to be a girl.

Black Saul asked, "Where's Kitty and your five boys?"

Margaret turned to look at Black Saul, and then stared at Doc before saying, "Allow me to tell him, Robert."

He nodded.

"A little more than a week ago, Kitty passed away. That's why I brought the stew. She was buried just east of here about a thousand feet from the Willamette River on that high hill. The children are staying with different families."

Doc frowned, "I can't handle the five boys without Kitty. Especially the little two-year-old. Joe Meek has my older boys."

"I've been coming from time to time to comfort Robert and bringing some food, but I really must be getting back to my husband." Margaret turned to explain to Mattie, "I'm married to Dr. William Bailey. He was away doctoring a neighbor when I left. Black Saul, maybe you would escort me home after we eat."

"Sho nuff, Miz Margaret, I'd be happy to. It ain't far to go. Doc, I sorry 'bout your wife."

Doc nodded.

"Why don't we ladle out some stew and talk while we eat." Margaret went to the hearth.

The cabin – twenty feet by twenty – was built French Canadian style, with the posts in the ground. It had one big room called the keeping room for doing everything – cooking, eating, sitting with guests, working on projects, and sleeping. There was a bunk bed standing in one corner and a larger bed – covered with a patchwork of deerskins sewn together like puzzle pieces – in the opposite corner with a rope attached high on the walls for a curtain to provide privacy around the bed when needed. A ladder leaned against one of the beams supporting a small loft where his older children had sleeping mats. In the northeast corner was the hearth with two pothooks, which swung out. A Dutch oven hung from one. The rocking chair sat on the other side of the fireplace and a large desk with books and papers scattered on it was in the southeast corner of the room. Several open books were stacked facedown one on the other, waiting for the reader to return to the unfinished pages. The wall behind the desk held the spread wings of a scrub-jay and the cinnamon tail of a red-tailed hawk. The floor beside the desk had a stack of grayish-brown peltry intended for lining in shoes or gloves. The highlight of the cabin was a chifforobe, which covered most of one wall; it had three doors and the center door had a hand-carved design of ribbons in an oval shape. There was only one door in the cabin to go to the outside.

Black Saul slid onto a bench under the window where the table was. Behind him, an oil lamp stood on a wide windowsill and provided light for the whole room. Margaret approached with the Dutch oven and placed the hot pot directly onto the homemade, rough wood table. Doc began to pour stew into the various unmatched bowls with a wooden ladle.

After Margaret removed her apron, she smoothed the skirt on her plaid, merino dress and sat on a chair opposite Doc, saying, "Matthew, come eat. You must be hungry. Doc, would you slice up that Johnny cake so we all could have a piece?"

Mattie sat on the bench next to Black Saul who was taking his first bite of the deer stew.

Never one to mince words, Margaret asked, "Matthew, what are you doing out in the dark by yourself and how old are you?"

"Eleven."

And Margaret continued by saying, "Why did you run away?"

At that very moment, Mattie had just picked up her spoon and Doc had placed the steaming bowl under her nose. Mattie looked to the food and then glanced up to Margaret with doleful eyes.

Margaret relented. "Eat! Just eat. I will ask the question again after you finish your food. Here have a slice of bread, and these jars have sweet jam to put on it."

Mattie smiled and filled her mouth with stew.

Margaret turned to Black Saul and asked, "Did you know that Robert has become a director of the newspaper out of Oregon City? It will be the first newspaper in the west."

Black Saul swallowed and replied, "That so? When?"

Enthusiasm filled Doc's voice, "Yes! Hmm, let me see." He tapped his fingers and seemed to count off items to be done. "Yes, in two months, all should be ready. Maybe in February we'll run the first copy. I need to write up some ads for that first printing. It is to be called *The Oregon Spectator*. Do you like the name?"

"I sho do! You know I can't read, but I could put an ad for my transportation business. Ain't that right?"

Doc slapped his hand on the table. "Of course! By gum, you could advertise about your fiddling, too."

While chewing on a piece of gristle from the venison, Margaret could not speak for the moment, but raised a finger to indicate that she wanted to say something. Finally, she just swallowed the tough lump and said, "I have a writing project as well as Doc. I am working on writing a book, though it might take me ten years to finish it."

Doc looked at her in amazement. "I didn't know you wanted to write a book. Oh, you were supposed to bring me copies of some of your poems. Remember, I picked a few to publish in the newspaper."

With a sly look in her eye, Margaret joked, "I brought up this topic hoping you would remember about my poems. I will bring them tomorrow. Since you just lost Kitty, I didn't know if you were ready to get back to work." At that moment, she had a thought about Matthew speaking well for a Negro and his light coloring made it obvious that he must have a white father or mother. She decided to ask a question that might reveal more information about him. Margaret asked, "Matthew, do you know how to read?"

"No, Ma'am. But I know my letters. My Grandpappy was teaching me my letters and how to read, but he died a while back."

Margaret's face contorted and she said, "I'm sorry for you." Deep in her subconscious, Margaret's sorrow was more for Mattie not knowing how to read than the loss of a grandfather. Anyone who knew Margaret would know that she loved books more than most things in life.

And Robert Newell had a similar love of reading. He was especially fond of Shakespeare and would often surprise people with a quote. In fact, books and the written word were what held their friendship together. Often Margaret and he talked endlessly about a book. Or they discussed a newspaper article or politics. But Robert Newell's heart had a pang of pity for the boy when he heard about the loss of his grandfather. From the one sentence Mattie said, Robert knew the grandfather had loved the boy deeply if he would go against the law to teach him to read.

Black Saul spread some huckleberry jam on a slice of the Johnny cake and asked, "Doc, was anything importan' in that letter I brought ya?"

"Thanks for delivering it." Doc explained, "It was from Joe Meek, and there's a meeting tomorrow night." He figured that Mattie may not know Joe and said, "Joe Meek is a friend of mine and always leaves his messages for me at The Hudson's Bay Company. They send them down with a messenger, like Black Saul."

Mattie batted her eyes in confusion before she realized that Doc was addressing her. She nodded to show understanding.

Margaret asked, "Oh, where's the meeting?"

"It's up at the Fort."

No one could live on the west coast and not know The Hudson's Bay Company at Fort Vancouver. Even a child like Mattie knew. She also knew that The Hudson's Bay Company was Great Britain's fur trapping organization and important to anyone living on the west coast. And she knew 'the Fort' was what people called it.

Doc began to eat again and then looked up from his food. "Let's all go to the meeting together."

With his mouth still full, Black Saul was quick to respond, "No thank you. I ain't going."

Doc looked to Margaret. "The meeting has to do with the British Crown wanting more information about the Northwest. I tell you, the United States can lose their foothold here. We have to get Oregon into the union."

Margaret cradled her coffee cup in her hands. "Maybe I'll go." Then she put her cup down and started complaining. "The United States just riled Mexico by annexing Texas into the union. Do you think they have time for any thoughts on Oregon? Not now! They're headed for a war with Mexico. I tell you, slavery drives America."

Puzzled, Black Saul asked, "Whacha mean?"

"Ha, I should have said that the slaves make America!" Margaret began a rant of how the Negroes are needed for the economy in the United States. "The rich get free labor, our country produces more goods and gets even richer, and those poor people just want to live free." Runaway slaves were a big problem. Back when Spain owned Florida, slaves would run to their freedom and be welcomed across the river from Georgia on the Spanish lands. During the Seminole wars of 1835-1842, runaway slaves fought alongside the Indians who had provided them with a haven from slavery.

More recently, slaves were running to Texas to be free. "Those Southern planters want to make it more difficult for the slaves to run to free land. I know, as soon as they have laws written for Texas, those laws will stop free Negroes from living there. And look at Oregon, trying to find a way not to deal with the Negro. How can we have a law stating that slavery is illegal and, at the same time, beat a Negro if he stays here? What sense does that make? Black Saul is a free man, so why should people be able to use the Lash Law against him? That law may have been repealed, but I know we are heading toward an exclusion law so Negroes can't live here."

Doc sat motionless for a few moments, "Margaret, please, let's not get started on slavery, Mexico, and Oregon. Let's stop all this kind of talk right now."

Before the meal ended Margaret decided to go to the meeting with Doc. They would take Matthew along, but it was decided that the boy would stay overnight right where he was – not at Margaret's place because her husband might be drinking.

At the door, when Margaret was leaving with Black Saul, she called her dog and then turned to Mattie and explained, "I'll see you tomorrow. I want to know you better and see how we can help. Good night."

After they were alone, Mattie began to stack the dishes.

Doc insisted, "Just leave them on the table. We can wipe them in the morning. Why don't you sleep in the loft; it's warmer up there than down here." They walked over to the bunk beds where he pulled a chamber pot with a lid from under the bed. "You can go out and pee tonight, but I'll put this here for you to take a dump. In the morning, I'll show you where to empty it." He stopped talking to give the boy a chance to say something. When the silence prevailed, he continued. "If you don't need anything else, I'll say good night. I'm going out to the barn to check on the animals first."

Mattie said goodnight and climbed the ladder. When she heard him leave the cabin for the barn, she rushed down to the chamber pot and relieved herself quickly before returning to the loft.

Sleep took her as soon as her eyes closed.

● ○ ●

During the night, Mattie woke with a start. A strange noise had interrupted her sleep. It was a low and mournful sound that seemed to be somewhere near. At first, she thought it was outside. Scooting quietly across the floorboards in the loft, she came to the edge near the ladder and realized the sound was in the cabin. On her belly, she peered into the downstairs and saw the cause. Doc sat on the edge of his bed with his face buried in his hands that held some kind of cloth. His back undulated up and down while the low and mournful sound oozed from him.

Mattie watched as he raised his head and peered at the cloth in his hands. *He's holding a dress!* The dress had rows and rows of colorful beads sewn on the bodice. Mattie's fist went to her mouth when she realized what she saw. *He's crying!*

Joseph Lafayette Meek, Mountain Man
Circa 1830-1840
Photographer unknown.

CHAPTER 2

DECEMBER 20, 1845

The next day before sunrise, Doc had gone out alone in the early morning fog to set some traps within a mile of his house. He leaned into the trap to set the pan and had a rush of sadness surge through his loins as he thought about Kitty. He pushed his thoughts away and murmured, "I must stay busy." He mounted his horse to go and set another trap deeper in the woods.

But his mind was dead set – like his traps – on thoughts of his past life and Kitty. He finally just let the memories fly back through the years. *I've come a long way from Ohio.* He was born in Zanesville, Ohio, in 1807. *When I went to Cincinnati to learn the saddler's trade, hmmm, that sure was a mistake. I was bored before the age of twenty. It took me until I was twenty-two to start my real life.* That was when he went to St. Louis and met a man named William Sublette who introduced him to trapping. *Those years as a fur trapper were good. Especially being with Joseph Meek. Everybody called us mountain men. What a friend I have in Joe!*

Doc dismounted and grabbed another trap. He headed down a slope to a creek. At the water's edge, he knelt to prepare this next trap. *When I met Joe he was just a lad of eighteen or nineteen. I may be the older one by four years, but he taught me as much as I did him.* With his next thought, he ached for Kitty. *Joe and I met our wives together. I remember it was in 1833 when we were with the Nez Percé and, a year later, I married Kitty on Ham's Fork of the Green River. It was good that we married sisters. It made our families even closer. Two daughters of a sub-chief. Two wives of friends.* Doc stopped, took a serious look, clenched his jaw, and wiped his nose on his sleeve. *Kitty was beautiful inside and out. More importantly, she was good for me.*

While Doc worked on the trap, more than his past life was being awakened. As the chain rattled and the trap clanked, Doc woke a sleeping black bear. But minutes later, and before the animal came from his den, Doc rode away, leaving the encounter for when he returned.

Mattie awoke to a deafening quiet in the house and a bawling cow in the barn. She had slept in her clothes to avoid the possibility of someone seeing that she was a girl, so in minutes she was able to be out in the barn. She hummed some hymns like her mother used to do while milking. And she heard her mother's words as if they were being spoken at that moment: "Always hum while you milk a cow. It relaxes them. There was a cow in the barn when Jesus was born, and the hymns bring that time back to the animals."

After the milking, Mattie fed the chickens. While flinging the chicken feed with a sweep of her hand, she scattered little glimpses into her mind's eye of past times in the McAlister barnyard with her Grandpappy. And she heard Grandpappy's voice in her memory: "I can fiddle and dance. Can you sing and dance?" She smiled.

As she walked the milk pail into the house, her mother's voice filled her head again. She remembered the day when she was taught how to make fresh cheese. So, Mattie busied herself making fresh cheese with most of the milk and sang *The Wayfaring Stranger* aloud, with her mother's voice in a duet in her head.

> I'm just a poor wayfaring stranger
> A trav'lin' through this world of woe
> But there's no sickness, toil nor danger
> In that bright world to which I go
>
> I'm going' there to see my mother
> I'm goin' there, no more to roam
> I'm just a-goin' over Jordan
> I'm just a-goin' over home.

She built up the fire in the hearth from last night's coals. In a pot she stirred the milk to let it thicken and listened to her mother's voice each step of the way. A thinly woven cloth hung on a nail by the hearth and, when the milk was ready, she draped the cloth around the pitcher; the cloth served as a sieve. The whey went into the pitcher and curds remained in the cloth. She pressed the curds into a round and stored it in a basket on the table. It was ready to eat.

Finally, she cleared the dishes from last night off the table, dipped a clean cloth in the water bucket, and wiped them clean.

Upon Doc's return, the day was still more night than morning. He pulled off a splinter of wood from the woodpile and sat on a bench outside the door. He didn't feel like talking to anyone, especially the young boy in his house. After he picked and cleaned his teeth, he chewed on the splinter. All of a sudden he had a realization and spoke aloud. "Crap! There's no time to cook today even if the traps catch some critters. I'm going up to The Hudson's Bay Company for that meeting. What a fool I am to set traps!" *Kitty, I don't think straight with you distracting me.*

He headed toward the barn for the morning chores and Mattie saw him passing the kitchen window. She rushed to the door and shouted, "I milked the cow and fed the chickens already."

Doc turned around and nodded. *Ha, I have to remind my boys to do their chores.* He waved and smiled to show he understood and went into the barn to put out some hay.

A little later, as they were putting food on the table – apple butter, dried venison, the fresh cheese, and some pan bread Doc made – Margaret rode up at a gallop.

Doc turned to Mattie to say, "She loves to ride. Oh, look! The two girls are coming up behind her in the wagon. No, it looks like three." Crow ran with the wagon.

They walked out the door to greet the visitors as Doc continued talking. "Margaret is raising two young girls called Sarah and Eliza Flett. Their mother died. She promised their father that she would teach them cooking, sewing, and everything a woman needs to know."

Margaret overheard and interjected, "Yes, the two sisters have been with me for almost a year." She turned and called out, "Sarah! Eliza! Come meet Matthew. He's going with us today and will ride in the wagon with you."

The two girls were helping a smaller child from the back of the wagon

– a small Negro girl.

When the four children were face to face, Mattie felt shy and just said, "Hello."

Margaret continued saying, "That's four-year-old Mary Jane Holmes. I'm looking after her while her mother has another baby. Robert, I don't think you know the Holmes family, but they came on a wagon train in December of forty-four. They live south of here."

Doc put his hands on a couple of the children's shoulders to herd them into the house. "No, you're right, I don't know them. Girls, come in and eat something before we leave."

While they were eating, Doc talked about preparations for the trip. "I need to take my papers before we head out for the Fort, and we need to take some grub to eat on the ride up and back – like some apples and *charqui*. I don't know what kind we have at this time – probably bear or deer *charqui*. I like the beef best, though. Kitty used to make a lot and store it all in the root cellar. Sarah, Matthew, and Eliza, after we finish eating, will you go to the root cellar and get *charqui* and fruit? Whatever kind you want. Take a basket," and he pointed toward the corner where several were piled."

"The girls and I brought some muffins, nuts, and fruit."

Doc smiled. "That sounds good. By the way, I must be on time for the meeting tonight. I don't like being late."

Margaret nodded. "I know. I don't either."

Now another horse was heard approaching the house. Doc stood and went to see. Black Saul rode up.

"You're just in time to eat. Did you smell the food?" Doc jested. "Come in for some bites. We'll be leaving for the Fort soon. What brings you today?"

Black Saul left his horse in the grass to graze and walked into the house. "I got more letters. Two is for Miz Margaret and Dr. Bailey. The other's for you, Doc." He pulled out the four folded papers as he squeezed onto the bench with some of the children. He handed them across the table and explained, "They's in-veetations from Dr. and Mrs. McLoughlin for their Christmas party. An' the other is an in-veetation to a holiday party at the Meeks' house an' I fiddlin' there."

With a twinkle in her eye, Margaret raised an eyebrow and asked, "You didn't open them and read them, did you?"

"Why! Miz Margaret, you knows I don't read."

She patted Black Saul on the forearm and smiled to him. "I know."

Mattie asked, "How long is our ride to the Fort?"

Doc told her. "The Fort is about twenty-five miles north of my place. It's a few hours. Not a hard ride. But with a wagon and all you children, it may take a bit longer than usual."

Margaret looked to Black Saul, "Will you ride with us some of the way? I know you don't want to go to the meeting, but we would enjoy your company."

He swallowed his food and grinned. "Sho nuff, Miz Margaret."

Doc asked him, "Last night on your ride, did you tell Matthew all about yourself?"

Between bites, he said, "I sho did. I told how I got here and why I stayed and what I do." Black Saul stopped eating and looked Doc in the eye, "I wonderin', did Matthew tell ya what happened ta us?" Without waiting for a response, he pointed his fork in the air to declare, "Six men came after me, wantin' to give a lashin'."

Both Margaret and Doc became wide-eyed; each started talking at the same time.

"Do you know who they ...."

"Why did they try to ...."

Black Saul laughed. "Jus' listen. They saw me comin' on Cricket and stopped me. Since I didn't know 'em, I thought they want to ask directions or somethin', but they done pulled me off my saddle. They start pushin' me around and hollerin' at me. Then other men came over and they start to argue, so I jumped back on Cricket and got away." He took a deep breath and continued, "They went for their horses, so I got a head start. Finally, I jumped off an' hid at that tree where I found Matthew. Cricket's smart and she disappeared and hid, too. I ain't a-goin' past those new houses again. They was places I never saw before – houses for the newcomers."

Doc nodded, absorbing it all, and said, "I want you to show me those houses. That law is null and void. This makes me angry."

"Don' you worry, Doc." Black Saul held out his plate, "Just a little more of those vittles. I is real hungry."

Doc insisted, "I need to make them understand that the Lash Law is done."

Black Saul changed back to the first topic, "Oh, I tol' Matthew about my farm, too."

Margaret asked, "Did you tell about Cockstock?"

Black Saul frowned and shook his head. "I wantin' to forget 'bout all that."

"Oh," Margaret said as she considered. "Do you mind if I tell him? It will help Matthew understand some of the attitudes people have in the meeting tonight. There might be problems there."

"Okay. I goin' ta eat and not listen, if that's all right." He took another piece of the flat pan bread and reached for the butter plate.

Margaret began a story about another Negro called Winslow who, in 1834, had come from California in a party of eight men with a herd of a hundred horses and mules. Years later, in 1843, Winslow settled on a farm near Oregon City in Clackamas county and hired a Wasco Indian by the name of Cockstock to clear some of his land. The payment was to be a horse. "But before Cockstock finished the work, Winslow sold the farm and horse to Black Saul."

Sarah, who was a mature young lady, had been listening with intent. She drew in her breath and said, "I see trouble coming."

"Yes," Margaret agreed. "Black Saul had bought the farm with the horse, not knowing about the prior agreement. So when Cockstock came for the horse, he didn't get it. Angry, Cockstock came back and stole it. That's when the local Indian sub-agent, Elijah White, made him return the animal. Cockstock threatened revenge and kept coming back to molest Black Saul and Winslow. Finally, last winter, Cockstock came with five others and started a melee in Oregon City. Sadly, Cockstock and two white men were killed. Since then, the Wasco Indians have been up in arms about the disservice done to their people.

"The trouble was that people got things mixed up and thought the Negroes and Indians were going to unite to attack the white settlers. It's not clear how that story got started. Elijah White gave Cockstock's widow some kind of compensation – I don't know what – and this calmed the Wasco Indians somewhat. But some white people claimed that Black Saul threatened to rile up the Indians against the white settlers, so there are still bad feelings. In fact, three witnesses testified against Black Saul in a court trial, and he was found guilty. They kept him in custody for several weeks."

Mattie gasped and asked, "You mean behind bars in a jail?"

"No, we have no official jail. No cell with iron bars and a lock on the door. He was in custody at someone's home. Finally, he was released and told to leave the area."

Black Saul wiped his mouth with his sleeve and looked up. "That's why I ain't goin' to that meeting. Winslow is a nigger like me and he did me wrong. Cockstock, an Indian, did me wrong. And now these three white folks lied about me, doin' me wrong. No tellin' who might'n do me wrong again. Goin' ta that meetin' could jus' be trouble. People want me gone an' I ain't plannin' ta leave Oregon. Doc, you can give me a report if there's anythin' interestin' I needs to know. Oh, please tell Mr. Joe Meek that I is ready to play the fiddle at his Christmas party on Monday night."

"I will tell him." Doc addressed the children, "I'm always happy to see my friend Joe Meek. None of you know him. Is that correct?" Many heads shook. "I think you'll like him. He's known for fighting bears and, what he calls, *Injuns*. I hope he shows you his flair for stories tonight at the meeting." Doc stopped and seemed to be remembering or even reliving a time with Joe. All of a sudden his face beamed and he laughed a hearty one. "Joe is an outstanding character. Like I said, he tells good stories, but he is a leader of men. He has been elected sheriff for the last three years. When you meet him, you'll see what I mean."

Margaret frowned, "Do you really think the children should go to the meeting?"

"Yes, the older ones need to understand about our lives. Joe mentioned in that note that he was bringing my two oldest boys." Stretching their ages to the next year to justify his logic, Doc said, "Francis is almost eleven, like Matthew here. William is almost eight and old enough. I expect them to be there. They need to understand that Britain wants to claim the Northwest and that we American settlers are working to have Oregon claimed by the United States."

"I know. I know. But the meeting could be long and boring."

"Margaret, how can you say that there is anything boring about our future here in the Northwest?"

She grimaced and retorted, "I don't like the attitude of how we're claiming this land. The Manifest Destiny attitude."

Mattie had been following their every word. She asked, "What's Manifest ... you know, what you said?"

Sarah and Eliza looked bewildered as well and looked to Doc for understanding.

Doc liked explaining and teaching children. He sat a bit straighter to display his teacher characteristics and addressed all the children. "Manifest Destiny – you asked what it means. Well, people seem to think that we Americans have special virtues and rights. They think that Americans are destined to expand across the continent and claim what they want. Some think that it's a divine destiny under God's direction. All this is called Manifest Destiny." Doc stopped to think and continued, "There's no concern about the people who live on the land that we want or ...." He stopped again. "How'd we get talking on this? I'm starting to feel riled."

Margaret agreed, "Yes, let's get ready to leave. Children, we can talk on the ride there and back. We'll answer any of your questions. For now, the men can clean off the table and I will take the girls to the root cellar."

Margaret picked up a lamp and lit it before they went outside. Pointing, Margaret indicated the door, "See, it's out by the barn." It began to drizzle as the girls walked toward the root cellar – a windowless room built underground.

Next to the barn the land sloped upward forming a small hill and there was a doorframe built into the hill. Margaret opened the door and extended the lamp in front of her. "Be careful, there are three steps down." When inside, Margaret hung the lamp on a metal hook from a beam in the six-foot high ceiling. The room had dirt walls and floor. There were cut tree trunks in the corners supporting two main beams going across the ceiling with plank boards holding up all the dirt from the hill above. Shallow wooden shelves lined the walls to the left and right and from floor to ceiling. Potatoes and turnips were spread in single layers across several shelves, apples and pears on other shelves. The ceiling had onions hanging from their braided tops and bunches of carrots, as well as inverted plants – basil, parsley, and dill – drying.

Eliza asked about the inverted flowers. "How do they use the little daisy-like flowers?"

"For tea. That's chamomile. I usually make mint tea for us at home, but I have some dried chamomile in the house in tins. Did you ever notice them?" Without waiting for an answer, Margaret pointed to the ham and thick slabs of cured pork hanging from the ceiling in a corner. "Doc keeps no pigs, so I always give him a Christmas ham and some small barrels of pickled pork that I make."

Little Mary Jane asked, "What's pickled pork?"

"My goodness, Mary Jane, you don't know about pickle pork?" Impatient with ignorance even in a child as young as this four-year-old, Margaret answered. "It's a process to keep pork from turning bad, for up to a year or so, by packing it tightly in these barrels with salt, saltpeter, and spices. Eliza and Sarah helped me make it. I'll teach you when you're older." Margaret pointed to some crocks. "Sarah and Eliza, see the crocks on the narrow shelves facing the entrance? Those are the crocks of pickled beets, cucumbers, and preserves that we made for Doc and his family. Remember? We used all the extra vegetables from our garden."

When they started for Fort Vancouver, the sun was out, and the day remained dry during their trip north. The breeze sent a smell of freshness into their faces. They were quiet for a time and watched a kettle of turkey vultures circling in the distance. Near them, smaller birds chirped and flew from tree to bush and back again —goldfinches, chickadees, and bushtits. A woodpecker out of their sight burrowed into a tree trunk with a rat-a-tat-tat.

"Matthew, tomorrow we need to go check my traps. There was no time for me to see if something was in them before we left. Besides, if I caught something, there was no time to clean and skin any game either. I just hope no animals are in the traps and going to suffer until I get to them tomorrow."

Mattie smiled at him. She liked the idea of helping get food for the table. Living on a sheep farm, she had only seen traps with rats caught in them.

Much of the terrain was flat with large areas of grasses. Doc explained that they were passing grasslands that the Kalapuyan Indians had burned for centuries. "They burned the dried camas plants to have a better crop in the spring for making their camas cakes. That was their main winter food. The Kalapuyans didn't know it, but they were also making the land ready for fields of wheat and corn for the settlers."

Listening to his voice lulled Margaret, and her eyelids felt heavy in the warm sunlight. She knew about the prairie burns by the Kalapuyan tribe, but didn't feel like talking, only listening. She studied his face from time to time and smiled to herself. She liked how Doc was always explaining to the children.

But after a couple hours, the children were impatient and complained wanting to know how much farther they had to go. Far above, they heard geese that had flown south to winter in Oregon.

Margaret reprimanded the children, "Listen to the geese squawking like all of you." She made a high and loud voice, squealing, "Squawk, squawk, how much longer?"

Doc sat up and his face took a serious look. "Yes, I know some words of Shakespeare that tell it better than the geese." He quoted:

Wisely and slow;
they stumble that run fast.

And he talked for most of the trip. As they approached the Fort, his mind turned to the upcoming event. He remembered something and asked Margaret, "Did you hear what happened to Dr. McLoughlin?"

"What do you mean?"

Doc told her, "Though the meeting is at The Hudson's Bay Company, McLoughlin might not attend. His status has changed. I don't believe he holds the position of Chief Factor anymore."

"What?"

"This is a difficult time for John McLoughlin. It seems that this year, a few months ago in June, London set up a three-man board to take his place. Oh, he's one of the three men along with James Douglas and Peter Skene Odgen, but I heard that he had no suspicion that this was in the making. I'm not sure if he retains the title of Chief Factor, but everyone still uses it."

"Why did this happen?"

"A while back, Joe Meek told me that London had gotten word of the large amount of unpaid credit that McLoughlin had extended to the settlers – to both his retired fur trappers as well as to people like me. I am so grateful to him; I couldn't have made it here without his loans. I couldn't have fed my family. Why, he loaned me wheat seed and oxen to plant the seed. He said I could pay him back after I raised my wheat. He let me buy other equipment I needed from the supplies of The Hudson's Bay Company. I say *buy* loosely because I had no money. I got supplies that were to be used by people working for him, but he let me buy them. Yes, he's a man of integrity and I paid him back for all my purchases. But many people still owe him."

As soon as they arrived, they left their horses to be brushed down and fed in the Fort's livery stables. Doc went to the meeting. Margaret took little Mary Jane to stay with a woman friend at the Fort before she and the children headed to the meeting.

The room was full. After Doc had asked some people to make a space on their bench for Margaret and the children, he went up front, as the representative of the Oregon Legislative Committee and the Speaker of the Assembly, and sat next to Joe Meek. Lieutenant William Peel and Captain H.W. Parke were representing the British Crown and sat at the same table with them.

The audience was a mix of men and women settlers, people from the tribes – Chinook, Wasco, and Cayuse – and residents of the Fort. All the seats in the room were filled and men stood two and three deep against the walls.

The chairman slammed the gavel against the table with a bang, silencing the talk, "The Chief Factor has asked me to open the meeting. He will join us later. I want to welcome our distinguished guests, Lieutenant Peel of the British Navy and Captain Parke from the Royal Marines."

The lieutenant began, "Thank you. It is an honor to be here and I want to thank all who are attending tonight. Since receiving my orders to come, it has taken me over a year to arrive. Most of us know the difficulties one faces to make this trip, whether by land or by sea. I started on the *HMS Collingwood* flagship and changed to the ship *Cormorant* in Valapariso,

Chile. Finally, I took the frigate *America* and, after it docked in Puget Sound, I rode here to the Columbia River. I have heard that my trip was preceded by the arrival of two British army officers, Henry Warre and Mervin Vavasour, who are at this moment seeing the Willamette Valley here in Oregon. My orders were to allay any fears you citizens may have; as you can hear by the description of my trip, Britain's navy and army are willing to go great distances to protect you." He stopped to look at his notes.

Hearing his words, people frowned and whispered, sending ripples of murmurs around the room. When he looked up, the disgruntled voices faded.

Seemingly unaware of the negative reaction, the speaker continued, "As everyone knows, The Hudson's Bay Company has been here representing the British Crown in North America since the English Royal Charter of 1670. That's over one hundred and eighty years. We have provided the opportunity for each of you to settle here and make your homes with the help of The Hudson's Bay Company, which was the only place to provide you with the supplies needed to survive. You are welcome, but it is our place to emphasize that this is a British ...."

People stood and shouted. They raised their arms, shaking their fists and complaining. The gavel banged over and over.

Once the crowd calmed, the lieutenant seemed to have nothing more to say. He mumbled and stumbled through some comments about the situation needing resolution. No one was interested, and the people in the audience chattered among themselves:

"I hear that Peel's only nineteen years of age. Who does he think he is to tell us anything?"

"He is the son of the Prime Minister. Is that supposed to impress us?"

"I saw a British battleship in the Columbia last week. I heard that McLoughlin was angry and told them to leave."

"Yeah, McLoughlin knows that riles us."

"I saw the ship, too. It was flying the British flag."

What people had seen was an eighteen-gun sloop called *Modeste* that was commanded by Thomas Baillie. People had heard that McLoughlin had recommended to the ship's captain that it was not wise to make a show of force and that they should shift to Puget Sound.

When Lieutenant Peel sat down, the captain was asked if he had anything to add.

With a stern face, Captain Parke stood and began a rant. "Mister Chairman," he made a slight bow to the Chair and then turned to the audience with a raised voice. "Great Britain has been here with the Hudson's Bay Company longer than any of you. We have made it possible for you to successfully settle by lending tools, seeds, and other supplies. On our books, there exists an enormous unpaid debt." He leaned forward and slammed his fist to the table. "How dare you shake your fists at us." With an extended arm, pointing to the audience, he shouted, "I refer to your debt to The Hudson's Bay Company! When our retired fur trappers were lent supplies, they paid back their debt in three years. You," and he spat out his next words in a sarcastic tone, "of this Provisional Government, shirk from paying. And what does this meager Provisional Government mean? You have no army, no protection other than us." He stopped, took a deep breath and pulled on the coattails of his uniform to straighten the jacket. In a firm, but normal voice, he addressed the chairman, "I stand down in disgust."

Doc raised his voice and said, "Mister Chair, I request to take the floor." After a nod from the chairman and a tap of the gavel, Doc began, "I am Robert Newell, but you are welcome to call me Doc or Bob, as most people do. I am here as Speaker of the Assembly to represent the Oregon Legislative Committee and to inform our esteemed visitors that this organization has been in existence since 1843 when we voted, on May second of that year, to form our Provisional Government." He paused and took a breath. "We knew we were laying the foundations of a great state. Our two years are miniscule compared to the time you mentioned – nearly two hundred years on this continent. But we have accomplished much for the people who live here. We have been making laws and upholding justice; we also established the first uniformed taxation. The Oregon Legislative Committee consists of nine elected representatives who are working on land claims, appropriations, military formation, on judiciary needs, and districting. We the people of Oregon have realized that we need laws and order. We want you to know that we are here to stay as American citizens, in America, and it is only a matter to time before that is official. Also, to emphasize our organization and dedication, I want you to know that I am the director of The Oregon Printing Association and by February of next year, we will have a newspaper called *The Oregon Spectator* that will be printed in Oregon City. We are a society – organized and devoted, working together to help each other grow and prosper in all ways. For food and shelter, our people have built and run grist and sawmills, have warehouses for grain, and organized community gatherings to share ideas. For development of our minds – for we are more than fur trappers or passing visitors – I have formed The Oregon Lyceum, a literary and debating society to further literature and scientific pursuits," Doc smiled to relax the discussion and added, "however, often at the meetings of The Oregon Lyceum we end up discussing local politics." A few people laughed at his humor. "The point I'm wanting to make is this: we are not here to gather furs to sell or to accumulate other products to be sent back to Europe. We are here to live. This is our American home."

Most of the audience stood to cheer. Applause filled the room.

Even with the banging of the gavel, the people continued to clap and shout. Soon they began to chant, "Oregon is America," over and over.

That is when Doc noticed that John McLoughlin, the Chief Factor of The Hudson's Bay Company, was standing in the back of the room. Doc leaned to whisper to Meek. "Look who has joined us. How long has he been here?"

Meek frowned, bobbed his shoulders to indicate that he didn't know. He turned to the audience and, in a loud voice above the crowd's chants, he asked, "Permission to speak?"

"Sheriff Meek has the floor."

As he stood, his chair fell down with a bang. Everyone strained to see what made the loud crash and the commotion in the room dissipated to complete silence. There stood Joseph Meek, looking more like a beady-eyed bear than a gentleman. He stood six feet two, the size and shape of a grizzly. For the occasion, he had slicked down his almost-black hair on the top of his head, but the wild beard and mustache covered his face and was framed by the long dark hair from his head that fell down his back. Adding to the bear-look, he wore a dark beaver skin vest, a long-tailed black coat, and even his legs looked like an animal's haunches with the rumpled and mud splattered trousers. All eyes were on Joe Meek, and he smiled.

Doc started to pick up the overturned chair, and Joe put his hand on Doc's shoulder. "Thank you, Mr. Newell, I can quiet the crowd with my gavel by myself." He picked up the chair and, with two fists clutching it, he banged it down on the floor several times.

Everyone laughed.

He began, "Esteemed guests and all here tonight, I've but one item of interest to mention." He looked around and hiked up his trousers by the belt at his waist. "This here room is crowded, but it barely represents us Americans who came here to live. Most jus' don't know how crowded it is here in the Willamette Valley." He stopped for emphasis before saying in a raised voice, "But I do!" Then he shouted, "'Cuz this year I took a census." He paused again. "And I took this census of our people before the wagon trains of 1845 war here. 'Course, it's like countin' jack rabbits, but the counters did a good job." He turned and stepped up onto his chair to bellow, "Thar are more than two thousand one hundred and ten American people living in Oregon."

Hats flew into the air with whoops throughout the room. For many minutes the din continued with the gavel banging in the background. John McLoughlin slipped out of the room during this time; Doc noticed a smile on the Chief Factor's face when he made his exit.

Finally, as Joe stepped down off his chair, the chairman declared that the business of the meeting seemed concluded, and he asked for questions from the audience. One of the newer arrivals from a wagon train raised her hand. "I have a question for Sheriff Meek, if I may."

Meek stood and made a slight bow. "My pleasure. You are Mrs. Victor, I believe."

"Why, yes, thank you, Mr. Meek. My question is: If I am correct that you have lived a long time here in Oregon Country and have witnessed the transformation of our society, surely you have observed equally great changes in nature. Can you tell us what you have seen, whether it be about the rivers, prairies, or mountains, for instance?"

Meek nodded and replied, "I reckon so." He waved his hand in the direction of the majestic Mount Hood, and said, "Mount Hood is white with everlasting snows and towers thousands of feet above the summit of the Cascade ranges." People seemed to slip to the edge of their seats waiting to hear. "But when I came to this country," he stopped and everyone held their breath. Then he shouted, "Why, Mount Hood war only a hole in the ground!"

The walls shook with guffaws and applause. Everyone enjoyed a good story from Joe Meek as well as a good laugh after the tension that had filled the room. No one tried to quiet the people.

After a few moments with Joe Meek still standing in front, the room became quiet in anticipation of more fun from him. But a man from the center of the room stood and asked a very serious question, "Mr. Meek, since our government has annexed Texas and riled Mexico, do ya think we'll have a war?"

Joe Meek sat down and leaned his whole chest up against and over the edge of the table while displaying a frown that demanded everyone's attention. "I'm afraid President James K. Polk is the only man who can answer that thar question, though I've been known to give my opinion on such delicate matters." Some heads nodded and people began to buzz among themselves like crickets until Joe raised both his arms out over his head and returned to his feet. The atmosphere of the room quieted like the silence before a storm – tensions grew again as they sensed his answer. Joe let his eyes pass from head to head around the room; they saw distress in his eyes. "I think thar is going to be no choice. We have to fight Mexico." With that said, Meek quickly turned to face the two representatives from Great Britain. People started to talk, and Meek looked over his shoulder toward the audience and threw out his arms like lightening bolts. Instantly people quieted, and they waited for the thunder of his words. A squeak from a chair leg against the floor preceded his exploding voice, "And everyone needs to remember ..." he inserted another one of his pregnant pauses before he leaned on the table and into the lieutenant and captain's space. "I don't mean to lock horns with you gentlemen, but we Americans are known to fight for the land we live on."

Cheers burst forth.

MOUNTAIN LANDSCAPE
Painting by John Mix Stanley.
WIKIPEDIA – PUBLIC DOMAIN

CHAPTER 3

DECEMBER 21, 1845

As planned, after the meeting, Doc and Margaret spent the night at Fort Vancouver in two rented rooms. However, for Mattie, there was an uncomfortable aspect of the night – one room was for the girls and Margaret; the other room was for *the boys* – Doc, his two oldest boys, and Mattie.

Mattie lay awake on the lower bunk, listening to the howling wind whistle through the window cracks, and she wondered how much longer she could pretend to be a boy. She remembered the big, broad smile of Joe Meek when he reached his bear paw of a hand out to shake hers. She remembered Meek's voice when he had said that he figured that she'd fit right in with Doc's boys. At that moment, droplets of nervous sweat popped out on her forehead, right there in front of the two boys. In the bunk, she gave a shiver from the memory of her embarrassment.

She turned on her side and pulled the blankets up to her nose. The room was full of soft breathing from the boys and a snore now and then from Doc. The night made a silver light in the room, and she watched reflections from the trees playing on the walls. These people were so good to her and she marveled at her good fortune. At the same time, she worried about her lie and how she would ever tell them. Sleep finally came to her as she wondered what Joe Meek would say when he learned that he was a she. Soon she was dreaming:

> *In a flock of chickens, two of them fluttered about with the heads of humans – Margaret and Black Saul. In between pecking on the ground, they told the other chickens all about the strange boy living with Robert Newell. A man walked into the dream – only his bandy legs were in view – but he purchased a chicken to eat and walked over to the chopping block, holding his dinner-to-be upside-down and by the legs. Before that chicken's head was cut*

off, it told another chicken, with the head of Joe Meek, about Matthew being Mary Anne. Mattie came into the dream with an axe and ran after the Joe Meek chicken. The dream went on and on with the chase going around and around the barnyard.

Finally, Mattie woke herself from the repetitious dream and smiled at the silliness. Soon, she slipped out the door and went around the corner of the building to pee. Upon her return, she climbed back into the warm bed and slept a deep sleep.

In the morning as they dressed, the children noticed Mattie had slept in her clothes. William asked, "Why'd you sleep in your clothes?"

Mattie shrugged her shoulders. "I don't know."

Francis, the oldest, asked, "Where'd ya get these shoes? Aren't they too big for ya?"

Mattie was lacing the left foot.

He picked up the right shoe and turned it over. "Did you steal them? Pa says you're a runaway."

Mattie finished tying the first shoe and reached out to snatch the other from his grip. She snapped, "Give it to me! They were my bigger brother's shoes. They don't fit him no more."

The boy gave her a push and wouldn't hand the shoe to her, "Ain't so. I think you're lying."

Doc blurted, "Francis, stop that! Remember that you are not to use *ain't* and I find your actions and your tone of voice to be disrespectful."

The boy bowed his head, looked to his feet, and apologized to his father, "Sorry."

While Mattie put on the second shoe, the too-wide legs of her long breeches exposed the hem of her dress.

William, the younger, asked, "Whatcha wearin' under your breeches?"

Hiding a smile, Doc reprimanded the children, "No more questions. We need to ride out of here. The cow needs to be milked, the chickens fed, and I have traps to check. As it is, we won't get home until late."

Everyone finished dressing in silence.

Once outside at the stables and before Doc mounted his horse, he lifted his seven-year-old into the saddle with him. He told ten-year-old Francis and Matthew to ride in the wagon.

Intuitively, the children were uncomfortable. They knew there was something strange about Matthew. A secret.

Margaret had started to suspect something, but couldn't figure out what was wrong. She did notice that Matthew was awkward around the boys.

No one talked much.

In her head, Margaret made a relentless search for a way to make Matthew comfortable with the boys. She wanted to talk it over with Doc to learn if he had any ideas, but talking in private was impossible while riding horses.

Doc was puzzled, too. He kept thinking about the morning scene with all those questions from his boys. He saw that Matthew was having a difficult time and he wondered if he could have handled it better.

From time to time, Doc commented on the wildlife – an osprey high overhead and deer in the distance. After an hour of riding down slopes, crossing creek beds, and searching the distance for the open French Prairie, all the remaining apples and *charqui* had disappeared into the stomachs of the children and they were still hungry.

Margaret insisted, "No, we will not eat what's in my basket until we stop."

Even Eliza and Sarah, who sat on the wagon bench, didn't talk. They looked sleepy. Matthew and Francis were in the back with little Mary Jane and had nothing to say. The ride was too quiet.

Suddenly, Francis let out a flatulence of such force and loudness that everyone in the group turned to look at the others to decide how to react. Matthew glanced at Doc, who was waving his hand in front of his nose. William craned his head back to see if Margaret had been offended. Sarah and Eliza had scrunched up their faces with the smell and peered back at Francis in disgust.

When Mattie pinched her nose with her fingers, Francis started to grin and then he began to giggle.

Margaret surprised herself and laughed loudly. And that was an indication to the children to have some fun. Even Sarah and Eliza, who were being trained to be ladies, became silly little girls. One of them exclaimed, "That stinks, Francis!"

The laughter was contagious and finally Doc said, "I'm going to ride faster to get rid of this smell." And they all laughed again as both horses were encouraged into a gallop. Finally Sarah gave her horse full reins and the wagon followed Doc and Margaret's horses.

After they all slowed, Margaret suggested they stop to eat the food from her basket; it wasn't much, but would fill their bellies enough until they got back to Doc's cabin. While eating under a tree, Margaret thought of the perfect topic to interest the children. "You children know that everyone thinks highly of Ben Franklin. He was a very intelligent and industrious man. And, in honor of this great man, your father has named one of his keelboats after Ben Franklin."

Both the boys and the girls bobbed their heads. They seemed interested in knowing where this conversation was headed.

Doc's curiosity was piqued, as well.

"Well, in one of my college classes, we had to read some essays written by Ben Franklin. One of them was called 'Fart Proudly.' Yes, it's true." Margaret started to giggle when she looked at Doc, but she kept her composure.

Doc was frowning, yet curious.

Margaret continued, "This is really true. In jest, Ben Franklin sent the essay to a friend of his. Years later many of his essays were published. So let me explain why he wrote this one essay that he called 'Fart Proudly.' He stated that there should be a scientific pursuit to find a way to learn what foods to eat to make the flatulence smell better. He even hoped that scientists could make a fart as agreeable as the smell of perfume."

Now Margaret started laughing and could barely talk. The boys looked to their father, who started to laugh. She strained to get the last line out of her mouth, "And at the end ... " she giggled, "he made a pun about other scientific investigations not being ..." she burst out with uncontrollable snickers, "he made a pun that stated that other scientific investigations aren't worth a *fart-hing*."

It had only taken a minute of this kind of fart-talk and the children were acting as old friends. Even Mattie, who had never played with children her age, was being accepted.

Doc knew that this was a favorite topic of boys, so he let the conversation about farts continue while they prepared to leave until Francis discharged a second fart. Doc showed anger. "Francis, no more! I imagine your first flatulence was an accident, but this was not. No more! We've had our fun, but you boys know that none of this – both your flatulence and this conversation – is proper in front of ladies. And, Margaret, I know you agree that these bad manners must not be encouraged."

The boys and girls removed the smiles from their faces.

Francis tried to sound serious when he said, "Yes Sir," but they all laughed again. The boys and girls snickered just looking at the other one. "Excuse me, Pa. I'm trying to stop."

Finally, as they continued south, Doc realized that he needed to find a topic for discussion. "Let's tell Matthew about ourselves." He looked at Mattie and said, "I used to live up on the Tualatin Plains where Joe Meek lives. I planted wheat and did some farming, but I got bored with that. I decided it was a better value to have a location upon a navigable stream, so I got this place on the Willamette River." He tapped William on the shoulder and said, "William, tell what waterways we have on our land and why they're important."

"Why, Mission and Champoeg Creeks run through our land. Pa, has 'bout a square mile of land. Oh, and Champoeg Creek is important 'cuz it has a gristmill on it."

Doc asked Francis to tell about their place.

The boy squirmed in his seat to look back and smile at his pa, "Golly, Pa, I could talk all day about that. We got lots of trees; it's thick with fir trees 'cept along the creeks, a'course. There grows the cottonwoods and, in between, the land is mostly oak. You see deer and bears besides all the little critters like rabbits, fox, lynx, otter, beavers and muskrats. Why, I even saw an ermine once. Pa says that they sell the ermine furs to kings and queens." He smiled at Margaret and took a deep breath. "Out on the west side of our land is a prairie that goes up to the Willamette River. Pa is makin' a town there. He calls it Champoeg. He's working with Mr. Longtain on making and selling lots. Pa says it's advantageous ...." Francis stopped and asked, "Did I say that right?"

"You did, son."

"So, it's advantageous for people to live in his town because they can use the Willamette River to travel. I especially like all the birds we see. Why we got bald eagles and osprey all year round. I go to the river and watch how them birds dive at the fish. We have red-tailed hawks and cooper's hawks and night hawks and ...."

Doc interrupted, "Thank you, Francis. I'm sure everyone found your information interesting, but you're correct that you could talk all day. Especially about the birds."

Margaret smiled at Francis. "I'm especially fond of birds, too."

The wagon and two horses were riding side by side and Doc announced, "We're almost home." He pulled his pocket watch out to look at the time. "We should be there a little after noon. After you boys put the horses in the barn with feed, I want the three girls to get some baskets and go gather all the eggs and then I'll warm up some of our Johnnycakes from the other day and fry some pickled pork and eggs for all of us. Matthew will you milk the cow again?"

When the chores were done and the meal cleared from the table, Doc went out to hook up a horse to his wagon, preparing to go look at the traps. "We have about an hour of daylight left; we need to go."

As Margaret mounted her horse to head back to her place with the girls, she commented, "This has been a wonderful day, hasn't it?"

There had been the usual amount of rain all through autumn; in Oregon, rain started in October and didn't stop until spring. But it was almost the first day of winter and the sun had shone all day. That's how Oregon was.

He turned to answer Margaret's question. "That's one of the reasons that I like living here. We appreciate the sun more. The old sun just fills us up with love for living because we never can take it for granted."

Margaret said her goodbyes.

Doc said to Mattie and his boys, "Let's go see if the traps caught anything. If my traps killed something yesterday, the turkey vultures ate it yesterday. If something was injured, it may have died overnight and be no good for us – again, the vultures have a meal. Nevertheless there's always the possibility that something is alive in the traps, and we'll have a good supper tonight." The boys went to the wagon.

Doc walked to peer into the wagon bed and began checking on the contents, "Where's the axe I always carry in the wagon? The hatchet's here. Francis, run in the barn for an axe." Doc turned and walked into the house with William. They returned with a couple of sheathed hunting knives, a Hall rifle, and two crocks. He slipped the rifle under the bench where Mattie sat.

Mattie asked, "Why are you taking a rifle?"

The heads of the children whipped around to give Matthew a puzzled look. Doc found it amazing for a boy to ask such a question, but he just stepped up into the wagon and sat down. He adjusted the reins and hollered, "Everybody climb in." He said a *giddy-up* before answering the question. "Matthew, there may be a hundred reasons for that rifle. Let's see if it comes in handy."

Hearing Doc's answer, Mattie realized that her question must have been close to stupid. Although no one could see it, she felt a blush heat her face. That's when she decided not to ask why he was taking the crocks.

They rode parallel to the Willamette River though not next to the water. The leaves were off the deciduous trees; the wagon wheels rolled over downed acorns. The huckleberry bushes kept their leaves all year and Doc pointed to one. "Let's remember to stop at that bush on the way back, it still has some huckleberries. Even a few are better than none. They're so tasty."

Mattie had a thought. *Oh, the crocks are for things like berries.*

At the first trap, a plump rabbit was caught by part of its back paw. When Doc examined the furry critter – as he called it – he found it was a female and had teats full of milk. "We can't take her. She's got a litter somewhere – a litter of very hungry little ones after this much time. Well, I can't tell how long she's been in the trap; maybe she was caught this morning. Appears she's not too hurt since the trap didn't cause any bleeding."

William asked, "Can we follow her and get one of the youngins for a pet?"

"No, son." Doc opened the jaws of the trap and the rabbit scampered off under some bushes and was out of sight in a blink. As he dropped the trap into the wagon, he noticed how quiet Matthew was. Now they headed away from the river toward some hills covered mostly in conifers. Doc stopped the wagon near the edge of a ravine. He picked up his rifle and then looped the reins over a low branch, leaving enough play for the mare to lower her head and graze. Doc started loading the rifle as he talked, "Let's go see if we got something. There's no vultures overhead, so maybe we'll get lucky."

His Hall rifle was a single-shot breech-loading rifle with a percussion cap. It had a special feature where the breechblock could be detached and then it could be carried as a makeshift pocket pistol. Doc detached the forty-inch barrel and opened a chamber that pivoted for loading. He loaded the ball and charge front to back. The United States Army had been using the Hall breech loading rifle since the eighteen thirties; it was known for being built from carefully machined components to form an effective seal while still allowing enough tolerance for the breech to be opened easily. When it was loaded, Doc picked up one of the sheathed knives and slipped it into his waistband. Francis picked up the other ten-inch hunting knife and did the same.

Doc took the lead, followed by the three. He walked toward the edge and stopped to peer down the ravine. A small stream flowed at the bottom. The trap was fifteen feet away from him and near the water. "There's something in the trap. I can't make out what it is, but it's not moving. All of you stay here." He scrambled down the slope covered in loose dirt, brush, dry leaves, and bushes, grabbing at the bushes to stop his slipping. When he came to the trap, he tensed!

It was only a raccoon – the ringed tail identified it – but it was mutilated and the blood was fresh. Really fresh! He knew that the raccoon was killed by something other than the trap. Something had been trying to pull it from the trap and tore it up. In fact, it was so bloody that it appeared that parts of the raccoon might have been removed. Doc said aloud, but to himself, "The blood puddles are so fresh that I know it just happened minutes ago, or possibly seconds ago. That's why the vultures aren't here. A cougar would just sit and eat it. Did we spook him?"

He scanned the area.

His heart jumped when he saw a large, downed tree that had been uprooted along the side of the ravine from floodwaters in some past year. The vast root system of the tree stood seven-feet high with debris and dirt still clinging to the entwined tentacle-like appendages that curved where still attached to the ground; it formed a cave. With his heart throbbing in his temples, his gaze went to find something that he feared would be on the ground.

There it was! A ten-inch anal plug that a bear discharges after waking from his winter dormancy! A bear eats pine needles, leaves and maybe some of their own hair to make an anal plug; it stays in place and is voided when the bear comes out and drinks copious amounts of water. Doc chastised himself in his thoughts. *This was a perfect place for a bear in the winter – a cave created by a mass of roots making a hole where the tree used to sit. Why didn't I see this when I set the trap? I probably disturbed the bear when I set the trap because it's too early for him to have come out.*

Only a second or two passed as all these facts raced through his mind, nevertheless, it was too long. When he turned to tell the others to get back to the wagon, the bear was up there.

He was a big black bear, ambling along the ridge toward Mattie and the two boys who, at that moment, were looking the other way. All of a sudden, the bear growled and rose up on his hind legs, becoming five-feet-tall. Then he roared.

Doc roared, as well, "No! Look out! Bear!" He knew he could get a shot off, but if he aimed for a sure hit to the body, it wouldn't instantly kill that bear. He needed to make a hit to the head and, for that, he needed to be closer.

Without thinking, the three turned to see. Doc started scrambling up the incline. He grabbed at the bases of bushes to stop his slipping because his feet could find no firm foothold. Small rocks and dead leaves flew from under his shoes.

In the same moment, the bear made his move by dropping down on all fours and heading toward the group of three. His fur stood straight up along his neck and back as he lumbered with an amazing speed and snarled, showing his forty-two teeth – long bicuspids and sharp incisors. Clumsy, but heavy and deadly, the bear came at them.

The boys started backing up very slowly. Mattie grabbed William's hand and started pulling him along, "Come on, let's run!" she cried out. The boys knew not to run; that was the worst thing to do with a bear.

Francis fumbled with the sheath to get out the knife as he backed away. Mattie hollered at him, "No knife, he's too big for you. Just run!" That was the moment William stumbled and fell next to a fir tree, knocking Mattie down with him; they collided against the trunk. Francis saw and rushed to pull them up, but the bear was there and, when the boy glanced over his shoulder, he tripped and fell flat on his back next to Mattie. Instinctively, she curled over the two boys – exposing only her back. And the bear arrived.

The bear reared up again and whipped out his paw. His growl was deafening! With front claws an inch and a quarter long, he swiped at the cowering group.

A shot exploded as the paw descended toward Mattie. She screamed! The impact of the paw thrust the huddled three into the trunk of the tree with a thud and her clothes turned red in lines across her back.

Doc was close enough to knife the bear, if needed, but it fell instantly with the shot to its head. When Mattie opened her eyes, she saw the black fur inches from her face; she screamed again, not knowing if the animal was alive or dead. Doc knelt to examine her while the boys squirmed away. Mattie's shirt and breeches were in shreds – around her waist and into the back – in perfect strips the width of the claws. Doc pulled her shirt out of the wound and ripped it open to the neckline to expose the damage.

Like the reaction to a loud clap of thunder, the three males jerked.

Seeing two small well-formed breasts startled them more than the attack of the bear. Their mouths fell into a gap and their eyes widened. Mattie's bleeding brought them out of their shock and Doc whispered to her, "It's not that bad. Just hold still." Gently, Doc pulled at parts of her torn clothes to cover her chest.

Francis handed over his shirt for Mattie.

"Thank you, son." Doc pressed the torn shirt firmly against the wound, raising it from time to time to see the blood flow. Francis handed over his belt, too.

Doc worked to secure the cloth to the wound, saying words unheard by Mattie; she had passed out. He told her that the wounds were not deep and that the bleeding had stopped. A lump formed in his throat when his thoughts made it apparent how foolish he had been not to see all her feminine ways. *She cleared the table and cleaned the dishes. She did chores without being told. She made cheese. How could I not think something was amiss when she made cheese? And then, her comment about the rifle.* To calm himself in front of his boys, he said aloud that he had herbs at the house and he would clean and dress the wound when they got back. With teary eyes, he leaned close to her ear and whispered, "I'm sorry I didn't protect you."

Once Doc had the bleeding stopped and the wound covered, he carefully turned her over and saw that Mattie had gained consciousness. She had beautiful large eyes with lashes that touched just below her eyebrows. With her honey-colored skin and soft curls, Doc wondered. *How could I not see that she was a girl?*

Confused, like waking from a deep sleep in someone else's house, Mattie looked to Doc with searching eyes. The pain caused her mind to clear and reminded her where she was. She recalled black fur coming at her, a horrible smell, and the force of the blow followed by an intense burning on her side. But the worst part wasn't over for her – she still felt afraid because she knew they had seen she was a girl.

Doc calmed her fears with his smile and simple question. "So, what's your real name?"

"Mary Anne McAlister." Tears puddle in her eyes. "But everyone calls me Mattie."

When they had seen her breasts, the boys were ashamed at being mean to a girl. Now they felt protective.

"Boys, give me a hand."

The boys helped Doc prop her against the tree, taking care to move her gently. William offered his shirt to cover her for warmth. Squatting at her side, Doc asked if she was comfortable enough because it was important not to delay the gutting of the bear. "The meat could spoil," he said.

She nodded and closed her eyes again. The whole incident had filled her with more fear than she had ever experienced in her life, and it exhausted her. She noticed that relaxing against the tree stopped the pain; it only hurt when she moved.

The bear was flipped to his back, and Doc exclaimed, "Man alive! He's heavy. William, come help us drag him over there." The three of them tugged and pulled the hulk to a place inside four trees. With some ropes from the wagon, they spread the rear legs of the bear, tied them to a couple of trees, and did the same for the front paws.

Before they started cutting, Doc asked William to go back and stay with Mattie to make sure she was okay. "Let me know if she starts bleeding more or if there's anything unusual." The boy nodded and stood tall next to this girl.

Doc inserted his ten-inch knife into the cavity formed at the base of the bear's throat and cut the jugular vein. They had placed the bear on an area with a slope for the blood to drain away from the carcass.

Watching, Mattie could see that Doc and Francis had done this before; they worked with few words, anticipating the other's next move.

Francis took his knife and cut the fur-covered skin in a straight line from the breastbone to the base of the bear's jaw, exposing the throat. Doc cut the other direction from his son's cut – straight down to the anus. Now, Doc picked up the hatchet and handed it to his son, who placed it on the breastbone. Doc stood, took the axe, and slammed it down on the hatchet to break the breastbone. It took two hits for the bone to crack.

Intrigued, Mattie eyed the whole affair with awe. Doc and Francis each grabbed one of the ropes around the front paws and pulled away from each other with all their strength to open the chest cavity. Doc returned to work on the abdominal muscles by carefully cutting into them, deeper and deeper.

All of a sudden, the foulest odor made its way to Mattie.

William saw Mattie watching and sat down by her side to ask, "Do you know about skinning a bear?" She shook her head and he asked, "Want me to tell you?"

She nodded and rubbed her nose before saying, "It sure stinks!"

The boy giggled, "Yeah. But it's really more smelly over there." William let his giggles turn to a smile in his eyes before beginning to talk. "What's most important is not to cut the stuff in the bear's gut. It'd ruin the meat."

Again, Doc and Francis picked up the hatchet and axe; in the same manner that they had broken the breastbone, they broke the pelvic bone to help splay the legs and to facilitate the removal of the urinary and fecal tracts.

From time to time, the pain from her gashes surged. She clenched her fists until it subsided and returned her gaze to the scene. She did not want to complain about her pain and was thankful for the distraction of watching.

William continued, "Now they have to cut the diaphragm so they can spill out all the innards. See how my brother has to pull all that stuff, like the intestines, colon, and liver? Francis pulls it all to one side so Pa can see where he's cutting. Remember, if he accidentally cuts anything inside the bear, like the stomach or bladder, it'll ruin the meat." William giggled again before sharing his thoughts, "Francis and my pa are going to smell just like that bear on the ride home. Phewy!"

"Oh, no!" Mattie said with a scrunched up face. "And we have to sit next to them." She found it delightful having William explain everything. She said, "I've skinned a lot of rabbits with my Grandpappy, but rabbits aren't like this."

Doc was leaning inside the bear, working with the knife as his son pulled innards this way and that. With a jerk Doc stood, he stretched backwards from the waist with his arms dangling down from his shoulders and he whooped, "Damn I'm stiff and tired." Glancing for a moment at Mattie, he smiled and, before he walked to the tail, asked, "Can you smell the stink over there?" Not waiting for their answer, he cut a circle around the tail and put his knife down.

"Okay, son, you untie the front paws and I'll undo the back legs." Then they rolled the bear and dumped all the innards out on the ground, again making sure that everything drained away from the bear.

"Hell and tarnation! I missed something! Looks like I didn't cut all the lungs loose." Doc wiped his face with his upper arm sleeve, the only part of his shirt that was clean. "Francis, hold the bear down. William, come over and hold down the other side." Doc saw that Mattie was intently watching. He smiled again and got back to work, "Okay, boys, I'm grabbing the windpipe to rip the lungs out. Hold him down with all your strength." With a yank, Doc removed the lungs and more of the bear's insides. He tossed the mass of organs as far as he could fling them. Doc turned back and picked up his knife while saying, "Now, I'll clean out anything that's left. William, you go get the bag of rags we have in the wagon." The two boys wiped the cavity clean while Doc wiped off all the tools.

On the short trip home, cold winds blew against their faces and helped take away some of the stink. Doc talked nonstop, "Boys, normally that bear would have slept longer. Bears aren't true hibernators, they just go dormant and everything inside them slows down. They can be instantly active if disturbed. We saw that! If he would've come out next month, when the new grasses, sedges, and buds start growing, he would eat those. Oh, they love to eat the flowers off skunk cabbage. Or ants, beetles, and eggs when the birds started laying. I know I woke him when I set that trap. I should have shown you the plug he crapped out. A plug of leaves and hair keeps his whole system – the intestines and stomach – from working while he sleeps."

The boys asked some questions and Doc glanced back at Mattie from time to time. She seemed to be sleeping.

As they got closer to home, Doc's thoughts changed, "Francis, you and I need to get some soap and head to the river when we get home." Then his thoughts shifted topics again. "We have enough meat to share with our neighbors. Francis, after you're washed, I want you to ride over to Margaret's tonight. Sure glad she only lives a couple of miles from us. Let her know to come tomorrow. Did you see all that yellow fat? Must be four fingers deep from him gorging last fall on acorns, chestnuts, Oregon grapes, and huckleberries. I promised Margaret that she could have the fur of the next bear I killed." Doc looked back at Mattie. Her eyes were open and he explained, "Dr. Bailey doesn't do any hunting; his doctoring takes all his time." He slapped his knee and let out a yelp, "Whoopee! This feels so good. What was I saying? Oh, yes, Margaret. She's always sharing her hogs with us. Oh, and the sweet preserves and jams. I owe her. Boys, you get to keep the long curved claws. I'll help you auger holes to string them. We'll hang the carcass in the root cellar when we get home. It'll be safe from varmints in there 'til tomorrow. Oh, ask Margaret to bring Black Saul and have her invite Joe Meek, too. This will pay Joe back for putting you children up at his place. Besides, I could use some help butchering the meat, and they can take some for their families. This bear isn't the biggest I've seen, but there's plenty of meat to share."

The boys said, "Yes, sir."

"Oh, we'll eat well tonight. It won't take long to cook that liver with onions and boil up some potatoes. Boys, you can help me cook since Mattie can't." Then Doc had an important thought. "Oh, tell Margaret that we need a dress and other things for Matthew." He laughed, "Of course, you will need to tell her about the new name."

The excitement flowing out of Doc's words assuaged the pain of her wound. Doc had explained that her wound wasn't too deep because he had killed the bear before the force of the swipe connected with her side. She was glad to be alive.

Mattie carefully shifted to her side while trying to find a comfortable position in the bed of the wagon. In a quiet little voice she began to sing to forget her discomfort. William slept, oblivious to the bouncing, the smell of the bear, and her song. Upon hearing the softly sung hymn, Doc and Francis glanced at the other and grinned.

Tucked near her head and under the driver's bench stood one crock with the bear's liver and the other crock with the heart – no berries. The wagon jerked; she squealed and Francis left the bench to get into the back with Mattie. Doc turned to see what was happening just as Francis covered her with his jacket. Her mouth stretched into an ear-to-ear smile at the boy, and her big, dark eyes beamed, as well.

United States Post Office on Commercial and Ferry Streets in Salem, circa 1880

This photo shows the dress of the times.
(Employees of Post Office: left to right, Ben Taylor on penny farthing bicycle, George Hatch, Sadie Palmer, Rich Dearborn, Ella Dearborn, Captain L. Scott, and Scott Bozarth.)

CHAPTER 4

DECEMBER 22 – 24, 1845

In a matter of minutes, people began arriving early across the frosty landscape, leaving wheel marks on the icy road. A clear night and freezing temperatures had created a sunny but cold day. The yard between the barn and house first had one wagon, then another, and soon children were flying around like bees in the sunshine – running around the trees, hiding under wagons, or chasing each other in a buzzing frenzy. A huge oak and bigleaf maple stood leafless with dark arms stretching and yawning against the morning sky.

Margaret had brought her girls, the sisters Eliza and Sarah, as well as Mary Jane Holmes and Crow; Meek and his wife, Virginia, had come with their children and the rest of Doc's boys. Even the two-year-old Thomas Jefferson Newell ran around on toddler's legs with all the others, giggling and following his brothers. Crow barked constantly and ran with the children, making more commotion. Black Saul sat on a bench on the front porch, picking his teeth with a wood splinter as he watched them playing; he was smiling wide with the sun making his white teeth gleam.

When Francis and William came out of the barn with the milk pail full and held between them, they passed the watering trough on the side of the barn where all the horses stood and came to a dead stop to watch all the children. The siblings glanced at each other with an unsaid message, started walking, and soon increased their pace, at the expense of milk sloshing to the ground; they headed for the house. In a blink, they were back out again to join the frolicking.

An hour ago, Doc had started a fire out in the smokehouse. He also replenished the hearth with new oak logs and placed five winter squashes around the edges in some of the coals from last night. Mattie had been ordered to stay in the rocker by the fire, "You're just to sit. Well, you can talk, but I don't want you up or helping. Using the pot under the bed is the only place you're allowed to go today. I don't want your wound to open and start bleeding."

Mattie promised to stay seated and found herself listening more than talking. Meek's wife Virginia and Margaret were preparing a hunk of bear meat.

Virginia was talking. "I learn to hunt rabbits with shotgun, but my man he trap so much I no need to hunt. I do all the skinning for small ones, like raccoons and squirrels, and I like to skin. But to skin a bear needs more people. With bear I do cooking and eating; I like better to eat. No skin a bear for me.

Margaret interrupted, "When the smokehouse is ready, we'll have a lot of work cutting that bear for *charqui*. We'll have to make really thin slices or it will be too tough."

Mattie asked, "When my Grandpappy killed a lamb, it was so much more tender than the sheep. I guess it's the same with bear meat."

Meek's wife nodded, "Course, you right, if you have a young one, all tender. Today that bear an old-timer. He going to be a tough one. You lucky he not kill you."

Mattie remembered an unfinished conversation. "Margaret, you said that you'd tell me about Mary Jane and her family. Mary Jane is the cutest little girl."

Before beginning, Margaret grimaced while cutting through some gristle. "There was a wagon train with over five hundred people that arrived here in forty-four. It was the largest westward train to ever come, and a Negro, Moses Harris, was the guide. Like many men who guided the wagon trains, he had been a trapper and explorer. He may be the best guide there is. Mary Jane's family was among the people on that train. On the same wagon train was a man called Nathaniel Ford and the Holmeses came as his slaves. Ford was the leader of the wagon train.

"After they had been here a few months, I met the Holmeses at a religious meeting and we became friends. Remember, I told you that Mrs. Holmes is having a baby right now and, until she is up and about, I promised to care for Mary Jane. But I told Mr. and Mrs. Holmes that Oregon is a free state and they should be free. They said that Mr. Ford had promised them their freedom if they came with him to Oregon and helped him set up his farm. When they agreed, they didn't know that the law forbids slavery in Oregon. But they wanted to keep their promise to help set up Mr. Ford's farm. Then they'll legally have papers that state that they are free. So, I'm just watching. I don't trust Mr. Ford and I told him to his face that I'm watching."

Mattie asked, "Can't the Holmes family be set free?"

"No one wants to interfere. The law states that Ford has three years to set them free. One year has passed already. So, I'm watching."

The women were quiet for a while. It was one of those moments when the three women filled the room with thoughts about the injustice toward others. If their thoughts could be written into the space of the cabin, it would have crowded the air; as it was, they felt they were suffocating in the inequity – not only for Negroes and Indians but also for themselves, women. It gnawed at one's soul, yet women had no power to change things. Oregon was a man's world. Margaret had scars and bruises to remind her; Dr. Bailey often hurt her when he was drunk.

Mattie sat and worried about what was going to happen to her.

"Oh," Margaret stopped cutting and turned to face Mattie, "where are your clothes that were torn? Possibly I can fix them. Those were good breeches, and Doc's sons could use them. I'll soak the blood out first." Margaret rinsed her hands in a basin of water for that purpose and dried them on her apron. "Don't move! Just tell me where the clothes are."

When Margaret came from the corner with the tattered clothes; Virginia was kneeling at the hearth, placing metal skewers with small fingers of bear meat near the fire. She smiled at Margaret and said, "I a-goin' to watch these little tasty pieces while you get those clothes in saltwater. They should just take a few minutes to cook 'cuz these are the tender parts of that bear. I like 'em crisp and black on the edge. When you come back in, we need to cook up all these eggs. Why, Doc ain't been here much and the chickens don't stop droppin' 'em. That's good! We got a lot of people to feed."

"Bear strips, squash, and eggs, that sounds like a good breakfast." Margaret said with a smile.

Virginia commented, "Too bad the bear fat not ready. I like to cook with it."

Margaret explained, "So do I. I will render my share tomorrow. I do lots of cooking and frying with it, too. I even make biscuits with bear fat."

Mattie wondered aloud, "Do you use it for other things?"

Margaret looked up at the girl. "My, oh my, yes! I shall tan the hide of that bear using its own fat. Well, once it is rendered."

"I use for medicine and soap." Virginia interjected. "And it have lots of other uses, too."

Doc and Joe were outside skinning and cutting flesh from fat when Dr. William Bailey rode up. "Morning, everyone. I came to see our new bear rug and that girl who got bloodied from the bear. My, he's a big one. Look at him!" Pointing to the carcass where the men were working, he said, "Without his fur he looks like a human."

Doc nodded in agreement. "Good morning, William. Yep, he does look human. Thanks for coming. Your wife said that we can stop skinning for some breakfast in just a few minutes. We cut off some choice tender slabs of this bear for this morning so go check the girl's wound and then get ready to eat."

As Dr. Bailey approached the house he found Margaret wiping the scuffed knee of little Thomas Jefferson Newell – the two-year-old. Mattie's torn clothes were in a bucket of saltwater under the tree where she worked. He extended his hand to pull her up to standing, complaining, in jest, "Hey, that's my job – doctoring the wounded." He put a peck of a kiss on her lips as the little Newell boy made a foray into a bunch of wrestling boys. Margaret and her husband walked to the house together amid all the outdoor activities.

Inside, Margaret said, "Meet Mary Anne McAlister, formerly known as Matthew." When Margaret saw Mattie looking at Bailey's disfigured face that had a ghastly scar along his lopsided jaw, she explained, "This is my husband, Dr. Bailey. He was attacked by Indians who made this scar on his face with a tomahawk. You were lucky that the bear didn't get your face, especially since you will never have a beard to help hide it, like he does." Without further comments, she walked away and grabbed the flour, lard, and baking powder to start biscuits. She pinched some salt from a wooden bowl into the mixture and kneaded it ten times before dividing it between two Dutch ovens that swung over the fire. "I'm going to the root cellar for more butter for this crowd. Need anything else?"

Virginia called out to Margaret as she walked out the door, "Cut some dried rosemary and parsley for us to use in the eggs and on the meat."

Dr. Bailey had raised his eyebrows and widened his eyes upon hearing her name before he set his bag next to the rocker. "Mary Anne McAlister is a fine Scottish name. I'm a Scotsman. Maybe we are related!" Bailey was practicing his bedside manner with the conversation. With much care, he picked up the small girl and placed her on Doc's bed to examine her. He kept talking to calm her.

Finally she smiled and asked, "Are you a real doctor or like Doc?"

"Now there, Doc did a good job with these herbs, but he never went to school to learn like me. Actually, I am a surgeon as well as an everyday doctor. And I am going to be the surgeon right now. I pulled some pieces of fabric out of the wound. I need to pour something on it and stitch you up."

"Like sewing?" Now her beautiful eyes looked amazed and fearful.

"Yes, just like sewing. It will hurt. Do you think you can be brave?"

With a dubious look she nodded.

"Margaret, come be with Mary Anne while I close the deepest gash; the other slashes don't need stitches. Wash your hands first." He turned back to the girl and teased, "We don't want any biscuits growing in you from her hands." He gave a little chuckle before continuing to talk. "There is something you must do. I am the doctor and I say that you must scream; that's important to make all this work. Do you think you can give me the biggest scream you have ever made?"

Puzzled, Mattie nodded.

While Margaret held Mattie's head in her lap, she gripped the girl's hands. Husband and wife gave a nod for a go-ahead and Bailey poured some of his spirits over her wound.

Mattie screamed like the sound of a locomotive coming into the terminal. Virginia jumped and dropped her knife onto the floor. Joe Meek came running in the door and was calmed by his wife. He returned outside, explained to everyone, and then remembered a story. "Why, that reminds me of the time ...."

Bailey smiled at Mattie, "That was the best scream I've heard in a while. That means you are going to get well quickly. Now, take a small sip of my horrible tasting magic potion and then I will sew. Virginia, bring her a wooden spoon to bite on. No need to scream anymore. You will feel little pricks like you're touching a thorn on a rose bush. I think I will make ten stitches."

Mattie was groggy from the laudanum when he finished. After wrapping her rib cage in clean bindings, he left her on the bed. He knew she would sleep.

Bailey went outside and told Doc in private, "A young man was asking around about a Negro girl. He wanted to know if we had seen a girl about eleven years old by the name of Mary Anne McAlister. He said the family called her Mattie and she was his slave."

"No!" Doc held his bloodied hands out in front of his chest. "Damn it all! Let me clean my hands. We need to talk to Joe about this. By gum, she was safer while pretending to be the boy Matthew."

When breakfast was ready, the plates were placed in a stack on an outdoor table next to the flatware that was all jumbled in a drawer they had pulled out of the cupboard. The mugs for coffee were in the cabin on the floor next to the hearth for the grown-ups to pour their own from the coffee pot. Tin drinking cups were filled with milk for the youngsters. Crocks with apple butter, small wooden plates of butter, two steaming hot iron skillets with eggs, Dutch ovens with biscuits, slices of winter squash, and skewers of roasted bear meat were placed directly on the wooden planks of the table. People filled their plates and sat on the edge of the porch or along benches leaning against the house or with their backs to a tree. All the hustle and bustle of the morning stopped. Yet, nothing stopped the excitement as laughter and conversation were enjoyed as much as the food.

Mattie was taken outside to be with everyone. The four men had picked up the rocker with her in it and taken her out.

Doc reminded her again, "Don't you walk any! You could open your wound. You're not worth shuck if you get sicker and I want you well to make more of your fresh cheese." Doc interrupted his talk to put a kiss on her forehead. "Remember that Dr. Bailey said if you split the wounds open they could get infected. And did you hear him say that he liked that I put a poultice of yarrow to stop your bleeding?"

Mattie nodded and replied, "He did tell me."

"I'll go get us some food." When he arrived back at her side, he placed her plate in her lap and put his on a stump that was to be his chair. He didn't sit. "I'll be right back, Mattie."

Doc headed toward the barn where Black Saul and Dr. Bailey were standing with their backs to the group. They didn't notice their host heading their way until Doc put his hands on their shoulders. "Gentlemen, I would appreciate if you would honor my rule of abstinence on my property. And I mean my whole mile-by-mile square property."

With a sheepish look, Dr. Bailey turned to face him and slipped his tin flask back into his jacket pocket.

Doc insisted, "Black Saul, please water the ground with the contents of your coffee cup." The black coffee mixed with hidden booze drizzled to their feet. "Now, let's enjoy this glorious day and return to the group." Doc had the two men laughing with a story before they had crossed the barnyard. Neighbors were too close and too needed for anyone to hold grudges. Besides, they had a lot more work to do that afternoon, as friends.

By the time the three men arrived back under the trees where everyone was eating, they heard Joe Meek telling one of his stories.

Joe called out, "Doc, we watched Black Saul pour out his spirits and I thought about the fools and maniacs at the rendezvous we mountain men and trappers had most years. Remember back in July of thirty-two?" Now Joe turned to his audience to explain further. "Thar always was some kind of alcoholic beverage – diluted and foul, but better then none at all. I remember the time one redheaded trapper said he weren't ne'r baptized. So one of the men poured his kettle of spirits on all his red curls and started spouting some biblical verses to baptize him.

"Wal, it were unfortunate, but another crazy was dancin' round with a flamin' stick, and it bobbed onto the red hair. Whoosh! Men jumped up and started beatin' the fire with saddle blankets and hats. The beating was as bad as the flames. Why, it nearly proved fatal. He got a baptism by fire."

Many gasped, but Joe Meek slapped his leg and howled with laughter at his own punch line. Soon everyone laughed along.

Doc chimed in, "After the rendezvous, we took off with Milton and William Sublette, Bridger, and some others. Remember, Joe? After one day we came upon a battle between the Blackfeet, Nez Percé, and Flatheads. Naturally, we got pulled into the fight and it went on for days. William Sublette got seriously wounded. At that time, lots of Indians were dead and one night, after they buried theirs, they just disappeared. We wanted to leave, too, but William Sublette couldn't travel. Joe, you volunteered to stay back with him, travel slow, and nurse his wounds. So we split up.

"I went off with Bridger and Milton Sublette with his wife named *Umentucken Tukutsey Undewatsey.*" Doc hesitated with an aside to explain, "Her name means Mountain Lamb." Then he continued, "We went north and, on the first day of August, her baby was born. The very next day, we traveled fifteen miles and so did Mountain Lamb with her child. She was a beautiful woman and as hardy as any man."

"Ho!" Joe shouted, "Watching all of you with bulging mouths full of food, I remember another part of the story. Me and wounded William Sublette went south where the Injuns war friendlier. We zigzagged along the Snake River until we got lost. Wal, not jus' lost, we war hot and hungry. It war the land of sagebrush and thirst." Joe stopped and picked up a pitcher of water before adding, "Jus' thinkin' 'bout that time makes me have a thirst." He drank down the whole pitcher and wiped his mouth with his shirtsleeve. "I gotta admit that I saved William's life. I nursed his wounds and fed him good. Let me tell you how. Thar weren't any buffalo or deer; we were in a desert. So, I held my right hand in an anthill 'til it was covered with those ants and then I licked them off. Then I put my left hand in the anthill and let William lick that hand clean. I took the soles from my moccasins, crisped them in a fire, and we had a good supper. Another day, I found some large black crickets and threw them into a kettle of boilin' water. When they stopped kickin', we ate. That's how we kept alive."

People laughed or nodded in appreciation of Joe's stories. Listening to his tales was good entertainment after hard work. Sometimes it was the only entertainment available, and not everyone had the gift of gab like Joe Meek.

◆ ◆ ◆

After eating, everyone got back to work. Mattie stayed outside under the huge oak tree and slept again. The rocker was wide with a high back lined in cotton padding on the rungs, with a seat displaying a soft, embroidered pillow, and with armrests made round and smooth from use.

When Mattie awoke much later she met Doc's youngest – little Thomas Jefferson. His eyes were fighting sleep when he found the new girl in the rocker, and he began to bring her things like acorns and oak galls. They talked about the objects accumulating in her lap and looked at birds that happened to fly their way. Not that the boy talked much. He made one-word comments and pointed. Finally, Mattie placed acorn caps on the ends of her fingers and began some make-believe where her fingers were puppets; she made the voice of a man and another of a child and one of a villain. Little Thomas Jefferson climbed onto the stump to hear the story. Also looking sleepy, little four-year-old Mary Jane wandering up to them and stayed to hear the puppet tale. She nestled herself at Mattie's feet. Before long and before the story ended, Mattie had two little ones dozing, among the hem of her dress. Mattie began to sing softly, and Crow came by to join the group, curling next to Mary Jane. Mattie closed her eyes, rested her head against the high back, and rocked, humming. This felt like home.

By the time the light disappeared, the five Newell boys and all the Meek children were in the wagon beds, sleeping among slabs of bear meat and buckets of fat for making soap, lighting lamps, and all the other mentioned uses. The smokehouse held more meat for them to pick up on a later date. Doc asked the Meeks if they could care for his boys a while longer because he was planning a trip. Then the Meeks drove away with Black Saul riding alongside.

An hour earlier, Dr. Bailey had left by himself, after checking Mattie's wounds one last time and warning her not to do anything except rest.

Inside the cabin, Margaret had her three sleeping girls nestled on blankets in front of the hearth and a wooly bear hide in a roll at the door. "I'll start tanning that bear tomorrow. An old Indian gave me an obsidian scrapper that I use on my pigskins. Works better than any other tool I know!" Margaret had wanted to be the last to leave because she had something to say. "Robert, I can see you are feeling responsible for this little girl, but it's not proper for her to stay with you alone. I want to take her home with me tonight."

Doc looked at Mattie, asleep in the rocker. He understood why she needed to go but had come to like her company. He nodded his head and gritted his teeth, knowing that, when they all left for the Bailey's place, his thoughts would return to Kitty and death.

Into the back of Margaret's wagon Doc dropped Mattie's pillowcase, containing her Grandpappy's tinderbox and hunting knife. He waved, watching the wagon pull away with all the sleeping girls.

He returned to his door but sat on the porch and pulled off a splinter of wood. While picking his teeth he succumbed to dark thoughts.

Death was something he had seen over and over while fur trapping in the mountains with Meek. Death couldn't be avoided. He witnessed many deaths of Indians and deaths of other mountain men. When it came to trying to understand death, it didn't matter how they died – an accidental slip from a cliff, an arrow to the chest in a violent fight, or just the wasting illness that slowly decays away the flesh. But now – this time – it was different. His woman had died. *How can I fight this death that torments me? It's invisible; I can't touch it, smell it, or hear it. But it lingers near me.*

He took a deep breath and sighed into the night air.

An owl flew silently by and carried Doc's thoughts of death away for only a moment. Like the bird that disappeared into the darkness, Kitty was gone into obscurity. She had been here – to touch and hold, to laugh and tease, to work and birth – and now she was gone. He stared into the direction of the bird's flight and marveled at how it had seemed to melt into the blackness. *Just like Kitty ... just like Kitty disappeared from me. So sudden it was to have her near one day and then cut out of my life the next day. It's like I can't think straight. She vanished from my sight, but I hold on to her in my thoughts. And she calls from the grave to my loins. I still desire her.*

He tried to consider where he was going, what he was to do, and how he would make it through another day. Then he thought of Mattie and smiled. *That little girl sure gave me back some of my life. She was only here a few days and I was my old self. Her singing takes me to another place. I wish she was here right now. I would go inside and watch her breathing in her sleep and feel full again.*

All of a sudden, his heart jumped in his chest. *I forgot to tell Margaret about the young man looking for Mattie! I must go to the Bailey's first thing in the morning to talk to her. Joe, Bailey, and I never talked about what we need to do for that little girl.*

The weakness in his limbs, the despondency in his mind, and the thoughts of death slipped away from him as he found someone who needed his help. He stood and walked to the leafless bigleaf maple in his yard and relieved himself. Then he went to bed.

In the morning, he changed his plan and first rode to Joe Meek's house. *It's interesting how our minds keep working even when we sleep. I hadn't thought enough about Mattie's situation last night. I went to sleep and woke up seeing the depth of this problem.* Doc realized that the law was on the side of this young man looking for Mattie. Oregon law allowed an owner of a slave to keep them until they reach the age of eighteen; then they would be free. So Doc wanted to go to the law; Joe was the sheriff. *I also realized that Mattie has not told us her story. We really don't know much about her except that her grandfather died just before she ran away.*

By the time Doc and Joe Meek were riding toward the Bailey's place, they had many other questions. Doc emphasized other problems. He told Joe, "We don't know where she came from either. Was she living in Oregon or California or somewhere else? Mattie must tell us her story."

"That's right. We war so busy yesterday. We had no time to think this through."

Like Doc's house, Margaret lived in a square house of hewn logs, but the floor plan was different. It had two rooms on the ground floor where there was a fireplace, four windows, one piazza out the front door, and a flight of stairs up to the garret – not a ladder. She had been there since she married

Dr. Bailey in March of 1839; nevertheless, it looked quite different than when she first arrived. There were some sheds and a barn now. In those seven years, the Baileys had accumulated animals – twenty-one cows, thirty horses, eighty-six sheep, three pigs and some piglets, and a dozen goats. Margaret had planted both a vegetable garden on one side of the house and a flower garden in front. There were other places with flowers scattered here and there around her home. Nothing was blooming, since it was December, but the dried stalks and leaves gave an indication of where those flowers had been, and in the summer there would be onions, cabbage, turnips, cucumbers, and corn on the side of her cabin. There were three goats tied to a stake, and they wandered among the remains in the vegetable garden. Sounds of cows could be heard coming from the barn.

On the side of the house opposite the vegetable garden, Sarah and Eliza were hanging some washing onto lines between two oak trees. A sledge with a leather dog harness sat next to one of the oaks and was stacked with stones that had been cleared from the garden; it was ready for Crow to drag it to one of the fields where Margaret was making a stone fence. The girls called out a hello and waved when they saw Doc and Joe. Little Mary Jane was sitting on the piazza eating from a wooden bowl with a spoon; she waved, too. Next to Mary Jane sat an old man eating from another wooden bowl without a spoon.

Margaret came from the open front door, drying her hands on a calico apron. "Hello, Gentlemen. Come in and have some coffee or tea with the biscuits I made for breakfast. Oh, and, if you are really hungry, I can rustle up some other fixins for you. I bet Doc has not eaten breakfast."

"You know me too well, Margaret."

Joe took Doc's reins and led both horses to a hitching post where there was a thick growth of green grass. He passed stacks of split logs, all neatly arranged with the wood crisscrossed at the ends so none would slip or roll. Next to the stacks was a large tree trunk with a cut branch still attached at an angle to form a crotch for holding the logs securely before splitting. The axe was parked with the blade deep in a stump where it waited to be used.

As the men arrived on the piazza, Margaret introduced the old man, "Oofaaf, stops by from time to time. He is my friend and we speak in Chinook Jargon. He is blind now and his people are almost all gone. He is

Kalapuyan." She placed her hand on the old man's shoulder and asked him to meet her friends. "*Oofaaf, chako kunamokst sikhs. Kloshe tumtum.*"

The old man struggled to his feet and made a small bow before speaking, "*Klahowya. Oofaaf wawa sikhs kopa Miz Bailey.*"

First Doc and then Joe reached to take the old man's hand to shake.

The two girls came a running to the house and Margaret asked, "Did you finish hanging all the clothes? If not, go back out and finish. Then we can all visit, knowing our chores are done for the moment."

Sarah and Eliza turned in disappointment and went back, dragging their feet.

Oofaaf said, "*Mahsie,*" before he waved and wandered off.

Joe shouted after the girls, "Hurry and finish. We want you here when we talk."

Startled, Margaret looked at Joe and said, "Is there some problem?"

Jesting, as usual, Joe replied, "No problem, jus' some trouble coming your way."

Doc was still standing and looking around the keeping room, "Where's Mattie?"

"Here I am," said a small voice from the middle of Margaret's bed in the next room. "I'm not supposed to move around. Dr. Bailey brought me down from the garret to his bed. Now I'm closer to everyone."

Within minutes, the men had eaten and the girls had hung all the wash. The group sat around a circular table. Mary Jane sat on Margaret's knee and Mattie remained in bed, but she could see and hear through the open door.

Doc asked, "Did your husband tell you about a young man inquiring if anyone knew the whereabouts of an eleven-year-old Negro girl named Mattie?"

"No! Willy was drunk last night and left early, still rather drunk. What does this mean?"

Mattie made a whimper and Doc walked to the bedside and sat. He told her, "Stay calm, Mattie. There's no need to cry. You're with friends who want to help you. We want you to know that we'll stick with you till the cows come home. Understand?"

She nodded.

Joe walked to the bed and smiled, "Why, yar talking to the Sheriff Joe Meek and we wants to help all we can. First, ya need to tell us your life story. We gotta know everythin' 'bout ya."

Doc took her hand. Margaret picked up her chair and came to sit by the bed. Sarah and Eliza did the same.

When Mattie finished, Doc stood and started to pace. "All right, it seems that her grandfather owned her mother. Mattie thinks this young man looking for her is one of her half-brothers. You said either Tom or Jed McAlister?" When she nodded, he asked, "Joe, if the grandfather was the owner, do they have the right to claim her as their slave?"

"You know, I don't know the answer. We need to talk to a lawyer or judge about that."

Margaret spoke up, asking, "She lived in California. Can they come into Oregon and use our laws to claim her?"

Joe shook his head and muttered, "Got me a-gin. I jus' don't know." He walked closer to the bed and touched Mattie on her head, "What you did – walkin' all that way – you took the bull by the horns. That's over two hundred miles!" He leaned over to kiss her forehead and noticed that she was clutching something. "Whatcha got there?"

"It's my Grandpappy's tinderbox. No, it's mine. He gave it to me when I learned how to use it to make a fire in his room each night."

Doc stood and looked at the tinderbox in the open palm of her hand. He picked up the thin rectangular wooden box with a tin lid. He slid the tin lid and opened the box for all to see. "This is a mighty fine tinderbox. And look, he had his name punched into the tin lid. Doc showed the letters: M c A L I S T E R.

Doc lifted the D-shaped firesteel out of the box. "This is of really fine quality. And look at the little compartments: one for the charcloth and another for long narrow wood splinters. Oh, what's this?" Doc asked as he brought the nail and fishhook out between his two fingers.

Mattie smiled, "Oh, the nail is for nothing, but that's where I keep my fishhook so it don't stick me. I like to fish."

Joe shook his head. "Mattie, I'm disappointed. I jus' don't like eating fish much. It jus' don't fill me."

"Me and my Grandpappy loved eating fish."

Doc laughed as he turned to Joe to say, "Be careful what you say to this girl, Joe. She just might make you eat crow."

Without even blinking or thinking, Joe retorted, "I don't like eating crow either whether it's a bird or a dog."

Everyone laughed.

Before Doc and Joe left they established some rules and swore everyone to secrecy. Sarah and Eliza promised not to talk about Mattie to anyone.

Little Mary Jane had fallen asleep in the corner on a blanket and heard nothing about keeping this secret. Nevertheless, no one could expect a small child to keep this kind of promise, so Margaret swore to keep her close at all times.

Margaret got out her rifle and loaded it, placing it near the door, ready to use. "William carries his colt revolver with him. Maybe he will let me use it for the time being."

Doc commented, "At least Mattie is in bed for a while. No one will see her walking around outside." He sat down and took Sarah and Eliza's hands into his before saying, "This is a situation where you must tell a white lie, if the need arises. If someone asks about Mattie or Mary Anne McAlister, you must deny knowing of her. Can you do that?"

They nodded.

Margaret stepped in and took their hands from Doc. "I want to say something more. I don't want to embarrass anyone, but facts of life are the facts of life. Mary Anne told us that those two half-brothers of hers came to her bed and forced themselves on her. She protested and screamed and their mother and father did not come to help her. I have talked about the marriage bed with you two girls, so you know what happened to her."

All of a sudden, Margaret got a hateful look in her eyes and spit out her next words, "No man is a man who forces his male desires onto a female of any age. They are beasts, not a man! If you deny knowing Mary Anne, God would not think it a lie. You will be protecting an innocent girl."

Joe agreed, "Margaret's right." And he promised to make it his job to try to find the half-brother asking for Mattie.

Margaret decided not to go to the McLoughlin's Christmas party. "Doc, I'll stay here with Mary Anne, but would you take Sarah and Eliza? I don't know if my husband will be drunk or sober and the girls deserve to go. I have been teaching them how to eat properly, carry a fine conversation, and dance. This will be their first opportunity to practice what they have learned."

Joe slapped his knee and laughed, "I got me an idea. My holiday party is about a week away and Mattie should be mostly healed. Margaret, I want ya and Mattie ta come to my party. Dress her like a boy and call her Matthew. She'll be safe. These are different people than those who go to the McLoughlin's. Thar won't be any strangers from wagon trains 'cuz they warn't invited." And he let out one of his horselaughs.

On the evening of McLoughlin's Christmas party, it was dark at five o'clock when the guests began to approach Fort Vancouver. A soft drizzle did not dampen the excitement for Sarah and Eliza as they rode up to The Hudson's Bay Company's complex. Within this kingdom on the Columbia River there were over forty buildings – housing for all of the Company's trusted men and their families, a school and library, a chapel, a pharmacy and hospital, as well as storage for grain, a blacksmith, and more. There was a long line of wagons full of guests as Doc approached the gate and walls made of twenty-foot high vertical logs; the Fort was 750 feet long by 450 feet wide. To the girls, it seemed a well-protected kingdom, complete with armed guards.

Sitting under umbrellas, the girls looked around and Doc gave one of his lessons. "All the fields and orchards you see belong to The Hudson's Bay Company. What you see outside the walls is everything they need – a dairy, vegetable gardens, a tannery, a shipyard, grist and sawmills, and a distillery. There are shops to make clothing and leather goods. All the homes are for the workers. Look over there at the stacks of barrels. A cooper made those barrels for packing furs to send to the East, for pickled salmon, and all sorts of foodstuffs. And look the other way at the wheelwright's shop with all the wheels and boards to make wagons. He continued pointing and describing the Kanaka Village that surrounded the Fort until they arrived at the gate. Doc showed his invitation to a man with a rifle slung over his shoulder before proceeding forward into the Fort.

Eliza scowled, "Did you smell the smoke from the pipes of those two Indians that were standing outside the gate? It smelled horrible."

Sarah agreed that it made a stink, but was curious. "I have never seen Indians with flattened heads like that."

"To have flattened brows is a sign of status in the Chinook tribe. They are noblemen in the tribe."

Walking into the home of Marguerite and Dr. McLoughlin was like entering a house in Europe or New York City. The décor was elegant, with velvet draperies, plush sofas, huge mirrors, and a mahogany table to seat twenty-two guests, although on this night there was no sit-down dinner. An assortment of delicious food filled the table on large platters and in bowls; Doc showed the girls how to take a small china plate and a piece of silverware to serve themselves from the many dishes.

Three men with violins were playing softly from a corner of the dining room while the guests mingled and ate. Doc noticed that many of the guests were British men who worked for Hudson's Bay Company or who had come on one of the ships docked in the harbor. Doc was acquainted with most settlers – the Americans and the retired fur trappers – but not the British. At one point, Doc wondered where Joe was. Soon he knew that Joe Meek was there because he could hear Joe's loud guffaws across the room.

"There must be at least fifty guests here," Doc told the girls. "It's just my estimate, but with the hoopskirts of the women's gowns, it seems more crowded."

When it was time to dance, those with a partner went through French doors into a room that had been cleared of furniture. The men with violins stood by a harpsichord and the music began again with very traditional tunes for dances. *The King's Head Reel* was playing.

Sarah felt shy, but delighted, when a man asked her to dance. Doc offered to dance with Eliza. In all the dances, they formed long lines or circles where the partners separated and passed to another partner.

It was later in the evening when Doc was dancing to the tune *Soldiers' Joy* with Eliza again – passing to another woman and back to Eliza, over and over – that he came upon a beautiful young woman and lost his heart. He could not remember ever reacting to a woman in that manner. He found he could not take his eyes off her even when she progressed around the circle with other partners. Everyone seemed to disappear from his sight and he barely noticed that he had circled with other partners. He stared at her, waiting to touch her again when she came around the circle.

After the dance finished, he could not find her until the party was ending. There she was across the room and he didn't even know her name. He was frantically trying to squeeze past people to get to her and introduce himself. But then, she vanished.

Sarah and Eliza came up to him with their wraps on. "This was wonderful. Thank you for bringing us."

Doc seemed to not hear as he craned his neck to see above the crowd.

Sarah asked, "Who are you looking for?"

"The woman in the green dress with a yellow sash."

"Do you mean Miss Rebecca Newman?"

John McLoughlin, Chief Factor of Hudson's Bay Company
Photograph from Project Gutenberg Archives.

CHAPTER 5

DECEMBER 26 – 30, 1845

Another crisp day with sunshine arrived and inspired adventure. Doc awoke with an idea and rushed through all his chores. The cow complained about his rough, impatient pull to her teats and the chickens only got half the normal feed before he saddled up and headed over to the Bailey's farm. On the ride, his motive lifted his spirits and made him want to shout aloud in joy. He was hoping to find where Miss Rebecca Newman lived.

When he got to the Bailey's farm, he suggested to Margaret, "My keelboat *Ben Franklin* is still at the water's edge. Let's take a trip to Oregon City. Have the girls been there?"

"No, they haven't."

He faced Mattie and explained, "Oregon City is located right on the Willamette Falls. Those falls are beautiful! Have you heard of Willamette Falls?"

Mattie shook her head, and Margaret furrowed her brow, starting to object, but Doc continued.

"Right now I don't have any Kalapuyans working my keelboats, but I can man the oars alone since it's all downstream. Mattie won't have to move much in the boat. It'll be a smooth ride. And we can dress her in her usual disguise as Matthew. Surely her wounds have scabbed over enough." Doc would not stop talking. "She can relax and watch the scenery instead of sitting here recuperating, and then we can have breakfast at the Moss Hotel." Again, before Margaret could respond, his enthusiasm carried him on, "I need Black Saul's help today to make some benches for Joe's party that's in a couple of days. We'll find him and borrow his wagon to come back. I'll leave *Ben Franklin* docked at Oregon City to wait for some business. It's not the time of year for shipping supplies, but someone might want a trip to Champoeg."

Margaret acquiesced.

They left her horse and wagon at his farm and walked to the water's edge; Doc carried Mattie to *Ben Franklin*. On the start of the journey, the sun had slipped behind clouds and the Willamette River was shrouded in silence from fog. Enclosed in the quiet of a cathedral made by nature, they floated without words. Doc maneuvered the boat with an oar. The visibility was dense enough that, here and there, they startled a heron and some ducks; the racket of wings hitting water and the squawking seemed sacrilege. Then, around one bend, they left the fog behind. Ahead, a snow-covered Mount Hood burst into view, and on their right was the rich bottomland stretching south. Growing close to the river's edge, trees blocked their view from time to time and then created an opening to show hills covered in timber of fir, oak, white maple, and white ash.

"See these grasslands around Champoeg?" Doc pointed with a sweep of his arm and he switched to his teacher-of-children character. "Remember I told you that the Kalapuyan Indians created them by seasonal burns? I never saw them burning and I guess they stopped because there aren't enough Indians living here now to continue their practice. They never planted these fields, but they were making the land ready for us to farm wheat and oats. Do you remember what I said? I told you why they burned these fields when we were riding to the Fort."

All of the girls shook their heads.

Doc said, "I'll explain it better, so you will remember. When Lewis and Clark were here in 1805 or so, Clark saw the fires and wrote about them. It's known that the Kalapuyans were burning the dried grasses of the camas plant so it would grow better in the spring. They processed the bulbs of the roots to make cakes in ten-inch rounds; it was their food through the winter months. And they traded their famous camas cakes with other tribes for seafood, shells, or other things." Doc took a breath, "Of course you girls are familiar with the purple-blue camas lily flower that blooms in springtime?"

Sarah nodded, "I am."

Eliza said, "Me, too."

Mattie said, "No, I don't know it. Could I meet some of the Kalapuyans?"

"Aren't many around."

Margaret interrupted, "You met one. Remember Oofaaf? He was at my place. Oh, you were in my bed! I guess you didn't see him."

Doc continued his lesson. "The year that Jason Lee started the Methodist Mission back in 1835 or so, eighty percent of the Kalapuyans died that first winter. I don't know who brought in the diseases that caused the deaths, but the remaining Kalapuyans are not the same as years ago. With so few in their tribe, they cannot sustain themselves. It takes many working together to have the life they once knew. Now, those who remain are sickly and sad."

"But you said that you hired Kalapuyans to man the oars for these keelboats when it's the season. Could we go see them?"

"I don't know where they are right now. It's December, and if they want work in springtime, they'll come to me. I don't know where to go to find them. They don't have a village or even houses; they live under evergreen trees."

Eliza worried, "But who will bring the *Ben Franklin* back to Champoeg?"

"It can stay at Oregon City until someone wants transport; anyone can man the keelboat. They can ask at the hotel or livery stables. When they arrive they pay me for the trip and I'll pay whoever was the oarsman."

"Oh," Eliza responded, "but why does someone want to come to Champoeg? There's not much there."

Doc huffed, "That's not so. The Hudson's Bay Company has a granary with a store in Champoeg and there's a house for the caretaker who handles any business with the granary and store. Andre Longtain has a house between the granary and mine. And we have a ferry that goes across the Willamette River. That's plenty of reason to come to Champoeg if you have grain to sell or want a store. Besides, if someone wants to go south to Mission Mill, they have to go there first. The Methodist Mission relocated in Mission Mill, fifteen miles south of Champoeg on the new road that was built last year. The river gets too many rapids south of us so people put in at Champoeg. Probably the most important new construction is Mr. Pettygrove's warehouse for grain; he put a thorn in The Hudson's Bay Company's side with his competition. People come to his store and sell their grain and wares. Yes, Champoeg is growing."

"I didn't see any of those places."

Margaret helped Doc, "Girls, remember, it was foggy today. The buildings are far apart and out of view from Doc's cabin. Oh, Robert, you didn't mention that Howard's Tavern is in Champoeg." She often cursed the tavern because Dr. Bailey went there, gambled, and got drunk.

"Yes, John Howard has a farm not far from Champoeg and he opens a tavern with drink and gaming in the summertime, when there are more people in the area." Doc knew of Margaret's contempt for the place. He coughed and continued, "His tavern is closed for the winter."

Mattie asked, "Why do you call him Robert when everyone else calls him Doc?"

Margaret was sitting with Mattie's head in her lap. She looked down at the girl and said, "Robert is a name not to be discarded. It is strong and feels good on my tongue whenever I pronounce it. I call my husband William unless I want to tease him. Then he is Willy." A gust of wind raised skirts, and Margaret grabbed her bonnet. "And I am going to call you Mary Anne. Every time I hear *Mattie* I think of what you told us about your brothers making fun of your beautifully curly hair."

A huge bird seemed to come from nowhere and careened toward the river a few yards in front of them. Margaret pointed to the bald eagle as it headed away with a fish in its talons.

Mattie exclaimed, "Oh, that was exciting!"

They floated quietly for a time before Doc picked up the topic again. "I'll give Mattie a little geography lesson. John McLoughlin laid out a town plan for Oregon City in 1842. It's located just beyond Willamette Falls. We'll be there soon and you'll see a city that's doing quite well. And Portland is north of Oregon City on the Willamette River. But it's my idea to make Champoeg the heart of the government, so I plan to donate land for that use."

Approaching the falls, Doc veered toward the southern bank, where a slough went around an island in the river below the falls. Each girl clutched the edge of the boat with both hands to steady against the rush of water while Doc exerted great effort to row the boat into a natural lagoon and finally toward the bank. They each relaxed when the boat touched bottom and slipped onto the shore.

The island held two large buildings owned by The Hudson's Bay Company, a sawmill and a gristmill, which had been productive for years. One of John McLoughlin's responsibilities was to make sure there was ample food and shelter for the thousands of employees and their families in his area – a wide span of land from the Rockies to the Pacific and from Alaska to California – where he had twenty-five settled outposts or forts stationed with people growing crops and cutting timber.

Doc jumped from *Ben Franklin* and hauled it farther onto land. "Like I said, John McLoughlin made the plans for all of Oregon City." He stopped pulling the boat and pointed up a slope. "You can't see the city just yet. It's up the bank and behind me." Doc turned to point the other way to the island. "Back in 1829 he had those mills on the island built for The Hudson's Bay Company."

He extended his hand to help each girl from the boat. "We only need to walk a block once we get up this steep bank to the walkway. I'll carry Mattie up this hill. I mean Matthew."

The girls looked back at Willamette Falls and Mattie exclaimed, "My goodness, I have never seen anything so beautiful."

Doc interjected, "You should see Celilo Falls up past the Dalles on the Columbia River. They are majestic."

"I would like to see them. Could we take a trip there sometime?" Margaret said as she adjusted her bonnet.

"Oh, Margaret, let's not bite off more than we can chew. That's a two-day trip on horseback. Not as easy as today with my keelboats. But maybe someday we'll go. Mattie could see Indians like she wants, too. Not the Kalapuyans, but many other tribes."

As they walked up the slope from the river's edge, first a church steeple poked above the top of the hill and into their view. Soon lines of smoke, floating up from chimneys, started to appear until finally they saw building after building lining a finished street. Most were wooden structures except for a large brick store. They saw people bustling all over the place – not just a few, but dozens.

Mattie exclaimed, "I didn't think there was any place like this here in Oregon. This is a real city. Look at all the people!"

Sarah said, "Where are all the people going?"

The look on Doc's face reflected hurt.

Margaret leaned closer to Doc and spoke in a soft voice. "Robert, we saw no one in Champoeg. You can understand why this really looks like a city to these girls. And it's early in the day and the streets are full." Instantly, Margaret regretted implying that Oregon City was more advanced than Champoeg. She knew his plans to make Champoeg a great place and his hopes to have it the capital of Oregon.

Doc changed the subject. They were standing on Water Street at Third Street. "Look, they're finishing up McLoughlin's house," he nodded toward a two-story frame home where a couple of men worked with hammers and saws. "And the building across the street is where the newspaper resides. Yep, *The Oregon Spectator* is going to be real in just over a month. We'll go inside later." Pointing, he said, "That brick building belongs to Mr. Abernethy; it's his general store and everyone calls it The Brick Store."

"Let's go there, too!"

"I reckon we can do that, but now we need to head for the Moss Hotel one street up on Main. We need to eat and I need to ...." Doc saw someone coming and indicated for everyone to wait where they were. He stood Mattie on the wooden walk and ran into the street. He stopped a horse rider and then returned to his group of girls. "I asked that gent to give a note to Black Saul. I'd hoped to see someone heading out that way. That was lucky. Remember, Black Saul is our ride home this afternoon."

They continued strolling down Water Street with *Matthew* in his arms and passed an alley on the other side of the McLoughlin house. "This is the Cliff House and the Masonic Hall that they're building. Just up the street is the First Protestant Church. I understand that McLoughlin donated a whole block for a Catholic Church up on Tenth Street." With no hands free, Doc pointed with his chin extending in the direction of Water Street, explaining, "That's where it's to be built. McLoughlin converted to

Catholicism just a couple of years ago, so he wants a Catholic Church."
When they reached Fourth Street, there were smaller sheds and buildings
between them and what looked like the end of town where rock bluffs rose
up more than one hundred feet and surrounded the whole city.

Once they were settled at a table in the hotel dining room and waiting
for their food, Doc walked to the hotel desk and returned with a sheet of
paper. "Look, girls, this is the competition for *The Oregon Spectator*." On
the table he spread a page with the words, *The Flumgudeon Gazette*,
handwritten across the top. They laughed as the girls practiced reading the
news about some baked goods for sale, someone offering his services to dig a
well, and Mrs. Smith's lost dog.

"There's another paper like this. See, it's tacked to the wall by the
door," he pointed. "It's called *Bumble Bee Budget* and they leave copies here
and there – on a post in the general store, here at the hotel, and the wall at
the post office. All handwritten."

Margaret bragged, "I don't think you have any competition. *The
Oregon Spectator* will be the only real newspaper."

While the girls read the paper on the table, Doc confessed to Margaret
that he had another motive to come to Oregon City. "I met a young lady at
McLoughlin's party and I would like to get to know her better. Do you
know Miss Rebecca Newman?"

Margaret was pleased to hear of his interest. "I'm sorry, but I don't
know her. I spend so much time on my farm. I just have no time to
socialize."

"Well, she attends Mrs. Thornton's boarding school here, and I
thought I would go to the school to inquire where her parent's live."

The waiter came with the food. It smelled delicious and the girls asked
if they could begin eating.

"Yes, let's all begin to eat so we can go find information about this
young lady." Margaret smiled and said just to Doc, "Robert, I am happy you
have an interest. This is good for your health and state of mind."

Dark clouds had rolled over to cover the sky while they ate, but they didn't
notice as they walked. Laughing at some comment, Margaret slipped her

arms into the elbows of Sarah and Eliza as they strolled back down Water Street. Mary Jane ran ahead. They headed toward The Oregon Printing Company.

Margaret came to an abrupt stop, "Look, Robert! That must be John McLoughlin standing down there in front of his house. There can't be anyone else as tall as he with wild, white hair like that!"

"Yep, that's him and his wife, Marguerite. You can hardly see her. She stands, more or less, five-feet to his six-foot-four. Shall we go greet them?" And so they approached the McLoughlins, who were giving instructions to their workmen.

"Hello, Robert, what brings you to Oregon City?" McLoughlin said, with an extended hand. Introductions were made and each girl curtsied, even little Mary Jane.

Margaret gestured to the child in Doc's arms. "Matthew has stitches from an injury. Dr. Bailey said he should not walk much today."

"I see," McLoughlin said, "Excuse me while I translate for Marguerite, since she speaks in French. We are from Quebec and that is our native tongue. Well, she also speaks Chinook Jargon, but to use it would limit our conversation, and I don't believe any of you speak French. Am I correct?"

Margaret smiled to Marguerite, "*Je parle un peu français.*"

"Wonderful, wonderful," McLoughlin said in a deep, strong voice, "I appreciate the respite from translating. I shall speak English for Robert. Would you and Robert like to have a tour of our new home?"

She answered the question with a simple, "*Oui.*"

"Today, Marguerite and I came with some housewares. We hope to move into the house in the coming month. The house needs only a few final adjustments, but we can't move until they finish constructing the detached cooking house. That's what they are working on over there."

They entered a large entrance hall with a wide staircase, "The double doors have not been hung for the parlor or dining room. I asked the workmen to start a fire today in the parlor, let's go in there. I want to see if it has a good draw. I have my office off the parlor." They walked to one side of the room to see. "And the room opposite my office is a sewing room for Marguerite. To show how Americanized I am becoming, I plan to have my furniture maker at the Fort produce one of those American ideas for a chair

94

– a rocking chair for myself and another for her." He laughed "A large poppa bear size and a small mama bear rocker."

After they toured the four upstairs bedrooms, they talked about the extra large dining room. "We have a table that seats twenty-two people." McLoughlin made a little chuckle before saying, "Not that they sit on the table; we have chairs to go with it." Now he laughed harder and longer. "As you may know, we do enjoy visitors and entertaining." When they finished the house tour, the women wanted to go to Abernethy's Brick Store.

"Robert, since we have many young girls with us who may not know about Mr. Abernethy, may I give some background on him?" Not waiting for a reply, McLoughlin faced the girls and began, "This year, George Abernethy was elected to be the provisional governor of Oregon. And it is of a humorous note to tell you that it was months before he learned of the honor because he was at sea." McLoughlin allowed himself a hearty laugh again at his own good humor before continuing, "He deserves to be given the position of governor; he is a very capable man. He is also treasurer of The Oregon Printing Company, where Robert is a director. And he was an accountant for the Methodist Mission until he realized the complete mess that they had made of their record books and store organization. He no longer works for them."

They crossed Water Street and headed for The Brick Store. McLoughlin continued his commentary. "He built this impressive building to be in competition with The Hudson's Bay Company, which has been the main provider of supplies to everyone in Oregon Country. Since I am no longer the Chief Factor, I had planned to shop here when we move, but Marguerite tells me that I am to be disappointed. You may or may not know how difficult it is to obtain all the goods for a general store." In French he asked for his wife to elaborate.

Marguerite explained in French, "In a moment, when we enter the doors to The Brick Store, you will see what we mean. Of course they have no molasses or sugar, that is understandable, but you will see no kettles, no tin pans, not one blanket, nor any leather parts for boot repair."

After Margaret translated for the girls, Sarah asked, "Why is it so difficult to get supplies?"

Doc began the answer, "All goods must come by ship and the ships arrive once or twice a year. It usually takes nine months to travel around the horn of South America. Abernethy has lumber and flour he receives as payment from people, and he ships it out for England or the eastern states to sell, but it is difficult for him to find a ship to return with the supplies he wants. He needs his own ship and his own man to sell his flour and lumber and then to buy the supplies he needs."

Soon the group of four adults and four girls was walking around inside the store. Mattie, as Matthew, was allowed to walk a bit. At one point they passed a case of candy; Dr. McLoughlin reached into his vest pocket and produced a few coins and said, "May the children have a sweet treat at my expense?"

"Yes, they may. Children, please thank Dr. McLoughlin."

Marguerite made comments from time to time. "Look, there are no pants or suspenders. I would love to be able to buy some sewing supplies, like bonnet silks and buttons. I can only hope he receives some goods on the next ship."

Margaret had an idea – a way to discreetly ask about Rebecca Newman. "Marguerite, may I call you by your first name?"

"Of course."

"At your party, a young lady named Rebecca Newman had on a lovely green gown. Sarah loved the fabric and I would like to inquire where she bought the fabric. Do you know where they live?"

"Oh, that is Mr. and Mrs. Samuel Newman, who brought their lovely daughter to our party. Can you believe that she is but thirteen years old? She appears to be seventeen, don't you think?"

Margaret's heart jumped upon hearing the age, but she maintained her composure. "Yes, my girls said that she was quite mature in her manners as well. And where do they reside?"

McLoughlin answered, "In the Champoeg District on a farm just a few miles north of Robert's place. Oh, I stand corrected. I understand that the Champoeg District no longer exists; it has been divided into four counties. Hmm, I do not know if they live in the newly named Marion County or Washington County."

Robert overheard and glanced to Margaret with a wide grin and grateful eyes.

The adults walked to a wall in The Brick Store where some hand tools were hanging. Doc noted, "I don't see a hoe, scythe, or hand axe. Let's look in the nail barrel." It was down to the bottom with only a handful of nails. He asked the clerk, "Have you any hinges or door latches? I need some back home." They had none.

There were some bolts of calico fabric that Margaret touched to feel the quality before asking, "How do people make an equal exchange. You know, if I had a barrel of flour to exchange for a small amount of tea, that's not equal. What do they do?"

Marguerite's face brightened before explaining, "Oh, that Mr. Abernethy is very clever. He has these triangle rocks that you call ...." she turned to her husband for help.

McLoughlin translated into English and filled in the word. "Oh, she means *arrowheads* from the Indians. Abernethy gives you an arrowhead for change after writing the value on a paper and gluing the paper to the arrowhead. People walk around with a little sack full of arrowheads and everyone calls them Abernethy Rocks. Since Oregon is not a part of the United States, the settlers have no official money, so they exchange the rocks among themselves for other things. You understand that these rocks have become a medium of exchange now because George Abernethy is highly regarded here in Oregon Country. People bring them to the Fort to pay for goods and we accept them, as well."

When they left The Brick Store, they had agreed to walk together to see The Oregon Printing Company.

"Ah, yes, I forgot to mention that it was George Abernethy who obtained the press to be used for The Oregon Printing Company. His contact with Mr. Francis Hall of New York is the reason that they have a press with all the supplies needed to print *The Oregon Spectator*. Is that not correct, Robert?"

Doc agreed, as McLoughlin held the door for all to enter.

Black Saul pulled up in his wagon after they had been inside for a while. He waited outside, and Doc walked out to invite him in, "If you'd rather wait here, that's fine. We'll be finished in a few minutes."

Mr. Fleming, the man who was hired to set the type and run the printer, was there making adjustments to the press. He explained that he could print 150 to 200 impressions per hour.

Doc said, "We plan to print the newspaper twice a month and hope to have enough news for four pages." He turned to Mr. Fleming to ask, "Have many subscribers signed up for the newspaper so far?"

"Yes, we have ninety people on the list, and it is growing."

After Mr. Fleming cranked the wheel and demonstrated how to print one page, Doc apologized to the McLoughlins. "Margaret and I have obligations and must leave soon. Thank you for sharing time with us." He turned to Mr. Fleming, "This was satisfying for me to see the equipment working and to hear how many subscribers we have. This newspaper is becoming a reality!"

Down the road in the wagon, Doc talked with Black Saul about the help he needed making some benches for the party at Joe Meek's place. They talked about how they were going to make them and how much wood Doc had back in the barn.

Black Saul bragged, "I good with the hammer and saw. We can git this done mighty quick."

Finally Doc began to discuss with Margaret how he was going to find Rebecca Newman and talk to her parents. He wanted to get permission to take her to the Meek's party, and asked Margaret to be the chaperone. "This shouldn't be as hard as finding a needle in a haystack. By gum, I bet Joe Meek knows the family and how to find them."

"You need to put on your charm, and I suggest that you shave off your beard. You look as rough as an uncurried horse. That's a little scary for an innocent young girl."

"I do not! Do you think I should make magic potions and trick her into liking me or just be myself? Black Saul, I don't look scary, do I?"

Black Saul, who was oblivious to what the conversation was about, insisted, "Now don't ya tell me what ya gonna do. Magic potions and tricks? I knows your talk makes me scared. It sound like witchery to me."

Doc started to say something.

Black Saul waved his hand in the air. "No, no! We jus' need to work. I is gonna help make benches, jus' don't talk 'bout what else ya gonna do."

Doc laughed and agreed. It was a private matter anyway; Doc didn't want to let everyone know how he was taken with this thirteen-year-old girl.

Margaret finished the topic by saying, "Robert, take my advice and shave off that beard. Besides, not that you are old, I just am saying that clean-shaven you will look younger. And give me your dress clothes to wash before you try to bewitch her."

On the night of the holiday party, the thirtieth of December, it was raining. Doc had borrowed a fancy surrey with a covered top. Margaret arrived in her battered and weatherworn wagon with Black Saul on the bench next to her and the bed full of three girls, holding umbrellas, and dressed in their finest frocks. Matthew sat with the girls in boy's clothes. They would head for the party at the Meek's home after making a stop at the Newman's house.

As Margaret and Doc walked to Rebecca's front door, the girls waited in the wagon bed and Black Saul held the reins. Margaret commented, "You certainly made a bee-line to this girl. I'm amazed how quickly you found her house and convinced her parents to let you court her."

"Margaret, how insulting of you. Why, I'm a wealthy man and well-known in Oregon. I am quite a catch." He grinned, "However it could have been my clean-shaven face that did it."

With a twinkle in her eyes, she turned to look directly at him and said, "Yes, wealthy and well-known, as well as, overly confident and a bit egotistical."

"I am not!" His agitation showed in his posture with hands on his hips and his head cocked in her direction. He quoted his favorite poet again and said, "Might I say that 'She speaks, yet she says nothing.'"

"I'm pulling your leg, Robert. You know I think you are the most wonderful and intelligent man I know. You are a valued member of Oregon and, I agree, you're quite a catch."

He rubbed his clean-shaven face and straightened his clean dress shirt before knocking on the door of the Newman house.

The Meeks had a new house built from lumber cut at Oregon City. The twelve-inch by sixteen-foot boards had been hauled by ox wagon to Tualatin County to become the first frame house in the area. The boards were nailed horizontally to upright hewn logs and poles; the roof was shingled. His home was quite a change from the existing cabins that would soon be replaced by more lumber homes. However, no matter how old or obsolete, no cabin was left empty. When Virginia and Joe moved out of their cabin, a family with nine children moved in the same day.

The Meeks' new house was big and very different from their prior cabin. Like the McLoughlin's home, an outdoor kitchen for cooking was constructed off to one side of the house with a hearth that was two-sided – the one chimney had an open fireplace for cooking in the kitchen with the same fire open to the keeping room. When Doc's surrey and Margaret's wagon arrived, there were several wagons out front and many horses. Doc said to Rebecca, "Just wait 'til you see their house. It's big and made for a holiday party."

They hurried inside, out of the rain. Margaret and her group followed close behind and were greeted by cheers. The fiddler had arrived!

The main room was quite ample, but as more and more people arrived the place became quite crowded with people bumping shoulders on the dance floor – no one minded. Throughout the evening, Black Saul repeated the few reels and jigs he knew, over and over to the foot-stomping guests. *The Wind that Shook the Barley* was the favorite of the guests.

The Meeks' party was not the formal affair that the McLoughlins' had been; yet Doc and Rebecca addressed each other properly as Mr. Newell and Miss Newman throughout the evening. When Doc presented her to the Meeks, Joe had to tell a story.

Joe put his arm around his wife and asked, "Has Doc told you about how I met Virginia?" When Rebecca shook her head, he grinned and began talking loud enough for most to hear. "In the winter of 1838, when me and Doc finished trappin' and went to be with the Nez Percé tribe again, we fell in love with two sisters whose father was Sub-Chief *Kowesote*. My first wife had died, but I found another beautiful woman in Chief *Kowesote's* daughter." Joe put a kiss on Virginia's cheek and continued, "But he said I war already married. He war talkin' of my second wife. When my second wife told him she didn't want me, he ordered her to give me back my little girl, Helen Mar. This time, with Virginia, I had a woman forever. I called her Virginia like my state of Virginia; that's whar I war born and raised. I love my state and I love my wife. Not necessarily in that order." He chuckled, always first to laugh at his own humor. "I been with Virginia ever since. We have three boys and three girls."

The guests who had been listening gave Virginia and Joe a cheer and clapped. Doc turned to those near and introduced Miss Rebecca Newman to everyone.

A beautiful clock stood on the chimney mantel as the centerpiece of the keeping room. It ticked loudly, asking to be seen. Doc walked to it with Rebecca and explained, "Joe is proud of his clock. As you may know, anyone with a clock must pay an annual tax. Now, since he is Sheriff Joseph L. Meek, this clock not only displays the time but also demonstrates his stature. Anyone who can afford to pay taxes for having the luxury of a clock is considered to be above the average homesteader." Doc had already told Rebecca of his past relationship as a fur trapper. "Yes, Miss Newman, Joe Meek may have been trained in the wild as a fur trapper and bear-fighting mountain man, but he is more. He is on his way to a career of life-long leadership and accomplishments for Oregon. He has a quick wit and sound judgment. Without a doubt, he is independent, reliable, and an asset to Oregon."

When Black Saul took a break, Margaret came to sit with Rebecca and Doc to talk. As Margaret often did, she started a conversation, hoping that the young mind could absorb the realities of Oregon. "Recently we went to a meeting at the Fort and Sheriff Meek said there are two thousand people living in Oregon now. Everyone was amazed at that number. Of course, the people here tonight are mostly old-timers, not the new people from the wagon trains."

With a puzzled look, Rebecca asked, "Why is that?"

Doc warned, "Margaret, please don't open a can of worms."

Margaret ignored him. "I believe there are a couple of reasons. We learned that Black Saul almost got lashed the other night. Many newcomers don't want Negroes living here in Oregon. Well, they'd accept a fiddle-playing Negro for one night, if they were dancers, since we don't have many fiddlers. But we do have many people who don't dance because of their religion. So that's one reason.

"Then there's the problem that many of the newcomers who came last year want to drive away any family with an Indian wife."

Doc nodded to Margaret. He realized that he could learn about this young girl by broaching serious topics, so he finished the thought. "So, they don't want to come to this house and party. Joe is Sheriff Meek, so by gum they can't do anything to him except talk behind his back."

Rebecca became wide-eyed and said, "That's not how a Christian should behave."

Margaret interjected, "Many of those same people confront the children all the time. They call them half-breeds."

Doc shook his head and frowned, "That has become a bad word. I have taught my five boys to walk tall and ignore those people. Here in Oregon we usually say the French word, *Métis*. I thought their religion taught them to welcome the little children, but they don't."

Black Saul started playing *The King's Head Reel* and it was impossible to talk. Margaret started tapping her foot and was delighted when one of her neighbors came to ask her to dance. Doc and Rebecca joined two lines of people covering the floor, and much to Joe's delight a caller started the Virginia Reel.

In the wee hours of the morning when the party ended, Doc went out and hitched up the horse to his loaner surrey. Rebecca had fallen asleep on Virginia and Joe's bed, so Doc lifted her into his arms to carry her outside. She awoke when placed on the seat and told him that the evening had been the best in her life.

Men from the party had helped Margaret put all her children into the wagon bed. Margaret, who sat waiting to leave with Doc, overheard Rebecca's comment and whispered into the night, "Well, at thirteen you haven't seen much yet, so saying it was the best in your life doesn't say much." No one heard her sarcasm.

Soon the two wagons headed south.

Doc felt the same as Rebecca. This had been the best evening in his life, and he was beaming.

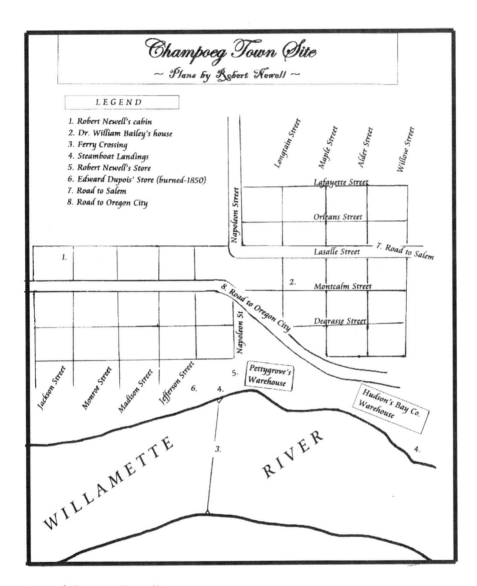

Layout of Champoeg Town Site

Many more homes were built from 1846 through 1861, and then the flood of 1861 destroyed all structures and washed away any trace of them with one exception – the Hudson's Bay Company's huge warehouse moved fifty feet and was damaged to such an extent that it was never used again.

CHAPTER 6

JANUARY – JUNE, 1846

Robert Newell was a thinker and a planner. Starting the day after the holiday party at the Meeks', he began to prepare to make a proposal for the hand of Miss Rebecca Newman. He decided that he would take her on outings around the countryside and to a play on a ship in port at the Fort. *Here in Oregon a man can't take care of children or run a farm alone, and a woman can't expect a courtship for a year like they do back East. Why, a woman in Oregon can't even expect a courtship for months.*

But she was not just any woman in Oregon; she was young, beautiful and smart. At that moment, he realized that she could marry any number of men. *I need to convince her and her family that I am the best man.* He was standing in the doorway of his cabin looking at the small keeping room and the disarray everywhere. For his wife Kitty, he had put down the wood floor. He remembered how thrilled she was. *And Kitty had been raised in the most primitive of living quarters. If she was so happy to have a new floor, I imagine Miss Newman would be pleased if I made this cabin a better place to live. I'll ask Margaret's advice on what to do.*

Within the week, Margaret and her girls came to clean and rearrange his cabin. He was given instructions on how to keep things more orderly. Margaret had suggestions: from simple ones as putting dirty clothes on the bottom of the chifforobe, off the floor and out of sight; to complicated ones as building a bedroom.

Margaret explained why she thought a bedroom to be important. "She lives in a house newly built with cut boards and has her own bedroom. You must make her feel it is an advantage – a step upward – to be with you. However, you have five boys and that is a more important reason for building a private bedroom with a door."

"A bedroom would be so expensive."

Margaret raised her eyebrows, "Well, if you win her hand, you will have won a prize. Is she not worth the expense?" Margaret was washing his knives, forks, and spoons. "Look at your disgraceful eating utensils, Robert!" First she held up a fork with bent tongs and then a twisted spoon. "Did you see what the McLoughlins used at their party? Have you noticed the fine flatware that I have? Mine is not fine silverware like the McLoughlins', but mine is respectable. A man of your status in the community should have more pride in his home."

"Ah, 'A word and a blow' from a friend." He grinned with his beardless face – winsome creases shot from the corners of his mouth and eyes.

"Save your Shakespeare for Rebecca, Robert."

During the first week of January, Doc visited the Newman's home and, while there, invited the family to Champoeg. He said, "Here, I'll show you a map I made of the Champoeg Townsite." He went to his saddlebag that he had dropped by the front door and pulled out some papers. "Mr. Longtain and I own all this together. I'm going to divide my land and sell lots." They were sitting at the dining table and Doc moved his cup and saucer to smooth out the map. "See, my cabin is here, only four blocks from the Willamette River, where the ferry crosses." On the map he pointed to the streets marked as LaSalle Street and Jackson Street. "See, I can just walk down Jackson Street to the river; like I said, it's only four blocks away. That's where my keelboat *Ben Franklin* is sitting right now. Before my wife got sick and died, I was caulking and greasing my keelboats to be ready for next year. *Ben Franklin* is ready to use, but I haven't finished greasing *Mogul* yet."

Mrs. Newman asked, "More tea, Mr. Newell?"

"No, thank you, ma'am. If you come with us tomorrow to Champoeg, there is a nice general store owned by Mr. Edward Dupuis." Gazing at the map, Doc placed his finger on the store's location, "It's right here."

"Oh, thank you, but I have other plans that I cannot change. Mr. Newman and Rebecca will enjoy the trip, I'm sure."

Mr. Newman, puffing on his burl pipe, asked if the store had any tobacco. "I'd like to get some Virginia blend."

* * *

During the second week of January, Doc invited the family to a play up at the Fort on the British ship *Modeste*. More importantly, Doc began building a new room onto his home – that bedroom that Margaret had suggested.

On the third week, the Newmans went to Oregon City with Doc in his keelboat. They dined at the Moss Hotel and he gave them a tour of The Oregon Printing Company. Doc said, "This is where the first newspaper in the west will be printed. Next month, *The Oregon Spectator* will be printed for the first time."

They talked a while about newspapers in the East, and then Mr. Newman added his name to a list for a subscription to *The Oregon Spectator*.

Doc said, "I've also started The Oregon Lyceum. I've always liked to read and, since books are hard to come by here in Oregon Country, I figured we needed an organization to spur literary discussions and scientific pursuits. I started The Oregon Lyceum three years ago." Pride oozed from his every word, "I try to read all I can on scientific ideas."

At the end of January, the Newmans invited Doc to dinner at their home. He brought one of his books of Shakespeare and read from it after the meal. The whole Newman family gathered to listen. Applause filled the room when he ended the reading. Then, much to the chagrin of Doc, the women went to work in the kitchen, and he was left with only Mr. Newman who started a conversation that would last an hour.

He said, "I cannot abide by the backward methods of handling money here. Goodness, in this day and age, how can Oregon still be buying and paying by the barter and trade method?" Mr. Newman took a puff on his pipe and waited for Doc to reply.

"Humph," Doc cleared his throat and glanced toward the kitchen. Knowing Rebecca was not returning anytime soon, he jumped into the conversation to defend his Oregon. "Before you arrived, this topic had been on the Provisional Government agenda frequently. In 1845, we passed legislation defining our currency. Legally, we created various methods, which included gold and silver, treasury warrants, and of course, wheat –

both delivered at market and to where no particular contract had been made. We made a very flexible financial system, which works. We approved available orders on wheat, beef, pork, butter, lard, tallow, hides, lumber and many other articles that were being exported from our territory. We are prosperous and growing."

"Mr. Newell, that is what I am saying. This legislation you described is a barter and trade system." He leaned forward in his chair and pointed to Doc with his pipe stem, "What you are saying tells me only that Oregon has progressed from using furs as money to using wheat and other products as the currency of the land." And Doc knew Mr. Newman was correct. At that moment, Doc hoped the Abernethy Rocks would not come into the conversation.

By the time February arrived, Doc talked to Margaret and lamented that he had not gotten to know Rebecca. "We are never alone."

"Robert, it's simple. The next time you go to their home, pick a warm, sunny day and ask permission to sit on the grass with Rebecca. Take a blanket of your own and spread it where the parents can see you from a window. Then you can talk."

One afternoon in the first week of February, the blanket was spread between two trees, so they each had a place to lean back and relax. Doc suggested that they tell their life stories. "So we can get to know each other better."

Rebecca suggested, "You go first. I don't have much to tell."

"Well, let's see. I was born in Zanesville, Ohio in March of eighteen oh-seven. When I left home I went to Cincinnati to learn the saddler's trade and was bored by the age of twenty. It took me until I was twenty-two to start my real life; I went to St. Louis, and a man named William Sublette introduced me to trapping. I became a mountain man and met Joseph Meek while I was trapping." Doc stopped his story to comment, "I'm always happy to see Joe. We should plan to spend some time with the Meeks. I guess you know that Joe's known for fighting bears and, what he calls, Injuns."

She nodded.

He continued talking, "In 1840, the American Fur Company broke up after I'd been trapping for eleven years. I decided to come live here in the Willamette Valley with my family. So I piloted some missionaries from the Green River to Fort Hall; they paid me with a harness and two wagons. When I got to Fort Hall, I sold one wagon and commissioned Joe Meek to drive the other to the Whitman Mission, twenty-five miles from Fort Walla Walla, which he did. That trip through the Blue Mountains was amazing. Sometimes we traveled through bunchgrass as high as the backs of our horses. Joe and our party made the first wagon trail to the Columbia River back in 1840. No one thought you could get a wagon through that river, so Joe made the decision to leave it behind. We went on foot and by boat to the Willamette Valley. Then in 1841, I went back to claim my wagon and took it down the Columbia on a raft and had the first wagon to come into the valley from the East. We had traveled the plains, mountains, and that Columbia River to get here. The Indians didn't know what to make of a covered wagon coming down that wild Columbia River on a boat. They had never seen such a sight. Ha, most had never seen a covered wagon."

Rebecca asked, "Where did you live when you first came?"

"Near Joe Meek and his family in the Tualatin Plains. After that, Kitty and I moved to Oregon City, and finally to my place at Champoeg. The cabin already existed, but had been deserted. In fact I know the whole history of my cabin. A man named John Ball built it in 1831 and lived with J.B. McKay, who made leather harnesses at that time. This John Ball had been educated in Connecticut and, I understand, was a bit uppity, if you know what I mean. Soon John Ball got sick and returned to the East Coast. He had come with Nathaniel Wyeth back in thirty-one. So when Ball moved out, Wyeth moved in; that was 1834, and he stayed until 1837. The last person to occupy my cabin before me was a gunner on the *U.S.S. Constitution*. Let me see, his name was Johnson. Yes, a William Johnson, and he left to build the first cabin up in Portland. Then I took it over."

Doc noticed that Rebecca didn't seem to find all those facts too interesting.

She stood and suggested that they walk a while.

"Okay, what else can I tell you?" Doc took a deep inhale, "Have you heard that I have an apple orchard and make a fine profit from my apples?"

"No, I didn't know that. I do know that you are on the legislative committee."

Doc bobbed his head in agreement and repeated about his keelboats. "You know that I have a transport service with two keelboats. I started with a couple of *bateaux* that I fixed up and now I have two keelboats with sails, if needed. I named them *Ben Franklin* and *Mogul*. Kitty used to joke with me that I named them after the two men I most admire – Ben and myself." He grinned at her and continued the subject. "I have a couple of men from the Chinook tribe and a few Kalapuyans to man the oars; they alternate on the trips – it's easy going north with the current, but hard work coming back to Champoeg. I make the trips as captain, from time to time. I haul freight and passengers between Champoeg and Willamette Falls at Oregon City."

"Does Black Saul compete with your business? He said he has a *bateau* for transport."

"No, no," Doc said, "He has a different route. He goes from Astoria up the Columbia River and back."

"Is your transportation business profitable?"

"It's getting there. I've only had it for some months. I need to write up some advertisements to put in the newspaper that's coming out in February. By gum, I forgot! This is February. Would you help me?"

She beamed. "Oh, yes! Hmmm, we could go inside and do that now. I have an idea. Do you remember what you said when you told my father about your keelboats? You said some words I didn't understand – greased and chalked. Or something."

Inside the house, Rebecca went for her ink box and paper. Mrs. Newman served some muffins and coffee.

As Rebecca smoothed her dress to sit, she said, "Oh, Mother, we are going to write a real ad for *The Oregon Spectator*. Remember, that's the new newspaper in Oregon City." She opened the ink box and turned to Robert. "Let's get started."

By the time their food had been eaten, Rebecca and Doc had completed the advertisement to their satisfaction.

For *The Oregon Spectator* in spring of 1846:

FAST RUNNING KEELBOATS FOR HIRE

Have well caulk'd, gumm'd, and greas'd the light draft and fast running boats, *Mogul* and *Ben Franklin*, now in port for freight or charter, which will ply regularly between Oregon City and Champoeg during the present season.

Punctuality to the hour of departure is earnestly requested. As time waits for no man, the boats will do the same.

Contact: Robert (Doc) Newell

When Doc was ready to leave, Rebecca asked her parents for permission to walk outside with him to say goodbye.

As they strolled toward his horse, she told him, "I do know some things about you that you didn't tell me. Mr. Meek said that you love books and always carried a Bible and book of Shakespeare with you when you were trapping in the mountains with him. He said that the other trappers were eager to listen to you read Shakespeare by the campfire." Rebecca swallowed and looked into his eyes, "Mrs. Bailey said that your heart was not into farming and that is why you moved from the Tualatin Plains – because you wanted to create and promote the new town of Champoeg. Is that correct?"

"Well, I've never been known to brag about my capabilities or deny that I couldn't do something. Yet I would have to say that farming – the kind that grows wheat – is not my choice of a daily activity. I enjoy working with *forming* our community and a government."

Rebecca found his play on words amusing. "Without a doubt, you're the most clever person I have ever known."

The weeks passed. Doc went to the Newman's place whenever Rebecca was home from her boarding school – one or two times a week. The rest of the time, he worked on his affairs and on building the bedroom.

Constantly, Doc looked for events to attend with Rebecca and was happy when an invitation came about a house-warming ball for the inauguration of Dr. McLoughlin's newly built gristmill in Oregon City. The Newmans were invited as well. It turned out to be quite an affair.

During the ball, Doc noticed that Lieutenant Peel and some of the other British officers were acting ungentlemanly with the Métis girls who were present.

Doc excused himself from Rebecca's side and went to Lieutenant Peel with a warning.

The lieutenant claimed that he had done no harm and Doc insisted, "May I present my opinion that you would not act in the same manner with a young lady from London."

"As you say, that is your opinion, Doctor Newell. Let us make this an amusing endeavor. I bet you a bottle of wine that more of the men on this floor tonight would agree with us British and our actions rather than with you and your opinion."

Doc accepted the wager.

Doc won.

Other than that incident, the festivities were delightful and ended with everyone in good spirits. Although Rebecca rode with Doc to the party, at the end of the evening her parents found it proper to take her home with them.

On February 19, 1846, The Oregon Spectator ran an account of the ball:

> *There was a brilliant assemblage of the "fair sex" of Oregon and, although in the far west, with the gay display that night, we are proud to state that the infant colony can boast of as pretty faces and handsome figures as the mother country. Reels, country dances, figures eight, and jigs was the order of the evening; and if we do not yet claim that fashionable dance the polka, still we live in hopes of seeing it soon introduced at our city balls.*

In late March, Doc went to Mr. And Mrs. Newman and asked for the hand of their daughter in marriage. He explained that he had not said anything to their daughter and wanted to speak first with them.

"Oh, no! Rebecca is only thirteen years old." Mrs. Newman stated firmly. "She is my oldest child and quite capable, but I am not ready to have her marry and leave me."

Mr. Newman took his briar burl pipe from his mouth and spoke up, "Humph, Mother, it sounds like you are thinking about yourself, and not Rebecca. We should make a decision that is best for our daughter, not you, my dear." He cleared his throat again, "Humph, Rebecca is attending Mrs. Thornton's School to better herself as a lady and to know what is proper. I believe she has learned enough." He replaced the pipe and puffed contentedly, knowing that Robert Newell was quite a catch for his daughter.

After thirty minutes of Doc reiterating his worth in assets and capabilities, and after many more minutes of Mr. Newman presenting the loss they would have to endure without the oldest girl who helped with much of the household needs, it was decided that she would be allowed to wed when she became fourteen years old in June.

Doc, wanting to be honorable and proper, asked, "Then, do I have your permission to broach the subject of marriage directly with your daughter? I would not want to marry someone who did not want to share my life."

Smoke wove thin tendrils around Mr. Newman's head as he took a couple of puffs and thought. Soon he leaned forward from his overstuffed chair; with an elbow on his knee he said, "Of course you can make a proposal. However, a girl of her age does not know what is best for her. I believe this is a decision to be made by the three of us. I will consider her to be betrothed to you as a result of our conversation today. I will not wait for a young girl to decide."

Mrs. Newman shifted on the settee and smoothed the lap of her dress before rising. Her face reflected sadness as she asked, "More tea, Mr. Newell?"

"No, thank you, Mrs. Newman." Doc took a deep breath, "Then it is settled. I will plan to wed your daughter in June of this year of 1846.

However, I would ask that I be the one to first speak with your daughter about this marriage. I would like to spend more time with her and tell her about this discussion at what I consider to be the proper moment and place. I would like to have it be a moment to be remembered fondly by her."

"Humph, I think that is acceptable." He turned to his wife to say, "I think we can keep this a secret for a couple of weeks." His wife nodded and took her handkerchief from her pocket to dab the corner of her eye. He continued to puff slowly on his pipe.

When Doc next came calling in early April, her parents allowed them to leave on a picnic without a chaperone. It was springtime and he picked a budding wildflower to hand to her as he leaned to her face to give their first kiss. Respecting her youth and inexperience, he put his hands behind his back so only their lips touched and the touch was for the briefest of seconds. With serious eyes, he spoke some Shakespeare:

This bud of love, by summer's ripening breath,
May prove a beauteous flower when next we meet.

A few days later, they received permission to drive alone to his cabin, where they were to have lunch with his two oldest boys, Margaret, and her three girls – Sarah, Eliza, and Mattie. Mary Jane Holmes was back with her family and a new little baby brother.

Doc wanted Rebecca to get to know his two oldest boys, but more importantly, he could show her the new bedroom that was finished.

On the wagon ride he saw a sword fern. Stopping the horse, he walked over to it, pulled off a couple of the fronds, and dropped them in the wagon under the bench. When they arrived at his cabin, the boys and girls rushed out to greet them. Doc grinned and reached for the sword ferns. He handed a frond to Rebecca.

She held the long green stem covered in small leaves and puzzled, "What do I do with this?"

William leaned across and took the other frond from his father's hand. "See you pull off the leaves and say 'He loves me' and pull the next and say 'He loves me not' until they are all gone. The Indians play this game to see if someone loves them." He continued pulling off leaves until the last one was, "He loves me." In a high falsetto voice like a girl he tittered, "See, Pa loves me."

Rebecca was not shy and giggled in amusement.

Instantly, Doc employed Shakespeare and said, "Remember that 'Home-keeping youth have ever homely wits' so they say."

Margaret had come out the door when William was saying his last 'He loves me' and just before everyone laughed at his antics. She cocked her head and asked Rebecca, "Has he been wooing you with Shakespeare?"

Now Rebecca blushed upon hearing the word *wooing*. Nevertheless, she was as quick as Doc, "And reading Shakespeare to my parents, as well."

Doc let his thoughts form his words before continuing. "I think of Shakespeare's wisdom often. But, as you can see, my not-at-all-shy boys receive the applause more often than I do."

With that opening, Francis asked of Rebecca, "Aren't you going to pull the leaves from your fern?"

Rebecca smiled coyly, "I already know that my father loves me."

And so the afternoon went. After all, with the not-at-all-shy boys and the mature Rebecca who was quick with retorts, the group spent most their time in mirth.

Everything grows in May. A few more times together – without a chaperone – and a few more kisses secured the vine that was growing around the two. Soon the vine began to flower because Doc was wise in his wooing, and the fruit of the vine ripened because he watered it often in playfulness.

He liked to make mischief by chewing on splinters of wood, stalks of grass, bay leaves, or berries before he kissed her. He would ask, "What do I taste like now?"

Rebecca was good at the game and usually guessed correctly, unless she wanted another kiss. "Hmm, I don't know. You will have to kiss me again to give me another hint."

"I'm glad to oblige," he said, as he kissed unlike their first kiss. Now their kisses were shared with her face in his hands or with his hands around her waist or with their arms embracing the other. And often Shakespeare enhanced the kiss.

She asked, "Do all couples kiss as much as we do?"

Doc let Shakespeare tell her. "'They do not love who do not show their love.'"

Another day, when they were alone at his cabin, he started to lean into a kiss and stopped, "Oh, I forgot. 'There's something in the wind;' please wait." He ran from the keeping room, out the front door, but within moments, he was back at her side and chewing on something. "Wait until you taste this one. You'll like it." They stared mischievously into the other's eyes while he chewed; the moment was delightful until he spit into his hand.

She screwed up her nose and made a face, "That was disgusting. Is that the same mouth that quoted Shakespeare and then displayed that loathsome act?"

"Ah," he feigned sadness and defended his actions. "I say 'Those words are razors to my wounded heart' and I want you to know that I was being thoughtful. You don't want leaves in your mouth. Do you?"

She shook her head and a loose curl bobbed back and forth.

In a soft voice he asked, "Now will you kiss me?" And she did.

She eased back from his lips with a grin and said, "Mint! You taste like mint."

And, at that moment, the look he had in his eyes told her he was going to say something serious. He smoothed some strands of hair from her face, "I feel for you, like I never felt before. I know how a man desires a woman, but this is different. I love you more deeply than I can express with my own words or with the words of Shakespeare."

Rebecca's eyes filled with tears. "You barely know me."

Doc took both her hands into his. "Rebecca, I know you. By gum, you couldn't hide who you are even if you tried. Would you consider being my wife?"

She inhaled a deep breath and put her head against his shoulder. When she sat up, so close and face to face, she asked, "I don't know what is proper to do. Should I say that I need some time to think about your proposal?" She hesitated a long time before saying, "No one taught me what to say or do."

Doc started to speak and she put her forehead to his and said, "Shhh, I'm not finished."

He feared that he had failed in convincing her. His stomach turned.

But his fears vanished when she said, "All I want to do is jump for joy and say that I will marry you. Is that proper?"

He squeezed her into his arms and kissed her all over her face. Then he stood with his arms still wrapped around her and circled around and around, raising her feet from the floor. Her skirts furled and fluttered in the twirl. When he stopped and put her down he expounded, "I don't know what's proper. Who cares? This is about us and what we want to do."

"Well," her face changed to an impish grin, "you don't even know if I can cook."

While Doc and Rebecca promised their heart and lives to the other, Margaret was meeting Mattie's half-brother on her doorstep.

"I knows she in there! MATTIE I KNOWS YOU'RE IN THERE!" He stood fifteen feet in front of the front door between the rows of pink foxgloves and the clumps of bright purplish-red begonias. His right boot had trampled on one of the foxgloves when he slipped off his horse. He stood in a collarless waistcoat and a striped work shirt. His hat was cocked on his head and was stained from dried sweat around the band. He had a pistol tucked at his waist.

Margaret stood just inside her open door. Out of his sight, the rifle leaned on the doorframe to her right. The day was ending and the sun just had dropped behind the trees, though it was not yet dark.

McAlister's shouts stopped the three girls from working on their slates. Margaret had them practicing their letters as they did every evening before supper, and she had lit the oil lamps in the keeping room to help them see. He could easily see into the house, but the girls were off to one side and not completely in his view.

Mattie stiffened.

Sarah turned to her and whispered, "He can't see you, only me. Go hide in the corner behind Dr. Bailey's desk. Go!"

Mattie scampered over to the other side of the room and squeezed behind the desk. She was to the left of the open door and had slipped into a tiny space where the desk angled out from the wall in the corner.

Little Mary Jane was napping on some blankets on the floor, seemingly undisturbed by the loud voices.

Sarah and Eliza crept up behind Margaret and looked out to see him just as Margaret demanded, "Who are you to come on my property and scream at me? There's no Mattie here! Get off my property."

"People say that you have a Negro girl here. I'm looking for Mary Anne McAlister, a nigger. I call her Mattie and she's my slave."

"The Negro girl who is here is Mary Jane. Those people told you wrong."

"I ain't wrong!" He seethed. Then he tilted his hat back and made a threatening statement. "You is alone here, ain't you." It was no question; he knew no man was there.

Margaret took that as an invitation to show she was not alone, "No, I have my rifle here with me." She grabbed it and pointed it directly at him. "Don't even consider touching your gun or I'll shoot." Without looking away from him, she called to the girls, "Sarah, show this intruder that Mary Jane is not the girl he wants. But don't come to the door; just stand behind me."

Eliza was waking little Mary Jane when Sarah took one of her hands and stood her up to walk. Eliza took her other hand and they moved behind Margaret, but in view of the man.

"Here she is Mrs. Bailey," Sarah muttered.

Margaret took a step out the door to allow him to see Mary Jane. "See, this little girl is not your Mary Anne. Whoever you talked to is confused. Mary Jane? Mary Anne? They got the name wrong. Now get out of here and don't come back. My husband will be home soon, and I plan to tell the U.S. marshal that you came here and threatened me."

McAlister looked at the little Negro girl and clenched his jaw. He pulled up into the saddle and jerked the reins to one side. His horse circled, trampling all the flowers. Glancing over his shoulder to catch Margaret's reaction to the destruction of her garden, his expression changed. That's when he saw it!

And Margaret noticed the change in his demeanor.

His grandpap's tinderbox sat on a bench on the piazza where Mattie had forgotten it. A wicked look appeared on his face as he started to leave. "You better be careful, I might come back." And he took off.

Waiting for her heart to slow, Margaret kept an eye on the disappearing figure that faded into the distance. Turning, she put down the rifle at the door. "Sarah, you like to ride bareback. Go to Robert Newell's cabin and tell him we need help tonight. I never know if Dr. Bailey is coming home or not and he may be too drunk to help us. Please ride like the wind."

Mattie came from behind the desk, crying.

Margaret held the girl on her lap and thanked the Lord that little Mary Jane was at their house for McAlister to see. It was just a coincidence that Margaret had gone to get Mary Jane from her parents the day before. Margaret had said she wanted to sew the little girl a new dress, and that's why Mary Jane was there.

In the dark and an hour later, Joe Meek and Sarah rode up to the Bailey farm. Through the lit window, he could see Margaret working inside. "Everything looks okay. Sarah, take the horses to the barn. I'll tell Margaret I'm here, then I'll come help ya put out some feed."

When he walked into the cabin, Margaret welcomed his presence. "Joe, thank the Lord. How did you know we needed you?"

"Oh, Sarah went to Doc's place when I war jus' leaving. Maybe it war luck or, like you said, maybe the Lord knew you needed me tonight."

Soon they all sat around the table where the supper dishes remained from earlier. Margaret served Sarah and Joe.

Joe talked between bites. "Like I tol' ya I would. I been askin' around 'bout the stranger lookin' fer a Mary Anne McAlister. In the last six months, I think he asked at ev'ry cabin 'tween California and the Fort."

Sarah asked, "How do you know that?"

He swallowed and grinned, "I'm the U.S. Marshal. I know everythin'. Wal, that war a bit of an exaggeration. Sarah, I have work to do all over Oregon and I have men workin' fer me all over Oregon. I war down south jus' last week and heard 'bout his travels and questions. Seems that he came in January, then went back home and came a-gin. Maybe even a couple of times." Joe took a drink of his coffee and then looked to Mattie, who sat across the table from him. "He sure wants to find ya."

"Joe!" Margaret exclaimed. "You don't need to say things like that and scare this girl any more than she already is."

Once the girls were put to bed up in the garret and the dishes cleared from the table, Joe and Margaret sat and talked quietly.

"I'll bed down in front of the door on the floor tonight. Jus' git me a couple of blankets. I brought my saddle in for my head. It'll be like me sleepin' with the mountain men." And he chuckled.

A little after midnight, Dr. Bailey came crashing in the door and fell on top of Joe. He had been at Howard's Tavern over in Champoeg and was quite drunk. There was such a ruckus that the girls woke and were scared that it was McAlister.

Margaret served warm milk to the girls and coffee to her husband while they explained the presence of Joe sleeping on the floor and told about McAlister's visit.

Finally everyone went to bed again. Sleep didn't come easy to anyone except Dr. Bailey who began to snore as soon as his head met the pillow. An hour passed and then another. Some of the girls were dozing lightly, but not Margaret or Joe.

It seemed that Crow – sprawled on the floor near Joe – was asleep until he started a low, deep growl.

Joe's eyes popped open and the dog raised his head, continuing the soft growling. Joe listened intently, but couldn't discern any noise. Then he heard it; it was a soft sound. There had been no sound of a horse coming; he knew he would have heard that. He willed himself not to move, only listen.

He strained his ears without closing his eyes. He concentrated on looking at the window for any sign of an intruder though it was quite dark. There had been a new moon that night.

Then he heard it again – a light rasping sound of something brushing against the boards on the piazza like a skunk or raccoon might do. But he needed to check if it was only an animal. Soundlessly, he rolled out of the blankets and onto his knees before going into a squat. Crow stood and moved toward the door. Joe eased his pistol from under the saddle, trying not to make even a rustling of his clothing. As he went to stand, willing his strong bear-like legs to quietly lift his heavy body, the door burst open and hit the dog.

Joe stood face to face with McAlister and a colt revolver.

Without taking his eyes off Joe, McAlister screamed, "MATTIE I HAVE GRANDPAP'S TINDERBOX IN MY HAND!"

At that moment, Crow recovered and came from behind the door, lunging at the stranger and biting into his right calf.

McAlister let out a blood-curdling cry and frantically shook his leg. He still held his gun in one hand and the tinderbox in the other as he jumped around.

Joe watched the gun move here and there while he tried to find an opportunity to grab it.

The girls cowered up in the garret, looking over the edge and crying loudly. Little Mary Jane was screaming in confusion and fear. Margaret had jumped from her bed in the next room – the door was closed – and wished that she had brought the rifle to bed with her. Dr. Bailey was snoring as she searched his clothes on the floor for his revolver. She found it and crept to the door.

McAlister finally freed his leg and gave Crow a hard kick before firing his gun at the dog. Crow was motionless on the floor. "MATTIE GIT DOWN HERE!"

At the sound of the gunfire, Margaret froze behind the door she had cracked open.

Joe huffed loudly, "Mattie, don't you come. All you girls stop screamin' and git away from the edge of the garret."

As he spoke, Joe made the mistake of making a slight turn of his head in the direction of the girls and McAlister raised his gun and brought the butt down on Joe's head. Joe didn't flinch from the blow even though he started to bleed. But he used the moment when McAlister's gun was pointing downward from the blow and took a step forward, grabbing at McAlister's gun arm with his free hand. The two men backed into the doorframe with arms locked and two guns pointing at their faces and then at the ceiling and then to the floor and back to someone's face. They struggled and twisted away from the door and onto the piazza until McAlister took one too many steps backward and stepped off the edge and fell, with Joe going down on top of him.

One of the guns discharged!

Margaret, who had cracked open the bedroom door, saw the struggle until they disappeared from her view onto the piazza. With the second discharge, Dr. Bailey finally awoke and got up. He came to Margaret's side and they both crept to the front doorway.

The two men were motionless at the bottom of the four steps.

Finally, Joe rolled over and off of McAlister. Joe struggled to standing while saying, "He shot himself. I think he's dead. Will you see if that's so, Dr. Bailey?"

Within a minute, the doctor declared, "He's deader than a doornail."

Margaret returned inside and stood at the stairs to the garret. "Girls, come on down. McAlister is dead."

Eliza rushed to Crow, calling his name.

The dog stirred just as Dr. Bailey confirmed he was alive. "Look here," he said, putting his finger into a hole in the floor, "he missed Crow by six inches."

Sarah arrived at the dog's side. On their knees, the girls hugged and petted the dog. Crow's tail thumped against the floor.

Joe asked Mattie, "Can you identify him as your half-brother?"

With her hands, she wiped her tearstained face, mixing dirt and tears into a smeared mess. She walked outside and peered down at the body. "Yes, that's Tom McAlister, my older half-brother."

Joe bent down and pried the tinderbox from his fist. "Is this your grandpappy's tinderbox like he said?"

Mattie nodded before saying, "I forgot and left it out here on the bench."

Margaret gasped, "He saw the box earlier. I remember seeing a change in his facial expression when he was looking toward the bench. I didn't know what it meant until now."

Joe came up the steps, "This war some day. First I stop at Doc's place and learn that he's going to be married in June. Then I come here and fight for my life."

Margaret gasped again and then reprimanded Joe, "You didn't tell me about the wedding plans of Robert and Rebecca."

"Humph, once I got here I plumb forgot 'bout that. Well, as Doc says, 'All's well that ends well.'"

Dr. Bailey corrected him. "It was Shakespeare who said that."

THE WHITMAN MASSACRE.

Time-Stained Document, Which Gives the Names of Those Killed.

PORTLAND, Feb. 15—(To the Editor.)
There lies before me, as I write, a sheet of blue foolscap paper, time-stained with its 49 years of age, reminding one of the awful massacre which took place at the Whitman mission, a few miles from what is now the city of Walla Walla, Wash., November 29, 1847. The document is in the handwriting of Peter Skeen Ogden, an influential factor of the Hudson's Bay Company, at Vancouver. Prompted by humanity, and without waiting for orders, as soon as he heard of the massacre, he went to the place with an armed force, and held a council with the Cayuse Indians, ransomed the prisoners – 53 in number – and took them to Oregon City, arriving there January 10, 1848. For this act, Mr. Ogden, whose son, William Seton, married the daughter of Thomas J. Dryer, founder of The Oregonian, and was well and favorably known among the early settlers of this city, should always have a warm place in the hearts of all true Americans. Years ago it was charged that Mr. Ogden sought to arm the Cayuses against the Americans because a little ammunition and a few guns made up part of the ransom given to free these helpless women and children from a captivity worse than death. No pen can depict the fearful experiences they were compelled to endure, and no ransom was too great for their release. The names of those killed and taken prisoners, given in Mr. Ogden's words, follow:

"List of persons killed at Doctor Whitman's mission: Doctor Whitman, Mrs. Whitman, Mr. Rogers, Mr. Hoffman, Mr. Sanders, Mr. Marsh, John Sager, Francis Sager, Mr. Kimball, Mr. Gillen, Mr. Bewley, Mr. Young, Jr., Mr. Sales.

"List of names of the persons from the mission of Doctor Whitman:

Mission children – Miss Mary A. Bridger, Miss Catherine Sager, 13 years; Miss Elizabeth M. Sager, 10 years; Miss Matilda J. Sager, 8 years; Miss Henrietta N. Sager, 4 years.

"Mr. Joseph Smith, Mrs. Joseph Smith, Miss Mary Smith, 15 years; Edwin Smith, 13 years; Charles Smith, 11 years; Nelson Smith, 6 years; Mortimer Smith, 4 years; all from Du Page county, Illinois. Miss Eliza Spalding (the second white child to be born of American parents west of the Rocky mountains; (date of birth, November, 15, 1837); Mrs. Rebecca Hays; H. Clay Hays, 4 years; from Platte county, Missouri; Mrs. Mary Sanders, Helen M. Sanders, 14 years; Phoebe Sanders, 10 years; Alfred W. Sanders, 6 years; Nancy J. Sanders, 4 years; Mary A. Sanders, 2 years; from Mahaska county, Iowa. Mr. Joseph Standfield, Canadian. Mrs. Harriet Kimball, Susan M. Kimball, aged 16 years; Nathan M. Kimball, 12 years; Byron T. Kimball, 8 years; Sarah S. Kimball, 6 years; Nina A. Kimball, 1 year; from LaPorte county, Indiana. Mr. Elam Young, Mrs. Irene Young, Daniel Young, 21 years; John A. Young, 19 years; from Osage county, Missouri. Mr. Josiah Osborn, Mrs. Marguerite Osborn, Nancy A. Osborn, 9 years; John L. Osborn, 3 years; Alexander A. Osborn, 2; from Henderson county, Illinois. Mrs. Sally A. Caufield, Ellen Caufield, 16 years; Ascur Caufield, 9 years; Clarissa Caufield, 7 years; Sylvia A. Caufield, 5 years; Albert Caufield, 3 years; from Mahaska county, Iowa. Miss Mary E. Marsh; Miss Lorinda Bewley.

"Mission children deceased since the massacre: Miss Hannah S. Sager, Miss Helen Mar Meek."

It is not known how many of the survivors are alive today, although an effort is being made by the under signed to find out. Eight of them were together at the annual pioneer reunion last June. Every survivor seeing this is requested to send his or her name to the secretary of the Oregon Pioneers' Association, giving postoffice address and sketch of life.

GEORGE H. HIMES.

Newspaper article from 1896
Located in a scrapbook at the
Oregon Historical Society.

CHAPTER 7

1846 – 1849

After the last of the guests had left from their wedding celebration, Rebecca snuffed out the lamps. Walking to their bedroom, Doc realized that he had not shut the barn door after all the guests had gotten their horses. He told his wife, "I'll be only a minute or so."

In the bedroom, she finished unbuttoning the thirty buttons down the front of her wedding dress and slipped out of her dress and corset. She was nervous and thought a drink of water would be calming, but the pitcher on a table near the bed was empty. So she stepped back into the dress and pulled it around herself before going in search of water. She didn't button even one button.

With only the light streaming from the bedroom's doorway, she found a metal pitcher with water beside the hearth and bent to pick it up while whispering to herself, "Why am I so thirsty?"

Out of nowhere, he spoke from directly behind her, "Oh, I'm sorry. I forgot to fill the bedroom pitcher."

Startled, she stood quickly and whirled around; the dress flew open and slipped from her left shoulder to expose soft, baby-like skin from her neckline to her belly button. "I didn't hear you come back in," she blurted.

He was inches from her, and they both froze in place. She heard him swallow. She tightened her grip on the pitcher because it seemed to grow heavier with each beat of her heart, and she naively hoped that it afforded some cover to her nakedness. She also considered reaching with one hand to pull the dress up on her shoulder, at the expense of dropping the water pitcher, but decided against it. Finally, she looked into his eyes and her mind shifted; she decided that she didn't want the moment to end.

Without moving his feet, he reached, taking the pitcher from her hands to place it on the floor. When he stood back up she was grasping for her sleeve to cover herself, and he placed his hand over her hand, stopping her. He slipped his other hand into her fine soft hair and cradled her head as he leaned to her. They kissed a soft, gentle kiss.

He moved a hand into the small of her back beneath the fabric of the dress and felt her firm back muscles and narrow waist. With his touch to her back, her up-tilted breasts hardened against his chest, and she shivered. He kissed her eyelids and cheeks and ears – each kiss placed delicately and carefully – before returning to kiss her lips. These were kisses after an evening of him searching her eyes in hopes of seeing that she wanted him as much as he wanted her. These were kisses mixed with some pain from losing his spouse and thinking he may never have intimacy again. He knew that love abides because he loved this young woman deeply. What he didn't know was how much she could love him after never having experienced even the kisses of another man.

Doc lifted Rebecca into his arms and carried her to their bed. They did not stop kissing as he stood her on the floor to let her dress drop around her feet before lifting her again and placing her on the furs that covered his bed. He walked to the window, opened the curtains, and turned the gas lamp off to let moonlight fall across the bed.

Watching Rebecca slip under the covers, he pulled all his garments from his body and climbed onto the bed.

Rebecca recalled the discussions presented by her mother, who mentioned that she "must know her obligation" and "it shouldn't hurt much" and "blood will come from you." None of those vague phrases prepared this fourteen-year-old for her wedding night. She had certain fears and expectations – like in a fairy tale – that vanish in a matter of seconds when the whole act of consummating the marriage was over. She stared out into the dark and puzzled about it all as Doc rolled off her and fell asleep.

Later that night, Rebecca struggled out of the warmth of the blankets to use the chamber pot. He awoke to see her naked; her bare shoulders, curving into a tapered waist, appeared bluish-black in the shadow of the moonlight. Her fine hair billowed like tall grasses in the wind when she bent to pull the pot from under the bed. When she disappeared from his view, the sound of her relief produced an unseen grin across his face. Finally, she stood to peer from the window into the Oregon night before returning, shivering to his side. They cuddled a while. In his thoughts, he kept seeing her standing at the window until he felt aroused and wanted her again.

Now he took his time and time stood still for Rebecca.

Time is so elusive. It passed, but they each had different concepts of its passage. Was it a minute or an hour? He only knew that he reached a moment when it was the right time, and he felt an explosion like he had never known.

For her, this lovemaking seemed to last forever. It seemed to be longer than each year of her life as she climbed in ecstasy, reached the mountaintop, and flew into the stars.

With her body completely spent, her mind continued on and she wondered why no one talks about this marvelous aspect of being married. Why is it a secret?

With the light of another day, they awoke to thoughts that stung like the cold morning air. One had lost a spouse only six months ago and he worried if he had waited long enough before marrying to show respect for his first wife. The other worried if she had fulfilled her wedding night responsibilities to his liking. So, even in the most forgiving of worlds, worry played a role in their morning awakening. A hawk high above sounded a piercing cry; and while enveloped in the warm bed within the other's arms, they listened for other birds and delayed the time when they must open their eyes.

Doc cooked a hearty breakfast of pickled pork and eggs with pan biscuits slathered in butter and preserves. Sipping their hot boiled coffee while eating, they discussed how they felt giddy, like carefree children. After taking a spoonful of the preserves, Doc leaned over to Rebecca and kissed her, asking, "Aren't I tasty? Can you tell what flavor that is?"

"Give me another hint."

And he did after another spoonful and another kiss.

"I don't know. It tastes like apples, but it's the wrong color."

"Bunchberry. They taste a bit like apples. Margaret makes wonderful preserves and always brings me some."

They kept kissing between bites of food and kept laughing until a serious thought interrupted their glee and sadness rippled down his face.

"With all this happiness you give me, at the same time, I remain sad about my wife," he puzzled. "How can that be? May I quote Shakespeare to tell how I feel at this moment?" He let the master say his inner emotion:

> It is too rash, too unadvis'd, too sudden;
> Too like the lightning, which doth cease to be.

Rebecca swallowed her last bite and scowled in amazement, "I can't quote Shakespeare, but I hear your despair. All I can share is my own confusion." A sob caught in her throat. "How do I say this? How do I ask?" Rebecca looked to Doc and whispered, "Since you miss your wife, maybe I did not please you."

He stood and went to her, taking her hands and bringing her up to stand against him. "Oh, Rebecca, you were wonderful last night. I love you."

She rubbed her nose against his cheek and whispered, almost in embarrassment, "Do you want me as much as I want you?"

They returned to the bedroom for just one more time, but Doc insisted, as he removed his clothes, "Listen, this must be quick. Hear the cow bawling? She wants to be milked. Kitty always did the milking. At least there is only one animal to milk; I put the rest out to pasture to get ready for calving time. Can you milk her when we're done?"

They undressed and rolled into the bed as Rebecca told him, "I don't know how to milk a cow."

Doc no longer was listening to her words or anything else as legs wrapped around legs and arms entwined. Making love took them to another dimension within themselves; it separated them from their present world and created silence, even from a bellowing cow.

Much later, Doc threw his feet off the bed and sat up. "Did you say that you don't know how to milk a cow?" He slipped into his flannel shirt, pulled on his pants, and grabbed his galluses – still buttoned to his pants – to lift them over the shirtsleeves.

She giggled, "Yes, I did."

She hurried to dress. They had brought all her personal clothes and things to his cabin the day before yesterday. "You need to teach me how to milk that poor bawling cow." As she buttoned, she wondered why her parents had not taught her how to milk a cow.

He grabbed a splinter from a log on the woodpile as they passed it.

"Doc, hurry! That noisy cow is getting louder. Oh, look at all the chickens. I know how to feed chickens and gather eggs. But I know I could not make a breakfast as delicious as the one you made me today."

Doc adjusted his galluses again and pulled at his shirt, "Feels strange, dressing twice in the same morning. Oh, the chickens? Yes, they're hungry. We need to feed them." Still chewing on the splinter of wood that protruded from the side of his mouth, he stopped in his tracks. "Let's slow down, I don't want this morning to end." He took her in his arms for one more embrace before the cow lesson. "I just want to tell you what Will Shakespeare is telling me." He shared:

> So we grew together,
> Like to a double cherry, seeming parted,
> But yet in union and partition;
> Two lovely berries molded on one stem.

She sighed. "Oh, Doc, that is lovely."

Not that she was thinking about their future; she just was assuming, though falsely, that life together would be exactly this way from now on – with their happiness and love overpowering reality. Rebecca knew that hard work was in her future, because the daily work of a woman in the mid-eighteen hundreds was backbreaking. She accepted this. She also knew the love she felt for Doc. But she had no way of knowing how daily life mellows lust and love. And not even Margaret would tell her this and crush the thrill of the beginnings of their marriage.

❀ ❀ ❀

In March of 1847, Rebecca gave a birthday party for her husband, who turned forty years old. No one knew that she was three months pregnant. In the middle of the festivities and outside among daffodils that decorated the grassy area where they sat eating at a table, Margaret asked quietly to Rebecca, "Did you invite Black Saul?"

"No one could tell me where he was," she answered.

Joe Meek overheard and bellowed, "Black Saul war arrested last December. But since we ain't got no jail, he disappeared from the house whar I had him in custody. It's been three months. We don't know whar he is."

Some of the guests asked about the arrest. Robert went to the house and returned with a stack of newspaper tied with a string. He undid the string and dropped the stack on the table. He riffled through the pages while saying, "I have the article about his arrest in December."

Doc had written the topic of each article in the top margin of the newspaper. When he found the article, he pulled it out and spread the newspaper on the middle of the table where all could lean over and read:

The Oregon Spectator – Dec. 24, 1846

A Negro man named James D. Saules was brought to this city recently from the mouth of the river, charged with having caused the death of his wife, an Indian woman. He was examined before Justice Hood, the result of which examination we have never been able to ascertain, but the accused is at large and likely to remain so we suppose.

Rebecca looked up to her husband, "Oh, no. Was this true?"

Margaret spoke, "Of course what you read did happen. Are you asking if he really killed his wife?" After Rebecca nodded, Margaret said, "You know Black Saul. What do you think?"

Everyone remained silent at the table. Scrub-jays flying above gave out their piercing call over and over until they disappeared in the distance. Margaret could not refrain from stating her opinion. "The jays mock us with their laughter. They know how prejudiced we are. A Negro has a harder road to walk. Not only here in Oregon but also anywhere in

America. The war with Mexico that has been going on and on has me so riled. Slavery runs America."

Doc shook his head and said, "We sit here eating sweets and among friends while men are fighting and dying in this senseless war." He emphasized, "Men from Mexico as well as Americans are dying." He pulled his stack of newspapers closer to where he sat and riffled through them again before he said, "I've been collecting articles from other newspapers since the beginning of our takeover of parts of Mexico. We fought from the spring of 1846 and it still is raging. Like Margaret, I get riled, too."

When he found them, he started passing cut newspaper articles left and right, "Here, read these and see some of the opinions on the Mexican War."

New York Herald, Aug. 1845
Our citizens cry out for war with Mexico.

News, Concord, Massachusetts 1846
Henry David Thoreau denounced the Mexican War by refusing to pay his Massachusetts poll tax. He was arrested and put behind bars. Friends came, without his consent, and paid the tax to get his release. One friend, Ralph Waldo Emerson, agreed with his views, but knew it to be useless to remonstrate. Emerson was reported to have told Thoreau in jail, "What are you doing there behind those bars?" Thoreau retort was, "And may I ask, what are you doing out there?"

Brooklyn Eagle, June 29, 1846
Opinion by Walt Whitman
As to a "Republic of the Rio Grande," such a formation would be but the stepping stone to furnish a cluster of new stars for the Spangled Banner. No small and weak power could, (or would wish to,) exist separately in such immediate neighborhood to the United States. We therefore think it every way likely that, unless the present war be summarily drawn to a close, Mexico will be a severed and cut up nation. She deserves this,...

New York Journal of Commerce
Satire
Why not go to war? The times are boring; we need excitement. Let us knock down cities that are not ours and rebuild our nation. What fun we will have.

New York Tribune, May 12, 1846
Opinion by Horace Greeley
We can easily defeat the armies of Mexico, slaughter them by thousands, and pursue them perhaps to their capital; we can conquer and "annex" their territory; but what then? ... Who believes that a score of victories over Mexico, the "annexation" of half her provinces, will give us more Liberty, a purer Morality, a more prosperous Industry, than we now have? ... Is not Life miserable enough, comes not Death soon enough, without resort to the hideous engines of War?

New York Herald, 1847
We the powerful people of United States can conquer the people of Mexico; and it is our destiny to civilize the backward peoples of this continent.

Before she finished reading all the articles, Margaret puffed up and had to say, "Remember, before they started fighting back in forty-five, I said that they were making this war because too many slaves escaped to Texas and were free. I was right. Even in Congress they discussed that. A handful of antislavery Congressmen voted against going to war, saying that some just wanted to extend the southern slave territory. How can the *New York Herald* print an article like this one? Humph, it's that Manifest Destiny."

North Star
Opinion by Frederick Douglas
... in the present disgraceful, cruel, and iniquitous war with our sister republic, Mexico seems a doomed victim to Anglo Saxon cupidity and love of dominion.

Handbill from *American Anti-Slavery Society*
Are our citizens' blind? The war on Mexico was started to gain
more land where slavery can exist.

Boston Courier
Satirical Poems by James Russell Lowell
(In words of Hosea Biglow, a fictitious farmer of New
England)

Ef you take a sword an' dror it,
An go stick a feller thru,
Guv'ment aint to answer to it,
God'll send the bill to you.

Ez fer war, I call it murder ...
They jest want this Californy
  So's to lug new slave-states in
To abuse ye, an' to scorn ye,
  An' to plunder ye like sin.

After the group finished perusing the articles, Robert said, "A man named Abraham Lincoln was elected to Congress in forty-six, just after the war began. He wrote some resolutions that have made him famous. He really has gumption and fears no one. He challenged President Polk about the reasons for starting the Mexican War by asking to be told the exact spot where American blood was shed on American soil. You see, everyone knows that our troops set up camp and started building a fort on Mexican soil, not in Texas."

Dr. Bailey shook his head before saying; "No war is pleasant, but even for a physician like me, the mutilation and suffering are indescribable. I hope never to have to work a war zone. They asked for doctors to join the troops, but I could not consider going for a moment. The loss of lives and limbs by the men on both sides are too high a price for taking California and New Mexico."

In her sarcastic fashion, Margaret spat out the words, "Oh, our government paid fifteen million dollars, Willy, so we didn't *take* anything. We paid for it."

Robert put an end to the topic, "That's enough about the Mexican War. Let's go walk on this beautiful day to settle our full stomachs.

And the years passed.

For Robert and Rebecca, life served up a platter of happiness that also came with a bowl full of tears and a few bittersweet morsels. Most people knew that life contained good times and bad times, and they hoped that the scale would weigh heavier for the former. If the latter side dipped down, one hoped the sadness would make them stronger. The Newells hoped for strength every day in the year 1848.

Rebecca had given birth to their first child in September of forty-seven; they named him James Henry Newell.

Sitting on the bed with Rebecca and his new son, Doc squeezed her hand and stated, "I am so happy for this beautiful boy and your health." And he quoted his favorite poet, as always:

If this rascal has not given me medicines to make me love her,
I'll be hanged.

Without hesitation, she retorted, "And you give me potions concocted from Shakespeare to make me love you."

Their eyes danced with the gaiety of those in love.

Their joy was brief. The baby boy died the next year, in June 1848, but between his birth and death, a disaster in Oregon brought sadness and fear into every home.

It happened on November 29, 1847, just two months after their baby was born. It happened near the place where the Snake River flows into the Columbia River at the Whitman Mission by Fort Walla Walla. From the

Willamette Valley, the distance was far – many days riding on a fast horse from Fort Vancouver – so no one knew until December.

The day before Christmas in 1847, Joe Meek rode up to the Newell cabin, shouting, "Doc, Doc, are you there?" Before Joe jumped from his horse, he bellowed, "Doc, it was a massacre!"

Doc rushed outside to see Joe's horse frothing at the mouth.

With his face distorted in anguish, Meek grabbed Doc by his shoulders to blurt, "They killed 'em."

"Joe, settle down. Who? Who got killed?"

Now Rebecca and Margaret came outside. Margaret had come to help prepare food for a Christmas party. Rebecca held the baby on her hip and jostled him. The child began to pucker up his face, knowing something was amiss.

Joe threw his arms to the sky and screamed, "The Whitmans at the Mission!" With that outburst, the baby bawled.

"Joe, Joe, please come in, sit down, and talk to us. Tell us what you know."

As everyone gathered around the table, they learned that many of the people at the Mission were dead. "Killed by the Cayuse!" Joe could not stay calm. Margaret got up and poured a cup of coffee for him.

"Joe, drink something and try to relax," she said, placing the cup on the table. "How do you know this?"

Joe took a sip and explained, "Some people escaped and hightailed it to Fort Walla Walla to alert 'em about the massacre. That's when they sent a man on a fast horse to The Hudson's Bay Company up at Fort Vancouver. That's how we know 'bout it. Mr. and Mrs. Osborne with their three small ones hid under floor planks until it war dark. They hear'd all the murderous goings-on. They got ta Fort Walla Walla after several days. Mr. Hall, a carpenter, left to go on to inform Fort Vancouver, but he never got thar. He ain't been seen since."

Doc was agitated and started to pace. "When, Joe. When did this happen?"

"The last days of November. Don' know what date. I war up at the

Fort today and the rider came in while I war thar."

Margaret asked, "How many were killed?"

Joe shook his head. "Don't know."

Doc lost his composure. "How would he know? People hid under the floorboards and could only hear the killing before they snuck out. They wouldn't stop and count."

Margaret frowned. "No need to bark, Robert. We are all upset like you."

Joe finished his coffee in one gulp and slammed the cup down, "Damn it all. Damn those Cayuse!" Then he calmed a bit and turned to Margaret and Rebecca. "Maybe you two don't know the story. Doc is right to be more upset than you. An' fer good reason."

Robert wiped his hands through his hair. Sweat was on his forehead. He nodded before saying, "Rebecca and Margaret, you may remember that my third son by Kitty is named Marcus Whitman Newell. He was born in the spring of 1840, and that was the year I had decided to stop fur trapping and come to Oregon to settle. My son was named after the missionary Marcus Whitman, whom I met and grew to love.

"Dr. Marcus Whitman and his wife Narcissa came to Oregon Country in 1836 to start a mission. They chose a site called Waiilatpu; it was about six miles from The Hudson's Bay Company's Fort Walla Walla. They taught their religion to various Indian tribes and tried to help them in any way they could. They built a large community at the mission with Americans helping the Indians. I admired Narcissa and Marcus more than anyone I know." A sob caught in his throat. "Joe, do we even know if they were killed or not?"

Joe put his shirt sleeve to his face and wiped. "No. But don't git your hopes up."

There were no Christmas parties that year.

To spread the word about the massacre, it was decided that Joe and Doc would have a meeting during the first week in January. But Doc couldn't wait to learn more and took a trip up to the Fort on Christmas day.

Dr. McLoughlin gave him more information. "As soon as we heard,

Peter Skeen Ogden took it upon himself to go, not to the Whitman Mission, but to the Cayuse tribe. He was concerned about the hostages. Armed forces were sent along to support and protect him. He has been gone a few days." Though Dr. McLoughlin did not hold the position and power he once had, he still maintained respect from people at Fort Vancouver. London had set his formal retirement date for the next year, June of 1849, so when this disaster occurred, he became involved.

It was winter, not an easy time to travel eastward. Doc and Joe wanted to go, but the Americans had no troops to protect them; there was no U.S. Army in Oregon. Joe Meek, as the U.S. Marshal, had the most authority. Doc and Joe decided they would go, without troops, as soon as the weather permitted. Until then, they relied on The Hudson's Bay Company to convey any new details.

On January 10, 1848, Peter Skeen Ogden arrived in Oregon City with all the prisoners who had been taken by the Cayuse. Doc and Joe went there to get the whole story. They were told by one of the survivors, "On that fateful day, after the massacre, the Cayuse and Umatilla tribes took all of us from the mission as prisoners and made us their slaves. We were fifty-four in number. They forced the women to be wives. We were so glad to see Mr. Ogden arrive."

Because Peter Skene Ogden went to negotiate with the tribes for the prisoners, results were achieved. It took him a month, but forty-nine were freed after Ogden arranged to pay a ransom of blankets, rifles, ammunition, tobacco, flints and other things. Only forty-nine of the fifty-four prisoners were released because five had died while living with the tribes. The daughter of Joe Meek was one of those taken, and she was one of those who died. His little Helen Mar was dead from measles.

While sitting and facing Peter Skene Ogden in Oregon City, Joe dropped his head into his hands and sobbed. Other people were present, but who could comfort a father who lost his beloved girl after she had been abducted in such a vile manner?

Hours later, Dr. Bailey, Margaret, Mary Anne, and Rebecca arrived in Oregon City to be with Doc and Joe at the hotel. They entered the Moss

Hotel, hung their coats, and joined the two men at a table. No one spoke, waiting for Doc or Joe to speak.

Doc began, "On November twenty-ninth last year, at two in the afternoon, the mission was attacked by Cayuse Indians and at least one white man named Joe Lewis. It was a massacre, and for reference in history books and newspapers – for the rest of time – it is to be called it the Whitman Mission Massacre. At least eleven people were killed, but Marcus was mutilated in the foulest manner; they dismembered him and left him in the dirt to die with severed limbs – a foot, one leg, and his arms. A white man named Joe Lewis entered their house and shot Narcissa in the chest, not killing her. Then, Chief *Tamtsaky* coaxed her down from upstairs to trick her into seeing what had been done to her husband. Once downstairs and as she stood above Marcus in the view of the enemy, they aimed their guns and, in a volley of fire from many, shot her to death.

"The massacre went on and on from afternoon until dusk. During all that time, the Indians were killing and torturing. From two until dusk! They brought death slowly for the adults, and they forced the missionary children to watch." Doc looked at nothing, yet was seeing what he described. "They sang and danced as they tortured with whips and war-clubs. Even the Indian women and native children assisted."

Mary Anne, now a young lady of thirteen, gasped, "Why did all this happen?"

Doc hung his head in silence for a while. When he began talking again, his voice was a hollow monotone. "Why did this happen?" He clenched his jaw. "Many reasons seemed to play a role in starting this. The white man who shot Narcissa was a bitter man who had just arrived last year from problems in the East. He started rumors that Marcus and Narcissa were poisoning the Indians. He talked with the Cayuse and Umatilla tribes. The Indians could believe the lies because their people were dying from measles and cholera at that time and, as you know, there is no cure. Also adding to the discontent was the politics of the religious groups. The Catholics wanted to buy the Whitman's Mission site, but Marcus refused to sell. Rumors have it that the priests started telling lies to the Indians about the Whitmans. Another factor: the tribes have laws that say that a medicine man, who does not heal, can be killed, and once he is dead the contagion should end. In their eyes, Dr. Marcus Whitman was their medicine man."

In 1848, three months after the massacre, Joe Meek and Robert Newell went to Waiilatpu, the Whitman Mission site. They had to see for themselves and, as the U.S. marshal, it was Joe's duty to report the massacre to the government in Washington D.C. It was March and bitter cold. The Mission was dismal and abandoned. Vandals had destroyed the house – no windows or doors remained. The wind blew through where life and laughter had once prevailed. Bones were scattered everywhere from wolves and other varmints uncovering the shallow graves that had been made. They found Marcus and Narcissa. Marcus was easy to identify without his arms and leg. She was in the same grave with him.

Meek rode on to St. Louis to spread the word and arrived on May 17, 1848. From there, he went on to Washington, D.C., arriving on May 28, and went directly to the White House. Being the cousin of Mrs. Polk, he needed no introduction. His words shocked Congress into action. Joe was the right man to go and tell the story.

As a result of the Whitman Mission Massacre, Congress established the Oregon Territory in August of 1848. The new territory embraced all of the Pacific Northwest south of the 49th parallel and east to the Rocky Mountains.

Months later, when Doc heard the news of Oregon finally becoming a territory of the United States, he shook his head and blinked his tear-filled eyes. "What a price to pay."

PART II

Albert Bayless, George Luther Boone, and Beaver Coins
Come to Oregon Territory
1848 – 1852

Traveling Blacksmith Working

Photo taken during the reenactment of old-time blacksmiths at Champoeg Living History: Blacksmith Day, July 2014.

Champoeg State Heritage Area
Oregon State Parks

CHAPTER 8

1848 – 1850

Some folks say that things happen and cannot be explained. Other people say most things happen because of luck or fate. And there are those who claim all occurrences are divinely planned. Albert Bayless disagreed with all of this. He believed that he made his own destiny. Off and on through his adult life, he had given this subject a lot of thought and the word *unbeknownst* always came to mind. This particular night he was determined to make his own destiny, but knew that unknown occurrences could thwart his plans. *But once I know about the problem, I work through it. So, there's nothing unbeknownst because I will always learn about it at some point in time.*

As he struggled through the swampy terrain near the Mississippi River in Tennessee, somewhere near the Kentucky border, the chains on his arms and legs got heavier by the minute; nevertheless, he knew where he was going and had no doubt that his strong thirty-year-old body could get him there. Another thing that gave him confidence: he had calculated that no one would know he was gone until daybreak. Ignoring the deep and bleeding cuts across his back – three days worth of lashes – was easy because he would endure any pain for freedom.

Until a few weeks ago when his owner died, he had lived life like a free man. His owner was kindhearted and a person who believed a man was a man no matter what the color of his skin. So Albert Bayless was taught to read by his owner when young and was taught the management of a farm when grown. They had worked side by side, running the farm, until his owner died and the relatives came to sell Albert like all the other farm equipment, animals, and furniture.

His chain caught on a broken branch and he slipped, falling in some muck. While pulling his muddy body to standing again, he smiled, thinking about his owner who had taught him. *He taught me so much. And none of that knowledge can ever be taken from me.* Albert was heading back to the only place he had ever lived until sold. He had a stash in the brick wall of the homestead. Some would say that it was luck that he was sold to the neighboring farm, because it was easier to get back to his stash. Albert knew he would have gotten back to it even if he had to travel across the whole state of Tennessee.

With his mind meandering through his past, he thought of his owner's wife who was kind and happy every day of her life. She had died a couple of years ago. *Good people raised me.* He often had wondered if they had formed his character or if he would have been the same person without them. He concluded that it was probably a little of both. His character brought out the best in people because Albert always wanted to help and to learn and to give and to make people happy. He was not going to change just because he was in chains and carrying wounds of a slave.

Ahead he saw the familiar homestead. No lamps were lit yet in the large brick house. He hoped the dogs were sound asleep and far from the wall with his stash. But the dogs knew and loved him; if they caught his scent, they probably would not bark. He only needed to pull out three bricks, grab the leather satchel, and leave. Albert hunched over to gather the loose chains between his ankles into a bunch, carrying them to lessen the noise they made. When he arrived at the wall, he put the chains down very slowly to avoid the unavoidable noise; the chains only rattled a bit, but when chains bumped the leg irons there was a clank, and he froze in anticipation of barking. No barks!

Methodically, he started removing the bricks. Without a clink of the first brick, he slipped it out and put it on the ground. The second brick began to make a slight rasping sound, and he stopped to wait and to listen. Sweat rolled down his back and stung the deep cuts. More carefully, he started again and removed the second brick and placed it on the ground. His hands were shaking now. When he wiggled the third brick, it came out silently, but he dropped it with a thud. The tension was too much; he grabbed the satchel and quickly replaced the three bricks, so as to not leave any clue of his visit.

Again he picked up the leg irons, and started moving as best as he could. He made a lot of noise, but he was two hundred yards away before he heard any barking. He just kept going. So far, everything was going according to his plan.

He headed for a blacksmith's shop in a small town about five miles away; it sat right next to the old muddy Mississippi. He knew the blacksmith there.

Knowing the morning light was soon to put him in view of others, he pushed himself to hurry faster than before. A little more than an hour later, he was at the blacksmith shop. Lester lived in a shed next to the shop. There was only room for a bed and a chest of drawers in the little shed, so Albert didn't worry about waking a lot of people. *No one else could fit in there.* He tapped on the window and Lester pulled aside the dirty sheet that hung as a curtain. Fear mixed with amazement when Lester saw Albert so he wasted no time in opening his door.

"Git in here 'fore somebody sees you. Let me get my pants on and pee. Then we can work on those chains."

"I need some clothes to look decent. I plan to board the steamer and go to St. Louis. I must look respectable. Can you help me?"

Lester looked out his window and a big grin with two missing teeth appeared on his paste-colored face. "The laundry from my boss' family is still out there on the line. I'll go get some clothes for you before the maid in the house is up. Here, clean yourself up with my water and soap. See the basin on top of the chest of drawers?"

"Grab a pillowcase off the clothes line, too."

Lester rushed out, peed, and returned with clothes and a pillowcase. "Lucky for you, Albert, I needs to put new shoes on some of the horses, so I'll be making clanging noises as soon as the sun is up."

It wasn't luck. Albert knew that. They would have thought of another guise if the horse shoeing had been another day.

While Albert washed, Lester squatted next to his friend and looked at the leg irons. "They won't be too hard to cut off. The cuffs are thick, but they used a puny lock to close 'em. I'll cut those locks off your legs and arms then you can come in here to dress and leave." Lester peeked out the window again and said, "It's almost light. I'm goin' to the house for my breakfast. Sometimes I git my own food when I gotta lot of work. I'll bring you back somethin' if I can." He scurried out the door.

Albert removed some of his money from the satchel and slipped it under Lester's pillow. He took off his torn shirt to dip into the water to wipe himself. Finally he cleaned his shoes, poured the dirty water out the window, and put clean water into the basin. He needed to wash at least twice to get all the muck and grime off. *Wish I had a hat.* Everyone wore hats.

Lester came back with day-old biscuits, a hunk of ham, and some cheese all wrapped in a cloth napkin that he had stuck into his pants pocket. "Here, put this in your satchel."

"I need to eat that ham right now. I'm starving."

"Well, eat up!" While Albert ate, Lester squatted in front of his friend and said, "Now, here's my plan. We goin' to the blacksmith shop together in a minute. I'm puttin' you in a corner behind a lot of stuff. After I start the forge a-goin', I'll go to the stable to git a horse. When I come back, the house should be awake by then and I can start bangin' on the horseshoes. I'll work on the shoes for a while just to see if anyone looks out, then I'll work on those four locks. When I done, you gotta go back into that corner until I is sure nobody's lookin' before you can head back to this room ta change. We say our goodbyes now. Understand?"

"You're a good man, Lester, to help a Negro. I'll repay you someday."

"Now, hows you gonna do that? You jus' git outta here without gettin' caught or we'll both hang." He smiled and carefully hugged his friend. He had seen Albert's back.

"Wish I had a hat."

Lester swallowed. The look on Lester's face told Albert that a solution was coming, but it was going to be a painful one for Lester. "I jus' bought the finest hat. One I been wantin' for a long time. An' shucks, I sayin' no more." He went to a shelf and pulled a hat from under some of his winter long underwear. "Hope it fits."

Albert beamed, "How much did it cost?"

"Oh, you don't need to know that. You need it more 'an me. That's all it matters."

"Lester, I can pay you. I saved money. How much?"

"It were twenty-five dollars. I was savin' for two years."

Albert smiled and went to his satchel and slipped another coin under the pillow. "Let's go work. Don't look under your pillow until I'm gone." They looked at each other and already they missed the friendship they had.

Five years ago, Albert's owner had paid Lester to teach Albert about blacksmithing. The two young men didn't have many opportunities to work with someone their age, and they liked playing pranks and jokes on each other while making metal tools and repairing broken ones. In this way their friendship grew. Now it was ending. Of course, Lester thought of this day as a special gift; he had concluded that Albert was gone from his life over week ago when sold.

In years to come, Albert could not put on a hat without thinking of Lester.

Albert looked like a fine gentlemen when he reached the steamboat docks. He was light-skinned, tall, confident, polite, and well-read. He could speak about current events, history, some literature, and most conversational topics while using proper English. No one would think him a slave. He had traveled with his owner many times from these docks, so he was not nervous about what he had to do.

Neither was he concerned about his appearance, even though he was missing a few pieces of clothing. Concerning his bleeding wounds, he surmised that the thickness of the pillowcase covering his back beneath his shirt would absorb the blood so it could not bleed through. What held the pillowcase in place was the strap of his satchel outside of his shirt, across his chest, and around his back. As he walked up the ramp onto the steamboat, he could see his ankles popping out above his shoes because the pants were a bit too short and he lacked socks. But he figured, *With Lester's handsome hat, no one will look at my feet.* He would buy socks, a coat, and belt in St. Louis.

While traveling up the Mississippi, he read a newspaper for the first hour and, when finished, he flipped the flap open on the satchel that rested at his hips and slipped the newspaper in next to another sheet of paper. Then he went to get some coffee and breakfast in a dining area of the steamboat.

That other sheet of paper stated that Albert Bayless was a free man. His owner had been wise enough to know that once he died, Albert would have difficulties. And Albert had been wise enough to know that the paper was worthless with the relatives; if he had shown them, they would have ripped it to pieces. So he had made this plan for an escape.

As Albert walked across the steamer to the dining area, he remembered the day he first saw his freedom papers:

"Sit down, Albert, and join me for some tea. Close the door behind you, Lily," the landowner called to the girl who had brought the tray of cups and saucers with the teapot.

Albert sat and said, "Thank you, Sir."

"Albert, I have written this paper giving you your freedom. I just hope you don't fly away tomorrow, but instead wait until I'm no longer here. I am old and ...."

Albert could not contain his surprise, "Thank you, but don't talk about dying. I'm not going to leave you. Why, you have more to teach me, I'm sure. I can't leave here until I know all that you know."

They chuckled.

The owner nodded and said, "One thing is for sure, you do know how to talk your way through any situation. Albert, I do so enjoy your company. Now, back to my topic. In this satchel is your letter of freedom. Keep the satchel, too, and ...," he leaned forward and hissed, "hide it! As we have discussed before, be prepared for the day I am gone. No one in my family will have any consideration for you. I sure have begot an ornery bunch of children. Thank heavens they no longer live in this house. I don't think I could stand being with them on a daily basis." He picked up his tea and took a sip.

Albert remembered the weight of the satchel and questioned why it was so heavy.

"Why don't you look and see?"

He looked into the satchel and found not only the letter of freedom but also a calfskin pouch with a drawstring. Inside the pouch were fifteen U.S. double eagles – gold coins worth twenty-dollars each. For Albert, a fortune!

Albert had a warm rush in his chest, remembering that scene from not too long ago.

When Albert strode down the gangplank onto the cobblestone streets of St. Louis he didn't fear being approached or detained because of his color. St. Louis had been the crossroads of cultures for over fifty years. Albert knew this. In the streets walked people from many places. Of course, the French had dominated St. Louis even after the Louisiana Purchase of 1803, however, an assortment of non-white people came and settled: Mexicans, Cubans, Creoles, Africans, along with the Americans from the eastern states and even gentlemen and ladies of Europe found their way to St. Louis – the place where civilization touched the wild west. Also, it was common to see delegations from various Indian tribes such as the Shawnee, Sioux, Kickapoo, and Cherokee. And it was a gathering place for the fur trappers before they set out for the west.

Since 1834, more people came because of the industrial activities sweeping across the entire country. The two most influential inventions of the era were the railroads and the steamboats and, because of them, St. Louis was prospering.

However, in 1848, throngs of people came because they had heard about the discovery of gold in California, and this is where they started their trip. Wherever Albert went – in restaurants and the hotel, at the corner newsstand and in a bar, even while sitting on a bench in the park – people talked with him about the gold to be washed out of rivers and picked from the hills in California.

Albert had lived in the Tennessee area all his thirty years of life. He had been to Kentucky and Missouri for brief trips, but nowhere else. As the realization of being free was seeping into his body and mind, he saw that he could go anywhere he wished for the first time in his life. He decided to go find gold. So he bought the recommended supplies and took a steamboat to Independence, Missouri.

Albert arrived in the rain with hundreds of people trudging through the ankle-deep muddy streets of Independence. It was early spring and everyone was eager to start this two-thousand-mile journey. *But how?* As he squeezed past people on the wooden walkway, he came to an old dilapidated building with a placard that designated it to be the post office and he noticed a paper on the wall. He read the flyer:

CALIFORNIA GOLD
Come find your riches!
Travel from Fort Smith, Arkansas
The shortest route to California.

Albert stared at the flyer and puzzled whether he had come to the wrong place.

Just then, a man bumped into him. "Sorry! Damn it all. Can't even walk in this place. Some fool pushed me as he rushed past." He looked at the flyer, "Hell, don't believe that! Who wants to go down to Fort Smith? That trail is new. It ain't been used long enough. Why, four thousand folks went on the Oregon Trail last year. If you're goin', take it cuz it's a sure thing. Tried and true."

Albert was relieved to talk to someone who seemed to know what was going on, "How do I find a wagon train to take me?"

"Some strangers from Illinois – three hundred of them – asked me to pilot their train. They want to leave from Westport in a day or so. I'm heading over there."

"Do you think I could go along?"

"I guess you could ask 'em."

"I'm an experienced smithy. They can always use another blacksmith."

With an outstretched hand, the man introduced himself. "George Luther Boone, here. I just got back from the Mexican War. My family left for Oregon a while back, and I want to join them."

"Albert Bayless," he said as they shook hands. "How did you get the job to pilot these people if you don't know them?"

George Luther grinned a wide toothy grin. "There's a couple of reasons. First of all, they ain't never seen an Indian and are a bit fearful about what to expect from those wild men. I know Indians. Also, they have no idea how long and hard it is to make this trip, and I've got traveling experience. Why, they've never even seen the plains or real mountains, like the Rockies. Mostly I think they chose me becuz of my name. I need to thank my great-grandpa, Daniel Boone."

Albert and George Luther went to the livery stables, bought a couple of horses, and traveled along the river to get away from the crowds. George Luther shook his head, "We could've bought a house for what we had to pay for these horses." They followed a path along the flowing water for a couple of miles, and came to Westport.

When Albert started wandering among George's wagon train, already the wagons were lined up awaiting the trip. He found a covered wagon with a limber hitched to it and knew that he had found the smithy.

The man was one of two blacksmiths for the trip and knew that he could not handle all the work that was to come his way. "Actually, our job on the trail will be more of a farrier, since most days we'll be repairing wagons and shoeing the animals – both horses and oxen. My twelve-year-old son knows how to help," he admitted, "but he's just a boy. Blacksmithing needs powerful muscles that he don't have yet." After the man walked back to the limber and traveling forge with Albert, he opened a box, which hung from the limber; it held all his supplies, "Albert, you're welcome to come, but I can't pay you. My wife'll cook and feed you to pay for your help. Here, have a look at what I brought." He had a 100-pound anvil, a four-inch-wide vise, a couple hundred pounds of horseshoes, iron bars about four feet long, and an assortment of hand tools. "I have bellows that are the best made anywhere and, in that other box, a couple hundred pounds of coal for my traveling fireplace."

Albert nodded his approval, and they shook hands on the agreement.

So, Albert left with the wagon train for the long trek across North America. He slept outside next to the blacksmith's wagon because, most of the time, they worked on shoeing horses or repairing wheels into the night. If it was raining, he slept under the limber. Whenever possible, Albert rode next to George Luther, who turned out to be quite a talker.

Albert asked a simple question, "Why didn't you travel with your family on their wagon train to Oregon?"

And George Luther spent the next hour talking. "A couple of years back, I was busy selling our family goods to get as much money for the family as I could. When I returned to Westport to leave for Oregon, I found my folks were gone, and there stood Colonel Doniphan recruiting for the Mexican War. While I was talking with the Colonel, in came a company of my old boyhood companions from Jefferson City. Why, of course, I went to war with all my friends. I sold my mules to the government for the war and was mustered in at Fort Leavenworth. In a couple of days I was on the march for Santa Fe.

"On Christmas Day in 1846, I was in the Battle of the Brazos, in Texas." George Luther shook his head and furrowed his brow at the memory. "Some of us soldiers got so sick. There was heavy dew in the tall grasses that gave our sentinels a fever that just kept coming back. They'd shiver and shake while burning up from fever." More than likely, they had malaria from mosquitoes, but he didn't know the illness or the cause.

Albert started to say something, but George Luther Boone was not finished with his story.

"Do you know," he stopped to point south, "down in Texas I met Meriwether Lewis Clark. He's the son of Captain Clark of the Lewis and Clark Expedition. Why, he was as red-haired as his pa! He was in charge of the flying artillery. He did a fine job. I was proud to ride with him."

A little more than a week on the trail and at noon on a sunny day, a huge flock of birds could be seen coming from the northwest. The sky darkened! When close, the air was filled with harsh sounds – keck, keck, kecking and tete, tete, teting. The noise became deafening. The birds formed undulating shapes that flowed like schools of fish swimming in the sky. The wagon train came to a stop as one driver pulled on the reins and then another. Everyone cocked their head upward and needlessly placed their open hand to their eyes to block the sun; in seconds, the sunlight disappeared behind the millions of birds. George Luther turned his horse around and rode back past every wagon shouting, "Wild pigeons! They're heading east to their nesting areas. Let's get some for our dinner!" His voice could not be heard in the din from the flock and that mattered little; everyone knew what he said and went for their fowling piece or shotguns.

At times a group of the birds dipped down in unison, so close to the wagons that it seemed you could pluck them from the air. Albert was amazed at how they twisted and turned in flight with a speed and maneuverability that he had never seen before. *They're better than falcons!*

When the volleys from all the guns began, it rained passenger pigeons. Though he had no shotgun, Albert went to gather some for the wife of the blacksmith to prepare. While kneeling and balancing on one knee, he measured the male birds as being longer than both his hands placed end to end. The birds were beautiful and colorful. The feet and legs were a bright red like the Indian paintbrush flower and a purplish eye-ring encircled the red iris. When he turned over a large male, the throat and breast were a pinkish-rufous color that faded bit by bit down to the lower belly. The neck had an iridescence that shimmered from green to gold to violet. Albert spread the wings open; they were brown to black with a white edge. The tail tapered long and to a point. The females were browner on parts and paler in color.

As Albert carried an armful to the wagon, women were starting the campfires. He had eaten this wild pigeon before, but had never seen the live birds dressed in its magnificent feathers. While his belly growled in anticipation of the delicious dinner that was to come, he cradled the birds, looked up at the still passing flock, and stumbled over other passenger pigeons on the ground. He stopped to watch. Peering in all directions, the birds filled the sky. He figured it might be a once in a lifetime experience, as he saw no end to the flying black clouds of birds. *And it's been over an hour ago since we first saw them.*

Hours later and after the meal ended, the passenger pigeons were still passing. George Luther said to a group of men sitting around the fire and scraping their tin plates for the last morsels, "They'll come down for the night when they find trees."

"Why that's 'bout a couple of hundred miles east of here!"

"That's right," George Luther said as he packed his pipe. "That ain't far for them."

◦ ◦ ◦

In the coming days, they started seeing Indians in the distance. The natives rode in small groups and didn't seem to be interested in the large wagon train. Albert was concerned and asked, "George Luther, like you told me, no one on this train of three hundred people had ever seen an Indian. So, naturally, they can't talk to them. Do you know how to speak their language?"

"I do, Albert, don't worry. Why, during the Mexican War, I was the only one in my unit who understood Indian talk. I went with a captain and seven commissioners to the headwaters of the Gila River at one point when we needed to make a treaty with the Navahos. Maybe you don't know that they use a sign language. You see, all the tribes have their own language. I don't know Navaho, but I'm skilled in the pantomime that the fur trappers and traders use with the Indians. This sign language is old and has been used by all the tribes for hundreds of years. I got a gold medal for helping with that treaty."

And then they started to see bison. The plains were black with buffalo as they traveled the North Platte. It seemed that the animals were heading down the Oregon Trail like the wagon train. On the second day of traveling with the herd, out of curiosity Albert and George Luther got on their horses for a closer look. A hundred feet away they dismounted and squatted to watch. The closest ones loped a short distance farther from the men before stopping and grazing again. The plains, covered with the new spring grasses, rolled to the horizon. As far as they could see the animals dotted the landscape and little birds with glossy black bodies and brown hooded heads were flitting on and off the back of the huge animals, walking and grabbing insects beneath the hooves, or standing in the shadow of the bison during the heat of the day.

George Luther commented in a soft voice, "I always see those birds with the bison. I call 'em bison birds – don't know the real name. Oh, look! See that bull rolling in that wallow of dust. I bet he peed there before he started squirming around. I think they do that to get all scented-up." He snickered and said, "Must be like perfume. Don't know if he wants to smell good for the girls or let the other men know who he is." After some time, they got back on their horses. "Let's get back to the wagons. I promised we could shoot some bison when we stopped to camp tonight. It's about time."

When men started shooting, the brown-headed cowbirds took to the skies in fright and the bison herd headed east on the run.

One evening, when they were only a day from Fort Laramie, a couple of riders came into their camp. One was the U.S. Marshal Joseph L. Meek.

George Luther and Albert were eating at the blacksmith's wagon when Joe was escorted to them.

Joe removed his hat, wiped the sweat from his hair with his shirtsleeve, and shook hands. "I'm on government business and been travelin' hard and fast. I sure could use a change of horse for me and my man." Then Joe smelled the buffalo meat. "I war ready to go on with a fresh horse, but your grub sure smells good."

As Joe ate his first plateful, he told about the problems the wagon train might encounter with the Indians, "They's on the warpath. You might ask the men at Fort Hall to escort your wagon train a-ways."

Albert asked why the Indians were fighting the whites and said, "We haven't had any trouble with the Indians so far."

Joe swallowed his last bite and a woman came with another ladle of food. Joe smiled at the woman before turning toward the men and grimacing. "It's a horrible story of how it all started. And a long one! Maybe I'll sleep a couple of hours after I tell you the story of the Whitman Mission Massacre that happened just months ago. I'm on my way to tell President Polk 'bout it, but you can hear it first."

Sometime during the night while everyone slept, Joe Meek and his companion rose from their brief sleep, mounted their fresh horses, and continued on to St. Louis. They would arrive on May 17, 1848.

The next morning, the wagon train was abuzz with the story Joe had told of the massacre near Fort Walla Walla. They rode in fear and worry for a few weeks until they were hit with something worse than Indians.

Cholera!

Thousands of people traveled on the Oregon Trail, passing and meeting others. George Luther wondered why they got the cholera when they did, but that question would never be answered. And the answer didn't matter at that point. No answers would stop the people from dying.

Albert learned that the medicine was gone before the family of the blacksmith came down with this scourge. First the man's wife died, then the youngest child, and finally the oldest boy. The blacksmith was deathly sick when he asked Albert to come and talk with him.

"I've two children left and they're going to travel with my sister and her family in the wagon just behind us. If I die, and I imagine I will just like my fine wife, well, my children will be raised by my sister. I would like to give her something to help raise them. All I have is this wagon and limber full of tools for blacksmithing. I wrote up a paper to give you ownership if you can pay for it. Are you interested, Albert?"

"Yes, I am." They made a deal, got two witnesses, and signed the paper. Now Albert had another important paper to slip into his satchel.

Within a fortnight, Albert became the owner of the wagon, the two oxen, and all the blacksmithing tools. And, like many situations in his life, Albert was amazed at the timing and coincidence of the next direction that his life would take. *Unbeknownst, a door opened for me! How does this happen? I want to make my own destiny, yet ....*

Just before they got to Fort Hall, another wagon train was coming up behind them. Albert knew that George Luther's wagon train was going into northern Oregon, and Albert wanted to go to California. When he learned that the train behind them was going to branch south onto the California Trail and finally onto the Applegate Trail, which headed into southern Oregon, Albert informed George Luther that he was going to join the other train.

"I want to get to California, not Oregon. I know you knew that," Albert explained. "I thank you for all you did to help me, and your friendship has meant a lot to me. But the gold calls me. Besides, it's a smaller group of wagons and they'll travel faster. I like that I'll get there sooner."

George Luther slapped him on the back. "We'll meet again. It's good that I have another blacksmith with us or your leaving would be a problem. But it ain't."

With the new group, Albert passed the City of Rocks, where the Salt Lake cutoff headed south; a couple of the wagons took that cutoff. At Emigrant Pass, no one talked about the Donner-Reed party from 1846, though everyone knew how they had been caught in deep snow and had to resort to cannibalism to survive. Finally, they turned the wagon train northward onto the Applegate Trail and, within weeks, they arrived in Oregon Country.

At Jackson Creek, Oregon, the wagon train camped. It was just a place, not a town.

That night, Albert learned that California was just thirty to forty miles south, so he decided to head out on his own for the gold mines. When the wagon train headed north the next morning, Albert went south with his traveling blacksmith shop.

By afternoon, he came upon business. A couple of riders paid him in gold dust to shoe their horses and, at the same time, gave him information.

Pointing, one of them said, "That's the Siskiyou Mountains, and when you reach the top, you're in California. Jus' follow the trail; you can't miss it. I guess the Injuns have been comin' and goin' on this trail for hundreds of years."

Albert reached the top and traveled until he saw a house in the distance. It was getting dark. When he approached the McAlister homestead, he was mighty hungry.

Standing on the back stoop and talking to Mrs. McAlister, he offered to repair tools or anything for a meal. She agreed to feed him and took him to the barn to show what needed repairing.

As he worked on a wheel out in the barn, he could hear the fighting in the house. He was almost finished with the repairs, when the barn door slammed. Without a word, a young man huffed past him, saddled his horse, and rode away.

Soon the woman brought out some mutton stew. She said nothing either, set the tin plate on a stump, and returned to the house. The food was a hearty portion and enjoyed by Albert, but when the yelling started again, he decided that it was his turn to say nothing and leave.

He headed down a scrubby trail to a dry creek bed and camped. In the morning, he dug around in the rocks and sand of the creek, looking for gold. He figured that gold could be anywhere. Not really knowing how to go about finding gold, he reasoned that he needed to find a creek with water. So, he hitched up his oxen and set out again.

Later that day, he struck it rich – no gold, just friendly people. He came upon another house, where a German man and his wife lived. "Ja, we got three other men staying here from Brazil. They sleep in that shed out back and look for gold all days. You welcome, too. Tomorrow, you talk with Brazil men about where to go for gold." That said, Jahn and Eliza invited him to join them for dinner, and Albert didn't leave for months. They became Albert's friends, and he would reach out for help from them in the years to come. For the present, Albert was content to have a bed to sleep in and fine people to eat with. "Eliza, this meal is the best."

She grinned, and buck teeth popped from her mouth. "It German dish I made with the mutton. I cut it real thin and roll into the little logs and cook for hours. It called roladin."

"Jahn, I saw that your wagon needs some repair work. I'll fix it in return for your hospitality to me."

"*Danke!*"

Soon, Albert was panning for gold on the Cottonwood Creek in Siskiyou County. He couldn't talk much with the three Brazilians, but the sign language, that George Luther had shown him, helped with communicating. They taught Albert how to pan and to keep the location a secret if he found gold. And he really did find gold. He put the sparkling grains into his calfskin pouch with the double eagles he had left.

He didn't pan much gold – a few grains here, a few more there, and one day a small nugget. But the horseshoeing business never stopped filling his pocket with gold. It didn't take long for the word to get around that there was a blacksmith who could fix things, trim and shoe hooves, as well as make tools. People passed the word of a Negro "over there" with the Germans or camping with the Brazilians. Albert moved about looking for gold in his traveling smithy shop and got richer on the customers coming to the blacksmith.

For Albert, the months flowed into another year while he searched for a worthwhile gold strike, and then he heard about placer gold to be found near Jackson Creek, Oregon. *That's where I was. It was just a place, there was no town.* So he left California and headed north into Oregon, back to the same area where he had first arrived with the wagon train.

As surprising as it may seem, when Albert made his way toward southern Oregon, so did Robert Newell, George Luther Boone, Dr. William Bailey, and a Negro named Alexander Louis Southworth. Few were the men who remained in Oregon, so it should be no surprise that these five were traveling toward the gold; it was like an uncontrollable force of Mother Nature – a twisting tornado that sucked people toward the gold mines. In the same days and months that these five headed out, there were hundreds of men from Oregon going south for the same reason. Within two years, thousands made this exodus and created great changes in the economics of Oregon.

In Oregon, between 1848 and 1849, the population was approximately 13,000 white people, mainly located in the Willamette River valley. Most of those people made their living in agriculture; by comparison, only a few were employed in the eight flourmills, fifteen sawmills, or in the handful of general stores, as furniture makers, blacksmiths, and other such individual businesses. During August of the 1848 harvest season, it was estimated that two-thirds of the adult population left to find gold. The gold seekers from Oregon, having only a short distance to travel, were among the first to arrive and became very successful.

Nevertheless, those who remained at home in Oregon profited greatly, if not more. While Oregon's population dipped with men leaving, California's soared. Almost overnight, there were 100,000 people in California, creating a demand for produce and everyday goods. There sat Oregon with the products and California full of people with gold in their pockets to pay. The ships arriving in Portland increased from five in 1847 to fifty by 1849. The price of wheat went from sixty-two cents a bushel to two dollars. Flour went up to $15 a bushel, potatoes were $7 a bushel and, before California had any sawmills in the mining areas, Oregon's lumber sold for $80 a thousand foot. Oregon, for about three years, sold its products at prices three hundred percent higher than the prices before the gold rush.

As a result of the gold mining and the end of the Mexican War, Oregon's currency system began to change. Silver coins of Mexico were in the pockets of the men returning from the war and on the ships coming into port to buy Oregon goods; there was no standard to determine the value of these coins. At the same time, gold particles and dust were being measured by the few who owned scales in Oregon, yet the dust often contained sand or other substances degrading the quality. People began to realize that they were suffering losses when trading with the gold coming from the mines. A stir developed as people talked of needing an Oregon mint or at least a standard for gold.

After 1849, few Oregonians returned home rich from gold mines; many ended up in the Rogue River War against the Indians; others succumbed to debauchery at the various mines. Dr. Bailey, Robert Newell, George Luther Boone, Albert Bayless, and Louis Southworth learned this first hand.

ROBERT NEWELL'S TREK SOUTH

Gold fever was truly like an unexpected storm that poured down on people and blew them to the gold fields. The logical and stable Robert Newell became drenched in the desire to head south to the gold. He abandoned the appointment that he had received in June of 1849 as Indian Agent to tribes along the Columbia River and in the Willamette Valley and decided to leave in early December to lead thirty men going to the mines.

Once they packed up and headed out, they wasted no time. Within two days, Newell and his group were more than one hundred miles south of Salem.

Being aware of the Rogue River Wars, Newell was extra alert when they came closer to the passes through the high summits. Over the campfire one night, he prepared the men. "I saw Indians watching us today."

The men stirred and looked to one another. Fear crept into the faces of many.

Newell continued talking. "We have troops down here, but they are few and far between. We can't expect any help." He pulled a stick from the fire and started drawing in the dirt. "All of you gather around me and look at my plan."

"Maybe we should turn back," someone blurted.

"Yeah, I didn't come to git killed."

Robert stood, "Calm down and listen. If you decide to go home tomorrow morning, then go. But listen to my plan now." Once encircled by the men he returned to his drawing. "I know the lay of this land. Tomorrow we will approach a narrow passage. By gum, I mean real narrow. We will have to go single-file. There's room only for a line of riders. If the Indians want to attack, that's where they'll do it."

Murmurs and grumbles circled through the group.

"Through the narrow pass," he pointed to the line he had made and said, "I'm going to send some of you as decoys."

Complaints were shouted, "Hell's fire, I ain't goin' to be no decoy."

"Damn it all, Newell, who do you think you are?"

Doc raised his arms and shouted, "Shit! Would you all shut up and listen. Let me finish and then you can tell me what you think." He started drawing again. "On this ridge above the pass, I want eight to ten of you men to cover the decoys. It is thick with wild plum bushes and you won't be seen. So while men hide in the bushes in the early morning hours, I will send another ten of you to circle around this hill," he drew a wiggly line on the other side of the pass. "That second group will circle behind the Indians and be able to shoot them from their backside. It will be a surprise attack. They will never suspect. I will go with this last group since I know every hill and creek. Weston and Howard, I want you in that group with me. By gum, men, we can do this!"

After a bit more talking, no one wanted to leave. They bedded down with two men as lookouts. "Sleep hard and fast. I need you alert for tomorrow."

Long before dawn, Newell headed out with his group. "No talking.

We'll have to walk some of the way with the horses, just follow my lead."

Just before dawn, the second group scrambled up the hill to hide in the wild plum bushes. They hunkered down and waited.

At dawn, the remaining men had breakfast and broke camp like everything was normal. They knew the natives were watching. "Can't see 'em, but they're out there somewhere." They hoped the natives didn't notice their shrunken numbers. Soon the men were packed and mounted on their horses. "Let's tell some stories and laugh a lot. We need to look like usual. Besides, talkin' will help us relax."

As the decoys approached the narrow passage, up on the hill the Indians were moving into position to shoot down on the single line of men, but they saw none of the men hiding in the bushes.

At the southern end of the pass – the place where the Indians expected the decoys to run away from the attack – more Indians gathered. Newell and his men could see them.

Someone fired a shot and the Indians were caught in total confusion. Men popped out of the wild plum bushes and killed the natives at close range, without taking a casualty. At the southern end, Newell and his men attacked, leaving the natives with only one possibility of retreat. Indians rode and ran along a bluff, but suddenly Weston came in with men to get the natives fleeing on the bluff. Newell and Weston had separated into two groups. Weston's men opened fire and Indians jumped from the bluff into a river. Now the natives were sitting ducks. Men took careful aim and started killing all the swimmers. The river ran red.

"Let those last two go! Newell shouted. "Let 'em swim away. Keep firing, but miss them. We want 'em to spread the word of our conquest. It'll put fear into the tribes so they'll think twice before attacking us again."

Newell and the thirty men arrived in Jacksonville without any other incident.

WILLIAM BAILEY'S DECISION

While Robert Newell was traveling south to the gold in December of 1849,

Baileys' life was deteriorating.

Mr. Flett came for his daughters, ending Margaret's life with Sarah and Eliza; the loss of the girls left a void inside Margaret. Her only solace was Mary Anne McAlister whose singing and companionship filled that empty space. Looking for other positive aspects of her life, Margaret was grateful that there were no other encounters with the McAlisters. However, Mattie knew she had not seen the last of Jed McAlister, though she never talked of her fear.

And there were other reasons for discontent in the Bailey household.

The Baileys fought daily, and Dr. Bailey drank incessantly. With the population of Oregon changing – his friends and neighbors leaving for the gold mines and strangers arriving on the wagon trains – he experienced a lot of theft. Neighbors weren't there to look out for neighbors and newcomers had no livelihood; the Baileys' cows and horses disappeared. What was harder for the Baileys to accept was that sheep and pigs were slaughtered with only the best cuts taken and the carcasses left to rot. Dr. Bailey was furious.

Then, out of the blue, Bailey's brother came to visit from New York.

Encouraged by his brother as they drank themselves drunk each night, Bailey decided to join everyone and go to the gold mines. They made the decision one day and left the next. He and his brother headed for southern Oregon in January of 1850.

GEORGE LUTHER'S LIFE BEFORE GOLD FEVER

A series of events occurred in George Luther Boone's first year in Oregon that would lead him to make a decision to go to the gold mines, too.

When George Luther had reached Oregon with his wagon train, he learned that the others in his family were well established in Oregon. His sister lived in Oregon City and was married to the editor of *The Oregon Spectator*. His brothers had homes, and his father, Colonel Alphonso Boone, had bought land and built a ferry – Boone's Ferry across the Willamette River.

During the winter of 1848, soon after George Luther had arrived, he was busy trying to make his own way in life. Not having a place of his own, he often stayed at the McLoughlin house in Oregon City, where many men had room and board. Billy McKay was one such man.

One night, while in their bunks, they talked and Billy said, "Hell's fire! They's so much gold coming here from men returning from the mines. You jus' can't imagine how damn much. I'm a clerk at The Hudson's Bay store in town, and I can't tell you how much gold flows onto our scales to be weighed for goods bein' bought."

From his bed, George Luther leaned up on his elbow and nodded, "I was jus' standing on a corner leanin' against a signpost and I heared a couple of men from the bank say to the other that two million dollars worth of gold has come into Oregon in the last two years. Can you believe that? I can't!"

Billy McKay pulled the covers up to his chin and rolled over, "Listen, come to the store with me tomorrow and you'll believe it. Let's git some sleep."

That next morning, while Billy worked in McLoughlin's store measuring out rope and putting away pants that had just arrived from England, George Luther walked around the place and watched. It was busy. In between customers, Billy stacked dozens of moleskin corduroy pants and striped hickory shirts. George Luther bent over to smell some tobacco – strong Brazilian rope type – and it made his head swim. He whispered to Billy, "Man alive, that stuff could stop a clock. I think that tobacco could git you as drunk as any booze."

People were busy buying, and George Luther saw Abernethy Rocks for the first time. A woman shook the arrowheads out of a drawstring pocket; they clattered onto the wooden counter. Billy started turning the arrowheads over to see the little papers glued to them. One could see Billy's concentration as he totaled the worth of each rock when he dropped them into his palm. He had gathered about twenty of them to pay for her yard goods. As she returned the unused arrowheads to her pocket, Billy wrapped her turkey-red fabric in brown paper and tied it with a string.

Then George Luther saw a Frenchman in a blue knit tasseled cap pay with more of the arrowheads for some sugar that was black as tar and labeled *From Honolulu.* He walked up to Billy and whispered, "What's goin' on with those arrowheads?"

"They's money. I can't talk now. I'll tell you 'bout 'em later."

As they walked the streets during Billy's lunch hour, the story of Abernethy's Rocks was explained. Billy said, "The United States Congress made us a territory, but we ain't got no currency. People still trade in wheat or oats. Mr. Abernethy invented a way to give people change by making these arrowheads have a value; he glues little papers to 'em with a number on 'em. They's jus' as good as paying in gold."

"Well, I heared paying with gold has its problems because it can be mixed with dirt or grit, makin' it hard to know the gold's weight."

"Yep, that's so."

While George Luther thought and digested his newfound knowledge about the currency problems in Oregon, many others were having discussions about the same. The men who held gold bullion complained the loudest; they started a movement to establish a value or rate of exchange that could not be raised or lowered randomly by anyone. The main complaint was against the many merchants who fixed a low price for gold dust in exchange for their goods. As a result of accumulating coins from their foreign relations, The Hudson's Bay Company pushed the price of gold dust down to $7 an ounce when it was worth $20 in London.

Within a day, George Luther got a bee in his bonnet. He was soon to learn that a lot of people had the same idea as he did. When he started talking to people, he found many who were interested in making coins from all the gold coming into Oregon. One evening, George Luther rowed to Portland with Mr. Curry and Archibald McKinley to see Captain Couch about the project of coining money from pure gold.

During the meeting, the excitement grew as the men tossed out their ideas:

"Ain't it unconstitutional to mint your own money?"

"Hell, we ain't the United States, we's jus' a territory. Besides, Abernethy has been makin' his own money for years with those Abernethy Rocks."

Someone else clarified the importance of that comment. "And George Abernethy is governor right now. He can't object!"

"Besides, we would jus' be making an exact measurement of pure gold with a label. That's kind of like gluing a paper with a dollar sign and a number ten on it, ain't it?" They all started laughing at that.

"Even the U.S. eagles and double eagles aren't pure gold. Our coins would be more valuable and save the merchants time from weighing."

By February of 1849, when the Oregon legislature met, many of the leading and influential people signed a petition determining the need for territorial coinage. One of the justifications for minting coins was the need for money to pay the debt created by the Cayuse Indian War. It was the legislatures' idea to split the difference of the price of gold set by the merchants and the true value; there was a wide margin. Using this line of reasoning, the individuals holding the gold and the territorial government would both profit accordingly.

The legislature deliberated from Tuesday on February thirteenth until Thursday February fifteenth and created a bill to provide for the weighing and stamping of gold coins. The official date on the passage of this bill became February 16, 1849, with eighteen votes for and two against. Those voting to pass were as follows: Applegate, Avery, Bailey, Cox, Curry, Hedges, Hill, Hudson, Lewis, Parker, Peterson, Portius, Thurston, Wilcox, and the Speaker, Rece. The opposed were Crawford and Martin, who stated that the bill went against the U.S. Constitution.

The preamble of the law stated the justification:

Large amounts of gold dust and particles mixed with other metals and impurities are being brought to and bartered in this Territory; and great impositions may be practiced upon the farmers, merchants, and community generally of the Territory by the introduction of spurious and impure metals, and great irregularities may exist in the scales and weights used by individuals dealing in the said article.

The Oregon mint, as they called it under the provisional government, planned to open on March 10, 1849 in Oregon City.

However, on the second of March someone arrived and changed those plans.

George Luther was at a meeting with a few others in Mr. Curry's house on the river in Oregon City when he saw a canoe slip ashore. It was flying the American flag held by two soldiers. Everyone stepped outside to see who was coming. Much to their surprise, Governor Joseph Lane, the new governor, stepped on shore. A second canoe hauled up and out stepped Joe Meek, the U.S. marshal. They had not come for dinner; they came to talk about the making of gold coins.

Before that evening ended, Governor Lane decided to pull the bill that the legislature had prepared because the territory didn't have the authority. Nevertheless, the reality of the times had not changed. Oregon needed coinage!

Within days, after Governor Lane killed the bill to make coins, the idea to make Oregon money began again.

One night in Oregon City, in the counting room of the Campbell and Smith's Store, a group of men met to form a partnership for the weighing and stamping of gold. They named their organization the Oregon Exchange Company. The partners were G. Abernethy (the former governor), Campbell, Kilborne, Magruder, Rector, Smith, Taylor, and Willson. Mr. Taylor was named the director and William Willson was designated the melter and coiner.

One of the men, Mr. Rector, was known for his mechanical skill. The group authorized him to build a rolling mill and furnish the dies and stamps. In Salem, he employed Thomas Powell, a good blacksmith, to do the forging for $10 per pound for the iron used.

But it was difficult to obtain iron to use. All sorts of things – old wagon tires and other scraps of metal – had to be broken down and welded together to make the dies and stamp. Powell used six pounds of iron and was paid $60 plus another $40 extra pay for doing the lathe work.

George Luther got involved in the Oregon Exchange Company. He talked up the idea with everyone he met, looking for people to invest their gold to be cast into coins. "We'll pay $16 an ounce," he told people. "They'll print coins with a symbol of a beaver on them." Soon, no one used the official company name of the Oregon Exchange Company; everyone talked about Beaver Coins.

In a little shack in Oregon City, the equipment was set up and coins were cast, making two types of gold coins – the $5 and the $10. To clarify the amount of gold in the coins, they were stamped:

130 G 5 D – to mean 130 grams for a 5 dollar value or
260 G 10 D – to mean 260 grams for a 10 dollar value.

On the reverse side of each coin were the initials of all the partners – K.M.T.A.W.R.C.S. – stamped around the edge and in the center was a beaver on a log with O.T. 1849 below.

Politically it was a confusing time. As the coins began to spit off the press on March 10, 1849, no one was sure who had the power to condone or reject these coins. President Polk had left office on March 4, 1849 and it had been he who appointed Joseph Lane, the First Territorial Governor of Oregon, back in 1848. Governor Lane had taken months traveling across the continent and had not arrived in Oregon until March 2, 1849.

An estimated 8,850 coins were produced – 6,000 of the $5 denomination and 2,850 of the $10. The United States government allowed them to circulate several years, until the coins of the United States mint in San Francisco came into use in 1854. That was when all the Beaver Coins were called from circulation and bought in exchange for U.S. currency.

Years later, the government requested information and all the machinery used to make Beaver Coins. Mr. Rector who was one of the partners of the Oregon Exchange Company wrote them a letter:

Oregon City, July 10, 1865

Hon. Samuel E. May
Secretary of State of Oregon

Sir:

In response to your request to give you the dies and stamps for the coins we minted, I write the following account: We petitioned the provisional legislature to allow our company, called the Oregon Exchange Company, to coin gold dust in the shape of $5 and $10 coins. It was granted and we had permission to make the mint, and also the money.

We went to work at once and I was asked to make the machine. I went to Salem and the shop of T. Powell, a blacksmith. He did the forging, while I supervised the work. I did the turning in Joseph Watt's shop on Mill Creek in Salem. Hamilton Campbell engraved the dies because he had the tools. I saw him put the engravings on the five-dollar pieces.

But I made a mistake in the order of the initials O.T. standing for Oregon Territory, they were reversed and read T. O. This was a source of great dissatisfaction and embarrassment for me but it would have required so much work to find the iron and make a new die. We let the mistake go. Before I left for the gold mines, I went to Oregon City and coined all the gold dust that the people brought in. We continued making the coins until September 1, 1849, when I left.

So that was the completion of the mint. The company then met and ordered the dies destroyed, and there was a committee of three appointed for the purpose. They were ordered to throw them from a high rock that stands below the falls at Oregon City. Whether they did so or not, I do not know and about the stamps I know nothing.

Yours respectfully,
W. H. Rector

With the termination of the production of Beaver Coins, George Luther was out of work. He told his family, "At least I get my $12.00 soldier's pension each month. I won't starve."

Even though all the other Boone men in his family were active, productive, and had good lives, gold fever spread to them like a disease that had no cure. Before long, the Boone men left their women behind and went south to find their own gold. It was the fall of 1849. George Luther went with them,

When the Boone men and their party neared the Rogue River, the Indians attacked. They kicked their horses into a gallop as arrows whizzed at them. Old Man Callahan, who rode with them, was hit in his breastbone. That night, nearing Jackson Creek, they camped and made a plaster of pitch to put on the wound. The party of men rested two nights until Callahan could travel.

When they arrived at the mining site for the placer gold, it was no longer just a place, it was a town called Jacksonville. A town of debauchery. Buildings stood shoulder to shoulder lining both sides of a dirt street— mainly saloons and hotels filled with women of the night and drunks. Oddly, a Chinese laundry was there and the Chinaman rented beds and had two tables in a small room that he called a restaurant. The Boone men learned all this from a large sign across the entrance:

GOOD CHINESE FOOD
LAUNDRY
AND
BEDS FOR THE NIGHT

The Boone men stayed with the Chinaman and his family on the first few nights before camping on the creeks and hillsides where they searched for gold.

When the Boones started digging around for gold, they were not far from the area where Albert worked a creek bed. However, George Luther and Albert had no idea the other was there. In due time, they would meet and have a hearty laugh that they were in the same place for months, unbeknownst to the other.

LOUIS SOUTHWORTH'S TRIP TO FREEDOM

About this same time, two men named Southworth were settling in Oregon, south of Salem. Though Mr. Southworth had come with his slave, he was a poor man because he had paid much for the trip and gambled away the rest during evenings when the wagons stopped. He was poor but fortunate because his twenty-one-year-old slave, named Alexander Louis Southworth, was industrious.

Since a slave could not own land in Oregon, Louis – for he went by his second name – helped a white man with a land claim. Louis told the white man, "I heard that your son abandoned his land and house, so he is goin' to lose his claim. I have a deal for you. My white master can't afford to build a house yet, but we'll live here until we get enough money saved for our own claim and a cabin. That'll give you some time to get your son to come back."

With a place to put their heads, Louis Southworth started to earn money doing what he loved to do: Louis lived to play his fiddle. The only problem was that fiddle playing did not make much money.

But Louis was smart and made another deal – this time with his master. Louis said, "Times are hard and folks can't pay much for fiddle playing. I'll go to the gold mines to make money for you on one condition. The condition is that the money is to buy my freedom. After I bring you one thousand dollars worth of gold, you must give me my freedom."

Such a deal! Louis Southworth headed to the closest place to mine for gold. It was the same place where Albert and George Luther were located – Jacksonville. But he didn't meet them right away.

After eight months, Louis had found about three hundred dollars' worth of gold and returned north to give it to his owner.

Louis told his master, "It was dangerous coming back here 'cuz the Indians are on a rampage and shoot at any person they see. I kept twenty-five dollars and bought a fine rifle to protect myself. If I can shoot back, they might leave me alone."

On the way back to the gold mines in Jacksonville, Louis met a company of volunteers under Colonel John Kelsay; they were on their way to the Rogue River War. Rifles were scarce, so the soldiers threatened to take his gun.

Just as they started to pull the rifle from his hands, their Colonel rode up and said, "You can keep your rifle if you come along and fight with us. We need volunteers as much as rifles. And the pay ain't bad. We pay fourteen dollars a month even when you retire from the ranks."

Louis did not want to part with his new gun. He needed it when traveling and for protection at the mines. So he went to war. Within a few weeks, luck came to him in the form of an arrow to his thigh. With the wound, he was released from duty. The medic removed the arrow and wrapped his wound. The next day, not heeding the medic's advice to rest for a week, he rode to Jacksonville with the leg bleeding.

During January of 1850, it was not only freezing cold in the valleys but also snowing hard on the summits. Going south, Louis had to travel through deep and falling snow over three passes. He had lost quite a bit of blood and had no food left. Staying on his horse became more and more difficult as he lost his strength, yet he knew he had no choice except to continue. He was shivering, so he took his bedroll and covered himself. Within minutes, the world went black as Louis lost consciousness and fell from his horse.

THE FIVE MEN BEGIN TO CROSS PATHS

On Dr. Bailey's trip to the gold mines with his brother, they encountered the same snowstorm as Louis Southworth. The snow fell heavily and was wet. Everything in the view of Dr. Bailey and his brother was white. Even the fir trees were covered with a blanket of snow and, with the thick falling snowflakes, the trees disappeared from sight. Only the lack of trees growing in their path kept them on the trail south.

Bailey said, "I remember when I came up to Oregon with eight men back in 1835. Trees covered all these hills as far as one could see. I mean it is thick with trees, endless trees. We just can't see them with this snow." He adjusted his capote – a blanket cut and sewn for use as a coat.

The days were short in January, so they didn't want to stop while there was light. They had good supplies and a tent that would provide cover when the time came to bed down for the night. Both men had long leather coats, heavy gloves, and capotes draped across their backs to keep the snow from accumulating and melting on them. As the snow got deeper, the going got slower, yet they plodded on.

Many large boulders were common in this area; the boulders created large snow covered mounds jutting up on the side of the trail. As they passed one small mound, Dr. Bailey slipped his flask from a pocket and took a swig before saying, "When it's dark, I just want to eat some cold biscuits and go to sleep. We can make a fire in the morning and have hot food and coffee." He spoke with authority, leaving no room for a retort from his brother; it was more of an order – plain and direct.

All of a sudden, his horse started to whinny and changed pace. Out from behind a boulder came another horse toward them. All saddled, but riderless.

"What the hell! Where did that bloody mare come from?"

Bailey leaned toward the mare and grabbed the reins with no trouble. "She's lost her rider. He must be around here somewhere." They turned their horses full circle and Bailey realized that the small mound was not a boulder. He slipped from his saddle and walked with the two horses. Brushing snow away with his gloves, he found Louis. Shocked at the find, he shouted to his brother, "Get off your bloody horse and help me. This man is half frozen, but alive. Damn, guess we stop here tonight. Let's put up the tent quickly."

Within the hour, the tent was up and, while his brother struggled to get a fire going, Bailey examined his patient. "He's got a bandaged thigh that's all bloodied. Help me drag him inside the tent where I can start rubbing him to get his circulation going."

Once the patient was out of the weather, Bailey's brother had to search for firewood. He let his foul mouth expel all his anger as he looked under the snow. Finally with an armful of wood, he kneeled and cleared a place for the fire. But he could not light the wet twigs. If curses could start a fire, there should have been a blazing one – but there wasn't.

Finally Bailey came out of the tent and mumbled, "Let me light the fire. You've been living in New York City too long to be of help. That man needs some hot drink." He gave his brother a push with his shoulder and said, "You go in the tent and keep rubbing him until I get some water heated for him to drink. He still unconscious."

When the fire was roaring and the coffeepot full of snow to melt, Bailey went to Louis' mare to unpack the gear and take the saddle off the horse for the night. He returned to the tent and ducked under the open flap where the warmth from the fire entered the tent, saying, "Look at this! We have a fiddler in our midst. Hope the cold didn't ruin his fiddle."

They completely undressed Louis and wrapped him in a dry bedroll while Bailey worked to remove the old bandage and check the wound. Once a fresh dressing was wrapped on his leg, the hot water was ready. Bailey had the man sip, little by little, until he seemed to be coherent.

"What's your name?"

"Louis Southworth." He drank more. "I'm heading to the gold. I came from the Rogue River War." Slowly a smile spread across his face as he glanced in the corner. Even though night had fallen, the moon and snow lit their campsite. "My fiddle. You brought my fiddle in from the snow. Thank you kindly."

"I'm Dr. Bailey. I saw your wound. There's no infection. If you can drink this whole cupful of hot water it would be best." Bailey nodded as the cup was emptied. "Now have a swig of some medicine to help you relax and sleep."

As Bailey fed some small pieces of dried meat and biscuits to him, the laudanum did its job and Louis started to nod off. When the three were bedded down for the night, they huddled with Louis between them to keep him warmer.

With the light of day, they found blue skies outside the tent. They fried up some pickled pork and pan bread that Margaret had packed for them and boiled some coffee. Louis dressed and looked well enough to travel.

"We'll go slowly today. Louis, you let us know whenever you need to rest. More importantly, you let us know when you feel strong enough to play a tune or two."

"Pass my fiddle, I'll give ya one right now."

While Bailey and his brother broke down the tent, Louis fiddled as he sat on a log at the fireside.

On the ride that day, Louis told his whole plan to buy his freedom. He explained that he had been at the gold fields. "They's close! That's right, there's gold in Oregon. I was there last month 'fore I went back ta Salem with gold to pay my master. You two could give Jacksonville a try. I hope the Chinaman still has a bed and board for me. I'm going to rest a few days when we get there 'fore I go out and camp to look for gold. This Chinese family runs a clean boardinghouse with good food."

When Jacksonville came into view in the distance, it looked like some wooden boxes jutting up in the middle of nowhere. As they got closer, it looked like any little town with nine buildings – five structures on one side of the dirt street, three across from them, and on down the street was the ninth place   the stables.

All the establishments were made from rough-sawed wood and had hand-painted signs that were done by no professional – "S A L O O N E" had an *E* on the end of it and the Adam's Hotel served "ALL YOU CAN ATE" on Fridays. The post office was located in the bank building that had living quarters upstairs for the banker and his family. Across the street from the bank was the Chinaman's place. The fifth building was another Hotel & Bar with signs for "ALL NITE POKER" and "LADIES." Then there was a General Store, Jail, and an Assayer's Shop, where two men with pistols on their belts stood on either side of the door.

As the three men rode down the middle of the street, they passed a wagon, hitched with four horses, from which men were unloading jugs of spirits and cases of wine for the saloon. Two guards stood with rifles as others unloaded. A couple of women in fancy and colorful dresses sat on a bench outside the saloon and smoked cigars while they watched the booze being carried inside; the breeze fluttered feathers in the one's hair.

Louis pointed, "The Chinaman's place is over there. See it? I'm headin' there to rest. You'll find the stables on down a-ways."

"I'd like to eat. A steak would be good."

Louis explained, "Mutton is about all we get here. Once in a blue moon the hotels have beef, but it disappears an hour after folks hear 'bout it. Like I said, the Chinese place has good food."

The Chinaman gave them a room with three beds, where they dropped their knapsacks before ordering some supper. While the food was being prepared, Bailey and his brother walked to the stables to feed and board the horses. They noticed the blacksmith clanging on an anvil as they left the stables. Albert was busy at work; he knocked a clinker to the floor and didn't look up.

At dinner, Dr. Bailey was not too pleased with all the rice and tea, but he ate the chunks of mutton, onions, and little specks of indiscernible greens. "I'm going to look around town," he said, as he donned his hat.

His brother got up, too. "I'll join ya."

Louis remained at the table, sipping his tea, as he watched from the window. Dr. Bailey and his brother went into the saloon, the one with an *E* at the end. The day was ending as the sun dipped below the horizon. Louis wanted to play his fiddle, but was too tired.

The little wife of the Chinaman came to his table, wearing a traditional Chinese dress with a high collar and long straight skirt with slits up to her knees on both sides. She started putting the dishes onto a tray and spoke. "Happy you back, Mr. Louis."

"Thank you, Mrs. Chen."

"You play music tonight?"

Louis explained about the wound on his leg and how tired he was. "I need to sleep tonight after my travels. Tomorrow I'll play my fiddle."

"That is good. I like." She made a little bow and took the tray to the kitchen.

Soon Mr. Chen was bowing to Louis. "We welcome you again to our humble place."

"Thank you. It's good to be here."

Making small shuffle steps, Mrs. Chen came back to his table. She made a little bow again and said, "I forgot to say. Another man who look like you come to stay with us. Maybe you know him. He look like your brother." And she giggled at her words.

Mr. Chen explained, "He Mr. Albert Bayless. He stay here for few days. He work at stables right now. He a blacksmith. You meet tomorrow?"

Mrs. Chen giggled again, "He a blacksmith and a black man, too."

Louis smiled at her little joke.

In the morning, Louis awoke to see that the other two beds had not been used. It seemed that Dr. Bailey and his brother never came back from the saloon to sleep.

Louis had breakfast alone and was told by the Chinaman that the blacksmith was back in the stables working again. "He leave very early. Say he had much work."

Louis nodded, finished his tea, and replied, "I'll take a walk to the stables to meet him."

When Louis was getting ready to leave and stood at the door in his hat, buttoning his coat, Mrs. Chen peeked from the kitchen door. "You take my pot to fix?"

He nodded and swung his fiddle case onto his back with the strap looping across his chest. Soon a young Chinese girl came out with a Dutch Oven; the bale was broken in half. Louis tucked the heavy pot under his arm and was putting on his leather gloves when a second Chinese daughter came out of the kitchen with her mother. This girl held up a skillet in one hand and the handle in her other hand. She giggled.

Mrs. Chen exclaimed, "More broken pot."

The young daughter said, "You always take your fiddle, don't you?"

Louis smiled and replied, "I do. It's a part of me. I wouldn't leave my arm behind either." Giggles faded as he closed the door.

The day was clear, cold, and cloudless. The blue sky rolled over Louis from one horizon to the other. He pulled his scarf higher on his neck against the wind. His thigh hurt as he walked, but Dr. Bailey had said he should walk, though slowly. He heard a bang of wood against wood – a sound above his head –so he looked up and across the street. On the second floor, woman had opened a window above the saloon and smoke billowed out, like a cloud, as she reached for a stick and stuck it under the sash. Although the street was empty of people, voices and laughter could be heard in the saloon. Louis surmised that Dr. Bailey and his brother were making some of that noise.

The street was dry though full of frozen uneven clumps from what had been muck. The bumps and chunks were a result of footprints and animal tracks hardening like adobe when the temperature dropped below freezing. To avoid tripping, Louis curved this way and that, like a drunk.

The large stable doors were propped open. The cold and wind entered with Louis, yet Albert was bare to his waist and sweating at the forge. A deafening clang rang through the rafters and bounced from beams as Albert's arm brought the hammer down to hit the red hot metal in his tongs. Louis watched from a distance until Albert seemed to be finished with the shaping of that piece. Louis had no idea what it was or where it would go to make something work.

Albert dipped the metal in water and put it down on a worn, wooden workbench before he turned to acknowledge the presence of Louis. "Howdy!" he said. "Oh, you must be the other Negro that Mrs. Chen has been telling me about."

Louis grinned and said, "She act like we ain't ever seen some other Nigger." He stepped forward and extended his hand.

Albert wiped his hand on his thick and filthy leather apron that covered his chest and legs. "I didn't get my hand too clean, but it's only dirt and will wash off."

They each said one word – their first names – and shook long and hard.

Albert commented. "Maybe it is Mrs. Chen who never has met Negroes before. Or never two in the same place." Albert's assumption was logical. There were only 207 *free colored* recorded in the 1850 census for the Oregon Territory, which was a huge amount of land from the Pacific Ocean to the Rocky Mountains and north of California to the 49th parallel. This was the area that would become the states of Oregon, Washington, Idaho, and a part of Montana.

Louis agreed with a bob of his head. "That sound right," he said and then placed the items to be repaired on the workbench. "These from Mrs. Chen for you to fix."

Looking directly in the other's eyes, they saw stories to be told and ideas to be shared. More importantly, with nothing said between them, they saw a friendship beginning.

Finally Albert ended the silence, "I have a lot of work. Can we talk over dinner?"

"Sho nuff." Louis turned to leave and Albert saw his fiddle.

"I've never worked to music. Would you be willing to play a couple of tunes?"

And Louis did. In fact, for over an hour he sat and played jigs and reels with the flames from the forge blazing and dancing to the music. The bangs from the pounding hammer seemed part of the concert; it all went together.

That night, as Louis and Albert sat at a table waiting to be served their dinner, Dr. Bailey came in with his disheveled and stumbling drunk brother, who went directly to the room to sleep. Bailey asked, "May I join you and your friend, Louis?"

"You sho can, Dr. Bailey. This is Albert Bayless." Silently, Louis puzzled about the doctor who appeared sober and alert after not sleeping in his bed. In a moment, it dawned on him that the doctor might have slept in someone else's bed. Louis thought, *That's why he don't look tired and why he ain't drunk.*

Wisely, when Mrs. Chen brought their plates, Bailey's portion had more mutton and less rice than the prior night. As always, she poured the tea, bowed, and returned to the kitchen.

Dr. Bailey began telling Albert how he had met Louis, stopping a moment to light a fine cigar that he had bought at the saloon.

All of a sudden, George Luther walked in the front door and saw Albert. Always polite, Albert stood and excused himself before rushing toward George Luther. They slapped the other's back and talked at the same time asking the same questions.

"How'd you git here?"

"When did you come?"

"How long ya been here?"

Finally, they laughed and Albert suggested, "Come join us. We just started to eat."

The dinner became a two-hour affair with each telling their own story of why they came west and how they met.

George Luther seemed to be the best storyteller and included scenes of the passenger pigeons flying over their wagon train. He told of his failed venture with minting coins and pulled a five-dollar Beaver Coin from his pocket to show them. "I have quite a few. We can use them right now. Someday, when Oregon's a state, they'll be collected up by the government. Then they'll be collector items and worth much more than their weight in gold. I'm goin' to try to hold on to mine."

Dr. Bailey bragged about his homestead, his wife, and all his animals in Oregon. It was obvious to all of them how much he loved living in Oregon, and the question was asked, "Why did you leave your wonderful life to come here?" Dr. Bailey explained about the population growing and how the new people were not the same as those who had come first. "They steal my horses and cattle. They slaughter a sheep for only the hind legs and leave the rest to rot."

Albert jumped into the conversation. "That sounds like it is here! When I came over a year ago, I came with a wagon and two oxen. One night someone slaughtered one of the oxen and butchered it on the spot. It must have been a group of men to do what they did in one night. Beef is hard to come by and drives men to do such things. I really didn't need that wagon, so I sold it. Actually, I traded the remaining oxen for a mule to pull my blacksmith limber and sold the wagon to the same man for gold. It was a good deal for me." He gave out a little chuckle. "The only thing that disappointed me was that I didn't get any beefsteak from the meat they stole." He held up his hand in the direction of the kitchen and commented to the men, "We need more tea; let me call my China Dolls."

One of the Chinaman's daughters came to the table with a new pot of tea, "I know what you want Mr. Albert. You talkin' so much I know you thirsty." Soon the second daughter was standing next to her sister – near Albert. Their affection toward Albert showed in their smiles and giggles.

Albert joked, "What would I do without you two taking care of me?"

They giggled more and their eyes twinkled.

Bailey asked, "Girls, do you have some wine? I'd like a glass of red wine. Would any of you men like a glass with me?" George Luther agreed to join him in a glass.

The older girl said, "We don't have wine, but my father can buy one across the street for you."

Dr. Bailey stated that it was to be added to his bill, and the girl went to tell her father.

Albert watched the littlest daughter of the Chinaman as she walked back to the kitchen with the teapot. He said, "When I lived in Kentucky, one day my owner came home with two china dolls for his daughters. The dolls were made with beautiful porcelain heads – fine white porcelain with hand-painted faces. Those dolls were delicate and beautiful just like these girls." He stopped his story while the Chinaman came with glasses and wine. The two girls stood at a distance talking and giggling. Finally, after the Chinaman left, Albert continued his thoughts. "So I think of these girls as China Dolls – sweet, flawless little China Dolls. Do you think they powder their faces to get them to be so white?" No one answered.

George Luther said, "That's a nice story, but we haven't heard why Louis came here."

Louis was the youngest of the group of men. He told of his father dying of smallpox in Missouri last year. "My pa ran the farm and my master was lost without him. So he sold the farm and we came west." Then he told of wanting to be free and how he was buying his freedom. "But it's dangerous traveling back to give gold to my master. I must do it 'cuz else he'll starve. Anyway, like Dr. Bailey tol' ya, I got this wound travelin' back from there. I gotta find another way to get money to him." Louis stood and reached for his fiddle. "I'm mighty tired, but I promised ..." he stopped and looked at Albert, "I ... I liked what you called the Chinese girls. I'm gonna use that name, too. I tol' the China Dolls I'd fiddle for 'em tonight. One waltz and I'm hittin' the hay."

After this first night, the four men planned to go gold panning or digging for five days a week and come back to the Chinaman's place to be together. "We'll work like the banker. He only opens his bank Monday through Friday."

Albert, Louis, and George Luther went off each Monday, separating at a creek or ridge, depending on their whims. But they camped together each night all week. Dr. Bailey and his brother had gone out to look for gold the first week and never did it again; the call of the saloon and women was stronger. Bailey drank, enjoyed the women, smoked fine cigars, and gambled, except on Friday and Saturday nights when he would join the others coming from gold digging. That's when the four men would have dinner at the Chinaman's place and talk for hours.

One Saturday night, just as the food was put onto the table, Dr. Bailey admitted that gold mining was not for him. Before anyone had time to respond to the news, Robert Newell walked in the door.

"By gum, this is a small world!" Doc rushed up to Bailey and they hugged while slapping backs. After introductions and explanations, the group of five acted like old friends each and every one. The stories and bantered went on and on. Dr. Bailey passed around his fine cigars and the smoke filled the room like the laughter. Just before midnight and while still sitting at the Chinaman's table among the dirty dishes, emptied glasses, and cigar ashes, they returned to Dr. Bailey's comment about leaving.

Bailey said, "Yes, I'll be heading back to Oregon in a few days."

Newell jumped in his chair as he exclaimed, "Me, too! This gold digging isn't for me. I'm leaving. We could travel together. It's safer. The Indians are still on the warpath."

Once the two had their plans, Dr. Bailey turned to the others and said, "I invite all of you to come stay awhile with my wife and me. Get to Champoeg and ask anyone where my cabin is. You're all welcome. Albert, I saw you teaching Louis about blacksmithing and we need good blacksmiths in Oregon. I'd help you both find a place to work. And we need a fiddler! Louis, the man who used to play for dances and other occasions is not around anymore. George Luther, you're welcome, too."

Albert brightened with the invitation. "I make more money as a Smithy than digging gold. And I would like to settle down and find a wife. Thank you for your offer. I will come."

Louis liked the idea but lamented with a shake of his head. "But I ain't free. I gotta make another payment, maybe two. Man-alive, I fear travelin'."

Dr. Bailey agreed to take his gold and make a payment for him.

Louis' face brightened. "If you do that, there's only one more payment. When I git enough gold for the last one, I'll come north ta stay."

❖ ❖ ❖

By the beginning of March in 1850, Robert Newell, Dr. Bailey, and his brother were back home from the gold mines. The doctor was poorer, not richer. He spent all the money that he had taken with him on spirits, gaming, and women. But mainly he was poorer because people stole many animals from his homestead while he was gone. Within days, the Baileys decided to sell their farm and go back to the East with the beautiful, fifteen-year-old Mary Anne. Margaret had taught her to sew, cook, read and write as well as all the proper ways of a woman. Mary Anne was eager to see New York City and Boston.

In April of 1850, just before they left their farm for good, Margaret got word that Nathaniel Ford freed the Holmeses. "To learn of their freedom before we leave is a godsend. Once we're on the ship, we'll know nothing about the happenings here in Oregon. I'm so happy for the Holmes family."

Her happiness was unfounded, for she did not know all the facts. Ford had not freed the five children – Harriet, Celi Ann, Mary Jane, James, and Roxanna Holmes. Only Mr. and Mrs. Holmes were free and, according to Oregon law, he could keep the children until they were eighteen.

When the Baileys drove away from their cabin, they didn't talk for the few miles between their place and the Newells. Thoughts filled their heads like the rain filled the land. It was pouring. The recent bad times may have been the impetus for the decision to leave Oregon, but the good times overflowed in their mind's eye.

They went to the Newell's home to say farewell. Margaret took Crow into the Newell's cabin and said, "Thank you for giving Crow a home. He's a good dog." Within the hour, they boarded the first steamer for Oregon City and then they took another steamer up to The Hudson's Bay Company, where they boarded a ship. They didn't own much anymore because they had sold most of their belongings, so their luggage was light, but Dr. Bailey's cash pocket was heavy from the sales.

They did not plan to return to Oregon.

Horse Fair in Salem
Circa 1880

Photo taken on NW corner of State & Commercial Streets, with First Methodist Church spire in the distance and, on far right, Land and Bush Bank.

Photographer: Cronise Studios.

CHAPTER 9

JANUARY 1852

With a depth of three inches, the snowfall was unusual for the Willamette Valley in Oregon. The breathtaking beauty – clumps of snow piled on bushes and outlining fir trees – made Albert pause to appreciate the sight. He took a deep breath as he patted the neck of his roan mare. The reddish-brown coat of his horse looked like snow had stuck to it; streaks of white fur were sprinkled throughout the darker. He put on his leather gloves again after examining why his horse had started to limp. "How far back were we when you threw that shoe? We both walk from here on."

While his gaze scanned the white landscape, he thought. *Sure glad I have good winter clothes.* It was January and, when he left the limber and mule down in Marysville with Louis, he had chosen only a few things to bring. He had come because of Dr. Bailey's invitation; he hoped to find a blacksmithing job. He and his horse started walking along the roadway.

Within fifteen minutes the snowfall stopped. All of a sudden, he noticed a speck of black in the distance coming toward him from the north. When he could make out the object, he saw a stagecoach pulled by four horses, coming fast. He stopped and stepped back to the edge of the road when the horses were getting close because it became apparent that they were not going to slow, much less stop. The driver bobbed his head as a greeting when he plowed past and then disappeared to the south. Albert stood looking at the disappearing sight. *First time in a long time since I've seen one of those. Not since Tennessee!*

The day was overcast, yet he noticed the temperature warming with the snow turning slushy under his feet. While gazing at the retreating stagecoach, he saw something else coming up from the south – a wagon with two riders on the seat. Albert watched as they came closer. He figured that they might give him a ride, since he was going the same direction.

A Negro man and woman stopped next to Albert.

Sitting hunched on the seat board with long dark reins drooping across the back of a thin-looking mare, the man asked, "Good morning, sir, do ya need a ride?" The wagon was old and the weathered wood was gray with boards missing along one side.

"Yes, thank you," replied Albert. "My horse threw a shoe. I'm going up to a friend's place. He lives south of Champoeg."

"That's right on our way and not far from here. We's headed to Oregon City. Come git up here wit' us."

After Albert removed his satchel from his shoulder and dropped it in the back, he tied his horse to the rear of the wagon and climbed up next to the woman, who smiled.

The driver continued talking, "Howdy do. This is my wife, Mrs. Holmes."

Albert held out his hand to the woman and then the man. "Pleased to meet you. I am Albert Bayless. Thank you for stopping."

"Much obliged," he replied as he pulled on the reins and the slack went taut as the horse started forward.

Albert began a conversation, "Do you live near here?"

"We's from Salem."

At that moment, a horse and rider was approaching them and, before the man rode past, Mr. Holmes raised his hat and dipped his head.

Albert asked, "What takes you to Oregon City today?"

Mr. Holmes answered, "Family's not too good. We's goin' to Oregon City to see a lawyer. Me and Mrs. Holmes were set free back in 1850 by Mr. Nathaniel Ford, but he done kept our son and girls."

"No!" Albert exclaimed.

Mrs. Holmes nodded, "Oh, yes, he done it. And our Harriet and Celi Ann died jus' a while back. That's when we knew we had ta do somethin' for the others – Mary Jane, James, and Roxanna."

Albert gasped, "How horrible for you!"

Another wagon approached and passed them. Mr. Holmes raised his hat again, and Mrs. Holmes nodded to the man in a wagon filled with what appeared to be sacks of grain. Albert noticed many tracks in the road from wagon wheels and horses. He wondered why it was so busy.

Mr. Holmes continued, "We hopin' this lawyer can help us."

Mrs. Holmes interrupted and repeated herself, "Our oldest girl, Harriet, died 'cuz Mr. Ford didn't feed her good. She was sickly and died. Mary Jane, James, and Roxanna is still wit' him an' I be so worried. They still his slaves." Her face showed a mother's anguish.

"How can that be?" A puzzled look crossed his face before he said, "I thought slavery isn't legal here in Oregon."

Mr. Holmes nodded, "We know'd that. But Mister Ford say he can keep 'em 'til they eighteen. He said that the law."

"That's right," the woman said.

Mr. Holmes leaned over to look directly at Albert, "You better tell us where you goin' or we might pass it."

Albert explained, "I'm going to the Bailey farm. I've never been there, so I don't know where it is exactly. I met Dr. Bailey at the gold mines in California. Do you know the Baileys?"

A curious look crossed Mrs. Holmes' face when she turned to look at Albert. "We do."

Mr. Holmes voice took on a high whine, "You don' know? The Baileys sold their farm and is gone. Besides, we done passed the turnoff to their place."

The tailgate fell open with a bang, and Mr. Holmes pulled up on the reins to stop. He climbed down and shut the gate, securing it with a stick shoved into the clasp on one side. He reached into the wagon bed and picked up a piece of rope to tie the other side. He talked while he worked, "They sold all their cows and animals. Miz Bailey was sad 'cuz she put so much work in her farm. But Doctor Bailey say he gotta sell. He say he so tired of people stealin' and killin' his animals."

Albert was amazed. "Oh, no! I can't believe this happened. I had no idea they were leaving Oregon." This changed all his plans.

Mrs. Holmes nodded to agree. "That's how it be. I miss Miz Margaret too much. She good to us."

Albert tried to digest all this news. Remembering how Dr. Bailey had described his farm and bragged about all the animals and his hard working wife, Albert wondered how they could sell their farm.

Another wagon, going south, passed on the road with a man and woman on the bench and the wagon bed full of children.

Albert asked, "Where is everyone going?"

"Oh, down to Salem. That's where we live now. This here is a new road built 'bout a year ago. It's a busy place now."

As Mr. Holmes finished with the tailgate, he said, "Oh, when we was freed, we took our savin's and bought some land in Salem." He told about their nursery business, selling plants and produce. He spent a lot of time explaining how they set up their business because the courts wanted them to prove that they could support the children.

And then Mrs. Holmes began to give details on all the vegetables they had planted last summer. "We still have winter squash, turnips, and potatoes to sell now."

When Mr. Holmes climbed back into the driver's seat, they heard whistles and looked up. Two men, waving their hats and whistling, were coming from the north, leading a herd of a dozen horses. A dog ran around the herd, barking and nipping at the fetlocks to keep the horses on the road. After the raucous bunch passed, Mr. Holmes started their wagon rolling again.

Albert twisted in his seat to watch the horses disappear down the road, "Where are they going?"

"Oh, there's a horse auction in Salem today and ...."

Albert stopped listening. As they rolled down the road, Albert tried to decide what he would do now that the Baileys were gone.

At that moment, Mrs. Holmes said, "Oh, we's here at the Newell's place. We jus' stoppin' to see if they needs somethin' from Oregon City."

Albert's ears recognized that name. "Is this Robert Newell's house?"

"Oh, you know Doc?"

Albert hesitated. He didn't have an invitation to come to the Newell's like he had gotten from Dr. Bailey. He explained, "Oh, I met Mr. Newell at the gold mines. I don't know him well."

When the wagon pulled up next to the Newell house, most of the snow had melted and left only patches of white here and there. The day was warming in the sunshine. In front of the house, there were bushes and a fence around a flower garden gone dormant for the winter. Albert scanned the barnyard and saw the door to the root cellar. He admired the well-kept place.

A very pregnant woman emerged from the house, "Good morning, Mr. and Mrs. Holmes, it is good to see you. Come in for coffee and some of my baked muffins."

Mrs. Holmes declined. "Oh, thank you kindly but we's got to git to Oregon City for a 'pointment. Me an' Mr. Holmes be much obliged, but gotta hurry. We jus' want to know if you need somethin' from town."

"Not today. Who do you have with you?"

Albert leaned over the side with an extended hand, "I'm Albert Bayless. I'm going to Oregon City with the Holmeses. I'm looking for work."

"Nice to meet you. I wish you luck." Just then, a child started to cry inside the house. Mrs. Newell gestured to the house, saying, "Excuse me, my little one is hungry." At the door, she turned and waved. "Goodbye, everyone."

The wagon disappeared down the road.

Later, noises outside took Rebecca's attention; the sound of horses' hooves told of approaching people who stopped at the side of the house. She remained seated, feeding her daughter in the rocking chair.

Laughter and talking drifted through the walls and soon boot heels made dull, heavy sounds across the wooden porch. The front door opened to Doc's congenial voice saying, "Let's greet Rebecca first. She will be so glad to see you and to learn that we will be neighbors. I'll get the map that I'm making of the Champoeg Townsite and then we can go back outside to pick where you want your house."

Another male voice responded, "I can tell you I want more than one lot. However, you need to quote a price before I say how many." The group of four laughed over that comment and entered the room.

Doc closed the door and noticed smiles on the faces of Margaret, Mary Anne, and William Bailey. He turned toward the hearth and faced Rebecca in the rocking chair.

"Mr. and Mrs. Bailey, you're back! Welcome," Rebecca said as she started to stand. "Oh, my! Is that Mary Anne with you? You have grown to be a beautiful woman."

"No need to get up," Doc said. He turned back to the Baileys and beamed when he said, "Yes, Rebecca is due to have another any day now. Can you see how big my little girl has grown? Remember when she was born back in November of forty-nine? Oh, what a thrill after six sons."

"You couldn't seem to stop smiling." Margaret told Doc as she approached the rocker and held out her arms. "May I hold her? She's beautiful." After a moment, she returned the child and took off her traveling hat and coat.

Like always, Margaret took charge in this familiar cabin. She reached for the apron hanging from a nail and, in a few minutes, Margaret had heated water for tea, made coffee, and noticed that the tin foot warmer at Rebecca's feet was cold. "Mary Anne, here's the fire-pan. Get some of those embers from the hearth and place them in the drawer of that foot warmer." When everyone was sitting at the table, Margaret asked, "Tell us what has happened in our absence."

Rebecca placed the sleeping child in a cradle. "Oh, we have new roads." She filled a plate with berry-filled muffins that she placed on the table before joining the others.

Robert was enthusiastic, "Yes! By gum, there are roads and more roads. Champoeg is a transportation center. There's a new road from Salem into Champoeg to the river where the road from St. Paul joins it and then continues east to Butteville and on to Oregon City."

Rebecca chimed in again. "We have stage lines and more ferries, too."

"There were many small changes that meant a lot to us." Doc mentioned, "Do you remember that in forty-six Champoeg was made into a postal stop on the route to Oregon City? Well, I was made postmaster of Champoeg Post Office about a year ago. Back in fifty-one."

Rebecca thought of something else. "Now we have steamboats."

"Ah, yes, that reminds me. The year I married Rebecca, my keelboats moved 15,000 bushels of wheat to Oregon City and collected cattle hides and deerskins for the Willamette Falls tannery. I had prosperous years until the steamboats came. They made transportation so easy; now the steamers move all the things I used to haul."

Dr. Bailey sipped his coffee and said, "That's too bad that you lost that income."

"Well, I didn't because ...."

And Rebecca finished his sentence. "Last year, Robert opened *wood saloons* at various places along the river. The steamboat captains can find dry wood at any season of the year. So we make good money from the steamboats."

Margaret reminisced, "I remember after the massacre in 1847, Doc, you became a commissioner with the responsibility to hold council with principle tribes of the upper Columbia. I know that you influenced the Nez Percé to stand aloof from the Cayuse War. Are you still doing that?"

"Yes, from time to time, because we are still fighting the Cayuse and other tribes."

They had finished their food and were feeling giddy from hearing about all the progress and achievements when Margaret bragged, "Speaking of personal accomplishments, I have finally started writing my book. Years ago I told you I wanted to write a book, and I finally have started."

Doc smiled, "I am happy to hear that. I hope you never stop writing. You write beautifully. You should submit something for *The Oregon Spectator* to print."

Dr. Bailey had something to add. "Robert, you didn't mention your general store here in Champoeg. When we stayed overnight in Fort Vancouver, we learned that you opened one. That's a new achievement here in Champoeg. I'd like to help stock it with some of the wares that I brought on the ship from the East. I brought a couple of fine scales back with me to measure gold for the sales of merchandise at the store. When I left for the East Coast, few people had scales."

Margaret reminisced about how it was before they went to the East and said, "I remember how people paid Willy for medical services – sometimes with eggs and other times in gold. If he got the eggs home unbroken, I was content. But the gold was a bigger problem. Like you said, people had no scales, and sometimes the impurity of the gold caused problems. We had no way to melt the gold out of a rock. We couldn't use it until it was processed. And, worse, no one used the same value for an ounce of gold."

Doc expanded on that idea and replied, "All of this is better now. The Beaver Coins helped. They didn't produce a lot of them, but just their existence has stabilized gold and forced merchants to offer a standard price of $16 an ounce in the whole territory."

The little girl woke and started to cry. Mary Anne went and lifted her from the cradle. Softly, she sang the cheerful Scottish song *Skip to my Lou*. The other two women joined the singing and then began to talk about babies.

Doc walked to his desk while saying, "Let's leave those three to women their talk and singing. Rebecca, I am going out with Dr. Bailey to look at lots. I have a customer in him." Doc picked up his map entitled, Champoeg Town Site.

Dr. Bailey was waiting on the porch, "Robert, I need to just look at the lots today, but I'm definitely going to buy. Are they all the same price?"

Margaret poked her head out the door. "Wait a moment, Willy. I'm going on the next steamer to Oregon City with Mary Anne." Margaret pulled out a flyer with the steamboat schedules and explained. "You and I have been staying at a hotel in Portland every night, so instead let's stay at the Moss Hotel in Oregon City tonight. I'll get a room for us and another for Mary Anne. I think the *Hoosier* steamboat is due to leave within the hour. If not, I will wait and get on the *Washington Steamer* later on. Willy, why don't you settle all your business and join us tonight for dinner."

He agreed.

Later, as the two women walked to the wharf, Margaret commented, "It was good to see the Newells, but I didn't think we should stay too long. Rebecca must be so tired and uncomfortable from this pregnancy. She is so big. That baby must be ready to come at any moment." She looked north down the Willamette River, hoping to see the steamer coming. "Mary Anne, do you remember that Rebecca's first child died the year before our trip to the East? He was only six months old. I was glad to see this healthy little girl."

Mary Anne nodded before saying, "Seeing their little girl reminded me, I wondered how Mary Jane Holmes and her family is doing. We should go visit them."

* * *

They boarded the steamboat *Hoosier* and talked the whole trip along the Willamette River. The day was beautiful out on the river, the scenery spectacular. But the two women were wrapped in their emotions and reliving times past. Margaret swallowed and shifted in her seat inside the steamboat's saloon, where they had been served two coffees and small cakes.

Mary Anne started to speak and stopped.

They sat without conversation for a while.

As often happens with the workings of the mind, a completely different topic popped into her head, and Mary Anne asked, "Do you think you and Dr. Bailey will start a farm again?"

"Oh, no!" Margaret complained, "Our place was a half-way stop between Salem and Oregon City; we were weary of being a free hotel for travelers who claimed to be our friends. Surely you remember how we gave accommodations to many and never charged a penny. It was good that we sold the farm for that reason and because it was so much work. We don't regret that we sold our farm, but we missed Oregon. It is good to be back. No, it is good to be home. Aren't you glad to be back?"

As with the Bailey's previous trip to the East Coast, after only a little more than a month on the East Coast, William Bailey missed the lush green land and the life he had had in the West. They had returned to Oregon in December, a few weeks ago.

Margaret repeated, "No more farming for us. In fact, Willy doesn't think he wants to practice doctoring anymore. As you know, we brought a lot of things from the East to sell. So, like he was telling Robert, he wants to stock stores and make money that way. I heard that the store in Champoeg that was owned by Mr. Edward Dupuis burned to the ground last year. The rumor is that his losses were over $7,000. That fire left Champoeg without a store and that's why Robert started a storefront. Willy will talk more with Robert today about stocking his store with some of our goods. I bought hundreds of buttons and a lot of paper for stock. There were never enough buttons or paper." Margaret stopped her rambling. "Mary Anne, are you even listening to me? You look so forlorn."

"I ... think, I mean ... I am worried." Mary Anne gushed out her fears. "I was so happy in the East that I forgot about the McAlisters. I fear they may still come for me. I am not eighteen and they can take me, according to

Oregon laws."

Margaret reached across the table and clasped Mary Anne's hands in hers. They sat quite a while squeezing hands and peering into the eyes of the other.

Mary Anne swallowed and bit her lip before she said, "Also, I wonder what is to become of my life. I can't live with you and Dr. Bailey forever. I never thought about this in the East, but now ...."

Like a disappearing sunset, bit by bit Margaret's smile faded to a dark look. "Mary Anne, as you know from our trip and all my problems with Willy's abuse, my marriage is not doing well. So, I worry about what you are saying as well. You see, I think I shall divorce. I should be granted by the courts half of the sale of our farm, but one never knows what will happen in this world run by men."

Mary Anne gasped. "No! A divorce?"

"Yes, a divorce. But it is too early to say more. I don't know if I really am going to do it. I have said nothing to him about my intentions. It is good for me to have someone who knows how Dr. Bailey is. Would you be a witness for me? Oh, don't answer that! I don't know what I am going to do." Margaret stopped talking a moment, smoothed the lap of her skirt, tucked a stray lock of hair back into her bonnet, and looked up at the passing scenery. "Let's talk about what we are going to do today and tomorrow. You know, plans we can really accomplish."

By the time the steamboat docked, it had been decided that this was the time to see more of Oregon. So they planned to take a trip to see Celilo Falls and to meet some of the Indians, like Mary Anne had wanted to do so many years ago.

Margaret insisted, "I don't even know how we can take a trip like this. We could never do it alone, of course. You know, two women can't travel alone." She shook her head.

After dinner that night, when alone in her room, Mary Anne could not rid herself of her fears of the McAlisters. She fell asleep in frustration.

Across the hall, Margaret was alone as well. Dr. Bailey had not joined them for dinner.

He arrived in the morning when they were heading downstairs to have breakfast.

Over breakfast, the Baileys and Mary Anne looked out the window of the hotel and made small talk, marveling at the growth and activity. They saw how Oregon City had thrived in the last few years. The town had more than doubled with what seemed like a hundred buildings. It was a Friday morning, and many of the shop owners were having breakfast in the hotel dining room; the fifteen tables were all occupied. Two men, at the table next to them, had pencils and pads in front of them, discussing some kind of business. Several people read *The Oregon Spectator* quietly while a group of three argued loudly about political issues and an article from the paper. Waiters shuffled around tables with trays above their heads, and no one seemed to be disturbed by the clank of dishes coming from the kitchen.

Dr. Bailey commented, "It's good that Oregon City has grown in the two years since we last saw it. That means the economy is good."

Margaret lamented when she said, "I hope our cities here in Oregon never get to be the size of New York or Boston. I yearn for things more natural, not all these manmade boxes we call buildings."

Mary Anne was quiet and content not to join in the conversation.

Red and white checked tablecloths covered every table; Christmas wreaths still hung in the windows with holiday garland draped around the walls. As they sipped the last of their coffee and finished eating, Robert Newell came into the room and headed to their table.

Margaret was the first to see him and exclaimed, "Robert!"

Dr. Bailey jumped up and pulled a chair out for him. "Here, have a seat. I forgot to tell the women that I invited you to come. Of course, I didn't know if you would."

Doc took off his hat and hung it on the wall next to their table. Hooks for hats and coats lined the room and most held woolen garments. "Good morning to all," he said. "I hope you had an enjoyable trip here on the steamboat yesterday and a good night's sleep. That was your first steamboat ride in Oregon, wasn't it?"

Leaving the question unanswered, Margaret, never one to mince words, asked, "Robert, what brings you here with your wife ready to give birth any moment?"

"Margaret!" Dr. Bailey huffed. "How can you greet our friend in that manner?"

Robert was quick to respond, "William, don't be angry with Margaret. She's my friend and always has been there for me. I enjoy her frankness and have missed her this past year." He made a little chuckle deep in his throat, "Besides, she never lets sleeping dogs lie." He raised his hand to signal the waiter to bring a coffee before turning back to his friends with a serious look. "Please let me explain why I am here."

Robert was very somber and began, "Last night, after the house quieted from the little one crying and while Rebecca slept, I sat staring at the fire. I sat there thinking, and the more I watched the fire, the more I wished I could revise the past. I know I can't but ...." He stopped and looked up into the six curious eyes. "Let me begin again. Have you ever had something gnaw at you, like some blunder you wish you could take back or something you wish you could have done differently?" He stopped again, for a moment, and looked down at his hands. "Something has been digging at me for years."

Still the three waited, unable to guess where he was going.

Robert continued, "I decided to come today to talk with friends. I realized last night that there are things I needed to tell you about .... Oh, I don't know how to begin. It's all about the slavery laws we have here in Oregon. They need to be changed. Why didn't I do something sooner?" He looked directly at Mary Anne. "I don't know how any Negro can live here and have any peace of mind."

The morning was ending; the breakfast room had tables here and there with soiled tablecloths, half-empty coffee cups, and platters with chunks of cold eggs; most guests were gone. Robert gulped some coffee and placed the cup back on the checkered cloth.

Awaiting his next words, Mary Anne scooted to the edge of her seat, and the Baileys leaned onto the table with curiosity in their eyes.

He suggested, "Let's leave the hotel and walk while I talk. Besides, I would like to go over to the offices of *The Oregon Spectator* to show you some news articles."

While Dr. Bailey paid for breakfast, they put on their coats and hats. Once outside Robert continued. "As you may or may not remember, years ago I showed you a newspaper article about Black Saul being arrested. Do you remember?"

They nodded their heads, not knowing where the topic was going.

The group of four arrived in front of the building that housed *The Oregon Spectator*. "Let's go in. First, I want to know if you have learned what has happened to Black Saul in your absence?" Doc pulled the door open for all to enter.

Mary Anne smiled. "No, how is he? I would love to see him."

Margaret, knowing the terrible accusation made against Black Saul about killing his wife, blurted, "Robert, what are you doing? We had a friendship with Black Saul. Just tell us what you need to say."

"I know, Margaret. It is because we were friends that I am having difficulty saying anything. I pulled some old newspapers before I went over to the hotel. First, this is the article I showed you at my birthday party when I turned forty. I pulled it out for you to read again, in case you didn't remember it."

After giving them time to read the article about Black Saul being accused of killing his wife, Robert said, "After this happened in December of 1846, Black Saul disappeared from our lives. We couldn't find him. He was hiding for years. But at some point Black Saul went to live in a cabin at Cape Disappointment, facing Baker Bay."

Excitedly, Margaret interrupted, "Yes, that's where Black Saul started out; that's where he met his wife. He had that transportation business with his boat and a place to live over there. He told me."

Robert nodded. "We know for a fact that he was there last year because Peter Skene Ogden bought the squatters' rights to the property where Black Saul lived. Ogden told us that he was intending to build a pilot's lookout and a British trading post there. Also, we know Black Saul was there, during the year of 1851, because his name is on ledgers at the Cathlamet Store."

Margaret asked, "So?"

"Please read this next article." Robert spread another paper on the table:

The Oregon Spectator – Dec. 30, 1851

We learn that three Negro men have been engaged for some time past in selling liquor to Indians, a short distance from

Milton, Washington County, and that the citizens of that place were so much annoyed by their continued drunkenness and debauchery, that several of the citizens started in a boat to take the Negroes into custody. This they succeeded in doing, and when taking them before the Magistrate, by some means the boat was capsized, and one of the Negroes drowned. For want of sufficient evidence to commit them, the other two were discharged.

Mary Anne was baffled. "I don't understand."

Margaret sighed before saying, "Since we just arrived back from our trip, I had not heard about this. Robert, do you think this is about Black Saul?"

"We don't know, but we think Black Saul was the man who drowned. A body was never recovered. But there have been no more debts in his name and no one has seen him. Of course, it is not even a week ago. I hope for the best. Chickens always come home to roost. Margaret, if Black Saul is alive, he probably will come to you or me."

Robert put the newspaper aside. "That's all I know about Black Saul. Now to another difficult topic about our Negro friends. Margaret, I remember you learned that the Holmeses got their freedom just before you left for the East. What you didn't know was that Nathaniel Ford gave the freedom only to the parents. He kept the children." He slammed his fist on the table. "Damn it!"

Margaret seemed to be in shock from the news about the Holmes children; she stood with her hand to her mouth.

Doc continued talking. "The law says that children can be kept in slavery until they are eighteen; that's abominable. Why didn't I try to change the law through the legislature while I could? I served from 1843 through 1849. Did you hear that I lost the election to Benjamin F. Harding in November of 1850?"

"No, we didn't know," Dr. Bailey answered.

Doc said, "I'm getting away from my point ... or maybe, avoiding telling you. I will just blurt it out – two of the Holmes children died recently while living with Ford and his wife."

"No, no, no! Who died? Do you know their names?" Margaret doubled over and held her waist. Mary Anne put her arms around her, but Margaret pushed her away to speak, "How did this happen?"

Doc's face darkened in shame, "I don't know the names of the children who died. I'm sorry, Margaret. Ford has the law on his side. Our hands are tied." He ran his hands through his hair. "Let me go on. There is more." He took Mary Anne's hand, "Joe told me about a month ago that there is another man asking for Mattie McAlister."

Margaret and Mary Anne collapsed onto a bench next to the table where the newspaper had been spread. They grasped the other's hands. Margaret looked to the men, "She was afraid this might happen."

Dr. Bailey suggested, "Let's go outside again, or maybe we could return to the hotel for some lunch while we talk."

Margaret asked, "How can you think of food? What time is it? Isn't it too early for lunch? I can't eat after all this shocking news."

Doc reached for his watch fob and said, "It is almost 11:15."

Dr. Bailey got back to the lunch decision. "I'm hungry and, Robert, you only had coffee at breakfast. Let's go back to the hotel."

Doc said, "I think that is best. Before noon, there will not be many people, and we can talk about what to do for Mary Anne and the Holmeses."

Out on the wooden walkways, their thoughts treaded along like their feet – sluggish and heavy. They entered the hotel, hung their coats, and went to a table. A waiter came and took their order for some sandwiches.

When seated, Robert leaned on the table with both arms and sighed, "No one has seen Black Saul, so there is nothing we can do. Joe Meek tried to learn more to no avail. No one wants to tell us whose boat it was because the boat owner could be accused of killing the one who drowned."

"What about the danger for Mary Anne?" Margaret discussed her desire to take a trip to Celilo Falls. "Mary Anne has always wanted to see Indians. A trip would get her away from here. Willy, until we have bought a house, we are just living in hotels and I have not much to do – no house to furnish. It's a good time for an adventure, but I need help finding men to go with us. Since Willy needs to buy a place and get us settled, he can't go. You, Robert, can't go because you have a wife who is going to have a baby and you must sell property to Willy. Can one of you help find someone to get us away from this area?"

There food arrived as Dr. Bailey mentioned, "We could look in the newspaper to see if someone is traveling."

Robert reached into his inner jacket pocket, "William, you reminded me that I have an ad for the *Oregon Spectator*. I need to walk back and leave it there." He put his handwritten ad on the table for them to see:

The undersigned has a very good assortment of
Goods & Groceries for the farming community:
Flour, feed, ham, pickled pork,
American and Indian horses
which he will give in exchange for
Wheat, Oats, Hides, Pork, Butter, Chickens, Eggs, or Cash.
Call anyway and see if you have letters at the Post Office.

Signed, Robert (Doc) Newell

Robert stood and dragged his chair around the table to sit next to Mary Anne. He took her hand, "You look so upset. Listen to me; you are safe with us. We'll learn more about who is asking for you. We'll get this settled."

"He's right," Margaret added. "Mary Anne, you're so quiet." Before she finished her thought, she looked out the window and saw the Holmeses. "Oh, look! Excuse me, I want to catch Mr. and Mrs. Holmes." She grabbed her coat and dashed outside.

Again Dr. Bailey volunteered, "Everyone seems to be finished eating, I'll pay the check. Let's all go."

When Robert, Dr. Bailey, and Mary Anne approached Margaret, they heard parts of the conversation.

"Oh, Miz Margaret, please help us. You jus' don' know how good it feel to be free. I can't be a slave again. Please come talk to this lawyer. He called Mr. Deady; he tell you true. We can't wait 'til our little ones are eighteen. Why, they be only eleven, seven, and five today."

"What has happened, Margaret?" Dr. Bailey stepped close and touched her arm.

Margaret turned and told the others about a letter. "As we know, Nathaniel Ford gave Mr. and Mrs. Holmes their freedom, but not the children. Later, Ford wrote to a lawyer named Mr. Shirley in Missouri to request that a federal agent come to reclaim the whole family and take them back to Missouri to sell; Ford would turn a fine profit selling them."

Mary Anne asked, "Can they do that?"

Dr. Bailey insisted, "That's the point. They can! They wouldn't have to sneak or come in the night; in daylight they could take this whole family. Do you think neighbors and bystanders would step up to stop them from taking Negroes?"

Mary Anne's face distorted in pain, but everyone was thinking only of the Holmeses. She realized that the same could happen to her. She also realized that this conversation contradicted what they had just told her in the restaurant about being safe.

Doc interjected, "If we are prepared and have law enforcement men of Oregon there at the moment the Missourians arrive, it can be stopped – if and only if the Holmeses have papers to prove they are free."

Dr. Bailey knew how serious this was. "Nathaniel Ford is a strong adversary and quite capable. He successfully led their wagon train and arrived here in Oregon in December of 1844. Since that time he has become a landowner, postmaster, school administrator and a legislator in the territorial government. I have worked with him. He is a forceful character. And I have to say that he is not quite fair at times. He can bend the truth to his benefit. He knows what he wants and what is good for himself and his family; he can manipulate a situation and ignore the rights of others."

Doc said, "I agree. He came to Oregon because of his careless use of money; his debts in Missouri possibly still weigh on his pocketbook. And people have told me that he is insensitive to his slaves. Be careful, Margaret."

Dr. Bailey kissed her on her cheek and said, "Margaret, Robert and I are returning to Champoeg. I know you want to help them and we support your efforts, so let us know if there's anything we can do."

Doc draped his arm over Bailey's shoulder. "Well said! As we know, when Margaret gets a bee in her bonnet, there's no stoppin' her. By gum, we may as well join her in her efforts."

Ignoring the lighthearted comment, Margaret was deep in thought. In fact, she already had hatched a plan. "I'm going to go talk with the lawyer now; they just came from his offices, but may not have clarified things. I don't think that they have papers proving they're free. And, when I can, I plan to travel south to see little Mary Jane and give Nathaniel Ford a bit of my wrath. I hope that little girl is doing well for his sake. Mary Jane is eleven years old, and he better not have touched her!"

It was a fact of life for slaves, former slaves, and even free Negroes that they could be abducted and sold, because they were viewed as less than human by many. Such were the times. And legally, since slaves were a piece of property owned by their master, the women slaves had to endure sexual relations whenever imposed. Rape? Few Whites gave any thought to sexual relations with a slave; if a white man took a slave to bed, much of the time, it was not considered to be an act of rape, even in the eyes of his wife. People in the slave states turned a blind eye or blatantly ignored lashings, hangings, and kidnappings of Negroes as well as rape. And rarely would any slave step up and help a fellow slave for fear of torture, suffering, or worse.

Most people in the free states found it best for their personal interests to step away from interfering with the powerful men who favored slavery. Margaret was different; she would not step away from helping the Holmeses.

Though exhausted by the conversations of the day, Mary Anne asked if she could help in any way. Margaret assured her that it would be better if she rested.

Margaret touched Mary Anne's arm and said, "You nap. I'll see you for dinner." She walked off with Mr. and Mrs. Holmes.

The two men walked Mary Anne back to the hotel. When she said goodbye to them she didn't notice that someone watched from down the street.

Jed McAlister had been studying her from afar. He was certain that she was his grown half-sister Mattie.

Oregon City
Circa 1850-1852
Painting by John Mix Stanley.

CHAPTER 10

LATER THE SAME DAY IN JANUARY 1852

A t the hotel, Mary Anne undressed to get in bed for a nap. She needed sleep because her waking mind was overwhelmed. Thinking clearly and logically about her life was impossible at the moment. She closed the curtains and slipped under the cold covers. Aloud she said with a shiver, "I knew today was going to be cold and hard." With that in mind she fell asleep and dreamed:

I knew it was going to be cold and hard. In the end it always is.

Flurries started to fall and the ground began to disappear into whiteness. The evergreens cradled the puffs of snow on branches. The wind came in gusts and, at times, swirled the snow into our eyes and noses. Men attended their horses, cinching straps and tightening their saddle-girth while a few stood facing their animal, speaking unheard words.

Shivering and stamping my frozen feet, I stared out at the one distant figure approaching with his long and confident strides; he passed the line of horses and nodded at the men. Still at a distance, a playful smile spread across his face upon seeing me. I puzzled as to who he was. Suddenly he was in front of me, but steps away.

He pulled off his gloves, crammed them into a pocket, and stopped so close I could feel his warmth. He leaned toward me for a kiss and slipped one hand to my nape and cupped my head; the other hand he wrapped around my back, and he pulled me into his sheepskin coat. I felt a thrill. His dark, wide-brimmed, leather hat stopped the wind from our faces for that moment.

"Look at you out here all unbuttoned and without a hat." *He knelt with one leg to start buttoning my long coat – he was finicky and liked everything in order. But I never could button*

this coat with cold hands.

"But I had the top clasp closed."

He rose off his knee and finished the last buttons and then he pulled the coat up to my chin. I took my blue woolen cap from the coat pocket and donned it. He shook his head, "If you're cold it won't do any good to only close the top clasp. I've said that to you so many times, haven't I?"

We smiled and gazed into each other's eyes, seeing what we felt reflecting back. He was taller than me, and especially with his cowboy boots with higher heels. I stretched up for another kiss and teased, "Aren't my kisses cold like ice?"

"No, your kisses are soft like snow and they warm my cold, cold nose."

I hugged him, enjoying his sense of humor, even in a snowstorm. But the moment passed and I whined like the wind, "Can't I ride with you?"

"You know I'm the boss and have to lead the men. I shouldn't have let you come at all, so don't complain. I'll ride back from time-to-time to see how you're doing."

I nodded with a pout.

He stuck his boot into the stirrup and mounted his mare, "The weather's getting worse; we're losing visibility. We must go."

I watched him ride to the front of the men and disappear into the snowfall. I got on my horse as the men started plodding away. I was last in line and didn't know anything – not where we were going, not why we had to leave, not when we would arrive, not anything. I didn't even know who he was. Those confusing questions clouded my mind like the snow clouded the way. Over and over I questioned where and why we had to make this trip, and I wondered why I had not asked. The monotony in my mind and the relentlessness of the storm was overwhelming, but I could not stop thinking about those questions any more than I could end the storm. And time dragged on.

As promised, he rode back to check on me. I didn't complain, and in the joyful moment of being with him I forgot to ask any questions. We held hands, and he laughed. Soon he rode back to the front of the line.

On his next visit to me, the snow was eight inches deep. I had no way of knowing the time, though it didn't matter; time had no meaning out here. The snow seemed to suck in the time and absorb all sounds. I no longer could hear the plodding of the other horses – even the sounds of wind and the groans of the evergreen limbs were gone. When he came to my side, nothing else mattered.

His first words made me smile, "Bet you have to pee."

With a nod of my head, I agreed.

He held his reins close while he spoke, "I told the men there was time for a quick break. You can go pee over in those bushes and none of them will see you. Don't be long, though. I have to leave soon." His horse pranced back and forth. In one easy motion, he dismounted and came to me, "I'll help you down."

I slid down into his arms not expecting to hear what he had to say.

He held me for a long moment before saying, "I love you, Mary Anne."

We kissed, and in a blink he was riding away. I watched him for only a few seconds because I did need to relieve myself. I walked off into the trees to find a bush some distance away from the men who were watering the trees.

Steam lifted from the yellowed snow beneath me, and I felt like it was turning to ice on my underside, so I didn't waste any time adjusting my drawers. "It had been easier to drop my drawers," I whispered to myself. Clutching the bottom of my long coat that I had refused to unbutton, I squirmed until they were in place.

When I emerged from the bushes, they were all gone.

I grabbed the reins that I had looped over a branch and flew onto my horse, screaming, "Hey, wait for me!" I nudged the horse into a run and then tried to go faster, but the snow was too deep.

Something seemed strange. Looking ahead of me, there were

no tracks. It wasn't snowing at the moment, and the blue sky hung over me. I stopped and shouted, "Where are you?"

Turning the horse full circle, I saw a horseman in the distance and wasted no time. I galloped to him, happy that I found someone. Suddenly I was there and looked at the rider. I screamed!

It was Jed McAlister.

A voice came from somewhere, everywhere: "Life is cold and hard. Tell me, where's my brother, Tom?"

Startled into wakefulness, she found her heart pounding as rapidly as if she had really lived the dream. Salty tears puddled in her eyes, and she swallowed, trying to remove the lump in her throat. In the warmness of the bed, she gave a shiver, thinking about the dream.

After her disturbing dream, Mary Anne arose to dress in the waning light from the window. It was time for dinner. The reflection she saw in the small mirror on the wall showed her sad expression. She puzzled over how to stop worrying about the McAlisters. A heavy emptiness pulled at her insides. She grabbed her hair and wound it all together at the base of her neck. Hurrying, so not to need to light a lamp, she poured some water from a pitcher into the basin and splashed her face. When drying herself, she rubbed harder on her cheeks to cause a flush of color. Now the mirror's reflection looked healthier, though not happier. She straightened the handmade quilt and pillows on the hotel bed before she furled the shawl around her shoulders and left the hotel room.

Mary Anne tapped lightly on Margaret's door.

"Come in," Margaret answered. She was sitting at a small desk with a goose quill pen in hand. The light from an oil lamp spilled across the paper. "Hello, Mary Anne."

"What are you writing?"

"Oh, just some thoughts into my journal. I am excited about taking a trip with you. Come see my thoughts." Margaret showed a page of her journal and Mary Anne read:

I have found the pull of Mother Earth, calling me to seek nature to heal my pain – mental or physical. I need the rain as I need the sun, not unlike the trees that reach for the sky; nature feeds my soul. But we have senses that the trees lack, allowing us to touch, smell, see, and hear the beauty ....

Mary Anne responded, "That's beautiful!"

Standing, Margaret commented, "Oh, I have quite an appetite, and we are going to be late if I don't hurry. Turning to the mirror, she tucked some stray hairs back with a hairpin. "We are meeting someone for dinner." Pivoting from the mirror to face Mary Anne, she held up her hands to stop any questions. "It is a surprise, so don't ask who."

Mary Anne surmised that things went well with the lawyer because Margaret's mood was lighthearted and gay.

They left the room and started down the stairway to the lobby. Mary Anne asked, "How was the meeting with the lawyer for the Holmeses?"

"We have a plan. Their lawyer, Mr. Deady, will write a standard document stating that Mr. and Mrs. Holmes are free. It just needs to be signed by Nathaniel Ford. An official, you know, someone with authority, must go to get it signed. I think our guest for dinner is the person to add the right amount of leverage. You and I must convince him to go and put the fear of God into this villainous Ford."

When they reached the bottom of the stairs and turned toward the dining room, Mary Anne asked, "Did you say 'you and I'?"

Margaret turned with a large grin. Without responding, she took Mary Anne's elbow and headed toward an occupied table. A large man sat with his back to them. Margaret continued, "He only needs to be convinced."

As he stood to greet the women, Mary Anne recognized him and cried, "Joe Meek!"

"No, no," Margaret responded, "May I introduce the United States Marshal, Joseph Lafayette Meek."

He grinned and made a deep bow. "Miss McAlister, how good to see you again after so many years. And Mrs. Bailey, I see you're back from travelin' to the East. If we're going ta use our formal names, you gotta call me Major Meek." He inserted one of his well-known pauses. "However, it sure tires me out saying all those extra words, 'specially if we're goin' to travel together to Celilo Falls."

The women bobbed with excitement. Margaret exclaimed, "If I were a child, I would jump for joy! How did this happen?"

"Well, I ran into Doc a couple of hours ago, and he told me about it after I told him my problems. I sure could use a break from politics; besides I got some business with the Injuns up thar at Celilo Falls." He jabbed his finger in the air to make the next point. "Before I commit to takin' you women along, I want a promise that you'll call me 'Joe.' By gum, I'm gonna use your first names."

True to his character, Joe Meek made the evening meal memorable with stories and gaiety. Sitting erect as always with his two-hundred-pound frame draped over the edges of the chair, he suggested that they order some wine with their dinner. When it arrived, the waiter poured a glass for each and took their orders.

Joe raised his goblet, "Margaret and Mary Anne, you were gone last year when everyone war vying to make their town the capital. Doc made a toast at the Fourth of July celebration that sums up what war going on. Allow me to repeat:

> Champoeg for beauty,
> Salem for pride;
> If it hadn't been for salmon,
> Oregon City would have died.

When their laughter stopped, Joe continued, "A log-rollin' bill passed, makin' Salem the proud capital and givin' Corvallis the University; not to be forgotten, Portland will git the penitentiary." He slapped his thigh and laughed, "but Oregon City got nothing." Ducking his head, he feigned fear as he looked to his right and left. "Maybe I should be more quiet here in Oregon City."

Margaret asked, "Joe, you mentioned that you told Doc your problems and you need a break from politics. Would you mind sharing what youmeant?"

"I reckon I could. Margaret, being a U.S. marshal is all about politics and money. And it's money I don't have; I should really say that it's money I never got paid. I war in charge of taking the census back in 1850 and had to get helpers to work for me; it's two years later and those men still aren't paid. I have to find people for jury duty all the time, and I haven't paid any of them, either. Haven't paid them in years." He pulled a paper from an inside pocket of his coat jacket. "Why, would you ladies help me with this letter that I wrote for Governor Joseph Lane? I don't spell too good ... so I been told. Tell me what you think." He unfolded the letter and smoothed it out on the tabletop with his huge and hairy hands. It read:

January th 3, 1852
Oregon City
General Jo Lane

Dear Sir . . they are hell in camp In this Countrey . . the Legislator is still in Sesion at Salem . . and the Supream Court and part of the Legislators at Oregon City have a Jurnd . . as you have Seen Mount hood it taint worth while to write you on this subject for you now all about it . . I wrote to you some time ago on matters of Bisoness . . I want you to see. A Holbrook he promised to make out my Reckquation on the Depart ment for money for to pay of the courts nex Spring he has all of my papers and can Do it   I want you to be shure to Se that he puts my Bisoness in proper shape with the Department and find out Something about the Louis county Court you know – they war a hevey Expence acurd there that the pople has not bin paid yet and they are after me all the time for the money . . Can you do any thing about it. I want you to see about the money for taking the Censis for they have sent none yeit and som of my assistant Sais that ihave got it and spent it but you know beter, I wish you would Pecure the Marshals office for me when my time Runs out or When the Administration chainges Write to me and let me Know the nuse and send Som papers aney thing for the Nuse. Nat is well the River is verey high, yours in haist

Joseph L. Meek

P.S. Have the Marshals fees Raised to the saim of the Mashals in Caloforna. JLK

The waiter brought their dinners as the women finished reading the letter.

After Margaret picked up the letter, folded it, and handed it back to Joe, she nudged Mary Anne lightly before saying, "Joe, the letter makes sense and it would be a waste of time to rewrite just for a few misspelled words. What do you think, Mary Anne?"

"Oh, oh, I agree. I can read and understand everything you say. I want to make only one point. You have tomorrow's date. It's important to always use the correct date."

Joe nodded, "I'll take it to the post office tomorrow. Then it'll be the right day."

"So," Margaret began, "these are your problems with money?"

"Oh, no!" Joe swallowed a bite and continued, "What you read in the letter war jus' the start of the rain, jus' a drizzle. So many people owe me money and jus' don't pay me. Like Nat Lane – yes, the Governor's son – he claims he's hard for cash and laughs, saying I don't need money with my salary. But I only make twenty thousand a year and use most all to pay the government debts. The U.S. marshal in California gets paid more than twice that." He frowned, "I like fightin' b'ars more than fightin' people to pay what they owe."

Mary Anne brightened, "Oh, Joe, since you mentioned bears, I would love to hear that story that goes with your famous bear fight."

Joe had ordered a double-thick beefsteak and it was almost gone. He stabbed the last cut and held his fork in the air, not taking the bite, as he began the story, "Ya must mean the contest back in thirty-eight. I tell ya the spring of 1838 war so bad; we lost many a horse and mule from starvation. But what war worse was the trappin' situation; the Blackfeet, Crows, and Snakes war our competition. They war trappin' and sellin' furs jus' like Doc Newell and me. Doc wrote in his journal, 'beever scarce and low like all the peltries are on the decline.' I remember that 'cuz I used his journal to practice reading when we war in camp. I only went to a schoolhouse for three months when I was a youngin. So Doc taught me to read and write."

Now Meek was ready to get into his story and leaned on the table with both elbows and with the fork and hunk of beef still in his fist. "But the b'ars war not scarce. They war plentiful and pesky when we left Crow country and headed into Yellowstone. We war near Cross Creek and at camp with our wives when a whole family of b'ars came in bowling over the squaws and knocking over the tents. What a sight it war. With wooden spoons those women were beatin' off those little black b'ars and bashin' them with kettles.

"We men war laughing and chasing the b'ars out of our camp, and I guess I started bragging that I was equal in strength to any b'ar. Well, one of the men challenged me to a contest with a b'ar. Not jus' any b'ar; he wanted me to show that I was up to a grizzly. It took a few days, but the day finally came when we had a grizzly in our midst."

Now Joe ate his last bite and chewed it thoroughly before continuing. "I saw this grizzly b'ar and recklessly approached her and struck her with my wiping stick. She reared up and, before that b'ar could blink, I fired so quickly and accurately that she went down. My luck held. Well, it held that time."

The women had finished their plates, and the waiter removed all the dishes and poured more wine. No one said a word until each had taken a sip and put their glasses down. Joe continued, "It so happened that an artist had joined our party of trappers and he war thar when I boldly decided to molest another grizzly. He painted this incident for posterity.

"First you need to understand that our guns are not sure-fire weapons. And I knew that. I war lucky with that first encounter. This next time I spied a large grizzly digging roots in a creek bottom. I had my two companions hold my horse for a quick getaway in case of trouble. And there war lots of trouble to come.

"I approached the grizzly and took aim. As I pulled the trigger, the cap burst and misfired, makin' a loud racket that rouse the b'ar. It came snarlin' at me. Well, the horses took fright with the b'ar runnin' at us, and they broke loose from the two men. I started sprintin' away and reloadin' my rifle on the run. That thar beast jumped on my back. They're fast runners. It was my luck that I war in a capote. The b'ar stripped off that blanket coat, scratched me some, but then went down on all fours when the capote slipped to the ground. Thar war time far me to turn before he raised up agin. I shoved my rifle right against him – I war that close – and blew out his heart."

Joe emptied his glass, while the two women sat wide-eyed.

"Ha!" he said, and the women jumped. Joe laughed, "That visiting artist, I think war called Alfred J. Miller, if I remember correct. He drew and exaggerated the picture with me holdin' a huntin' knife and jabbin' it into the jugular vein and me with missin' fingers. It weren't that way. They made a wax statue in the St. Louis museum showin' what he claimed to have seen. But it weren't true."

Margaret sighed, "What a story, Joe. Here I sit and hope never to be as close to a bear as you. Oh, I forgot! Mary Anne was that close, too. She has the scars on her side! You should tell your bear story to us."

"But Joe was at Doc's house the day when they divided up my bear. Do you remember, Joe?"

"I remember havin' bear for lunch at Doc's and about bringin' home b'ar meat. But I forget the b'ar story. Tell it again."

When Mary Anne finished, Joe raised his glass. "Mary Anne, your bear story sure sounds like one of my tall tales. Doc told me long ago about you and that bear, but I had forgotten the details."

The trio parted after Joe told them they should head up to Portland on the first steamer out tomorrow morning; he would meet them at the docks. "I'm going home tonight to see my family. I'll ready the horses and pack the mules with all the supplies. We'll leave when I have everything made ready." Joe suggested, "You might head over to Abernethy's Brick Store for a couple of capotes, hats, and whatever women might need. See you in Stumptown tomorrow."

As the women walked away, Mary Anne asked, "What is Stumptown?"

"Remember how all the streets were covered in stumps in Portland? That city grew so fast! When they cut down trees to make the streets, they didn't have men to remove the stumps. Don't you remember those white stumps all over the streets when we were there? Those stumps have been there for years so people whitewashed them to help see them at night."

"Yes, I didn't understand and forgot to ask you about them."

Tired and sated, Margaret and Mary Anne climbed the stairs without words. But once at their doors, Margaret asked, "Mary Anne, how are you feeling?"

Mary Anne began to cry and confessed, "Oh, Margaret, I'm scared."

Margaret suggested a talk in Mary Anne's room. They sat on the edge of the bed.

Mary Anne told of the dream she had had. "You don't know, Margaret. You just don't know how it feels. I don't want to be a slave, and Jed is so mean."

Margaret stood and paced the room for a minute before she turned to face Mary Anne. "You must stop this worrying," she said. "We are going to take a trip tomorrow – a trip of a lifetime. I am so excited to be able to travel with Joe Meek. You are going to see all that is beautiful in nature. You said that you wanted to see Celilo Falls and Indians, and now you will. On this trip we will make memories that no one can take from us for the rest of our lives." She stomped her foot. "Stop worrying!"

Mary Anne wiped her tears with her hands and nodded in agreement.

Margaret pulled a handkerchief from her sleeve, "Here, use my handkerchief. Wash it clean tonight, and tomorrow we'll buy a couple more at Abernethy's store for the trip. We'll put all we need for this trip on my tab. Oh, and I don't know how you feel, but I plan to wear my husband's breeches under my dress so I can ride my horse in comfort. I'll get a pair for you."

While Mary Anne blew her nose, Margaret pulled an object from a drawstring bag attached to her wrist and opened her palm. It was a small pistol.

Mary Anne's eyes grew wide.

"Yes, I have this Philadelphia Deringer to bring. I asked Willy if I could use it on this trip. He just bought it in New York. It is a new design by a man of the same name, Henry Deringer."

"Do you know how to shoot and reload it and everything?"

"I do. I wish I had one to lend to you. You may need it."

Celilo Falls on the Columbia River, Oregon (Circa 1900)

The photographer, Benjamin Gifford, operated a photography studio in The Dalles from 1895 to 1910. Throughout those years Gifford captured important images of the Columbia River Gorge and the native inhabitants.

Oregon Historical Society (Item number: 89622)

CHAPTER 11

HEADING TO CELILO FALLS, 1852

Heavy fog hugged the Willamette River and muffled the sounds of the paddlewheel as the steamer *Blackhawk* pulled in at the wharf in Portland. Barrels, bundles of furs tied with twine, leather bags labeled *U.S. Mail*, wooden boxes with *Abernethy* burned on the sides, crates of nails, and sacks of flour lined the wooden platform. A wagon with prancing horses and a driver waited for expected travelers; and people, bundled in winter clothing, were bustling up and down the streets. By the time Margaret and Mary Anne walked down the gangplank, workers were making the boat ready for the return trip to Oregon City by toting sacks of grain over their shoulders onto the steamer and by rolling barrels up a ramp. Dozens of people holding satchels, bundles, or suitcases fastened with belts waited behind a gate for the signal to board; at the blast from the horn, the ticket taker unlatched the portal and took tickets.

Peering this way and that, Margaret strained to see Joe Meek in the fog when she noticed a man jumping from one stump to the next, crossing the street in front of the pier. He approached her. She watched this Negro, the color of bronze and a head taller than most of the men on the pier; he carried his large frame with confidence and displayed a fine hat pulled down over his kinky hair. He was clad in a worn, wool coat that fell below his knees where dark trousers, encrusted in mud at the cuffs, protruded. Though he had hopped from stump to stump to avoid the mud while crossing the street, his boots were still muddy, like everyone's.

Removing his wide-brimmed hat, he asked, "Are you Mrs. Margaret Bailey and Miss Mary Anne McAlister? Major Meek sent me to fetch you." Albert recognized the two surnames – Bailey and McAlister – from his time at the gold fields, but said nothing for the moment.

"Yes, I am Mrs. Bailey. Where is he and who are you?"

With his hat still in hand and pulled to his chest, he explained, "My name is Albert Bayless. Major Meek is at the livery stables getting a horse shod. I was there asking for work because I'm a smithy. They didn't need any help, so the Major hired me to ride on your trip. He made me his deputy."

Margaret held out her hand. "It is nice to meet you, Deputy Bayless. I would like to go to my hotel and change clothes. Should I do that first or go to the livery?"

Mary Anne shook his hand and commented, "Nice to have you coming with us, but we decided to use first names on this trip. Please call me Mary Anne." When their hands met, something passed from one to the other. Her honey-colored hand was but a slight shade different than his bronze skin. They held hands longer than one usually does in a greeting. She looked from his eyes to the two interlocked hands and then they released their grip. For reasons she did not understand, she blushed. When she glanced back up to his face, he had a playful smile. A smile like the man she had kissed in her dream!

Mary Anne and Margaret hurried to the hotel to change and pack.

In early afternoon, the four riders and two pack mules headed east by northeast toward the Columbia River. The fog thinned off and on, and they could see the well-wooded land for some distance before clouds rolled back to shroud them in the murky quiet.

The group rode two by two with the horses, and the two mules followed behind on leads. Meek estimated the trip to be a bit more than one hundred miles. "We'll camp tonight when weary, and the day after tomorrow we'll get to Celilo Falls. Big Al says I met him back in forty-seven when I hightailed it down the Oregon Trail to tell the President about the massacre. But I war so tired that trip, I don't remember him. So, Big Al, tell us where ya came from and how ya came to be here in Oregon."

Albert Bayless let out a hearty laugh. "Big Al! I have never been called that before, but I like it." He lifted his hat and adjusted it again before beginning his story. "I was born a slave in Tennessee to a kind and good master who taught me my letters and gave me books to read. When I was thirty years old, my master died and I was sold to a cruel, ignorant man. That was in 1849. I read about the gold in California, so I escaped and came west. I found a little gold – not enough to buy new clothes, but sufficient to buy food and save some for emergencies– and I worked as a blacksmith in the gold mining camps when I wasn't panning for gold. I heard Negroes are free here in Oregon and decided to come last fall. I wanted to find work, settle, and start a family. Thank you, Major Joe, for hiring me today. Miss Mary Anne, do you have a family?"

"Margaret and Dr. Bailey are my family. I have lived with them for seven years."

Margaret joined in with her story. "I've lived in Oregon since 1836. That's sixteen years, if you don't count my voyages back to the East. My husband, Dr. William Bailey, and I are planning to build our home in Champoeg. The construction may be starting at this moment."

Big Al jumped at the sound of Dr. Bailey's name. "Why, I thought so! Down at the gold mines in Medford, I met a Dr. Bailey. He has quite a scar under his beard and across his jaw. I wondered if he was your husband. He spoke about you only as *his wife*, never mentioning your name."

"So, you met my husband. No one else could have a scar like his. And he went down to the mines briefly before we traveled to the East."

"I came up here because he invited me. He said maybe I could find blacksmith work. He named all these towns that were getting bigger and more populated by the day."

Mary Anne was amazed. "So you know Dr. Bailey already. Isn't this a small world?" She looked at Albert and her stomach fluttered.

"I also met a family by the name of McAlister on a sheep farm in Siskiyou County in California when I first arrived a couple of years ago. I repaired some equipment in exchange for dinner."

"That's where I grew up!" And they started talking about the McAlisters. Albert told how the family of three was shouting and fighting the whole time he was there. Mary Anne nodded in understanding.

Margaret noticed how Albert and Mary Anne were eager to talk to the other. Margaret let their conversation wind down before she smiled to herself and continued the prior subject by asking, "Joe, tell us about your family. I don't think I've heard the whole story. You lost a wife, if I remember correctly."

"I had me three wives!" Joe explained that he had become a fur trapper when he was nineteen, back in 1829. "Doc Newell and another man called

Milton Sublette war with me then. I can't 'member when Sublette took his Injun wife, but in 1834 he got real sick with gangrene in his leg and had to leave the mountains. He went back to the East for medical help and left his wife. So I took her as mine. Her name was *Umentucken Tukutsey Undewatsey*, and it means the lamb of the mountain, so I called her Mountain Lamb. She was the most beautiful woman I ever saw.

"When she was mounted astride her dapple gray horse, she made a fine show with her tomahawk tied to one side of the saddle up by the withers and a peace pipe on the other. And she knew how to use that tomahawk. She often wore a skirt of blue broadcloth and a tight bodice of scarlet red that matched her leggings. She wore one long braid draped over her shoulder with a scarlet silk kerchief over her head. That braid went down past her waist."

Joe explained that Mountain Lamb died from an arrow shot by a Bannock Indian in June of 1837 when the fur trappers were fighting with that tribe. "So I took me my second wife from the Nez Percé tribe, and we had the most wonderful little girl called Helen Mar. But my second wife didn't like me or my ways. She said I drank too much and was gone trappin' too long, so she left me. She tossed all my belongings out in the rain and mud and left them thar before she took down the tent and rode off with the tribe."

In the winter of 1838, when Joe and Doc finished trapping and came back to the Nez Percé tribe again, the two men fell in love with two sisters whose father was Sub-Chief *Kowesote*. "I found another beautiful woman in Chief *Kowesote's* daughter, but he said I war already married. When my second wife told him she didn't want me, he ordered her to give me back my little girl, Helen Mar. This time I had a woman forever. I called her Virginia, like my state of Virginia; that's whar I war born and raised. I love my state and I love my wife. I been with Virginia ever since. We have three boys and three girls."

Mary Anne interrupted and said, "I heard those exact same words from you at that holiday party you gave when I first arrived in Champoeg. You said EXACTLY the same thing about Virginia."

"I can't deny that I've said that before. But heck, I distinctly remember that you warn't at that party. A young boy named Matthew came, not you."

For the next hour, Albert heard Mary Anne's story of being Matthew.

* * *

When they came to the mighty Columbia River, the fog disappeared with the strong, cold gusts of wind coming across the steep and rocky bluffs. The banks of the river were high and, at that moment, the four of them rode among the foothills of the Cascades. The river flowed between two high bluffs and during this trip the width of the river would fluctuate from a mile across down to only one hundred and fifty feet. The riders now traveled single file along the river. When the going was steep and difficult, the horses began to sweat; frothy, white moisture formed around the edges of the saddle blankets and seeped into the riders' clothes where they touched the horses' flanks.

Joe stopped and said, "Thar's other ways to go, over the Barlow Pass or Lolo Pass from Oregon City, and it's wide enough for wagons. But I figured we war all good horsemen and can ride these high, narrow banks or low muddy ones until we get to Fort Drum, whar the Dalles are. It's a lot shorter trip this way, but sometimes we'll have to walk the horses."

They spoke little; the sights seemed to demand their appreciation through silence, and the path needed their concentration. At times it was as narrow as a deer trail. The quiet was interrupted every so often by the chink of a horseshoe on an outcropped rock. Soon they were deep in the foothills where a gap appeared, showing magnificent giant cliffs and peaks. Everything was stark and cold, but displayed a chiseled beauty of natural masterpieces. In the river, cascades flowed and bubbled for miles over rocky beds.

While they traversed the southern bluff above the river, Joe watched groups of Indians on the northern bluff throughout the day and said nothing to the others. He knew Indians well and could see that some were Cayuse and other groups were Wascos. Hours passed.

Finally, Joe stopped and turned his horse, "I know'd this trail real good. We're comin' to a place that widens. Thar's a wall of rock to protect us from the wind and, if we're lucky, the waterfall will be runnin'. It'll be dark in 'bout an hour, so we'll make camp thar. Big Al, I have a tent for the women. You and I need to set it up after we start a fire."

Mary Anne blurted, "I'll start the fire. She reached into her saddlebag. I have a fine tinderbox that my Grandpappy gave me."

Albert, with his back to the others, grinned. He liked this woman.

Joe nodded and said, "That's fine. Everyone's ta gather wood. Thar's even some nice bunchgrass for the horses."

With a blazing fire and bellies full of fried pork strips and day-old Johnnycakes that Virginia had packed, they sat on blankets facing the fire, holding tin cups of black coffee, warming their hands and innards. Billions of stars shared the sky with a gibbous moon. Though they had camped in a clearing, some juniper trees and scrubby bushes surrounded them.

Albert looked at Mary Anne and asked, "May I see your tinderbox? It looked interesting."

"Oh, yes." Passing it to him, she commented, "It has the family name on it. See, it says M c A L I S T E R." Without any prompting, Mary Anne talked for a while about her beloved grandfather.

When Albert passed it back to her, the touch of their fingers was no accident.

After the tent was ready, Joe looked serious, not his joking, jovial self. "I want to talk about the Injuns. The reason I came on this trip war to meet again with Chief Joseph of the Nez Percé tribe. W'ar meetin' at Celilo Falls. Remember I know him well 'cuz my wife Virginia is Nez Percé like Doc Newell's wife Kitty war. If you add all the time Doc and me lived thar with the Nez Percé, it's years. I speak their language and call many my brothers. Celilo Falls is bordered by Chinookan and Sahaptian speaking peoples, and the Wishram and Wasco tribes live north and south of the falls. The Nez Percé live farther east along the Snake River, but thar's dozens of different tribes 'roun' here. I tell ya this 'cuz the Injuns are not happy with us white people."

Joe explained that the explosion of discontent by the tribes started with the Whitman Massacre. At the same time, there was an epidemic of bitterness by white people, not only toward the Indians and *Métis*, but also toward The Hudson's Bay Company and the Catholics. "It war all so mixed up. People mad at people. Thar war a delegation tryin' to deprive John McLoughlin of all his property in Oregon City; others tryin' to get clemency for the accused Cayuse; Protestants against Catholics; and the usual bitter greed for land. Governor Lane was gone trying to round up deserters from the Mexican War when the five accused Cayuse Injuns came on thar own to Oregon City to face justice for their part in the Whitman Massacre. So I war the acting governor for all them problems.

"Those five Cayuse – *Tiloukikt, Tamahas, Klokamas, Isaiachalakis,* and *Kiamasumpkin* – came, knowin' they might have to give thar lives to free all thar people from shame and blame. To give your life for others is a code among some tribes.

"Thar war a great many indictments against those five, and a great many people in attendance at the court, probably two to three hundred. The grand jury found true bills against the five Injuns, and they war arraigned for trial. Thar war four lawyers.

"Mr. Holbrook, for the prosecution, laid down the case so plain that the jury war convinced before they heard any defense attorneys."

"Captain Claiborne led off for the defense. He foamed and ranted like he war acting in a play in some theatre. He knew as much about law as the Injuns he war defending; and his gestures were so powerful that he smashed two tumblers that the judge had ordered to be filled with cold water for him.

"Then came Major Runnels, who made a very good defense.

"Mr. Pritchett closed for the defense with a very able argument, for he war a man of brains.

"But the jury found 'em guilty. An' when Judge Pratt passed the sentence of death on them five, two showed no terror, but the other three war filled with fear and consternation they could not conceal. The day set for execution was the third of June in forty-nine.

"As the United States marshal, I always do my duty even when Joe Meek would rather do somethin' else. So it war my duty to bring forth the five prisoners and place them on the drop. Thousands of people were watchin' that day. It war at this moment that Chief *Kiamisupkin,* who always declared his innocence, begged me to kill him with my knife. Injuns fear a hangin'. As the U.S. marshal I could not do that. But I soon put an end to his entreaties by cuttin' the rope to the drop with my tomahawk. The trap fell, and the five Cayuses hung in the air. Three of 'em war dead instantly; the other two struggled a while. Little Chief *Tamaha*s went on the longest; he was the one who was cruel to my little Helen Mar in the massacre, so I put my foot on his knot to tighten it, and he got quiet."

With the end of his tale, they listened to the fire spit and crackle for a few minutes, but Joe was not done talking. "It seems I got away from the point I wanted to make. I wanted to warn the three of you that many tribes, mostly encouraged by the Cayuse, attack without reason. Our troops have been busy fighting Injuns since the Whitman Massacre. We need to be alert at all times on this trip." Joe took a deep breath and continued, "Tomorrow, I'm going to meet with Chief Joseph to make sure he's still on our side. He's a good man and has always supported us, but we need to keep meetin' and talkin' to have a good relation." Finally, Joe got as quiet as the night. There was nothing more to say anyway. Each sat with their thoughts on crime and punishment.

And those thoughts were to become apropos within the coming moments.

The fire was fading into embers when Joe stood and headed to water the trees. The other three, still sitting around the fire and staring into the warm glow, slowly started to arrange their bedrolls. Finally Mary Anne slipped off her capote and went to pee in the trees on the opposite side from Joe. Still silent, Margaret and Big Al began arranging their things. Big Al slipped out of his coat and pulled his shirt over his head before rolling it into a tight cylinder to use as a pillow. His skin glimmered in the night; it seemed to reflect the firelight.

Finally, Joe came back and squatted to spread out his blankets. Quite a few minutes passed before he asked, "Where's Mary Anne? It ain't gonna take this long to pee, is it, Margar ...?"

Before he finished his sentence a blood-curdling cry pierced the night from the direction that Mary Anne had taken.

The shriek came again, "EEEOW!"

Joe sprang to his feet while grabbing his rifle and hurdled over the campfire to the trees, screaming, "Big Al, the horses! Don't let 'em take 'em!" On moccasined feet, Joe slipped between bushes, junipers, and trees, barely making a sound.

Margaret sat bewildered for only a second before she realized. "Indians!" She guessed that Joe meant that Indians do not travel alone;

while one went for Mary Anne, the other would go for the horses. She put her hand on her hidden drawstring bag where the derringer nestled against her groin. Her heartbeat pounded in her chest as she pulled the gun out and began to load it.

Big Al picked up his rifle and disappeared into the darkness though only going twenty-five feet away to where their six animals were hobbled.

Margaret was alone but could hear their horses shuffling around. With hobbled feet, they could not walk anywhere unless someone removed those ropes from their forelegs. Her hands worked quickly; she placed the handgun on its half-cocked notch to prevent misfiring it. She uncorked the black powder bag and poured what she guessed was twenty grains down the barrel and then rammed a lead ball down onto the powder. It was a special ball with a patched surface that prevented burning powder from escaping between the barrel and the ball. Finally she put a percussion cap on the nipple and the gun was ready to fire. As she slipped it into her waistband, she reminded herself, "All I need to do is fully cock that hammer, aim, and squeeze the trigger." She didn't like being there alone and wished that she had gone with Big Al, but it was too late now.

Meanwhile, Joe was making his way closer to Mary Anne. He could hear her struggling with her feet kicking on dry leaves and downed branches. He knew the Indian had one hand over her mouth and her head tucked in his armpit while he dragged her along in that manner. Joe could hear that he was getting closer to them; he could hear her gagged squeals. He decided to circle around.

Suddenly, another cry filled the night. This was a different voice than the first and it was a shout in English. "JOE, HELP ME!" Mary Anne screamed. "Help, please, help!" All of a sudden, her voice became muffled and stopped.

Joe puzzled about that first shriek he had heard back at the campfire. The memory of the sound rolled around in his mind without a solution. He wondered who could have made that scream.

Suddenly, Joe could see them. Just like he had thought, the Indian had Mary Anne pulled against his chest, holding her mouth with one hand. Mary Anne faced away and squirmed with arms flying. Finally, she grabbed a small sapling, twisted, and pulled free from the man.

"HELP, JOE!" she screamed in a terrifying, high pitch.

The Indian pulled his knife. Mary Anne lost her balance when her hand slipped from the small tree; she fell to the ground, screaming again. He raised the knife high above his head – the blade was ten inches long – while trying to grab Mary Anne, who scrambled and jumped around. Finally, the Indian started a downward thrust ready to sink the blade wherever it would fall; and Joe appeared from nowhere, ramming his rifle into the Indian's gut while pulling the trigger.

KABOOM! The explosion from Joe's shot filled the air and echoed from the cliffs across the river canyon. Joe grabbed the black, braided hair, picked up the dropped knife, and swiped it across the Indian's throat. Taking only a moment to slip the Indian's knife into his own belt and to yank off a necklace of feathers, Joe spoke with an urgency in his voice. "Mary Anne, now that he went beaver, let's git out of here." He held out his hand with the feathered necklace dangling from his grip and pulled her up to a stand. "We need to run back to camp. Fast!"

But they were too late.

Panting and scratched from the brush, they arrived to the glowing coals. "Big Al! Margaret!" Joe called out.

"Over here with the horses," Big Al replied before he appeared, coming toward them. He was leading the four horses and the mules followed. His lanky and shirtless form displayed hard muscles, smooth and glistening like water on a quiet lake, until he turned to wrap the leads around a tree trunk. Startled, as if a stone was thrown into the quiet lake and water cascaded onto them, Joe and Mary Anne jerked with wide eyes; they gasped upon seeing his scarred back from lashings.

And that shock led to the next. Excitedly Joe asked, "Where's Margaret?"

Mary Anne panicked and cupped her hands around her mouth to call loudly, "MAR-GAR-ET!" Then she shrieked, frantic with fear, "MAR-GAR-ET, WHERE ARE YOU?"

Big Al grabbed his coat and slipped into it while Joe bent and perched on his heels to read the ground. "They struggled here and he drug her that way. That's two Injuns; the one I killed with Mary Anne and this one. Thar are probably more." Joe stood and slipped another knife in his belt, "Give me my horse. I'll ride bareback. Big Al, you stay with Mary Anne and the other horses. Keep the mules over har, too. And build up the fire agin so ya'll see them coming." Joe brandished a handgun that he pulled from his bedroll, "Mary Anne, take my Colt. If they git close to ya, shoot thar heart. That's the easiest to hit. That gun's got six bullets."

"I know how to shoot."

"Good," Joe said as he slipped the bit into his horse's mouth and secured the headstall. He flipped the reins into place and grabbed the mane to pull himself onto the horse's back. In a blink, Joe leaned into the withers and disappeared into the darkness.

The two worked quickly to fetter the horses again. "Maybe we shouldn't put these back on. Is it better if they are ready to ride?" Big Al commented as if to himself.

Mary Anne was crying while pulling one of the mules closer. She remembered the thrill when they had begun this trip – her excitement of going to see Celilo Falls and different tribes of Indians. But now, she feared losing Margaret. Irritated, she jerked the head of the mule, "Why are these animals so stubborn? Oh, Big Al, I can't relax. When that Indian was dragging me, I was more scared than ever in my life."

Big Al took the reins of the mule from her and touched her hand as he did. They looked at the other's face and froze. Embarrassment flowed, not from the touch, but from the feelings he was having for her. He reached for his handkerchief and started to hand it to her, but decided to wipe her tears himself. With the mule bumping his shoulder, he dabbed her cheeks; they stood only inches apart. All of a sudden, the mule gave him a push and his arms flew around her so as to not fall. She grabbed around his waist to maintain her balance and their faces touched. When he started to step back from her, he changed his mind and said, "I don't want to miss this opportunity," and he kissed her.

It was a long kiss, and when he stepped back he exclaimed, "Blood! Mary Anne, are you hurt? You have blood all over your neck and clothes."

"I'm fine. I'll explain later." This time she kissed him. Finally they got their wits about them and remembered that they were in danger. Mary Anne said, "I'm going to grab those downed tree limbs over there for firewood, but I want you to understand that I'm not going out of your sight to get more."

Soon the fire was blazing again.

All of a sudden, a shot rang out in the distance. Mary Anne and Big Al sat up straight and tensed. A minute passed and then several shots were fired from the same direction Joe had gone. Without words, they stood and held their guns ready to use.

"Let's stand back-to-back so we can see in a complete circle," Big Al suggested. He had both hands on his rifle and asked, "Is that revolver ready to fire? Make sure it is."

Mary Anne pulled back the hammer about half way and spun the cylinder to check. It was loaded and ready.

Big Al peered into the night. "I know nothing about Indian fighting, but the horses seem uneasy, and I don't like that."

"I don't know anything either, but animals seem to know when something is going to happen." Nervously she continued to babble, "Before humans know about a coming storm, animals sense something; they probably can hear better than we do, too." Mary Anne reached for her capote and put it on. The temperature was dropping, yet she shivered more from fear than the cold. "I can't stop shaking. I keep recalling being dragged through the woods. Why didn't he just kill me? What was he going to do with me?"

"Let's stop talking and listen."

From time to time, they put another piece of wood on the fire. Joe had been gone for quite a while. Mary Anne was tired and her legs ached. Clouds came in and a drizzle started. She put the capote over her head, and Big Al picked up his hat.

Even with the river quite a distance from them, a rumble from the flowing water filled the night. The river, the crackling of the fire, and movements from the horses were the only discernable sounds until Mary Anne detected hoof beats. She tapped Big Al's shoulder and pointed in the direction of the new sound. He nodded and whispered, "Get your gun ready to shoot." They each turned to face the oncoming thudding of the hooves.

Before they could see who was riding, Joe called out, "Big Al! Mary Anne? It's me and Margaret coming. Answer me if all is well."

Mary Anne screamed, "Joe, Joe, we are here!"

Big Al gave a more appropriate response, "All's well; no trouble in camp."

As Joe rode up, Margaret slipped down to the ground, holding the reins of two appaloosa horses behind her.

"Be sure to lower those firearms," Joe said as he dismounted. "We don't need any more excitement tonight with a misfiring."

Margaret exclaimed, "Mary Anne, you are covered with blood!"

Mary Anne pulled her capote aside and reached into the pocket of her skirt, "That Indian had his filthy hand over my mouth so I wouldn't scream, but it slipped after a while. One finger went between my lips and I bit him. See, I bit right through his little finger and had this in my mouth!" She held up the tip of his finger.

Joe reached out his hand, saying, "That's the first screams we heard. Am I right? The Injun screamed in pain."

Mary Anne nodded and dropped the severed joint into his palm.

"Well, ya women definitely have more gumption than I ever guessed. Margaret got out a little pistol hidden in her clothes and shot her Injun b'fore I was close enough ta help."

Margaret smiled. "Now that it's over, I can smile. But I was terrified. He was pulling me by my head with his hand over my mouth. I kept trying to reach for the gun tucked near my waist, but I couldn't get it. He kept bumping me into trees and bushes. I was afraid the gun would fall out of the pouch. Lucky for me, we heard shots ahead of us and he stopped. He dropped me and pulled his tomahawk. Well, I pulled my little pistol and shot him in the face. I didn't want to try for the chest and have him only half-dead. I knew if he had any strength after being wounded he would be ready to hack me with that tomahawk." Margaret took a deep breath, "Of course, I didn't know if my ordeal was over even with that dead Indian next to me. I was afraid to move."

Joe spoke up, "It war b'fore Margaret shot her gun that I war walkin' my pony so not to make a lot of noise. Then I hear'd Injuns talking. I mounted and rode up to the two of 'em to see if they war friendly or not. They made it clear they warn't! So, I shot one and, after the other tossed a tomahawk at me, I shot him, too. I dismounted and got thar horses and hid to wait to see if more war comin' or not. That's when Margaret fired her gun. I didn't know it war Margaret, but I went to see. I feared she war dead."

Margaret finished the story, "After I killed that Injun, I heard someone coming and was scared to death, not knowing if it was Joe or not. Finally he called out my name and I answered him."

Big Al went to look at the appaloosas, "Were the Indians Nez Percé? They're known for these beautiful horses."

Joe grinned, "No, no. These war Cayuse. The horses war stolen or traded. I know I told you that many tribes are on the warpath against all the Americans, but not the Nez Percé." Joe turned, "Let's talk tomorrow. I'm so tired and thirsty. After I guzzle all the water in my water bag, I'm going to sleep. Big Al, you have first watch. Wake me when you're tired. I jus' want to say 'All's well that ends well.' That's what Doc always said."

Mary Anne volunteered, "I'll stay on watch with Big Al. Four eyes and ears are better than two. Besides, the sooner I wash all this Cayuse blood from my dress the better."

Margaret agreed, "Yes, I'll go on watch with Joe. I'm still so scared. I'm not going to feel safe with only one person on watch. It's too easy to fall asleep and be attacked."

Late in the night with the flickering light of the fire presenting hypnotic illusions in her mind, Mary Anne relived her abduction by the Cayuse. She smelled the pungency of her attacker's skin and heard the forceful words he spat at her. His hate of her – of the people coming to live and take their homeland – was obvious. Mary Anne glanced at Big Al, who sat in silence with his own thoughts, and wondered if he hated the white people. She thought he had just cause from the scars across his back. Thinking about just cause, she believed that there is no true justification for giving someone a lashing. Mary Anne looked away from the kind and handsome man on watch with her and remembered his kiss.

The night passed without further incidents.

Young Chief Joseph with Family in Leavenworth

The photo was taken after they were exiled, at some time between 1877-1885.
He said, "From where the sun now stands, I will fight no more forever."

CHAPTER 12

ARRIVAL TO CELILO FALLS, 1852

Late in the day on Sunday, the four travelers approached Fort Drum, a settlement at The Dalles. In the late thirties, the Methodists had established a mission there under Jason Lee. It was called Wascopam, after the Wasco tribe. Joe recalled arriving at that mission years ago. "It war a Sunday jus' like today and we war starvin' and cold. But we came from the other direction – the east. Jason Lee refused to give us any food 'cuz it war the Sabbath. We left in the snow and came to an Injun camp where they fed us and offered all they had. I never liked Lee after that."

In the early forties, American settlers started to arrive at Wascopam with their wagon trains and found it to be the end of the trail for wagons. Joe said, "Doc and me, with our families, brought the first wagons here in 1840 and abandoned our wheels because there was no Barlow Trail yet. We walked the rest of the trip into the Willamette Valley. We traveled the same trail we rode yesterday 'cuz we had no horse for everybody."

After the Whitman Massacre, the Cayuse Wars began in 1848 and the missionaries at The Dalles abandoned the site; a volunteer militia soon occupied the buildings to fight the tribes; it was a never-ending war. Joe told his group, "A couple of years ago, 'bout 1850, the U.S. Army made this abandoned mission a post 'cuz they're still fightin' the tribes. So, we'll be welcomed here today." He laughed, "They can't turn away a U.S. marshal and his deputy like Jason Lee did. And it's sure they'll serve us some decent grub." In his usual joking way, he said, "Why, if you have any letters to mail, thar's even an official United States Post Office, too."

When they finished their meal and the military officials excused themselves from the table, Mary Anne asked, "Joe, I've been worrying all day about being attacked again. What would have happened to Margaret and me if you hadn't saved us?"

"Well, I don't rightly know. They didn't want to kill you or they would have. I imagine they jus' wanted to take you as slaves or wives. If they'd had the chance, they'd have killed me and Big Al for the horses."

Relief filled Margaret's voice. "I'm so glad we're in a fort tonight.'

Mary Anne added, "And surrounded by troops with lots of rifles."

"What's our plan for tomorrow?" Big Al asked. "You never told us a plan. I'd like to know if we have more days of possible attacks ahead."

"It's jus' an hour or more from here to Celilo Falls. We'll have the army escort us there, and they'll come with us on our way back to Portland, too. Days ago – before I knew that the three of you war coming with me – I sent word to meet Chief Joseph; he may be thar already. I want at least one of the officers from this fort to go with us. We men will sit down and talk peace with Chief Joseph."

"I thought you told us the Nez Percé are peaceful."

"They are. And last night I told you that Old Chief Joseph is a good man; he converted to Christianity and wants peace with us whites. He's not jus' a good man; he's smart. I came to talk to git his help with stopping the fighting of other tribes. He's a powerful man among the tribes." Joe continued to explain that Chief Joseph always comes to the falls at this time of year. "Do you know how important a place it is for all the tribes?"

Margaret said that she did, but Mary Anne and Big Al shook their heads.

Many times in the year, tribes meet at Celilo Falls, and they have done that for thousands of years. Joe smiled, "All the different tribes come to swap what they have, like dentalia, obsidian, and buffalo meat. As you know thar's no buffalo in Oregon, so I'm hopin' to eat some. At this time of year, they're probably going to exchange buffalo hides, wappato, pipestone, and slaves, too.

"It's quite a place. The Wishram and Wasco tribes are great fishermen and built wooden scaffolds out over the river below the falls. They got nets with long handles and spears far fishin'. To keep fish for winter or trading, they dry 'em, by smokin' or by poundin' with stones, after cooked, until real fine and that's when they press it real tight into heavy bales. Them squares they call pemmican. They catch lamprey eel, sturgeon, and different kinds of salmon. I don't much like to eat fish; I like buffalo or beef. And I prefer a slab of buffalo meat, not that pemmican stuff they pound up."

Big Al asked, "How long we gonna be there?"

"Well, I reckon jus' one night and then we'll head back to the cities. Thar's a trial, and I gotta be in the courtroom a week from tomorrow. I got the jury all lined up, but thar's a witness I gotta find."

Margaret leaned over to face Mary Anne. "So, tomorrow you will see the falls. Are you excited?"

Mary Anne nodded, "Especially now that I know the army will be with us for the rest of the trip."

Joe laughed, "I thought you war dead set on seein' Injuns. I guess ya got closer than ya wanted." Then Joe sobered. "Tomorrow you gonna meet many good people. The Nez Percé women are special to me. They'll make you welcome."

Margaret asked, "I know French, so I must ask something. Will they all have pierced noses with decorations?"

A horselaugh exploded from Joe. When he settled down, he explained that the name Nez Percé is a misnomer given by the interpreter of the Lewis and Clark expedition in 1805 when one tribe was confused with another. "They put the wrong name in their journals, on maps, in documents, and letters. It war a mistake that we still use today." In French, *nez percé* means pierced nose, but it was the Chinook tribe that had the nose decorations. "The Nez Percé people call themselves *Nimiipuu*, which means The People, but all of us use the wrong name. Well, when I am with the *Nimiipuu*, I don't."

They departed from Fort Drum before the first light, and while they rode the sun rose into a celestial explosion of fuchsia, pink, and yellow; the display disappeared in minutes and left blue sky with wisps of clouds on the horizon. A fierce wind was blowing. Leaving The Dalles, the group made an impressive sight as U.S. Marshal Meek led a long line of horses with Deputy Bayless at his side; the two women followed them and were comforted by the fact that a squadron of soldiers marched in the rear. It was a twelve-mile trip, and in less than an hour the roar of the falls could be heard before seen.

All of sudden, the scene opened into a panoramic view for miles with

Celilo Falls the centerpiece. Behind the falls, wavy hills rolled along the horizon above the Columbia River. In those few miles, the hills cascaded down to where the land was flat and filled with scrub before it reached the edge of the bluff that dropped to the river. There were no trees in sight. The rim rocks made sheer cliffs of stone that dropped straight down for what looked to be one hundred feet, and the river surged past and turned at the point the falls appeared. The crescent shaped falls were over one hundred feet wide. The riders stopped while facing the falls and could see the Columbia coming toward them; the power and beauty created foaming, rushing, and frothing waters that fell for eighty feet to explode upward into mist. The height of the falls was like the height of the bluffs but in contrast – one moving, roaring, and white – the other stiff, silent, and dark.

Mary Anne turned to Margaret and shouted, "Where does that much water come from? How can there be that much water going on and on, never stopping?"

The noise prevented comment or discussion; nevertheless, each of them wondered the same. Nature never ceased to amaze.

Finally, Joe led them away from the river toward the bluffs. The roar of the water abated. Many people of different tribes were in the area. Joe dismounted and walked back to talk with the army officer in charge before returning to Margaret and Mary Anne to explain. "This is whar we set up our tents, by those scraggly shrubs. It's more quiet so we can talk."

The place was a little village with dozens of groups working here and there – smoking fish, making nets, weaving baskets, cooking – and children running everywhere. There seemed to be as many dogs as children, but the dogs mainly were snoozing or resting next to cook fires, waiting for a handout. Many pole tents were scattered around, and with the arrival of troops, people peered from the doorways.

Joe explained that this time of the year was not the time of the big gathering when hundreds, if not thousands, would come to fish and meet. "Tribes from afar come when thar's salmon jumping up to spawning grounds. These people you see are more local tribes coming for a fresh fish dinner," Joe chuckled. "I don't see that Chief Joseph is here yet. Like I said, I hope he brings some buffalo meat. I ain't had none in quite a time. Why don't you look around? Thar's some men fishing off the wood platforms."

Margaret agreed, "Let's take care of our horses and go look around. I speak Chinook Jargon, so we can talk to the women. We shouldn't talk to the men; that's an insult if we don't know them."

People had erected different types of structures for sleeping and to remain out of the cold weather. Some used poles in the typical conical shape with hides draped over them. The discarded boards from the fishing platforms also were used to form a tent. Everywhere one looked were indications of how the Indians used the buffalo. Besides the obvious need of meat for food, fat for fires, and covers for their lodges, they used strings from guts and strips from hides for bowstrings, cordage, thread for clothing, and trail ropes for horses. Also, from the hides, they made boats and vessels for water storage. From the innards and juices the Indians made glue and medicines. Because of all these products, the buffalo was invaluable – for themselves and for trading with other tribes.

Mary Anne and Margaret walked over to watch a group of three women pounding something into a powder. Margaret talked with them and told Mary Anne that when meat was dried, pounded, and mixed with fat, it was called pemmican like Joe had told them; it could be stored for months. "Remember, when Joe talked about it, he said that he doesn't like it, but it can be stored for months, so it is necessary. Pemmican could be made from moose, elk, deer, as well as bison, and these women often fancied-up the pemmican with chokeberries, currants, or other berries. Another staple that they make to get through the winter is the camas cake from the roots of the camas lily."

"Oh, yes, I learned about camas roots from you and Doc. Remember?" Mary Anne said.

Here and there, men sat or crouched while smoking a pipe or eating; they sat with robes draped over their shoulders, against the wind and dropping temperatures.

Margaret and Mary Anne went to watch men fishing from the large platforms built out over the river; some used nets with long handles, while others had spears. The men wore tunics and leggings of deer skins decorated with beadwork and fringes. A few dressed like Joe.

After leaving the water's edge and walking back through the village, Mary Anne said, "Look at that woman weaving some kind of net. Can you ask her what it's for?"

Margaret and Mary Anne approached the woman, who sat alone beside a bush. They gathered their skirts into their arms to squat next to her and learned that she was weaving a snare. She explained that several women would drive stakes into knee-deep water and wrap the snare around the stakes; when fish tangled in the netting, the women removed the whole net with the fish wiggling and squirming to be free. Then the woman pointed to a fire with smoking embers where two other women worked, drying the fish they had caught. The fish had been filleted and spread on sticks, arranged in a conical shape over the smoking fire, only inches apart. Two native women walked around their smoker, turning each piece over and over, never resting. However, on some days the fish was dried with only the wind blowing through the slivers of salmon.

At that moment, Joe walked up. "Look, Chief Joseph is comin'. I'll bring Big Al and one of the officers with me so we can greet him. Just watch and talk with the women until I come for you."

Mary Anne counted thirty Nez Percé riding into the village area on beautiful horses; many were appaloosas. Chief Joseph wore a full crest of eagle feathers with braids at his temples and draped over his shoulders. He sat tall and graceful, with a buffalo robe tied at his waist and hanging loosely from his shoulders. A rifle rested across his thighs, and a tomahawk protruded from beneath his robe.

His son, a young boy, was at his side with the same temple braids hanging loosely and the rest of his hair pulled to the nape of his neck and decorated with feathers that flitted in the air; he appeared not to have reached manhood, yet he displayed the bearing and confidence of his father. He held a powerful-looking bow across the horse's withers and had arrows in a quiver made from dog skins, hanging from his shoulder down his back.

Behind them, the only man with face paint rode bareheaded and with unfettered hair. Beneath his open bearskin robe, a breastplate cascaded down his chest with a talisman of bones, lizard feet, and a wing of a small colorful bird tied to it. Hanging from his saddle was a medicine bag, whistles made from wing bones of the war-eagle, and pipes for smoking.

Two stunning women followed next. They were dressed in soft, white deer hides from neck to toe. Their unbraided hair had elaborate arrangements of loops and tucks all over their heads.

Margaret whispered to Mary Anne, "The women in the white skins must be Chief Joseph's wives and daughters. There is special clay found on the prairies that's used to chalk the skins. It's a sign of their family stature to be in white. Look at all the shells and sparkling trinkets they have around their necklines. They live far from the sea and must trade for the shells. Probably they trade at Celilo Falls, when people of many nations gather in the fall of the year. Watch when they take off those white robes they wear for warmth; you will see a lot of long fringe and colorful beadwork."

The different rank of the tribe members was shown by their order behind the chief. Various men came wrapped in cloaks of dark hides, and women followed clad in natural-colored deerskins or antelope hides. They were a tall people, straight and well-proportioned, with smooth and clear skin. They prided themselves on strength and stamina. Both men and women carried objects of war, such as lances with fluttering feathers; bows with arrows hung in a quiver down their backs, and tomahawks, but a few had rifles and powder horns. Children of all ages – some riding with their mothers and older ones riding two or three on a horse – were dispersed among the group. Scattered throughout the procession were dogs straggling alongside, and last came the horses and mules – some dragging lodge poles that made furrows in the ground, and others burdened with supplies.

With Celilo Falls the backdrop for this regal scene, Margaret watched them parade past. The whole spectacle, literally breathtaking, moved her soul. Yet, when the wind whispered their future fate, her stature sagged; she drew a deep breath and sighed while she thought. *Why can we not learn to live with them? Why must we take their lands? Why must we destroy their way of life?*

When the Nez Percé stopped, Mary Anne saw that Meek waited for them to dismount before he approached with Big Al and the army officer. They all shook hands, and Joe spoke. She wondered what he was saying. A few minutes passed in conversation before Joe and his two men turned and walked toward Mary Anne and Margaret.

Joe explained, "Chief Joseph said he'll meet with us three men after the sun goes down. We'll smoke the pipe, eat, and then talk. For now, his people are settin' up their camp and goin' to cook while he rests." Joe smiled, "He brought buffalo meat. He remembered how much I like it. Let's rest, too. It will be a long night."

Like the other evenings, Mary Anne retrieved her tinderbox and, in a few minutes, she had started the fire. Albert watched her and could not stop smiling.

Joe and Big Al reclined around their campfire. The two women sat. Before Joe closed his eyes, he began to talk of the Nez Percé. "Horses war a part of their ways for hundreds of years. Look over thar at those thar horses. See them gettin' 'em ready to graze. Those bridles war made from braided horsehairs, and the stirrups are wood covered in wet deerskins that shrinks to cover 'em tight. The Mexicans got saddles and stirrups that look a lot like those. So you see the saddles? Some are jus' stuffed deerskins. Those with wooden backs are for the important women. You know, the wives of a chief. They got different rankin' for a chief. The father of my wife, Virginia, war a sub-chief."

Mary Anne asked, "How long did you live with the Nez Percé?"

"Oh, I don't rightly know. Off and on for years. Like I said, horses are the most important part of thar lives. They really delight in horse racing. But I think thar favorite pastime is betting on the horse races. Ha! I been in many a race and lost all sorts of things with my bets. Even my pants!"

They took a minute to laugh and enjoy the humor through their mind's eye, which pictured Joe returning to his lodge without pants.

Margaret asked, "How far did they travel to come here?"

"No more than us." That said, Joe closed his eyes and, in an instant, dozed.

From the edge of the Nez Percé land, Chief Joseph's party had traveled westward nearly the same distance as Joe's group had gone eastward. The Nez Percé lived east of where the Columbia River turned north and where hundreds of miles of the Snake River cut through the middle of their territory. Their land was a place of many rivers and streams, yet, instead of having many canoes, horses were their means of travel. The Blackfeet, Shoshones, and Crows inhabited the land to the north and east of them and were hostile neighbors. With the dwindling buffalo herds, the conflicts were more frequent. Unlike the Indians along the Willamette and Columbia Rivers, who were great fishermen, these eastern tribes were excellent horse riders, even the women. A man's wealth was in horses, and some of the chiefs claimed to own fifteen hundred head. With the need for horses in hunting, travel, and warfare, many of these tribes were quick to steal horses. And in hard winters, when game was scarce, the horse was important for another reason; these tribes would subsist on horseflesh.

Margaret retrieved an old journal to read what she had written years ago. She spoke in a soft voice so as not to disturb the men. "While we still have light, I want to reread my old journal that I brought. Oh, Mary Anne, I am really making progress with my book. I am using journal entries from years ago."

Mary Anne nodded and stirred the coals with a stick before turning to Joe to say, "The sun is almost down. Isn't it time for you to go visit Chief Joseph?"

Joe threw out his arms to stretch and stood, "Yes, I see his lodge is up." He pointed, "Look through the cracks in the buffalo skins; I see a fire glowing, more important, outside the lodge I see kettles hanging from poles and meat strung across the cooking fire. So thar's no time to waste; I need to talk to you three. Big Al, are ya awake?"

"I am." He sat up with his blankets still around him and, hearing a raucous above, he peered to the sky.

Joe left to pee. "I'll be back to talk."

A dozen ravens passed, squawking and croaking, as they flew – buteo-like – toward their roosting site. A pair of ravens dropped from the group and did a somersault for reasons only the birds understood, making bubbling and clicking sounds during their acrobatics. Minutes later, the flock of ravens flew into the distant bluffs and landed to roost. Soon, a great blue heron floated overhead, and a flock of a hundred geese noisily came and went.

In a soft voice and with a far-off look in his eye, Albert began telling of the passenger pigeons he had seen. "When I came by wagon train, we saw the noisiest birds, and there were millions of them. The sky went black for the whole day while they flew over."

Margaret interjected, "Those were the passenger pigeons. Is that correct?"

"I didn't know their name. The pilot on our wagon train just called them wild pigeons. We killed hundreds to eat that day. No! Maybe thousands. When we drove away in the wagons the next day, the ground was littered with the remains and feathers fluttering in the breeze as well as carcasses of those we didn't clean and cook. There were too many."

Mary Anne looked amazed. "Why did they waste them?"

"We ate all we could and cooked more for the next day." Albert blinked a few times. "It felt wrong though to leave so many."

Mary Anne turned and said, "Margaret, do you remember when we were in New York City, and they were selling wild pigeons for thirty-five cents a dozen?"

"I do remember. Big Al, I am appalled to hear how those people killed the birds and then did not eat them. What's wrong with people? Don't they think? Don't they realize that everything in our world is balanced to work together. Take what you need, but don't waste. That is a sin."

The group of four was quiet and deep in thought for a few minutes while the people in the Celilo village bustled about, preparing for the end of the day. Many were gathered around their fires and eating.

"Listen, back to what I was sayin' 'bout it bein' time for me ta go." Joe began, "I war thinkin' 'bout what I can give Chief Joseph. It's polite to do that when ya meet a chief. The bag of coffee I brought ain't enough, so I decided that the three of you war a-goin' to be another part of my gift." He stopped talking to tuck his shirt into his belt.

"Okay, Joe," Margaret huffed. "I know your ways; you're waiting for me to ask you what you mean. But I know you're not going to GIVE us to the chief."

Joe sat down with the others and grinned from ear to ear. "Margaret, now don't spoil my fun. These other two don't know all 'bout me." He slapped his thigh and laughed before he proceeded to explain that he was going to present three unusual people to Chief Joseph. "I'll call you into his tent after we pass the pipe. So, wait outside and be ready."

Margaret was irritated, "That's all you're going to tell us. Do we have to prepare in some way?"

"Nah, I want to surprise you three." He began to leave and turned. "Oh, Margaret, that's a good idea. If you think of somethin' unusual that we could give to the chief, bring it along."

They watched Joe as he walked away, scratching his shoulder and then under his arm and finally lifting his hat and smoothing his unruly hair. He knew they were looking and wiggled his butt at them.

Big Al chuckled, "How'd he know we'd see that?"

Margaret said, "That's one of the reasons he's a good Indian fighter. He must have eyes in the back of his head. Virginia always says 'There's no man like Joe' and I agree."

"He's a good man. He's been kind to me," Big Al said before he went to the bushes.

Both Mary Anne and Margaret nodded in agreement.

Margaret picked up her journal and started to read again. She turned a page and it was empty. Surprised, she exclaimed, "Oh, somehow I skipped this page years ago when I wrote this."

Mary Anne cocked her head in thought for a moment. "May I have it? I know how important paper is to you, but I want to make a surprise for Chief Joseph."

"Ah-ha, you want my paper, but won't let me in on the secret."

"No, but I'll give you a hint." Mary Anne smirked. "It is something I learned when we were in Boston at your sister's house."

Celilo Falls provided a constant drone of soothing sounds in the distance. The moon rose in the east, quivering at the horizon; it was close to full, and an owl flew past making a silhouette within the huge, shining globe. On the way to Chief Joseph's meeting, the three passed a woman squatting next to her small lean-to with her dog at her side; she had made her lodging, with only enough space for her and the dog to sleep, from the boughs broken from bushes; her cook fire looked dangerously close to the greenery of her shelter. Mary Anne worried that it could burst into flames and start a wildfire. The native woman showed no worry and scratched behind the dog's ear. A chanting came from a distant part of the village and giggles rolled out of some lodges where children still played.

They walked to the edge of the bluff to view the falls. Mary Anne looked down, and a rush of vertigo encouraged her to take a step back. No one said a word, for the beauty and experience of being there was beyond words. Somewhere inside their chests, an unknown part of their anatomy filled with something more precious than gold, and it would last their lifetimes. Finally, content with the universe, they turned and saw the gorge in the night, stretching blue and purple west of the glowing, white waters of Celilo Falls.

They waited outside Chief Joseph's lodge for only a few minutes before Joe stuck out his head to beckon them to come in. They stooped and entered a cozy, smoky space filled with smells of cooked meat. They walked upon a soft floor carpeted with buffalo robes. Their stomachs growled, and they glanced to each other and smiled. They were hungry, but protocol demanded other formalities before food. Joe motioned with his hand for them to stop and stand as he continued forward. The bonfire in the center was embers and a trail of wispy smoke drifted up and out the center hole at the top of the lodge. Only a dull light from that smoldering fire lit the place. A dozen or so men sat cross-legged around the warmth, and Joe went to his place and joined the circle. Joe sat to the left of Chief Joseph; the chief's son sat on the right. Three of the army officers sat behind Joe and all of the Nez Percé that had arrived with Chief Joseph were scattered around the edges and against the walls of hides. Many were talking.

Joe began to speak in a strong voice, and the place became quiet. He spoke their native tongue. "Chief Joseph, to honor you I bring three unusual people. I want to share my knowledge of these friends of mine, and they will become your friends. They are people of value."

Murmurs passed between the men of the inner circle. Frowns were on some faces, for gifts were usually given, not just shown.

In English, Joe asked, "Big Al, will you step forward and enter close to the fire for all to see?" Then Joe returned to speak in their language, "This man is my deputy, Albert Bayless, and he carries his bravery upon his skin. I call him Big Al to honor him." When Big Al was close to Joe, people began to see he was a Negro who most had never seen. "His face is not painted like you sometimes paint your skin," Joe said. "He is a Negro from a land across an ocean far away in a place where all the people carry the night upon their skin. If you of the *Nimiipuu* nod your heads in kindness, I'll ask him to remove his shirt for you to see his bravery."

Everyone nodded, so Joe explained in English to Big Al, who agreed to show his torso. The lodge filled with sounds of amazement as the shirt was pulled over his head and dropped to the floor of hides. Big Al walked around the edge of the fire and, as he passed each person, all could see the deep and ragged scars from his lashings.

Chief Joseph stood when Big Al came full circle, "I speak English and want to talk with you. Joe said that you have the night upon your skin." The chief chuckled, "Joe likes to treat us like ignorant heathens." He raised his eyebrows and shrugged. "I like to play along for a while and let Joe feel like he understands the *Nimiipuu*. But I say to you that I know of a place called Africa where your brothers live. You are not the first Negro I have seen. I know of the slavery that your people endure. I see your bravery on your back. Are you a free man now?"

"I am." Then Big Al smiled and admitted, "I know about Joe's humor. I have heard his stories, and I know he is a good man. Joe has been generous to me, and I am thankful. So I agreed to show the scars on my skin because I understand the curiosity of people."

"Good! First, please shake hands with all my chiefs and elders in the circle. Let them touch your arms if they wish. Then I tell my people that you are going to sit at my side so they may pass to see your brave scars. Is that acceptable?"

"It is." When Big Al finished the handshakes, Chief Joseph told his people to come meet Big Al at his side." One of Chief Joseph's elders stood and asked a question. Quiet filled the tent and a full minute passed. Finally, Chief Joseph turned to Big Al to say, "I am the all-knowing Chief of my people, but I do not know how to ask what has been requested. I am embarrassed and glad that my people do not know English to hear my insecure words. Big Al, they have asked if they can touch your hair."

With a serious look upon his face, Big Al said, "I will answer your request in a language that all men understand." And a huge smile spread across his face.

Excitement filled the lodge.

As the people passed and touched – first tentatively with fingertips, then patting with open hands and at last with confident swipes with their palms – the chatter and talk increased to laughter. When all had passed and touched, Chief Joseph clapped his hands for quiet again.

Joe presented the second guest, "Margaret, it's your turn. Please step forward. I'll present ya in English and let Chief Joseph translate." He waited for Margaret to walk to him and said, "This here woman war the first white woman to work a homestead in Oregon. What I really mean is that she's the first white woman to work as hard as the women from tribes who married a white man. She and her husband got a farm with sheep and pigs and chickens and crops of corn and wheat. She also war the first person, before any man, to write poetry for the newspapers. That means it war preserved forever. Margaret, can you recite a short poem of yours?"

"Yes, I wrote one about the Indians my first year in Oregon Country. That was seventeen years ago. I had just come from the East where the people call the Indians by a horrible word." She turned and looked into Chief Joseph's eyes. "I am ashamed to say that they call you savages."

Chief Joseph nodded, "I know."

Margaret began:

We call them savage–O be just;
Their outraged feelings scan;
A voice comes forth, 'tis from the dust–
The savage was a man!
Think you he loved not? Who stood by,
And in his toils took part?
Woman was there to bless his eye –
The savage had a heart!
Think you he prayed not? When on high
He heard the thunders roll,
What bade him look beyond the sky?
The savage had a soul!

Chief Joseph stood and looked into Margaret's face. Then he stepped to her and extended his hand, "Thank you. That was beautiful. Please allow me to tell my people about you in our words. Please join our circle next to Joe."

Finally it was quiet again, and Mary Anne was summoned into the circle. Joe asked her in a quiet voice, "Did you bring a gift?" Seeing her nod, he said, "Let me introduce you in their language. What did you bring?"

"I have brought a piece of paper that I will make into a flying bird. While I work on making the bird, I shall sing life into it with my voice."

As Joe spoke, there were gasps and shared murmurs among many. When Joe finished, Chief Joseph rose to his feet and stood but four feet from Mary Anne. He said, "How can this be? I cannot understand. I wonder if this is a tall tale of Joe's making."

Mary Anne looked to Joe, who shrugged his shoulders, and she turned back. "Sometimes it makes more sense to speak about magic more than truth."

The chief nodded.

Mary Anne lifted the white paper above her head for all to see as Chief Joseph explained that she would make this white paper into a flying bird.

When she began to sing, she stood straight and quiet with her head bowing down. She started humming very quietly. She had chosen to sing *Amazing Grace*. When she was ready to sing the words, she took a step closer to Chief Joseph, where most could see. Singing, she held the paper high and started folding. The Nez Percé people had neither heard a woman's soprano voice nor anything like the clear, sweet sounds of a melody. They were accustomed to the deep chanting of men with the rhythm of drum.

Mary Anne sang quietly and clearly for the first stanza and made the first fold of the paper.

> Amazing grace! How sweet the sound
> That saved a wretch like me.
> I once was lost, but now am found,
> Was blind but now I see.

A triangle formed. She continued folding and increasing the volume of her song. The full and melodious voice became louder and rolled around the tent like an eddy in the river, flowing and washing over each person. She had chosen the correct hymn to create amazement; the astonishment showed on most faces.

When we've been there ten thousand years,
Bright shining as the sun,
We've no less days to sing God's praise,
Than when we first begun.

Chief Joseph's people had never touched paper and wondered how it could become a bird from the flat, thin sheet they had seen in the beginning. Gradually the paper became more and more angles and folds. Mary Anne repeated the verses as she worked. That the natives did not know the words or their meanings, did not matter; the sound of her voice and the tantalizing melody enthralled them. And rhyming words need no translation. Finally, when she was singing loudly, she turned in a circle for all to see the origami swan that moved its wings in flight when she pulled the tail.

Chief Joseph and his people smiled in their eyes and hearts. Murmurs between many filled the tent.

Mary Anne ended her song and handed the swan to Chief Joseph. He stood and pulled the tail to make it fly and then he gave out a hearty, full belly laugh.

"Bravery from one, rhyming words about our people from the next, and finally a flying bird that sings more beautifully than any we have heard. We are honored and thank you, but now it time to fill our bellies like you filled our souls.

First, the circle of elders and the guests were brought food. Boiled buffalo was ladled from the kettles with implements of horn.

Joe ate his buffalo meat through a long, relaxed meal.

At some unseen signal, the people outside the main inner circle started exiting. While they were leaving, Joe leaned over and explained that Mary Anne and Margaret should leave and go back to their tent, "It's time to talk turkey here. It ain't goin' to be a short meetin', either."

As Mary Anne bent to scoot under the flap to leave, she glanced back to Joe. With a stern look on his face, he held the feathered necklace that he had ripped from the neck of Mary Anne's attacker. One word, said forcefully by Joe, she could hear; he said, "Cayuse." Chief Joseph took the necklace and frowned. Then Joe showed the severed finger.

Hours later, Margaret arose from her blankets and left the tent to pee. She saw that Big Al was sleeping with his feet near the glowing embers and with his head resting on his saddle. He snored in a soft, irregular drone. Joe was not there.

Returning from the bushes, she stopped upon seeing Chief Joseph and Joe standing not far from the corner of her tent. In diminished voices yet distinct, she could hear every word. They were not aware of her presence.

Joe said, "But you agreed to accept a reservation of your tribal lands that includes the sacred Wallowa Valley."

Chief Joseph was emphatic, "Joe, I do agree, but I want more. I want an additional promise for my people, not just the land. We ask that the same laws shall work alike on all men. If an Indian breaks the law, punish him by the law. If a white man breaks the law, punish him also. Let me be a free man – free to travel, free to stop, free to work, free to trade where I choose, free to talk and think and act for myself."

Joe bobbed his head, "Equality of mankind. I understand and agree. But for many, that's a tall order." Joe held out his hand and they shook. "I'll do my best for you. Goodnight, *Tuekakas.*"

Gravestone for Albert and Mary Ann Bayless in
Salem Pioneer Cemetery on Commercial Street, Salem.
Lot: 369   Spaces: 1-2 NE

The Salem Pioneer Cemetery is cared for by:
City View Funeral Home
390 Hoyt Street S, Salem, Oregon
 (Offices located across from the cemetery entrance.)
www.city-view.org

CHAPTER 13

BACK FROM TRAVELS, 1852

Without a doubt and without opening her eyes, Mary Anne knew it was morning. The soft glow on her eyelids assured her of the coming of another day. However, to determine where she was greeting this day, she needed to open her eyes because she had traveled over an assortment of places in the last few days, and her mind was not awake enough to remember where she had gone to bed.

Mary Anne fluttered her eyelids and saw a hotel room, and she remembered. *Ah, yes! Portland! And Margaret is in the room across the hallway.*

Pleasantness filled her as she thought of Albert Bayless and she decided to lounge longer under the warm covers. "Well, after I use the chamber pot," she said aloud. When relieved, she slipped back into the bed and allowed her thoughts to travel back over the past days. The return trip from Celilo Falls had been uneventful. "Thank heavens!" Musing about the trip, her thoughts turned again to Big Al and her body tingled. She touched her lips lightly with her fingertips and relived the sensations of his kiss. "Albert," she said, just to hear his name.

Mary Anne wanted to tell Margaret about the kisses. She got up and dressed amid her contentment, not knowing that problems awaited her across the hallway.

Tap, tap, tap. With her fingertips, she knocked lightly on Margaret's door.

It opened a crack. Margaret peered out with one eye – an eye displaying upset – and cleared her throat before saying, "Mary Anne, now don't be alarmed when you see me. Let me say that I am going to live."

When the door opened wider, Mary Anne gasped, "What happened?" Margaret's face was swollen on her cheekbone, and her eye was black and blue.

Margaret frowned as she closed the door behind Mary Anne, "Last night, I upset Willy and he gave me a fisticuff." She stomped her foot and raised her clenched hands. "I am so angry with him." In her agitation, Margaret began to pace from one side to the other in the small room. Coming to an abrupt stop at the window, she pointed. "From this window, I saw him with an Indian woman in a doorway down the street, so I rushed out of this hotel and confronted him." Margaret went to sit on the edge of the bed and picked up a cloth from the basin; she squeezed out the water and placed it on her cheek and eye.

Mary Anne collapsed into an overstuffed, horsehair chair, "Oh, my!"

Margaret walked to Mary Anne, "I have never had a friend like you are to me. Thank you." They hugged. "I am so glad I can share my problems with you. Most women don't like me. I know the reasons: for one thing, I refuse to conform to their ways; also, I don't say what they want to hear ... no, it's not that I don't ... I *won't* speak in a way that they think is proper; lastly, I abhor idle gossip. Don't misunderstand me, I know the proprieties that society puts on women. I only wish they would stop and think about their actions and words. Of course, I am speaking of the American women. I have never had problems with the Indian or *Métis* women."

Margaret went to rinse the cloth in the cool water again and placed it back on her face. She sighed and sat on the edge of the bed. "Sorry about that outburst." They remained in silence for several minutes. All of a sudden, she had some kind of thought and started to laugh, but grimaced from the pain caused by her bruises, "Oh dear, that hurt! No laughing today."

"Margaret, what Dr. Bailey did to you is horrible. I have seen him drunk and know how mean he can be. How do you live with his meanness? He is a different person when drunk. How do you find any meaning in your life?"

"Mary Anne, my life is full of meaning. I love my life. What are you talking about?"

The girl swallowed, "Finding the right words is difficult. When we went on this trip to Celilo Falls, I was so glad to be away from here and in a place where Jed McAlister could not find me. But he wasn't the only problem; it was more. Before the trip, I felt lost. I didn't know where my life was going. It seems like I was searching for a meaning in my life."

Margaret frowned when she said, "I disagree. Most people feel like you when there's sadness in their lives, not because they're looking for the meaning of life. No, we seek experiences of being alive. We want to feel the rapture of being alive."

"What do you mean?"

"Being dragged by a Cayuse through the woods might have scared you and made you fear for your life, but when it was over, life looked different. Didn't it? You felt more alive. Happy to be alive, when minutes before you might have been worrying about the McAlisters and feeling sorry for yourself."

Mary Anne nodded.

"Of course, I don't mean to say that something horrible must happen to you to feel some zeal for being alive. Going outside into nature, working with the soil to grow food and flowers, and caring for the cows and sheep make me glad to be alive. The point is that both the good and the bad experiences give our lives meaning." Margaret sat back on the bed and continued, "Everything in the world is connected, and people seem to forget that. We all need the other. That is the key. We must value everything in nature, even the little worm that works in the soil to make my plants better. When I turn over the dirt and see the little worm, I marvel at being alive. I marvel at how it all fits together. That little worm makes the soil better with its droppings and, by crawling in it, loosens the soil up for the roots to spread. Because of the little worm, I have corn, carrots, potatoes, and herbs to eat. I love to think about all this."

"Yes, you have said it well. Our trip to Celilo Falls made me feel this way over and over." Mary Anne stopped and puzzled for a moment, "But I think about what Mr. Newell said about the unjust laws against Negroes. And, more importantly, just knowing that Negroes die at the hand of white people, like the two Holmes children and Black Saul, who was pursued so often and finally drowned."

Margaret jumped up to interject, "Wait, do not confuse death, bad laws, evil people, or all those things with having a desire to live. Storms come, floods kill cattle and destroy crops, people have unjustified wars, and life goes on. Mary Anne, think about all this! Life goes on. The plants grow again and a calf is born to replace the dead animal. Nature repairs itself and life continues. I love seeing that. I love the experience of being alive to see the spring replenish all that winter put to sleep and to see a tree grow on the grave of a loved one."

Mary Anne shook her head. "I understand and see what you are trying to teach me. Thank you, Margaret. But, when I knocked on your door, I didn't need this kind of talk. I wanted to tell you how happy I was feeling. I'm still scared about the McAlisters, but since I met Albert, I feel so happy. He kissed me!"

Margaret waved her hands in the air and tittered, "Oh, how exciting! I knew something was happening. I think Albert is a good man. We've only known him a few days, but no one can hide their character from me."

They stood staring into the other's eyes. Finally, Mary Anne whispered, "I just want to be with Albert."

"Good, because we are going to be with him today."

They chatted for a while longer before Margaret explained the plans for the day.

Margaret patted some face powder over her bruise before reaching for her bonnet. "Now, let's go fill our lives with more experiences. We are going to see if we can get something done for the Holmes family. I'm taking the early steamer to Oregon City. This morning I want to ask the lawyer, Mr. Deady, to start working on my divorce and, at the same time, I'll pick up the papers he was preparing for the Holmeses. So I'll go to Oregon City alone. We'll meet Joe and Big Al here at the hotel at noon to go south to Nathaniel Ford's farm."

Hours later, the four headed south on horseback from Portland below a sunny sky filled with fluffy, cumulus clouds. Reflecting on thoughts of the morning conversation with Margaret, Mary Anne marveled at the quiet beauty – Mount Hood stood in the distance. But still, she was sorting out the logic of that talk. She knew how Margaret could talk in circles and never make her point.

Mary Anne turned to Joe and asked, "How can we justify taking all the lands from the Indians? They have lived on those lands for thousands of years."

Joe blurted, "Oh, it's all legal." He took off his hat and scratched his head. "Let me think 'bout this. It war 'bout twenty years ago. Yep, in 1832,

Chief Justice John Marshall expanded the definition of ownership. It war stated that whoever discovered and saw the land first war the owner. Of course, the crux of the matter war that the person who saw it had to claim it legally." He plopped his hat back on, pulled his leather water bag up, and took a drink. "You see, 'fore the white man came, the Injuns believed that no one could own the land. I mean, thar beliefs are that humans can't own land. Chief Joseph made me understand how they think by askin' me if we white people thought that we could own the ocean. To the Injuns' way of thinkin', the land is the land for all to use jus' like the rivers and oceans."

Margaret watched the clouds shift and change. She thought of how life through the ages must change like nature, which is in constant change. "Progress and change is inevitable, I know. Even in nature there is change. Mountains are eroding, lakes grow old and dry up, and even trees can't exist forever. We were not meant to remain in a life as a caveman or a hunter-gatherer. My mind knows that, yet I can't accept what we have done to the Indians." A soft breeze rippled the dry grasses of last year, and the group rode without talking for a while.

Joe finished his thoughts, "Since we took away their right of ownership, all the Injuns got left is a right of occupancy. And thar's stipulations that they can only occupy with permission from the United States."

Margaret asked, "Do you think we are correct in doing this to the Indians?"

He frowned, "I may not agree with those thar laws, but as the U.S. marshal I'll enforce what my country asks of me."

Margaret turned to Albert. "Big Al, you don't say much. What is your opinion?"

Albert grinned, "Usually, no one wants to know what I think. In fact, depending where I am, it is wiser to say nothing. But, since you asked, I accept what is. Those with the power will always win. If we want to do things differently, we must obtain the power. Often power is with the people who have the greatest numbers."

Margaret argued, "But you could fight for making a change."

Albert's gleaming white teeth shone even more with that comment, "You speak as one of the people in power. There are but a handful of

Negroes here in Oregon. Don't misunderstand me; I am thankful that some of you are for the freedom of my people."

Joe inserted a comment, "Oh, I looked at the 1850 census because I wanted to tell you how many that handful is. I war thinkin' you might like livin' in Salem. There are nine Negroes in the Salem area of Marion County. I was also thinkin' that we'd go to the smithy in Salem and see if he needs help. I know'd the blacksmith. What do you think about doin' that?"

"I would be grateful for your help."

"By the way, we're almost at the ferry in Champoeg. I know that Doc ain't home today, so we'll stop jus' to see how Rebecca's doin'. Now, you women listen to me; thar's no time to sit and chat; we got business with this Nathaniel Ford and we got a-ways to go 'cuz he lives outside of Salem. So this here is a short stop."

When they arrived at the river's edge and dismounted, Margaret turned and said, "Have I mentioned that Doc plans to build a new house on higher ground? It will be a spacious, ten-room, two-story frame structure. He showed me the plans – nothing elaborate. Well, it is impressive for Oregon at this time. He starts the construction next month and thinks they will be finished in a couple of years. He's ordering things from the East, and that's why it will take so much time to build."

"Yep, I'd heard 'bout that. Not much happens here that this U.S. marshal don't know."

When they boarded the ferry, several other people boarded with them. Joe greeted them with a "Howdy. Grand day we're havin' ain't it?"

When the ferry started off, Joe chuckled to himself and began a story. "All my years as a trapper took me across many a river and stream. Thar weren't no ferries. We had to ford the rivers. Sometimes they war flooded and sometimes they war n'ar dry." He gave a little laugh, "And sometimes those rivers saved me from a chargin' b'ar.

"Once me an' one of my trapper friends took our rifles and shot across a pretty big stream and thought we killed ourselves a b'ar. We were hungry and war dreamin' of b'ar steaks. So we had to go git him. We tied the mules and dropped everything n'ar the tree – our guns, hats, and clothes. Yep, we took every stitch off except our belts that held the knives to carve up the meat. Then we swum over to whar that b'ar war.

"But he warn't dead! He jumped up when we war close and we turned and dove back in that water faster than lightning. I swam like crazy, but when I looked around, thar war the b'ar. He war swimmin' a fast as me and his beady eyes war glazed and crazy. My friend made it to the other side, but the current had me and that b'ar floatin' down the stream side by side. My friend – why he weren't too good a friend – he war whoopin' and laughin' at me and that b'ar as we floated away. Then my luck turned. The b'ar made it to shore opposite my friend and I swam like the devil. When my feet touched bottom across from the b'ar, I hightailed it on to the muddy land. By then, we war more than a mile from whar the mules war. Thar we war with a b'ar on one side of the river, and two b'ar arses on the other."

The ferry bumped against the shore with a load of rowdy passengers doubled over in laughter. The ferryman knew Joe; everybody knew Joe. The ferryman was still chuckling when he said, "No charge for this trip, that is, if ya let me tell about my trip with Marshal Meek and his story of the bear bottoms."

"Much obliged," Meek said, and they shook hands before everyone departed.

Now across the Willamette River, they went up to Doc's house.

Within minutes it was apparent that Rebecca shouldn't be alone. She could barely walk with her large stomach and she admitted to feeling poorly. Her little girl was crying incessantly. Mary Anne volunteered to stay at the Newell house. She took the hand of the little two-year-old and said, "Let's go outside for a walk while your mama rests." Mary Anne, holding the child's hand, waved goodbye to the others.

In the distance, the three riders heard her singing as they made their way south.

The group continued down the road through the French Prairie toward Salem for some miles until they took a side road to Rickreall. Meek slowed his horse, "Let's take a break. Everyone can water the trees while I read the papers again. Nathaniel Ford's farm ain't far from here, and I want to have all my facts straight."

Margaret reminded Joe, "We're trying to kill two birds with one stone.

Most importantly, we need him to sign that paper that states that Mr. and Mrs. Holmes are free. Don't let on that we have another document until he signs the first."

"I know, Margaret. And I know my job. What Ford is doin' jus' sticks in my craw. I have a couple of names for him that I can't say in the company of a woman. When I turn to introduce you, Big Al, put your deputy badge on the outside of your coat and make sure that it's shinin' and showin'. I want him to know that a Negro has come to serve papers on him. But stay with Margaret until I talk to you."

Margaret added, "And introduce him as Deputy Albert Bayless. Use his complete name. I want Ford to understand that the deputy demands the dignity that most folks don't give him as a Negro. And I want to see all three of the children. I want them to know what's happening. I need to see Mary Jane to know that she's all right."

"When I serve Ford with the second papers, he'll most likely be angry. That's when I'll introduce my deputy."

Albert asked, "What are the second papers?"

"Robin Holmes filed a lawsuit against Ford for the freedom of the three Holmes children," Margaret explained. "A while ago, in Oregon City, I learned that Nathaniel Ford wrote a letter to a lawyer called Mr. Shirley in Missouri. Ford wanted an agent to come and claim the Holmeses as runaway slaves and return them to Missouri to sell them. The Fugitive Slave Act of 1850 would allow that because the only evidence needed is Ford's word that they are runaways."

Meek grinned, "I see. He's trying to use a law of the United States – The Fugitive Slave Act. It don't work here in Oregon. California has got that kind of law, but we don't. Ha, that's why he needs them back in Missouri." Joe slapped his thigh and laughed. "But how did the Holmeses learn that he wanted to get them back in Missouri?"

Feeling anger, Margaret's face flushed as she told them. "The Holmeses learned about the letter from one of Ford's neighbors. Ford is such a fool! It seems that Ford had the letter ready to mail when a neighbor said he was on the way to the post office. Ford asked the neighbor to mail it for him and proceeded to tell the neighbor what the letter was about: he bragged that he was going to make a lot of money off the sale of the Holmes family. Well, the neighbor mailed the letter after he had written down the address. That's when he went and told the Holmeses the whole story.

"I don't know how it happened, but the prosecuting attorney for the Oregon Territory, a Reuben Boise, heard about all this and he wrote an order for the Missouri lawyer, Mr. Shirley, to send the letter as evidence in this case."

Meek interjected, "Oh, Mr. Deady is not representing Holmes?"

Margaret nodded. "That's correct. While we were gone, Mr. Boise stepped forward to become their lawyer."

Meek seemed pleased. He thought that Deady was pro-slavery, but didn't want to say as such. Meek did tell her, "Now, Margaret, I want you to know that the dockets are full and the case may not come to the courts until next year, but we'll get this done. Mr. Boise is an excellent lawyer. Because Ford wrote that letter to Mr. Shirley, there's proof of his wrongdoings."

With that said, Joe chuckled and said, "Talking about Mr. Deady reminds me of a story. Let's git goin' and I'll bend your ears."

When they mounted the horses again, Joe said, "I remember Deady's first time on an Oregon case. Yes, sir, when Mr. Matthew P. Deady came into the courtroom, his mouth fell open. I remember this like it war yesterday. Judge Pratt war presidin' over the court, and it war held in Jacob Hawn's tavern in Lafayette, Oregon. The bench war the Judge sat war made with a table balancin' on top of two benches. I had to make him sittin' higher than everyone else 'cuz the judge is looked up to. We had to improvise to make it court-like. People brought in some nicer chairs for the lawyers, but they sat at the round tables from the saloon. Afterwards, even Mr. Deady thought we maintained the dignity needed for a courtroom. I war right proud."

"Looks like the Ford farm ahead," Albert said, pointing.

Margaret commented, "It is his farm. He choose a homestead farther south than anyone else. I understand that it has the richest soil, but he and his wife are far from neighbors and schools for their children. They are out in the middle of nowhere – no stores or any conveniences."

In the distance, they saw a man watching their approach. He held a shotgun in his hands and a black dog barked at his side. He stood on the front stoop of a small house made from lumber. A barn and some small sheds were scattered around the house. A pig was tied to a stake and wallowed in a shallow mud puddle. A couple of broken chairs leaned against the house waiting to be repaired; the hammer and a tin of rusted nails sat in the dirt near the chairs. A bucket swung from the water pump handle and squeaked with each swing.

"Good afternoon. Am I talkin' to Mr. Nathaniel Ford?" Joe asked in a loud voice.

With suspicious blue eyes squinted at the four riders, he snarled, "Who's askin'?" Ford's bushy eyebrows furrowed as he, with white knuckles, clutched the shotgun in front of his chest.

Joe slid from his horse and walked closer to show his badge, "U.S. Marshal Joseph Meek at your service. I'm escorting this woman to Salem and stopped to git your signature on some papers."

"What papers you talkin' 'bout?"

"Well, you may know, then again maybe not, that the U.S. marshal is responsible for many legal things. I heard you freed two Negroes – a Mr. and Mrs. Holmes. When things like that are done, thar's procedures. I brung the papers for you to sign and confirm it."

"I didn't know I needed to sign nothin'"

Joe smiled, "These papers are jus' normal procedures. Oh, mightin we have some water for the lady? We done drunk all we had. While you get the drink, I'll pull out the papers."

Ford returned with two tin cups in the crook of one of his fingers. He still carried his shotgun in his other hand. Joe had tied up his horse and was sitting on a stump next to the front stoop. Margaret and Albert were standing fifteen feet away and next to their horses. They watched Joe put on his charms and tell a couple of short stories. While Ford laughed, absentmindedly he leaned his shotgun against the house to free his hands to sign the paper. Once the paper was signed, Joe folded up the document and tucked it into his coat breast pocket.

When Joe placed the one paper into his pocket, he pulled the second one out and stood. With a flick of his wrist, Joe unfurled the papers and turned to Big Al. "I'd like to introduce Deputy Albert Bayless." As Ford turned to look at Albert, Joe stepped between Ford and the shotgun. Big Al pulled his coat to the side to show the badge and took several steps closer.

With that, Joe said, "We have a second document to serve you."

Like an angry bull, Ford leaned forward with cocked knees, "What's this about?" His hand pushed back his black hair from his forehead.

Joe explained, "I understand you have kept the three Holmes children as your slaves. I need to see them. And I mean, right now! These papers are filed against you for the children's freedom."

Ford turned to reach for his shotgun. "You tryin' to take me for a fool?"

Joe pulled his pistol. "Hey now! Thar ain't no reason for any upset. We jus' har to give ya these papers. You can present your side in court. But I gotta tell ya that this here one paper signed by Judge Pratt states that you must show us the three children."

Ford cursed and grabbed the paper to read. A woman, hearing the commotion, came to the door, and he looked to her and said, "Woman, go git those damn niggers. This here U.S. marshal wants to see 'em."

"But the one's sick in bed," the woman retorted.

Ford's anger escalated. His face was red and his fists flew into the air, "Jus' go git all of 'em. NOW!"

When the group of three arrived in Salem, the afternoon had disappeared with the winter sun that set at five o'clock. At a boardinghouse on State Street they sat to eat, though they had little hunger. Their faces still carried the strain of seeing the three little children and knowing that they could not give them freedom overnight. Joe had made it very clear to Nathaniel Ford that a doctor would come the next day to see the sick child. Margaret planned to make the trip again with Dr. Bailey.

"When I hugged that little girl, she was skin and bones. I could barely recognize Mary Jane as the little girl I cared for years ago." Margaret's voice cracked and she rubbed her forehead. "My heart is in my throat. I cannot eat. Especially knowing that those children are hungry and I can't help them." Mary Jane Holmes and Margaret had cried upon seeing each other.

Albert nodded, saying, "I still can hear her weak little voice saying 'Miz Margaret' over and over. Her eyes got brighter when she saw you." Upon seeing the children, Albert experienced a flash from the past. The healthy and happy China Dolls popped into his mind's eye. As he remembered their giggles, anger fumed in him upon seeing such a contrast. *All children deserve to be cared for and adored.* Albert was shocked upon seeing the gaunt black skin and sad dark eyes of the Holmes children as well as their dirty hair and tattered clothes. *Ford knocked the spark of life out of them. They deserve to be happy like the China Dolls. All children are like fine china that breaks if not treated with care.* Albert told the others, "I felt so helpless."

Joe patted Margaret's hand. "I put the fear of God in him. He knows the authorities are goin' to come to see those children. And they better be healthy when he goes to court. He'll face jail time if he neglects 'em."

After drinking coffee and eating only toast, they decided to head down the street to where the blacksmith had a shop.

It was a day of contrasts. In a moment of exhilarating excitement, they witnessed Albert Bayless being hired to work at the blacksmith shop in Salem. He had put on the blacksmith's apron and demonstrated his ability to fire the forge and shoe a horse. The proprietor had a spare room at the back of the shop; Albert had a job and place to call home. He was to start work in a week.

Walking back to the boardinghouse, where they planned to spend the night, Albert started talking like never before. "I may not have told you that I own better equipment than you saw tonight at that smithy shop. I have a 100-pound anvil, a four-inch-wide vise, dozens of horseshoes, just as many iron bars about four feet long, and an assortment of fine hand tools. And I have a limber on wheels that holds my forge when traveling. Why, my bellows are the best made anywhere. A friend of mine whom I met down at the gold mines is using my equipment in Marysville right now. I taught him the smithy trade in between panning for gold. We made more money being blacksmiths than gold miners.

"We came up to this area from the mines together, wanting to find a job and start living a real life. We both would like to marry. He wanted to stay in Marysville – it's just a few miles south of Salem – while I came up to meet with Dr. Bailey. Do you know Marysville?"

They were inside the boardinghouse again and Joe slapped him on the back before saying, "I didn't know you could gab like that. Yep, I know Marysville. Don't forget, I'm the U.S. marshal of this territory." Joe held up his hands. "Now don't start talking agin, I want to say something." He pulled up his pants by his belt, "Look at this, I'm losing my pants 'cuz I'm so hungry. You gittin' a job made me happy and hungry. Let's sit down and see if they have something with beef in it. I knowed they don't have buffalo."

When they were eating some hearty stew, Margaret asked, "Who is this friend in Marysville? He must be a trustworthy man for you to leave everything with him."

"His name is Louis Southworth. He is trustworthy! And maybe it's because he's young, but he trusts others, too. He gave Dr. Bailey a few hundred dollars worth of gold to bring back to his master in Marysville. He had only known your husband a couple weeks."

"Oh dear," Margaret said.

"Don't worry! Dr. Bailey delivered it, and we brought up the rest of the gold needed for Louis to be a free man. He paid his master for his freedom and has it on paper."

"So Louis is a Negro? Or should I say, he's a free man, like you?"

Albert laughed, "He would prefer to be known as a fiddler rather than anything else."

Joe was sopping the last of the stew from the bowl with a hunk of fresh bread, but looked up and managed to say with a full mouth, "A fiddler! Why, we need a fiddler in a couple of weeks. Do ya think he might come up here?"

"I do think he would. He never turns down an opportunity to play his fiddle. And, he's good at it!"

The next morning, before the sun was up, the three riders started back north. They got to the Newell's house when the sun was peeking above the horizon. Joe headed on to his place, leaving Margaret and Albert as they dismounted.

A lamp was lit in the window and they could see Mary Anne inside, bustling around the table. When Albert opened the door, Rebecca greeted them from the rocking chair next to the hearth. "Good morning. Welcome back."

Mary Anne wiped her hands on the apron she wore and said, "Hello,

hello. You're just in time to help with all the morning chores. I put the kettle on and started the fire. Well, actually I emptied the chamber pots first thing. Now someone needs to milk the cow so we can have some milk for breakfast. Yesterday, I used what they had to make fresh cheese."

Albert spoke up, "Well, I'll take the horses to the barn, remove their saddles, and feed them, but I don't know how to milk cows."

The three women turned toward him but said nothing.

"Hey, I was not that kind of slave. I was learning to read and be a gentleman for my master. I didn't milk cows."

Rebecca laughed before saying, "I didn't know how to milk until I married Robert. Someone should teach you."

Margaret suggested, "Mary Anne, why don't you give Albert his first milking lesson while I get everything ready for breakfast here. Rebecca, you are not to move from that rocker."

Albert and Mary Anne crossed the barnyard with the two horses trailing behind. Margaret peered out the window and saw them chatting with love in their eyes. She remembered how she felt when being courted by her husband. It seemed so long ago.

While Albert unhitched one saddle, he told Mary Anne about his good fortune in getting a blacksmithing job in Salem. "At first I'll stay in the shack next to the shop. But I plan on buying or building my own place."

"Oh, I would think that you'd have to save a lot of money to do that."

"No, I have enough saved right now. But I want to choose the right location." He took a deep breath before he said the next sentence. "Maybe you could help me."

"What could I do to help?"

"Oh, I don't know," he said. He poured some oats out for the horses. "I guess I want a place that a woman would like. You know, one that has the right amount of space for a garden or things like that." He finished with the horses and turned, bumping into Mary Anne. As he caught her from falling, he pulled her closer and kissed her. "I want a place that you would like."

"Oh!"

"Would you help me?"

Mary Anne nodded and they kissed again and again. Finally she stepped away from him to say, "We best milk the cow or it will start bawling and Margaret will come out to see what we're doing."

Once the cow, the bucket, the stool, and Albert were situated properly, the milking lesson began.

After more than twenty minutes and many glances out the window, Margaret began to worry about what she had started. "Rebecca, since I'd like some milk with my coffee, I'm going to see if they are almost finished milking." As she approached the milking area, no one was there – not even the cow. However, the pail – full of milk – stood in the doorway. Glancing around, she heard whispers and saw movements in a pile of hay in the corner of the barn. Margaret barked, "Albert, that is not part of the procedure to milk a cow!" She waited a moment and added, "Breakfast is ready."

Back in the house, Margaret told Rebecca that the two had been in the hay.

Minutes later, as all four of them sat at the table with hot biscuits, apple butter, dried venison, and fresh cheese on the table, Mary Anne began to chuckle and leaned toward Margaret, saying in a whisper, "The udder was so soft and warm. And I had to lean into his back and reach around him to show him what to do. Between Albert being so close and the squeezing of the teat being so soft and warm, we became distracted. Do you know what I mean?"

Margaret's mouth opened and no words came out.

Rebecca had overheard and put her hand to her mouth to stifle a laugh.

Margaret continued to slice the cheese on a cutting board and glared at Mary Anne and then, over her shoulder, at Albert. He was facing away and filling their glasses with some water over by the hearth. Margaret could tell by the movement of his back that he was chuckling.

Mary Anne continued to tease Margaret. "I found the lesson so enjoyable. I had no idea that milking...."

Interrupting, Margaret threw up her hands and shouted, "Say no more!" She walked out of the house and started pacing on the front stoop just as Robert rode up. "Thank heavens," she said loudly. "Surely this will stop their romps for a while."

Margaret walked back into the house with Robert and could not resist saying, "Look who is here. Are you *udderly* surprised?"

While the three of them laughed, Doc walked over to greet his wife, who said, "Margaret is making fun of the milking lesson. Albert claimed that he didn't know how to milk a cow, so they went to the barn and, besides milking, they ...." She decided not to say more, but Doc had gotten the gist.

He walked to the hearth, grabbed the coffee pot, and said, "The coffee is ready. Anyone want milk?"

Everyone laughed again, like youngsters who had said a bad word.

Being a man who liked to make his own destiny, Albert proposed to Mary Anne within the week. She accepted and they planned to wed when the first flowers of spring emerged from the ground.

Margaret was insistent and complained, "No one knows when the flowers will emerge. We can't plan anything with such a vague date. Please use the calendar and set a real date."

They decided to wed on the last week in March.

Meanwhile, Rebecca and Doc had asked Mary Anne if she would stay with them and help until the new baby came. When the baby girl arrived on the eleventh of February, there was more work with a new baby than before the arrival, so Mary Anne was asked to continue living with the Newells.

"Only until you become Mrs. Bayless."

"Rebecca, of course I'll stay and help. Oh, I like the sound of my name-to-be, Mrs. Bayless. But, I'll need time to go to Salem and help find a place for us to live."

"Of course, you will have time to be with Albert. Oh, Robert and I would love to give an engagement party for you a week before the wedding." The party was set for mid-March.

A few times each week, Albert finished at the blacksmith shop in Salem and came over to the Newell's place. One such evening after days with no rain, Doc had flushed quail from a neighbor's weedy and dry cornfield and shot a dozen of the tasty birds. Mary Anne decided to make a culinary feast. Out she went to the root cellar to get ideas on how to dress up those birds and cook them. She grabbed a basket and dropped in apples, onions, a handful of dry sage, potatoes, and carrots to give the meal some color on the plate.

In the Dutch Oven, Mary Anne made layers of sliced potatoes in their skins, dabs of butter, thin slices of carrots, sprinkled flour, and bits of cooked pickled pork. Over and over she layered these things for about four layers and then she poured some hot milk in, put on the lid, and hung the pot over the fire to cook for more than an hour.

After plucking the birds and saving some feathers for Margaret, who liked to decorate hats, and after stuffing the birds' cavities with a mixture of chopped filberts, onions, apples, sage, and day-old bread, she carefully slipped thinly sliced pickled pork beneath the quails' skin. She ground some peppercorns in the mortar bowl with a pestle, added some salt, and lightly rubbed the birds on the outside with butter before sprinkling on the salt and pepper. Now they were ready to put on some pointed metal rods that Albert had made for her. "In New York they called them spits," she told him.

He had nodded knowingly, "I know."

Rebecca set the table with her best. A fine white tablecloth with lace, brass candlesticks that had been wedding gifts from the McLoughlins, and delicate plates made of fine china that usually remained in the buffet, never used. Doc opened a bottle of wine that the Baileys had brought for them from the East Coast and poured the pungent, red liquid into tin cups.

"Doc, I want some real wine goblets. Please, for my birthday or Christmas," Rebecca whined.

The four adults all helped serve the food before sitting. Steam rose from the little brown birds – four each for the men and two each for the gals. The aroma made mouths water. Doc held the heavy Dutch Oven as Mary Anne spooned out the soft, melt-in-your-mouth potatoes. Like she had planned, the white potatoes with orange carrots dotting them looked appetizing.

"Seeing this steam rise from the birds, reminds me of how I saw them," Doc said as he held the pot. "I knew there had to be a covey of quail when I saw the dust rising out of a bare spot in the dry corn. I ran for my shotgun and Crow. Crow is the best bird dog I've ever had." He took the pot back to the hearth and hung it, never stopping his story. "I figured those birds had to be taking their daily dust bath. Especially on a sunny day, like today, they like to burrow down into soft, dry soil and, using their underbellies, they wiggle and squirm, flap their wings and ruffle their feathers. Crow and I crouch quietly. I took one shot and they rose in a frenzy above the bent corn stalks, and then I shot again. Wish I had gotten more, but those little devils fan out in all directions and make it hard to hit 'em. And without a dog it's impossible to find all that you hit. By gum, Crow did a good job and rounded up a dozen."

Everyone sat and raised tin cups. Doc said, "Here's to Oregon that gave us these potatoes, carrots, herbs, and quail. And here's to the Oregonian who cooked them to perfection. To Mary Anne!"

Mary Anne complained, "No, I want Shakespeare. Quote me some Shakespeare."

Rebecca chided, "Oh, Mary Anne, be careful. You don't know what you're asking."

Without hesitating, Doc raised his cup again:

Who rises from a feast
With that keen appetite that he sits down?

And as they savored the dinner, Doc added more quotes. When Mary Anne licked her fingers, he quoted without hesitation:

Tis an ill cook that cannot lick his own fingers.

And when Albert leaned over to place a kiss on Mary Anne's cheek with an unheard whisper of some endearment, Doc grinned and quoted:

How silver-sweet sound lovers' tongues by night,
Like softest music to attending ears!

What an evening!

* * *

Within a week, George Luther rode up to the Newell's house. His father had died at the gold mines and he told the Newells, "So I came back here. It's the only home I have even though I have no place of my own. I'm staying with my sister's family."

Kind words were said by all; Alphonso Boone was a respected man. Doc reminded George, "Your father will be remembered forever because of the Boone's Ferry he put across the Willamette River."

After Rebecca gave her condolences, George Luther was invited to attend the engagement party for Albert and Mary Anne. "Have you even met the beautiful bride to be?" He hadn't.

Doc inserted a thought, "Do you know the fiddler? Possibly you met him at the gold mines with Albert. A man by the name of Louis Southworth?"

George Luther brightened, "Yes, I did meet him when we looked for gold. He is the best fiddler I have ever heard. What a party it will be."

In the time between his proposal of marriage and the pending engagement party, Albert and Mary Anne bought a house in Salem and grew more deeply in love.

When possible, they found afternoons to roam the countryside of the French Prairie, stopping to recline on mossy stream banks lined with sword ferns. Among the ferns, they planned their life in Salem, talking about their children and what names to give the girls and boys.

As the wedding date came closer, their desires could no longer be denied and they made love in the woods with the chickadees watching and the squirrels protesting. The blue-and-white checkered tablecloth, spread on the emerging camas leaves with the uneaten picnic lunch, served better as a bed. Their touches searched to learn more about the softness behind the ear or the crevices along the spine or the hidden place between the legs. Passion lit them like two candles burning with such heat that they melted into one. During these times, they formed a bond to never be undone.

"I love you," said one.

"I adore you," said the other.

⁕ ⁕ ⁕

The party was small. People who had known Mary Anne when she was Mattie or Matthew came: the Meeks, the Baileys, the Holmeses, Sarah and Eliza Flett, and Albert with two friends – George Luther Boone and Louis Southworth. And then there was the uninvited person, who was never seen by anyone throughout the evening.

Louis left Marysville in the morning. He had the longest trip, and he stopped in Salem to spend the day with Albert at the blacksmith shop. He watched Albert apply bee's wax on a wrought iron hanger to prevent rusting before he reached for an apron off the wall and dipped a kerchief in some water and tied it around his neck. They worked together and talked all day before heading north to the Newell's place.

Virginia Meek came early to help Margaret, Rebecca, and Mary Anne prepare food and drink. The weather had cooperated and the party could be out in the barnyard.

Everyone was there and the fiddle was singing when George Luther rode up. He arrived with his purchased laurels from the days of the Mexican War. He rode into the Newell's yard on his gaily caparisoned horse – on a red-fringed Mexican blanket was a Guadalajara saddle with a silver pommel and silver bells jingling from the edges.

Throughout the evening, people formed squares with four couples or just danced as two. Finally, toward the end of the evening, Joe Meek shouted that they should make two lines for the Virginia Reel.

This put an odd person out.

When George Luther took Sarah Flett as his partner, Mary Anne asked, "Albert would you dance with Sarah's younger sister, Eliza? I'm going to run to the house and see if the two little children are still sleeping. We're making a lot of noise out here." She gave him a little peck of a kiss on his mouth and hurried off.

Louis stepped up on the horses' watering trough. With his feet firmly planted, he straddled the trough, well balanced and bobbing to the beat of his fiddle music. Then he began shouting the calls:

Head lady out and foot gent, too,
Greet with a bow and back you go.
Now head gent out and hustle to meet,
Foot lady for a nice long twirl.

Head lady go meet the foot gent agin
And make a Do-Si-Do.
Head gent meet the foot lady, too,
And do a Do-Si-Do.

Head couple join hands
To gallop to the foot and back agin.
Now reel the lines.

Amid much laughter, Joe and Virginia, as the head couple, linked arms with the next couple as they swirled down the line, in and out of the couples. The dance repeated over and over until each couple had been the head couple.

When the reel ended, Albert looked for Mary Anne. He asked Rebecca, "Did you see her come back? She went to look at your children."

Rebecca started walking toward the house, saying, "No, let's go see if there's a problem with my children."

They went in and found the two girls sleeping soundly. They came out and walked around the house. They returned to the barnyard and asked everyone. Soon the music stopped and everyone was calling and looking for Mary Anne.

Mary Anne was gone.

PART III

The Power of Court Cases, Politics, War, and Mother Nature
as Oregon becomes a State
1852 – 1881

View of Robert Newell's office in his Champoeg home

The sorting box is the only original piece of furniture in photo; Newell used this box with many cubbyholes when he was Postmaster of Champoeg. It is only a portion of the actual box.

Newell House Museum Complex
Located next to
Champoeg State Heritage Area
Oregon State Park

CHAPTER 14

1852 – 1855

Dealing with death is one matter; dealing with a disappearance is quite a different affair. Time can heal the human mind, can allow for an acceptance of death, and can diminish the sadness or pain when the death can be confirmed. When a person is gone from people's lives, those people need answers to the what, who, when, and where questions to find closure. When someone disappears without a trace from one moment to the next, chaos results.

The night Mary Anne McAlister disappeared, everyone at the engagement party searched. The men saddled horses and took off in all directions trying to find her. It was assumed that her half-brother Jed McAlister had abducted her, though there was no proof. The logic of the group was that he could not have gone far with Mary Anne struggling, so they would find them. She had disappeared in the time it took to dance the Virginia Reel – a few minutes. Five minutes, at most!

In retrospect, Joe Meek wished they had not been so hasty; any tracks and evidence of a struggle had been obliterated when their horses trampled all the ground around the Newell's cabin. In the light of day, they found no clues. In the light of day, only their pain and guilt remained. How could she be gone? Where did he take her? They just disappeared? How did he do it? How did he overpower her without any of them hearing?

Of course, they could understand that it was dark, the music was loud, they were laughing and making noise among themselves, and the cabin was forty to fifty feet from them. Knowing those details, they could see how it happened. BUT – this was the large and heavy *but* that left them with guilt – they had known there was the possibility of danger for her, but they took no precautions.

In the coming days, with no sightings of Mary Anne with a man, they were baffled. Two people cannot vanish without a trace. Someone had to have seen them. They had vanished like the smoke that lifts from the chimney and – poof – dissipates into nothing.

At first, much had been done to find her. With all his connections from being the U.S. marshal for years, Joe Meek sent out word to many, without results.

Doc ran ads in *The Oregon Spectator*, requesting information and offering a reward. He received no responses.

Margaret got permission to tack posters with Mary Anne's description on walls of the steamers, in the post offices, at the banks, in the hotels, and anywhere she could. Nothing came of her efforts.

Albert Bayless was frantic. That first night, he rode all night looking for her. The following days, he went from house to house, methodically, circling around the Newell cabin – farther and farther in concentric circles – to find anyone or any evidence of where McAlister had camped or hid. Finally, he decided to ride south to Siskiyou County in California to where the McAlister's lived. He told his friends, "I've been there. It was by accident that I was at their house when I first started my gold mining days. At that time, I didn't know any of you."

Through logic, Joe Meek and Doc talked him out of going. "They won't help you. If they know about this, they are waiting for you to come and will be ready for you. They will hide their son and Mary Anne."

Albert nodded and agreed. He decided to write a letter to the German couple, Jahn and Eliza, where he had stayed in Siskiyou County. He would ask them to go over to the McAlister's place to see if Jed and Mary Anne were there. "I don't know if they can read, but they will find someone to help them with my letter. I'm going to send an envelope and paper for them to mail back to me what they find."

After more than a month, an answer came:

Dear Albert,

Me and Eliza go to McAlister farm. We say we on visit to meet our neighbors. Only Mr. and Mrs. McAlister there. They sad. They don't know what happen to 2 sons. Years ago, first one gone and now this Jed not come home. They going to sell most sheep. Can't take care of animals with no sons. The barn was falling and the house not have a back porch. It fall off. They want to sell the farm to us. We said we sorry, but not interest. Come visit or come stay with us again. We miss you.

From, Jahn and Eliza LoFiance

In the coming months and with their minds trying to cope with this unexplained mystery, not one of the people who had been at the party was without some form of guilt, remorse, or shame when a thought about Mary Anne popped into their heads. Why? Because after many months had passed, most of them stopped dwelling on the disappearance of Mary Anne as they continued to live their own lives. Only Albert continued to think and hope.

One evening in Salem, after Albert finished at the blacksmith shop, he went over to visit the Holmeses. He confided to Mrs. Holmes, "I'm hollow inside. I can't think of what more to do. Where can I look for Mary Anne? Where is she? Most nights, I can't sleep and my thoughts are crazy."

Polly Holmes nodded her head over and over as he spoke. Finally, she whispered, "I know. I have same trouble, but it's different. I know where my three little girls are, but I can't touch them or help them or do anything. I go crazy, like you, thinkin' 'bout that."

Robin Holmes came in the door and greeted Albert before telling about his day. "I been in Oregon City all day, working on my case with Mr. Boise. I wish I could read and write. Makes things hard that I can't. Sometimes I don't know if Mr. Boise tells me exactly what the papers really say. But ...." He left his sentence unfinished. "I go before the court next month. Hope I'm ready." This legal battle of *Holmes vs. Ford* would go on for fifteen months. Robin Holmes would demonstrate strength and determination, as he plodded through four different judges and the court system. He went and poured himself some water. "Hear anything 'bout Mary Anne?"

"No."

* * *

On another evening, Albert rode up to the Newells after his work. Margaret was there visiting, too. Again he wanted to talk to friends who understood. "What do I do? I feel like I'm not trying. I need to do something to find Mary Anne. You know, like Robin Holmes who is out there working and working on getting his girls back."

No one said anything for a minute. A long minute. They sat around the table, drinking tea. Rebecca was rocking the baby by the hearth. The rocker made a soothing squeak with each backward movement.

Finally, Doc put his hand on Albert's forearm and said, "Robin may end up just like you, with his hands tied. Do you realize that? It is impressive that he has gotten this far, but many obstacles are still in his way. However, don't compare your plight with his. Unlike him, you really have no where to go for help." With both his elbows on the table, Doc dropped his head into his hands and shook his head. "You do know that we are suffering with you, Albert, don't you? It's a horrible feeling not knowing where she is. And we have no clues!"

Margaret sat up straighter and leaned into the table, "There is one strange thing. When I came here to collect all of Mary Anne's things. I didn't find her Grandpappy's tinderbox." Margaret swallowed and a tear rolled from one eye, "Mary Anne took the tinderbox to New York City and back. She would hold it when we read books on the ships to and from the East. Since the first day I met her back in 1845, she slept with it beneath her pillow."

Doc said, "She must have had it in her pocket on that night she disappeared."

Margaret replied with a huff, "Don't you think that I thought of that? She was in her Sunday best for the engagement party; there was no pocket!"

Now Doc seemed irritated, "What are you saying, Margaret. What does it prove that the tinderbox is gone, too?"

Albert lifted his hands into the air to stop the disagreement and then he placed them on Doc and Margaret. "See how easy it is to get upset. Just be calm. Doc, Margaret has presented the first clue in all this time. I think it proves that Jed McAlister abducted Mary Anne. He would have wanted that family tinderbox."

Doc bobbed his head and replied, "You're right! We assumed Jed took her, but this gives us more assurance that it was he. Trouble is, he could be anywhere in the United States ... or even Canada or Mexico."

Though Albert Bayless filled his days with hard work, it didn't assuage his pain. He was waiting and hoping for his Mary Anne to return. He always talked about her. George Luther sat and listened one day.

"Albert, I feel bad for you. It just scares me so much to listen to how much you love Mary Anne and she's gone."

Albert cocked his head with a puzzled look on his face. "Why does it scare you?"

"I met this pretty girl at my sister's place. When I come here, I see everyone mourning the loss you have because Mary Anne disappeared and then I meet someone with a name that you jus' can't believe."

Albert waited and finally asked, "Well, what name is that?"

"Mourning Ann. Yes, that is her name – Mourning Ann. I tell you, before I heard her name I knew she was the one for me. But now, I'm scared ...." George Luther took a deep breath. "Her name reminds me of Mary Anne. We all are mourning for you and I think I might loose her 'cuz ...."

Albert burst out with a guffaw.

George Luther jumped. "What you laughing 'bout?"

"George, I didn't think you would be superstitious. Ask her to be your wife and, if she wants to marry you, do it. Nothing is going to happen like it did to me."

George reached into his pocket and pulled out a gold nugget, the first gold he had ever found, and said, "I thought I'd have this made into a ring for her."

Albert put his arm around his friend's shoulders before telling him, "George Luther Boone, just do what your heart tells you and be happy. You can't be scared because of my problem; you're like most men and are just scared of asking her to marry you. You're afraid she'll say *no* to you."

Within the week, George Luther was back at Albert's house. "She said that she would marry me!"

They wed in the winter of 1852 and went to live on the Pacific Coast.

Louis came from Marysville to visit Albert at his house. He rode up, leading Albert's mule that was pulling the limber. "Came to see how you're doin' before I leave for California again. I got tired of blacksmithing, so I brought back your equipment."

Albert poured out his heart to his friend. "I'm okay when I work. It's on Sunday and in the evenings when I can't stop thinking about Mary Anne. I want to do something to find her, but I don't know what I can do."

Louis shook his head, "You're going about all this wrong. Don't you know in your heart that she will come back to you if she can? You need to be waiting for her, not worrying like this."

"How will she come back?"

Louis punched Albert, "I don't know. But you need to believe and be positive that she will, if she can. In the meantime, do something useful in those evenings and on Sunday when it is hardest for you.

"Like what?"

Louis was adamant and said, "You tell me! Is there anyone who could use your help? Try to be useful to someone."

"How?"

"Damn, you being one stubborn man. You a blacksmith, you can read and write, you healthy and strong, you own a house, a horse, a mule...." Louis stopped listing Albert's assets. A thought popped into his head and he said, "Why, if I could read and write, I would teach someone else how to. Like little children or a friend."

Albert stood and went to Louis. He pulled him into a hug and started laughing. "You're just a twenty-two-year-old and you're wiser than I am."

"Ha, you thirty-three and jus' need to grow up some more."

"I know what I can do to help someone. I never would have thought about it without you. Robin Holmes is trying to get his three children out of slavery, but he can't read all the legal papers. I'll help him."

Later that evening as they prepared to have supper, Louis finally shared a problem that had cropped up. "I joined a church a while back and enjoyed the people and the worship. They is all white people, but they accept me. It made me feel good. But all that changed. To be a member of the church, they told me that I must get rid of my fiddle. They said it unbecomin' to a Christian."

"No!" Albert was placing food from the other night onto the table. His house was sparsely furnished, but he had a bed, table with chairs and a fine buffet. He opened the buffet and took out some plates and cups.

"My fiddle is my friend. You know that 'bout me. Everybody has their own way to look at things. Some people don't understand that I love my fiddle for many years and, like you know, I don't go anywhere without my friend. I find my fiddle makes other people feel good. It can't be wrong for me to play it."

Albert nodded and continued to listen, knowing Louis was not finished.

"I told those church-goin' Christians that they can take my name off their rolls if they must, because I can't part with my old friend. But I hope the Lord doesn't take my name off the Big Book up yonder. In fact, those who pass those pearly gates probably will meet many a fellow who remembers my fiddle playing because it helped them forget their troubles. And I told them that there are those up yonder who play the harp. I can't see how the Lord would take a harp and deny a fiddle."

They ate in silence and then Louis played a couple of tunes.

The next day, as Louis was leaving for California, he told Albert, "Well, I'll be back someday. Look for me."

As Albert thought of Mary Anne every day, he relieved his guilt and anger by beating the metal harder in the blacksmith shop. In a state of total exhaustion, after a day of banging and hammering, he collapsed and slept soundly. More than the passage of time, sleep helped him to heal, little by little.

But some evenings, and on most Sundays, Albert worked on the court case with Robin Holmes.

On Robin's first visit to court – that day that had so worried him – nothing happened. Nathaniel Ford claimed that he had misplaced the court papers, and he didn't bring the children because he could not afford that expense.

That evening, Albert told Robin, "Ford's stalling. Did your lawyer get that letter from Mr. Shirley in Missouri?" When Robin shook his head,

Albert emphasized, "Don't give up hope."

Time plodded on and a year passed since the Holmeses had filed.

Robin went to court again and again. Ford kept stalling. As did the judges. Even when the letter arrived that proved Ford had schemed to sell the Holmeses back into slavery, no judge wanted to favor a Negro over a white man. On June 24, 1853, Judge Cyrus Olney told Robin, "A new Supreme Court justice is due to arrive soon, therefore, the court awaits him. I will put this case on the dockets to be heard in October. Court adjourned."

President Franklin Pierce nominated George H. Williams to be the new chief justice of Oregon's Territorial Supreme Court and the U.S. Senate confirmed the nomination. George H. Williams came to Oregon.

Robin and Albert were concerned about this new judge. They talked:

"Williams is young, only thirty years old. He can't have much experience."

"Of course, I don't think it matters that he's never been to Oregon, but he's a New Yorker by birth. Do you think he can understand my problems?"

Much to everyone's surprise, the first order of business that Williams performed was to move the court date up for the Holmes case.

Only a few days after he arrived in July, he was in court with Nathaniel Ford and the Holmeses. He loomed tall, lanky, and heavy framed as he entered the courtroom with his black robe billowing open from his long stride. His deep-set eyes had a no-nonsense gaze and his receding hairline was balanced with long, bushy sideburns that joined at his mustache.

His words betrayed his youth. When Ford explained that he had given Mr. and Mrs. Holmes their freedom in exchange for keeping the children. Judge Williams stated, "Freedom was not yours to give. When the Holmeses feet touched the soil of Oregon, the laws of Oregon went into effect. Your relationship with them dissolved at that instance. They were no longer slaves."

Ford insisted that the Holmeses were harsh and not capable of caring for their children.

Judge William's words were recorded to be:

Nothing appears in evidence to show the charge of harshness to be true. Quite the contrary, there is an abundance of evidence, proving that the petitioner and his wife are affectionate, honest, and industrious people. The difference of color does not change parental authority in this Territory.

Against the overwhelming odds, on July 13 of 1853 in the Polk County Courthouse in Dallas, the three Holmes children – Mary Jane, James, and Roxanna – were permanently and legally free. Legally, they were under the custody of their parents. A fifteen-month legal battle had ended. Robin Holmes had won against a white man, against a slave owner, against Nathaniel Ford. Robin Holmes had won in an area of Oregon that was known to be sympathetic to slavery and slave owners. He was the only Negro to have his case adjudicated in Oregon courts. This was a landmark case that would help shape Oregon's policies toward slavery.

Robin and Polly went to Albert's house with their children to share their happiness.

Albert stepped out his front door onto his porch and encircled all of them with his long arms. "Look who's here! Why, I am so happy." Then he took a step back and looked at the children. He didn't know them too well; he had only seen them that one day when he went with Joe Meek to serve the court papers on Ford. But there stood two boys and one girl on his porch. "Am I crazy? I remember two girls and one boy. Yes, I remember that the legal papers listed Roxanna, Mary Jane, and James."

Polly started weeping, so Albert stepped back into his doorway. "Come in, come in. Let's go sit while you tell me what's going on."

Robin placed a hand on each child's head as he named them, "Roxanna, James, and Lon."

Polly was dabbing her eyes. "Lon, our youngest boy was born after we left Ford's. He only three. Nathaniel Ford never had him for a slave." She started crying again, "Mary Jane don't come home to us. She say she don't want to."

The adults sat at the table. Robin said, "Our Mary Jane is a young lady now. She goin' to be a thirteen-year-old. She been livin' with Nathaniel Ford's daughter, Josephine Boyle, doing house chores. She say she wants to stay and work for Mrs. Boyle 'cuz she get paid now that she's free. She wants to earn her own money."

Mr. Boyle was the first physician in Polk County, where he had built a fine colonial style house. Little, stout Mary Jane was a much loved house servant in the Boyle household and was recorded living with them in the 1850 census. Everyone loved the sweet girl who was generous and always helping, not only the Boyles but also all the neighbors.

Polly said, "She say our house too little and crowded. But I tell her that she my chil' and there's always room." Polly began to cry more.

Robin hugged her, "Mother, you have your other children. Mary Jane is a young lady who can decide on her own. She happy at the Boyles. Now, stop frettin' 'bout all this."

Polly, with pleading eyes, asked, "Albert, you helped Robin with the readin' for the court case. Could you help me git my little girl to come home? Please go visit Mary Jane and talk some sense into her."

Albert went to see Mary Jane, but never convinced her to go home. They got to know one another and he became a special person to her. She would call him Uncle Albert for the rest of her life, and he would always be there to help her in the future.

In the coming year, Margaret was making changes to her life. For her, the year of 1854 was filled with many painful events. Like Albert, she would have her future dreams vanish.

Margaret Jewett Bailey and Dr. William Bailey completed their divorce early in 1854. For her, the marriage had been filled with mental and physical abuses, but she was not relieved of hardships with the divorce. She walked away from the marriage with one hundred dollars, her clothing and personal effects, as well as her piano. She had no place to live – took a room in a boardinghouse – and had to rely on her skills as a seamstress, teacher, and nurse for her livelihood. Dr. Bailey took pity and signed over a house in Butteville and she went there to live. Slowly, she resumed her literary ambitions. She worked on her book day and night.

By May 1854, Margaret had a job with the newspaper, *The Oregon Spectator*, writing and editing three columns of the Ladies Department. She was clever and versatile – the column had riddles, fashion news, poetry and fiction. But the job ended after six weeks when she and her boss had disagreements; he wanted to limit her space and to decide himself on the topics of her writing.

She turned to teaching. A notice in the *Spectator* stated:

> We doubt not the young ladies and gentlemen in town would do well to attend Mrs. Bailey's class of instruction in grammar and rhetoric, which is held on Tuesday, Thursday, and Saturday evenings of each week, in the Baptist College.

Being a divorced woman, people talked and convinced the pupils that by being in her company they would be contaminated. That hope of a livelihood ended.

In July, in order to earn money, she made the decision to publish her book in monthly installments until it was completed. She got a few subscriptions to bring in money for food.

Finally it was completed. Margaret paid Carter and Austin of Portland to print her novel that was called: *The Grains or Passages in the Life of Ruth Rover, with Occasional Pictures of Oregon, Natural and Moral*. It was printed in two volumes. Margaret had chosen the pseudonym of *Ruth Rover* for herself in this autobiographical book and, in the coming years, people often referred to her as Ruth Rover; the references most often were made with a negative connotation. This may have been a result of the book's reviews. The reviews were not complimentary:

One reviewer from *The Oregonian* complained, "It is bad enough to have unjust laws – poor lawyers and worse judges – taxes, and no money, with the combined evils they saddle on us, without this last visitation of

Providence – *an authoress*. In the words of Homer (or his translator) we say 'and may this first invasion be the last.'"

Another reviewer, with distaste for a female author, stated, "Who in the dickens cares about the existence of a fly, or in whose pan of molasses the insect disappeared."

And the flurry of reviews continued for a time:

- "We seldom review, much less read, books of feminine production, believing their province is to darn stockings, prepare pap and gruel, and work on cookstoves ...."

- "To call it trash, would be impolite, for the writer is an *authoress*."

- "Maybe after reading this book attentively, one can conclude that it is more a story of *Grub-poling*." (Being politically astute and well-read, Margaret saw that this review referred to the political satire written by W.L. Adams; in that play, William H. Willson is a pseudonymous Grub. AND in her book, Margaret had written about her affair with the same, William H. Willson.)

To no avail, Margaret wrote rebuttals for many of these reviews. No efforts on her part could stop the written reviews or the verbal criticism coming from those living in her community. The people of Oregon disliked that she blatantly printed details about her four affairs, especially the affair with a man living amongst them – the respected Methodist Missionary William H. Willson. They disagreed when she criticized the lack of effort made by the missionaries to preach to the Indians or to establish schools. They were appalled that she saw the disasters that had occurred to Dr. David Leslie at the mission as a divine retribution of his bad treatment of her.

Although it is not known how many copies were printed, all the books disappeared. Where did they go? Did people destroy them in a bonfire? They could have been stored and washed away in a flood. Did someone buy all the copies to prevent distribution? Did Margaret regret all the negative responses and hoard the books, selling them no more? Or did they sit on shelves in homes, gathering cobwebs, to be forgotten and finally thrown away?

At the end of September 1854, nothing more appeared in any

newspaper about *The Grains*. By 1855, *The Oregon Spectator*, which had carried the most negative reviews and derogatory criticism, shut its doors; like Margaret's book, it was no more.

Like the Baileys, the Holmeses, and Albert Bayless during 1852 through 1854, Robert Newell was struggling.

Though Newell had lost in the election for the House of Representatives in 1850, receiving only 92 votes to Harding's 128 votes, he continued his involvement in the controversy to determine where the location of Oregon's capital would be. Champoeg was no longer a consideration, but he preferred Oregon City to Salem.

Politics were heating up in Oregon. Although President Zachary Taylor was only president for about one year, he brought the Whig party into Oregon by appointing John P. Gaines to replace Governor Lane. Oregonians were not happy; with Governor Lane, they had been led by a Democrat, like most people in Oregon.

During the time when Governor Gaines presided, an act of the legislature:

1. named Salem as the capital of Oregon,
2. chose Portland as the location for the penitentiary, and
3. selected Marysville as the location for the university.

But a question of the legality of this act went before the justices of the Supreme Court of Oregon because only one subject should be in a bill.

If this new act was to be void, the justices didn't know which way they should vote on the legality. There being only one Democrat judge, the two Whig judges ruled that the bill naming the capital was illegal; therefore, Oregon City was left as the legal seat of the government.

This controversy was not settled.

The men in government were stubborn. Most of the legislature was Democratic, so they met in Salem while the federal officers maintained their work in Oregon City.

On Christmas Day in 1851, Robert Newell had called a meeting of the people of Oregon to discuss the problem. Doc was chairman and explained that he wanted to know what the public opinion was. Those in attendance were adamant in their opinion – they decided that the legislature was wrong in disregarding the decision of the Supreme Court. Doc spoke and criticized those who supported Salem for the capital as selfish people who did not respect the authority of the courts.

Robert Newell was a Democrat who sounded like a Whig!

About this time there was a new weekly newspaper out of Salem called *The Statesman*. Asahel Bush was the owner and editor. He was a strong, relentless, and calculating man who would dominate Oregon politics for a decade; and he was a Democrat who wanted Salem to be the capital.

Newell and he clashed – head on, like two bulls.

Bush published an accusing article in *The Statesman* saying that Newell was a pretend Democrat who did the bidding of the Whigs who paid him for his services.

Newell answered the accusations with a letter to Bush and, surprisingly, Bush published it in *The Statesman*, as follows:

> Mr. Bush, you accused me of being hired at five dollars per day
> by the commissioners; for services I never performed. That is
> untrue like the rest of what you said and I can prove it.
> Signed, Robert Newell

Politically the controversy continued between the two men and between the Whigs and Democrats. In the *Oregonian*, the Whigs poured out their wrath toward Bush and his printed words. It got childish and nasty at times; a Mr. Dryer suggested that Bush should get a medal manufactured out of skunk's eyes, for his services to Oregon.

This fiasco went all the way across the country to the President of the United States. President Fillmore was asked by the Treasury Department, how to appropriate money for the erection of the Capitol building for Oregon without a location being known.

Again, the people met in Champoeg. At this meeting Robert Newell was selected among a committee of ten men to prepare resolutions for newspapers – *The Statesman*, *The Oregonian*, and the *Democratic Times*.

Soon the people located in the areas of Clackamas and Oregon City met to discuss the situation. But the quarrels continued.

After the elections of 1852, when the Democrats had a convincing majority, the location of the capital was resolved by a Congressional joint resolution passed by the House on April 26, 1852 and passed the next day in the Senate. Salem became the official capital of Oregon.

Robert Newell stepped away from politics for a time. In Champoeg, he was postmaster, had a general store, and finished building a large flourmill. Champoeg was still centrally located and the area where most of the wheat was grown in Oregon. Being back in his beloved Champoeg, he was happy. He removed himself from the public's eye for five years.

Louis Southworth sitting in his home with his fiddle and his favorite president.

Photo courtesy of:
Benton County Historical Society & Museum
1101 Main Street
Philomath, OR 97370
Telephone: 541-929-6230

CHAPTER 15

1855 – 1863

Albert Bayless had once championed the idea that he controlled the destiny of his life. Not any longer. Years ago, the three friends – he, Margaret, and Robert Newell – had had a talk about making their own destiny. They had agreed that they were successful at forming their lives. If the three would talk at this time, they would have to concede to a change of opinions. Now they were filled with doubts.

Since his wife-to-be disappeared, Albert felt defeated. He said to his friends, "Unbeknownst to me, fate stepped in and took my beloved Mary Anne. I could do nothing. I tried to find her to no avail."

Margaret admitted, "There are all these unknown factors that come to play in one's life. I could do nothing to make my marriage work or control how people accepted my book. I will not publish another word."

Robert was not yet defeated – tired, but not yet defeated. "Yes, I have had some disappointments that I didn't expect, but I am a wealthy man with a wonderful family and I live where I always wanted to live, here in Champoeg."

Robert Newell's disaster was coming, along with another for Margaret.

Margaret was forty-three years old and still quite attractive. She held herself straight and had sewn beautiful clothes for herself. When she had lived on a homestead with animals and crops, she could not use her fine frocks; now she did.

"Being a seamstress, I need to dress well if I want customers to come to me," she whispered to herself while dressing for a trip to Salem. She lived alone and often talked to herself to fill the silence. She had been asked to make a wedding dress for a fall wedding in Salem. Margaret took a stagecoach from Butteville to Salem.

Salem was small. Wooden storefronts lined Commercial Street, where the stagecoach stopped. In the distance, at State and Church Street, she glanced at the wooden building for the Methodist Episcopal Church to get her bearings. She walked briskly down the walkways on State Street in an unusual summer drizzle. Many of the stores had built roofs over the sidewalk to protect the customers from the rains of Oregon. Nevertheless, a fine spray blew at Margaret, so she opened her umbrella and tilted it against the rain to stay dry. As she turned a corner, she bumped into a gentleman and dropped the large cloth bag with her sewing tools. A scissors fell out and some thread.

"Oh, pardon me! How dreadfully clumsy of me," the man said in a deep voice. His umbrella was upside down and tipping this way and that on the planks of the walkway where it had fallen. He reached for the scissors and thread as Margaret crouched to retrieve the cloth bag.

When they each stood, their eyes met.

"May I introduce myself? I am the widower, Francis Waddell, of Eola Hills."

"How do you do, sir. I am Miss Margaret Bailey of Butteville."

They had made apparent both their marital status and place of residence before they turned, bid the other goodbye, and continued on their way.

He raised his hat, saying, "Good day to you, Miss Bailey."

"And to you, Mr. Waddell."

And so began a courtship.

Mr. Waddell had lost his wife in June of 1855, only a few weeks before meeting Margaret on the walkway. He had come to Oregon in 1852 and, as everyone knew, a man cannot live in Oregon without a wife. A household needed a woman to run it and work it.

Within a few days, Margaret had a letter at the post office from Mr. Waddell. He invited her to dine in Oregon City at the Moss Hotel.

After that, on her next trip to Salem for a fitting of the bridal dress, she lunched with him at his home in Eola Hills and met his sixteen-year-old daughter named Mary, who lived with him. The other two children were not present during the lunch; they were younger.

They met once a week, and then twice a week, and soon every other day.

By August they announced their engagement to be married; and *The Statesman* printed a notice:

In Salem, on the 4th of September 1855, Mr. Francis Waddell, of Polk County, and Mrs. Margaret Jewett Bailey, (her literary *non de plume* is Ruth Rover), will be married by Rev. O.S. Dickinson in a private ceremony.

Dr. William Bailey had married again in 1855, as well, to a widow named Julia Nagel Shiel. He went to live in her home on the French Prairie and took over her husband's medical practice. They would remain married for all his life.

Not the same could be said of Margaret's marriage to Francis Waddell.

After the marriage, Margaret moved to the lovely home in Eola Hills. She enjoyed the place; that is to say, after she redid much of the effects such as the curtains and other decorations. Early on, her stepdaughter Mary and she did not get along.

"Where are my mother's crocheted doilies that sat beneath every lamp?" Mary complained. "What? You gave them away? How dare you! Didn't you consider that I would like to have them? My mother made them."

And, in front of her husband, Margaret complained one evening during dinner, "Mary, we all share the dressing room and I would prefer not to see the results of your monthly woes. I do hope that you do not expect me to clean up after you. I am not your servant. And, as long as I am talking, I would think you quite capable of making your bed, since you do little else."

Mr. Waddell was appalled at the reference to his daughter's monthly menstrual cycle; he said nothing until Margaret and he were alone.

In a gentle voice, he suggested, "Margaret, can you be a bit more tactful and compassionate? I do realize that my wife spoiled Mary, but the girl lost her mother just a few months ago. She has many adjustments to make."

"She needs to learn what a woman needs to do. She will never make a good wife unless she learns cleanliness and housekeeping."

The conflicts between the two females continued for several months, and Mr. Waddell continued to try to calm Margaret until he finally lost his patience. They began to fight every night in their room.

Soon Margaret moved to the guest room to sleep. She explained to him, "I would rather not have arguments every evening. If I am not in our bedroom, you cannot fight with me."

After Margaret had said she was leaving his bed, he had insisted, "You are my wife and must sleep with me."

"I have made my decision." And Margaret held to her decision.

However, unknown to Margaret, a different reason existed for how she felt about sleeping with her husband. One morning when she was sipping coffee and watching the sunrise while everyone still slept, she gazed at the beautiful view of colors – purple, pink, and puce – from the window of the house and was struck with the realization that she no longer had sexual desires. She collapsed into a chair in her surprise, gasping aloud, "Something is wrong with me. I feel so different."

All her adult life, she had allowed her hormones to dictate decisions for her lusts, not consciously but endlessly. Now she had reached an age when the female desires lessened and eventually would disappear, yet she had no knowledge of this phenomenon. She had no mother to talk with her, no close female friends, and no literature available that would have warned her. Suddenly, with the beginnings of the *change of life*, she felt more neuter than a woman. And those were the words she used in her mind. *I no longer feel like a woman; I am neuter. Now, when I look back on my sexual exploits, it is like I am standing away from myself and seeing a maniac. How could I have been that way? Willy and I had sex every night when we were together AND even after he beat me. What was wrong with me allowing that? Oh, and those four affairs I had years ago!*

She placed the cup with her cold coffee on the table and stared into space. She remained motionless; this realization depleted her of energy. She would ponder this topic often in the coming days and weeks.

Months passed.

The dressing room in the Waddle household had a toilet, which consisted of a wooden chair with a hole in the seat and a chamber pot below. And there was a tub for bathing and a mirror. It was shared by all in the family and was entered from a doorway in the hallway; all the bedrooms had doorways into the same hallway, as did the guest room where she slept. Late one night as Margaret made her way to relieve herself in the dressing room, she met her husband coming out of his daughter's room. They startled each other and stood transfixed for a moment.

Finally, Margaret asked directly, "Why were you in Mary's room?"

"She's feeling ill and I took her some water to drink."

With a frown, Margaret accepted the explanation; however, from then on, she was alerted to watch for any nightly movements. She left the guest room door ajar to hear, but the floors and doors had no squeaks. Besides, she was a sound sleeper.

Nevertheless, evidence would soon surface to show that her husband and his daughter were having sexual relations.

One such morning, Mary rushed from the breakfast table to the dressing room. She had to vomit. After it happened a second time, Margaret knew what it meant. Pregnant woman have this problem – morning sickness.

Though Margaret was religious and believed the teachings of Christianity, she had had sexual relations out of wedlock with four men. She had berated herself for sinning and prayed for forgiveness. She surmised that the Lord forgave her because with the first two men she had believed that they had wanted to marry her. So, Margaret reasoned, it was her naivety that led her astray. With the next man, she was so depressed from her prior sins that she succumbed to temptation. She felt God forgave her for that as well. The fourth man really wanted to marry her and she was going to marry him until she learned that he had proposed to another before he had slept with her. She broke the engagement and explained that she could not marry a man who had promised himself to another woman.

Even with all her experience with sexual desires, she did not see that by depriving Mr. Waddle of the marriage bed she helped cause the pregnancy. Margaret only saw the horrific sin and deception of her husband.

When she confronted Waddle, at first he refuted her claim that his daughter was pregnant. When Mary's growing belly demonstrated the fact, he confessed to being the father of his daughter's unborn child.

In 1856, Margaret tried to obtain a quiet divorce through the Oregon legislature; they denied her petition by one vote. So, Margaret used the opportunity and bought property – unmarried women could not own property, but a married woman could. Soon, she separated from Mr. Waddle, and moved to her property on Commercial Street. She had paid $50 for the plot that was located on the north half of Lot 3 in Block 49 on Commercial Street in Salem.

Their situation became more complicated for two reasons: Margaret wanted the $1,000 that she had taken into the marriage, but Waddle had used it to begin a business in Salem and no longer had it; and she had asked a couple of men – her clergyman and Waddle's business partner – for advice after Waddle had told her that he had gotten his daughter pregnant. One of those men, or someone who overheard, must have told of the sexual relationship and pregnancy because the whole affair became public knowledge.

Now a one-sided battle began.

In February of 1857, Waddle published a notice in the newspaper to defend himself:

NOTICE:
A false report has been circulating about myself and my daughter. These slanderous ideas were started by Mrs. M. J. Waddle (Ruth Rover) and are false, without the shadow of a doubt.

I have not wanted to defame her name, but after she started these rumors, I must defend myself. Life in the past year of marriage to her has been hell. I needed a mother for my three children and for that reason married her; she was unkind and even starved my children while I was away on business.

I state that the black lie she circulated is false in every way and I shall hold every man accountable who talks about this lie.

Margaret made no answer to his notice.

Within two weeks, Mary Waddle had a notice printed in the newspaper:

NOTICE:

The lies invented and circulated by Margaret J. Waddle (alias Ruth Rover) in reference to the treatment of myself by my father are entirely false, malicious, and without foundation. This dependent never participated in the heinous crime as she claimed and pronounces that all such charges are false.

Again, Margaret made no answer.

In these first two newspaper notices, the specific charges against Mr. Waddle were never stated – everything was vague and left to the imagination of the reader. However, during the next week, Mr. Waddle made another sworn statement, which clarified the charge against him:

NOTICE:

The lies invented and circulated by Margaret J. Waddle (alias Ruth Rover), in relation to my having seduced my daughter, are false and without foundation. Margaret J. has evinced a devilish and malignant spirit, threatening to destroy not only my character but also that of my motherless children.

A divorce petition was presented to the court again and the divorce was granted in September of 1857 with each party retaining the original property that they had brought into the marriage. Margaret was awarded her $1,000.

Margaret continued to live at her property on Commercial Street and, one evening after dark, she had a visit from Albert Bayless.

"Albert! What a pleasant surprise. Come in, come in." Albert stepped in the door and was followed by another man.

Margaret squealed, "Louis Southworth! I didn't see you out in the dark. Oh, don't take that the wrong way."

"Oh, I don't. Lots of people call me a darkey. In fact, the creek that runs by my place is called Darkey Creek. It's on the maps. Darkey Creek! Why, that's an honor that the town named it for me. Miss Margaret, you don't have no creek named for you, do you?"

She smiled and said, "I don't. Now, tell me about your lives since I last saw you. I can see that Louis has come back from California to live in Oregon again. And I don't need to say anything about my life; all the details have been printed in the newspapers. It is apparent that I jumped out of the frying pan and into the fire." The men started to sit on a small sofa and Margaret said, "Let's go sit around the table like we have always done in all the years past. I'll make some tea and warm some sweet cakes from this morning."

"I ain't goin' to say no to that," said Louis.

Margaret had a stove in her kitchen, no hearth. She opened the fire door and plopped a few sticks of wood into it and said, "The stove is still hot. I just need a little wood to get some water to boil. It won't take long. Who is going to start talking and tell me about your lives since I last saw you?"

Albert began, "I wanted to come and invite you to my place. On Sunday next, Louis is going to fiddle at the wedding of Mary Jane Holmes."

"Oh my, oh my! What wonderful news you bring me. Do I know the groom?"

"His name is Reuben Shipley. I just met him. Do you know him? He farms over in Benton County and he came to Oregon back in fifty-three. He's a free man."

Margaret came to the table with cups hooked on her fingers and the teapot. "No, I don't think I have met him. I don't get to Benton County. Oh, I haven't seen Mary Jane in over a year. How is she?"

Louis took a sip of his tea, "Oh, that's too hot. She fine. She so happy to get married."

Margaret said, "I will come to the wedding. Let me write down the date. July eighteenth? What an exciting year! In 1857, I have a second divorce and Mary Jane a wedding. At least it is all happiness for her."

Albert shook his head and told of a problem. "Not quite all happiness. Margaret, you are not going to believe this. Nathaniel Ford had the last laugh."

"What?"

"Yes, Ford told Reuben Shipley that Mary Jane was still his property to be bought for $700, if he wanted to marry her."

"No! She is a free person."

Albert held up his hands to interrupt, "You and I know that. Mary Jane tried to tell Reuben the same, but he is a kind and just man who wants no trouble so he paid the money."

Louis joined into the topic, "Yes, it true! Reuben is a fine man. You wait and see when you meet him. I understand him. He jus' wants to make sure there ain't no problems later on. That's why he paid."

Albert added, "Reuben isn't rich, but he is a landowner and I would say that he is a man of means. He is fifty-seven years old and wise. You can imagine that he is too old to want to deal with the likes of Nathaniel Ford, who made the Holmeses struggle for years to gain custody of their children."

After they chatted a while about the wedding, Albert changed the subject, "Have you heard about the Dred Scott Decision? We thought you might talk with us about that."

Margaret put down her cup, "Oh, I forgot the sweet cakes. We'll need something to sweeten that topic." When she returned with the plate, she stated, "Ha, what's next for you Negroes? I guess you understand the basic idea – the Dred Scott Decision denies citizenship and constitutional protection to Negroes whether slave or free."

Louis nodded, "Sure, but what do you think it means for us?"

"Nothing!" Margaret stood and started to pace. "I think there are nine, maybe ten, Negroes living here in Marion County. I mean, we know that the voters here in Oregon approved Oregon's constitution with both a prohibition against slavery and an exclusion clause barring Negroes from the state, but did anyone come and tell you to get out?" She didn't want an answer; she leaned on the table and then pointed her finger in the air before blurting a loud, "No!"

Albert contradicted her, "Back in 1851, a man named Jacob Vanderpool was expelled. I didn't know him; I read it in the newspaper."

"Is that correct? How could I have missed that?"

Albert said, "It happened when you were on the ship coming back from the East."

"Oh, I do remember someone talking about that, because there were two Negro brothers in Portland that were told to leave that December when we returned in fifty-one, but a petition was circulated and a couple of hundred people signed it. So those two men were allowed to stay. I seem to remember their last name was a first name. Francis, I think." Margaret repeated her opinion. "I don't think the Dred Scott Decision will affect you here in Oregon. And, if someone tried to get you expelled, I'd fight for you with a petition and signatures."

Both men nodded.

Louis finished one of the cakes, "These are tasty. Thank you Miss Margaret."

"Don't act like a slave! You are both free men. I call you Louis, you call me Margaret in my house and Mrs. Bailey on the street where I will call you Mr. Southworth."

Albert slapped the table, "We came to the right person, Louis. She barks like a fighting dog to put everyone in their place. I believe you would help us, if we had trouble with the law." He gave out a hearty laugh.

Margaret remained serious, with her thoughts progressing to other ideas. "The Democrats are strong here in Oregon's government and they're against slavery. We still are not a state, but it will happen soon. I know it! Albert and Louis, listen to me. There is a movement brewing in the East to end slavery. It will happen. Not this year or next, but maybe in ten years. Just be glad you are here and not in the south of the United States."

Louis agreed, "I know you right, Miss ... I mean, Margaret. Why, there is always change. I come back here to the city of Marysville and there is no Marysville. It Corvallis now. It changed its name. Everything changes."

And the years rolled along with more changes.

In 1859 Oregon became a part of the United States as the only free state in the union with a Negro exclusion clause in its constitution.

In 1860 a new president by the name of Abraham Lincoln took office, and Robert Newell was elected to the House in Oregon. They were two good men who would be faced with rising problems in 1861. Both Mankind and Mother Nature wended unwanted changes. In the East, succession and war; in the West, destruction from floods.

* * *

The Democratic Party in Oregon was weakening. When the two Democrats, Robert Newell and Asahel Bush, fought for different locations of the capital, a crack was made in the party. Little by little, the split widened with Governor Lane pursuing a pro-slavery course in Congress; he alienated many of the Democrats who avowed the doctrine of popular sovereignty. With the hostilities in the Democratic Party reaching a peak in 1860, Robert Newell and fourteen other Democrats voted with the Republicans on the slave issue by voting for a Republican for the United States Congress, Edward D. Baker. This split of the Democratic Party was costly; they lost power.

Governor Lane was furious. "Damn it, Newell, how could you support Baker? He just moved to Oregon to get an office. He lost to the Californians, so he moved up here." Lane started to walk away, but turned. "And damn if I will introduce him to the Senate tomorrow. You will have to find someone else." It was December 5, 1860 and the senator from California made the introduction.

A despondent Robert Newell went home that night to Rebecca and his five children. Rebecca was due to give birth next month, so Margaret was there again, to help.

They lived in their new, large home on the hill above the townsite of Champoeg. The rooms were spacious, but did not seem to be; the house was full of rambunctious and noisy children with the oldest being only eleven years old.

Rebecca directed the shenanigans from the rocking chair, "Samuel stop that. If you continually hit Harvy, I must send you to your room without your serving of rice pudding."

Bending to kiss Rebecca's forehead, Robert Newell, reminded his wife what he had said, "I suggested that they never sit at the table side by side." With an impatience stemming from the tensions in Salem, he barked at his son. "Samuel, behave or we'll go outside together to discuss this."

Margaret walked into the room with the steaming pudding. "Good evening, Robert. Welcome home. From what I hear, the capital looks just like the antics at your dinner table. Fighting and excessive talk. Am I correct?"

Robert collapsed into his chair and began eating his dinner. They had not waited for him. As he gobbled some stew, he said, "Margaret, it is horrible there. Bickering on every issue, complaining about the slavery, and making surly references about who had voted for what. Even the Governor is acting like a child. He refused to introduce the new senator to the senate. I don't think things could get worse."

But they did – in the nation and in his home.

On December 20, 1860, South Carolina seceded from the Union.

By February 1861, seven states had declared their succession, formed the Confederacy, and met as an independent government in Alabama.

On March 4, 1861, Abraham Lincoln took office.

On April 12, 1861, the Civil War started with the Confederate attack on Fort Sumter in South Carolina.

Amid all the chaos at work, Robert had a tragedy at home. Rebecca gave birth to a son named George Edward Newell on Saturday, January 26, 1861 and the child died five weeks later, on March 2.

For the whole year of 1861, problems would rain on Robert Newell – literally, politically, and personally. He would never recover from the disasters of this one particular year.

Every year in Oregon, the rains began in September. Everyone welcomed the cool, falling water and accepted the rain as the way of the Northwest. People knew that, with the ninth month of the year, the heat of summer ended and the fall precipitation came. Leaves changed to brilliant colors, pumpkins and squashes laid ready to pick, and the cedar waxwings – passing on their journey south – took the last of the ripened berries from trees and plants.

Every year in Oregon, the rains continued through the winter months. So when the rain came harder than usual in November of 1861, no one gave it much thought. When the rain continued for days and days, it became apparent that the rain was not normal. What was normal for Oregon to have was a lot of drizzle and light rain, but this was a continual deluge.

By the end of November in 1861, the entire Pacific Coast – from southern California to northern Washington – experienced a nonstop downpour for eighteen days. At the end of the rain, the temperatures began to rise and people welcomed the warm weather and blue skies.

Margaret decided to venture into the clear day in Salem and walked over to the blacksmith shop where Albert worked. Margaret said, "I had to get out of the house. I'm so tired of rain." She came with food. "I made too much of this potato casserole. I need you to help eat it up," she lied. She liked making extra to share with Albert, who still lived alone and who still hoped for Mary Anne to return.

"Thanks, Margaret. Give me a minute to finish here." He knocked some clinkers from the fire before he put down his tongs and walked to her. "Just hearing you talk about food made me hungry." He took off his stiff leather apron and reached for a cloth to wipe his brow and hands.

Margaret asked, "What was that stuff you took out of the fire?"

He rubbed his shoulder as he explained. "Those are clinkers – impurities that get in the fire from the rust flakes that fall off the metal. If I don't take them out, they block up the airways and foul the fire."

"Did you hurt your shoulder?"

"No," he said as he rubbed more. "Sometimes I forget the technique of how to guide the hammer down and then let it bounce back up. That conserves my energy and prevents my shoulder from getting sore. If I don't loosen my grip as soon as it hits, all that vibration goes to my bones."

They sat on a bench side by side below a wall with an assortment of tools, hanging from nails.

Albert pulled open a drawer and removed a spoon. "I keep a big spoon here for these times. I guess you have noticed, since you come with food at least once a week."

Margaret nodded, but she was deep in thought. The blacksmith shop was closer to the Willamette River than her place. She looked out at the river and asked, "Is it rising?"

Albert didn't get the gist of her question until he saw where she gazed. He stopped shoveling in the food and turned to look for himself, before saying with a frown, "Yes, it is." He stood and placed the dish on the bench. "Let's go take a look."

They walked a short distance into a field of golden grass that had been beaten to the ground in the excessive rain. "The river really is high!"

Margaret turned to Albert and said, "But surely we don't need to worry. Look at all the distance between the river and Commercial Street. Must be a couple of hundred feet. After all the rainwater drains off the land, we'll see the river start going down. The rain has stopped."

Albert disagreed, "It's so warm. The rainfall waters aren't the problem. The snow is going to melt. The snow on all the mountain ranges."

It was November 28, 1861.

During the early morning hours of December 2 and before people were up and about, the Willamette River broke over the banks in Salem and, in ten minutes, flooded the field of golden grasses where they had walked the day before. In another ten minutes, waters swelled to a depth of four feet in the downtown and raged through the blacksmith shop.

Albert was still at his house, a couple of miles away. He was not there to see the force of the river that ripped the walls from the shop and broke them into boards that floated away. The bench disappeared first, as did the table with the drawer containing the big spoon, and all the tools hanging from nails on the wall. And it did not matter that the tools were heavy and metal, they disappeared. Even the anvil, that weighed more than one hundred pounds, was never to be found. The man who owned the shop lost his entire business in minutes. And the rain began to fall again.

Margaret awoke, unaware of the flood. When she arose, she placed her feet into water ankle deep on the floor of her place. She rushed to the window and looked out on a Commercial Street that was a flowing river. All the wooden walkways were inches from submersion. She saw a horse belly-deep and tied to a post. The water pulled at the animal. Without hesitation, she went out in her nightclothes to get the horse. Wading in water to her knees, she untied the mare and coaxed her up onto the wooden walkway. In those minutes, water covered the walkway and was up to the horse's fetlocks. She tied the horse to the same post, but now he was up elevated from the rushing water. She talked to calm the animal, saying, "Let me dress and I'll ride you to higher ground." Minutes later, she did.

In Salem, the flooding waters of the Willamette River spanned a width of more than one thousand feet, but did not quite reach Albert's house at

1891 Fourth Street; Fourth Street was separated from the river by Water Street, Front Street, Commercial and Liberty Streets.

Louis Southworth was visiting Albert and they walked outside to see the confusion. Soon they were helping people from their homes and carrying children while the parents waded to higher ground.

Farther downstream (north of Salem), the waters of the Willamette River were growing higher as more streams fed into it. Champoeg was twenty-five miles north of Salem. At the same moment in time, when Salem had four feet of water, Champoeg had thirty feet and rising!

By evening, Rebecca and Robert, who lived a half mile from the river in their new home, heard people calling. They looked from their porch as, in the distance, the flood took on biblical proportions; it appeared that the world was preparing for Noah. Smaller trees that they knew should be in their line of vision no longer existed. All they could see was water, which sped by with a sucking force, toppling everything. Robert pointed, "Rebecca, look!" They saw the roof of a barn floating – only the roof, no barn – and someone was on top!

Rebecca gasped and clutched Robert's arm. For the Newells, the year of 1861 had already been a disaster. She remembered her son who had been born in January and was dead by March. She touched her large belly, not knowing if she could cope with more deaths; she was with child again and due to give birth within the month. Her angst was justified; the child she carried would be born in January 1862 and dead by drowning by 1863, leaving her with only five of the eight children she had birthed. As she watched the water of the Willamette rage past, she saw their life being washed away.

"Oh, Robert, look! I see people getting into canoes from the second floor windows of Harvey Higley's new store." Higley's General Store was the tallest building in the Champoeg Townsite with rooms on the second floor used as the Free Mason's Hall.

Robert ran to his red barn as he shouted, "*Ben Franklin* and *Mogul* are in the barn. I must get them out." Just then, two young men rode up and Rebecca sent them to the barn to help Robert remove the two boats. They mounted them on wagons and hitched horses to pull the boats to the edge of the water.

The river had risen so quietly and quickly during the day that people had not noticed and were marooned in their homes. When they finally saw the deep water, their only option was to climb to their garret and out onto their roof.

Robert put the first boat into the water and one young man grabbed the oars out of the wagon bed. Robert pointed to a tree and shouted over the roar of the passing waters, "Get that person out of the tree!" He turned and pointed at another place, "and I think I saw people out on the roof of that cabin."

Robert's second boat was put in and rowed away as the canoe with the people from the Higley's General Store came ashore. The man with the paddles for the canoe turned it around and started back, shouting, "There's more people to git. Everybody from the town went to Higley's Store cuz its got two-stories. They thought they'd be high enough. But the whole building is rocking like it's ready to fall." Rowing away, he disappeared into the night while he continued to shout words that faded within the darkness, as well.

A home floated past with lights coming from the windows. "Let's hope the folks got out. They probably were in a rush and left the lanterns burning." All of a sudden, the house caught in an eddy and made a complete circle before proceeding down river and floating out of sight.

The rain continued to fall heavily as people were brought to the shore. Robert directed them to his house. Soon there were dozens of people heading to his house.

As the people arrived at the Newells' home, Rebecca started organizing. "I pulled all our blankets out and put them upstairs in the large meeting room. I want all of you women and children to go up and undress. We must get your clothes dry or you will freeze tonight. I do not have blankets for the multitudes I see coming."

She told the men as they reached the house, "All of you men must grab more of the firewood outside before coming in. And then go stoke up the fireplaces for me. We must warm the house so we can dry everyone's clothing."

From a hook at the back entrance, she grabbed a coil of rope that they used for clotheslines in the yard. Opening a drawer in the kitchen, she reached for a hammer and nails before walking upstairs.

"No, no, ladies, I said undress! You must get out of your petticoats and undergarments, as well as your dresses or nightclothes. You are soaked to the bone and this is no time to be modest." She set the tools down and continued to give orders, "Take a blanket to wrap around yourself after you remove all your clothes." She pulled out a chair and shouted a command to a young woman, "Climb on this chair and hammer a nail there." Rebecca pointed high on the wall. "Then we can string a line in front of the fireplace. We must dry all the clothes as quickly as we can."

The young woman protested, "But a nail will ruin your wallpaper."

"Wallpaper is not important! We need to keep people from getting sick from the cold."

Rebecca chose four of the women who would fit into her clothing and gave them some of her garments to wear. "You four women dress in my clothes and go downstairs to the kitchen to start cooking for everyone. I imagine that no one had time to have meals today. I will come and show you where everything is. You need to start making cornbread and ...." She turned to shout again, "One nail is not enough! We need nails on the other side. Ladies, help me help you. Think! Get this clothesline up, back and forth across the room." She turned to a small child crying in dripping clothes. "Why is this child in wet clothes? Who owns him? Get him naked! I will go get all my own children's clothing to put on the little ones. You two ladies come with me to bring some clothes back for the children."

One of the women said as they walked to the next room, "Rebecca, how else can I help?"

"Gertrude, get some of my children's toys and try to calm the little ones. They must be terrified. I am going down to help get the food started."

She started to the stairway and stopped to say to the man coming up with an armful of firewood, "Leave the wood stacked on the top step. The ladies are not presentable. They can stoke their own fire." She continued slowly down each step; she was too large with child to hurry.

Once downstairs, she shouted, "I need two men to go milk our cows." The house was teeming with wet, dripping men. It looked like a dozen men were in her parlor. "Please do not sit on my sofas with your wet clothing. When you have the fires roaring, please go feed the animals in the barn. Look for a place where you and your sons could sleep in the barn. Look for old blankets out there. We should have some in the barn." Before she huffed off to the kitchen, she threw out her arms and shouted, "Stop standing around! Be useful! We have much to do!" She stopped again and turned, "I imagine we will be living together for days. We need men to shoot some game. While you are still wet, some of you could split more logs. Don't sit here, feeling sorry for yourself and counting your loses; get to work!"

For hours, Robert supervised the work to save people with the boats while the river was rising at a rate of three inches per hour. The river continued to rise for four days until it crested. On December 6, 1861 it was estimated that the river rose to a height of fifty-five feet above its lowest level. That would be an elevation of 112 feet above mean sea level. The current flowed so rapid that all the structures in the townsite of Champoeg, save one, were gone.

The one remaining building was the immense and sturdy warehouse owned by the Hudson's Bay Company. It had moved fifty feet off its foundation but was so badly damaged that it was never to be used again.

When Robert finally came to his home it was close to midnight. He evaluated the situation and asked everyone to squeeze downstairs so he could talk, "Friends and neighbors, I have counted twenty families here tonight." He stepped up on a wooden chair, "Now we know how Noah felt!" He paused. "But I want to assure all of you that I will not bring the cows and horses into this crowded ark." No one laughed; only smiles showed their appreciation. He continued with a solemn face and serious words. "I, like you, have lost everything. But we are Oregonians who know hardship. We will rebuild and prosper again. For now, we must be mindful of the situation. I welcome each of you in my home and barn, but we must have some rules." Rebecca handed him a steaming cup of coffee and he took a sip before handing it back.

They discussed the size of the food portions for each person so his supplies would last, the procedures for the chamber pots and bathing, and work assignments. Robert was blunt, "Those of you who know someone in Butteville, Oregon City, Portland, or Salem, I want you to see if their homes survived; even Noah would find it hard to feed twenty families, each with many children." Robert asked for a show of hands and then assigned who would use his horse tomorrow and the next day to go and seek other quarters for their family.

"Tomorrow, I want men out at the river. Today, I saw pigs and cows drift by and had to let them go. I needed to bring in the people, but tomorrow I want volunteers with ropes to go to the river and try to capture any animals they can. I have five firearms for hunting; talk to me to borrow one when the sky clears." He stopped a moment and inhaled, "If anyone is missing a family member, raise your hand." No one did. "Does anyone know of a missing friend?" Again, no hands. "Let's bow our heads in thanks."

The next morning, Harvey Higley left in a wagon and found his damaged store, caught in hazelnut tree branches, a mile from where it had stood in Champoeg. When he arrived back at the Newell's he had a lot to tell. "My store was empty 'cept for these two bolts of cloth – some plaid wool and the other is toweling. We sure can use towels!" He let people smile at his humor before pulling out the chicken coop. "And look at this! We all goin' to eat well tonight." The coop had six chickens. "And we found a shed full of apples. It had slammed into my store and got lodged with the hazelnut trees, too." He also found a family by the name of Smith who agreed to let the Higley family of six stay with them so they would leave the Newells home the next day.

After that one warm spell that had melted the snow and caused the intense flooding down the whole Pacific Coast, the weather turned cold and the rains continued until July 1862. What cattle did not drown struggled to survive a bitter cold; many animals died from the low temperatures.

At Fort Umpqua in Douglas County, they kept records of the

precipitation from October through the end of March – 71.6 inches of water fell during that timeframe. In the Pacific Ocean, from the Columbia River to San Francisco and along the coastline for twenty miles out, one could find drifting debris from Oregon's destroyed structures.

The land values in Champoeg plummeted and the lots that Robert Newell owned were never sold. Even if he could have sold them, the original value of $500 had dropped to $50. He lost his store and all the contents, his large mill, all the structures holding firewood for the steamboats, the post office, and all the income that would have been derived from those investments. All of Robert Newell's businesses and means of livelihood were gone; and the flood washed away his dreams for Champoeg, as well.

What Champoeg lost, Butteville gained. It had been built on slightly higher ground and did not wash away completely. Oregon City and Linn City suffered greatly, but rebuilt.

Margaret, with her wry humor, commented afterward, "It was quite a show for many. People in Oregon City got to see the small side-wheeler *Saint Clair* ride over ripples in the river where the Willamette Falls should have been. People of Portland got to watch everyone's belongings from Champoeg and much of Oregon City float past them. And I understand the steamers could make quite a fast trip from Oregon City to Portland; it must have been like going on a carnival ride."

As much as he could, Robert Newell had come to his neighbors' rescue. When Margaret and Albert came to visit him to see how he fared from the flood, people were camped all around his house in the same fashion that she had seen the Kalapuyans camped around the Methodist Mission so many years ago. Under trees were families who had made shelters by leaning planks of wood against the tree trunk. In the small space beneath the planks, they had small fires burning for warmth and cooking.

"My house is full of my houseless neighbors, too," he told Margaret. "They have nothing, and what little I have left, I am using to feed and clothe as many as I can." Tears came to Robert's eyes, "Did you hear about my new son, Charles? He was born in January when it still was flooding, ..." He stopped to sob. Reaching for his handkerchief, his shoulders shook.

"Margaret, everything I worked for is gone. I guess I should be thankful for a healthy child."

Margaret grasped his forearm.

Unbeknownst to them, little Charles would drown the next year. And, fate was not finished handing out the catastrophes to the Newells; Rebecca would give birth to three more children, lose one of them within months, and then die herself in 1867 at the age of thirty-five.

But, for the moment, Robert regained his composure to say, "Charles is only six months old, but Rebecca has aged ten years since the floods. Every day she works her fingers to the bone, cooking and helping others. I have none of my businesses left here, and I must help her. I am moving my family to Idaho where I'll negotiate with the Indians and our government to acquire the legal title for Indians' land."

Robert Newell succeeded in his new responsibilities. In 1863, his work with the Nez Percé was recognized. However, the Nez Percé refused to cede any land or sign the treaty until the following article was added to the agreement:

> Inasmuch as the Indians in Council have expressed the desire that Robert Newell should have confirmed to him a piece of land lying between the Snake and Clearwater rivers, the same having given to him in the past and described in an instrument of writing and signed by several chiefs of the tribe, it is hereby agreed that the said Robert Newell shall receive from the United States a patent for the said tract of land.

Yes, Robert Newell had a moment of contentment among his longtime friends, the Nez Percé.

Mary Jane Holmes Shipley Drake
(A few years before she died in 1925.)

Photo courtesy of:
Benton County Historical Society & Museum
1101 Main Street
Philomath, OR 97370
Telephone: 541-929-6230

CHAPTER 16

1864 – 1875

Twelve years had passed since the disappearance of Mary Anne. Albert sat in his blacksmith shop eating a piece of unfinished toast from his breakfast and listening to one of her songs in his head; he still heard Mary Anne's sweet voice after all these years. On his property at Fourth and River streets, he had built his own shop from boards that had piled along the riverbank after the flood. He was located in a good place for business, only one block off the busy streets of Liberty and Commercial. He reached for a drink of water and, while he drank, he let Mary Anne sing her song to the end.

At this time in his life, he knew that he could not direct his own destiny because other people and Mother Nature often stepped into his path. But, at the same time, he didn't feel some force greater than himself was going to make all the decisions about his life; he had some say. And although he had acknowledged to himself that Mary Anne might never come back to him, he had never looked for another woman. The 1860 U.S. Census had stated that there were only twenty Negroes living in Marion County. "Not many women for me to choose from anyway," he mumbled as he swallowed his last bite. He sat and counted the Negroes whom he knew and got to the number eighteen. "I wonder, whom did I miss?"

Just then, three children came to the shop where the two barn-like doors were propped open with large rocks. "G'afternoon, Mr. Bayless," a little blonde girl said to him. "Can we come visit ya?"

"Of course, Miss Matilda, come on in. I've been talking to myself since no one was here. I would prefer to talk to you. Are you coming home from school?" Before he gave her a chance to answer, he noticed a new child, "Oh, who's this? Matilda, I know you and your brother Bert, but I don't know this little girl. I thought I knew everyone in the neighborhood."

Matilda blurted an introduction as she coaxed the little girl forward by pulling her by the hand. "She called Cynthia. She new in school."

"Howdy do, Cynthia. Have they told you what I have for children that stop and chat with me?"

The little girl nodded a nervous bob of her head while clutching Matilda's hand.

"What did they tell you?"

"Sticks of candy."

Albert turned, reached around a post, and pulled three peppermint sticks from a jar on his workbench.

A horse in a stall not far from the children made a loud neigh. Cynthia jumped in fright, Matilda laughed, and Bert said, "He wants one, too."

"I have a carrot for him. Who wants to feed him?"

Matilda reached for the carrot, taking it in one hand and a peppermint stick in the other. "I like to feed horses."

After the children went on their way, Albert finished trimming the horse's hooves and nailed on a new set of shoes. He hung his apron and took his hat before saying to the horse, "Guess I don't have to talk to myself. I can talk to you. Let's get you home like I promised." Albert grabbed the reins and tied them to the back of his wagon. He closed up the shop and headed down Commercial Street toward downtown.

After he dropped off the horse, he drove his wagon back onto Commercial Street and stopped not far from Margaret's place; she had invited him for lunch. First, he went and bought a copy of *The Statesman*. As he had done in Tennessee, he still read the newspaper. Sometimes he posted an article on the wall in his blacksmith shop when there was something worth saving. Like last year's issue in January of 1863, when Abraham Lincoln had delivered the Emancipation Proclamation and freed all slaves in the Confederate states, that newspaper with the two-inch-high headline still was tacked to the wall in his shop. He liked to look at it every day.

Thinking how good it was going to be to chat over lunch with Margaret, Albert headed that way, walking beneath the wooden sign – Starkey-McCully Buildings – swinging and creaking in the breeze. Women passed him in both directions with their skirts rustling and their gossip fading in the same breezes as Albert walked on. On a bench, a man sat and leaned against the wall of a store, puffing on his pipe; suddenly, he pulled his pipe from his mouth and stood as a penny farthing bicycle came with a ding-ding-ding; people stepped aside to let it rush past.

Amid all the quiet sounds, Albert's ears perked. Behind him he thought he heard a familiar name. His heart jumped when *Mary Anne* came again to his ears. Some man was irritated and, in a blustery voice, said words that Albert could not understand until *Mary Anne* was said again. Albert turned.

At the other end of the block stood a man who appeared to flay someone who was out of Albert's view. People stepped as far as they could from the situation and hurried past; a dog arrived and started barking at the man. The man gestured with large sweeps of his arms, put his hand on his hip, leaned toward the person, and, if Albert summed up the sight correctly, the man continued to castigate until Albert was a step away. Still Albert could not see who was getting the tongue-lashing.

"I brought you and your children across the continent; I fed you and helped in any way I could. Now you think I owe you more?" The man shouted. "Mary Ann, I have nothing – no money and only the clothes on my back. I can help you no longer. Mary Ann, stop looking at me with those doe like eyes."

In a little voice, she pleaded, "No! No sir, you don't owe us. I jus' don't know where to go or what to do. We git here and my boys are hungry. I don't know what to do."

Albert, in his usual erect stance and air of confidence, approached the man and stood next to him. There he saw the woman with the name Mary Ann – a very small and very black Negro woman squeezing two young children to her sides. With each burst of incriminating comments that rushed from the mouth of the redheaded man, the woman cringed and frowned.

Albert, who stood taller than the man and seemed twice as tall as this apparent Mary Ann, said in a forceful voice and an outstretched hand, "May I interrupt and introduce myself?"

The man jerked his head around and looked up to see Albert before saying with a huff, "No need to interrupt; I'm done here. And I don't care to meet another nigger." He walked off.

Albert removed his hat and turned to Mary Ann, "My name is Albert Bayless and I am a blacksmith living here in Salem. May I offer to help you?"

"Guess you know my name. He sure shouted it for all to hear. My whole name is Mary Ann Reynolds and these are my two boys." She made a little curtsy.

"This may seem to be a strange question, but do you spell your name with an *e* on the end?"

She did have doe like eyes, which first looked innocent, and then puzzled, just like a frightened doe might have looked when confronted with a confusing situation. All of a sudden her eyes started to twinkle and she chuckled, "Why, I not quite sure what you say." She was black like ebony – a face like shiny, polished ebony – with her hair pulled tight under her cloth cap that tied under her chin. Her pudgy arms and middle jiggled a bit as she chuckled. She seemed full of mirth.

Albert wondered how she could be so calm and chuckling after that man had berated her. He looked into her doe like eyes and began his question again. "I used to know a woman who was named Mary Anne and she spelled her name with an *e* at the end. Do you spell it that way?"

One of her boys, the larger one, spoke, "Ma don't read or write. She most likely don't know that she don't have an *e* on the end. Well, that's how I think it's spelt. You know, just with A-N-N."

"I see," said Albert. "Well, excuse me for confusing you with something that has no importance while all of us are standing here hungry."

At that moment, a couple walked past and greeted him. "Hello, Albert."

Albert responded, "Good to see you, Joseph. Drop by the shop tomorrow. I've finished fixing the buckle on your belt."

On the ground next to the Reynolds was a rug-like bag with two wooden handles. Albert reached for it. "May I carry this for you? Come, let's go this way. I think lunch is ready." As the group strode down the walkway, more people greeted Albert. He raised his hat each time. Margaret's door was at the north end of the block, and they were there in a minute. He knocked.

"Hello, Margaret. I found some new people who have come to town. I knew you would like to meet them." He grinned mischievously.

Without a look of surprise, Margaret pulled the door wider and said, "Come in, come in. Let's go to the kitchen where there is more room and then we can learn each other's names."

The first room in Margaret's house – converted bit by bit to be her workroom – was filled with bolts of fabric stacked here and there, half-finished dresses hanging around the walls, and a large table strewn with scissors, large spools of thread, measuring tapes, and all the paraphernalia needed for her seamstress business.

As they passed her workspace, Margaret said, "Someday I will have a storefront with a window to show examples of my finished dresses. I dream of a brick store."

Arriving at the kitchen table, Albert pulled out a chair for Mary Ann and said to Margaret, "It is good to dream. I have my own smithy shed now; I'm sure you will have your seamstress shop in due time. I just hope it won't take a flood to get you there, like it did me."

"Oh, it will. I already am close to flood stage. I have so many dresses to make that I am overflowing with business. Luckily I have the general store right next door in the Starkey-McCully Building. I am saved a lot of time because they sell dressmaking goods besides groceries and tools. But I'm afraid I need to look for someone to assist with all the sewing."

A young proud voice of one of the boys blurted, "My ma is good at sewin'. Ain't you, Ma?"

"If I weren't so black, you'd know I's blushin' but thank you, son."

Margaret eased the moment, saying, "We can talk about sewing after we introduce ourselves. My name is Margaret Bailey or Mrs. Bailey even though I am divorced."

After introductions and after the ravenous young bellies were filled, the group shared stories. Albert went first and told of how he came from Tennessee to the gold mines and up to Salem.

Margaret found the boys very interested in her trip to Oregon by ship and her tales of meeting many Kalapuyans when she was at the Methodist Mission. She omitted the ugly details about her marriages and divorces.

Mary Ann began with her freedom. "My life began when I got my freedom at sixteen and married my boys' daddy. His name was David Reynolds and we lived in Missouri. One night last year, our little house caught fire and I lost my husband and my two daughters. When it burned, my two boys and me were over helpin' some neighbors pick apples. That's who brought me on the wagon train; my neighbor, he named Mr. James

Ord. He weren't doing too good in Missouri and I surely wasn't either. So we came here to make a new life." Mary Ann turned to Albert. "He ain't like how you saw him today. He a good man, but his family is hungry and I was too much for him to worry 'bout, right then."

Albert nodded and asked the boys, "Did anything exciting happen on your trip here to Oregon?"

By the time all the stories were finished and the group was well acquainted, the whole afternoon had passed. Margaret asked, "Where are you staying?"

"Ma, we ain't goin' to sleep by the train tracks again, are we? I got so scared when the trains came and blew those whistles."

Albert spoke up, "No, you are not. I invited you to Margaret's for lunch and I'm inviting you to stay at my house to sleep." He looked at Margaret before saying, "Why, I've been waiting for a Mary Ann to come and stay with me. Isn't that right, Margaret?"

Ignoring Albert's reference, Margaret stood and picked up some of the dirty plates, "He has a nice but empty house. It could use some people. And, Mary Ann, please come back tomorrow to show me how you sew. I'll have you hem a dress." Margaret stacked more of the dirty plates and emphasized, "Now, don't get your hopes up because I am very particular. However, if I like your work, I will hire you."

It turned out that Mary Ann was excellent at sewing and Margaret did hire her.

One can't say that Albert fell in love with Mary Ann like he had fallen for Mary Anne. He had been younger back then, the times had been filled with excitement from the trip to Celilo Falls and from the near death experience with the Cayuse, but mainly the two lovers had had private romantic days with just the two of them.

Now, with this new Mary Ann, it wasn't easy to get to know the other. Each day he left for the blacksmith shop and in the house they were never alone with two boys in their lives. Nevertheless, their love grew day by day.

This new Mary Ann was not playful. She did not sing and fill the house with music. She was not tall and pretty to look at. But for Albert she was everything he wanted and had hoped for. This new Mary Ann came with patience – he marveled at how she managed her boys and settled arguments. To everyone, she was considerate, kind, helpful, sweet, thoughtful, and happy. She had life experience – she could cook, sew, and take care of a house. He thought it a bonus that she came with a family – he never thought he would have a house full of children. And full of children it was, because there were always friends of the boys in the house, too. However, there was one trait that won his heart – she gave him more love than he had ever thought possible.

They lived together for a year and never spoke of marriage. Nevertheless, in that year, they talked a lot. They shared stories of their days as slaves and their past lives. He could share his deepest thoughts and emotions with her, but he didn't want to talk about Mary Anne. "Please understand that I can't talk about her. It's too painful and I feel guilty. No, it's more. It's the not knowing! I hurt because I don't know what happened to Mary Anne. I don't know where she is. I don't even know if she is dead or alive. I failed her."

That night, after sharing the pain he carried with him each day, he had a disturbing dream:

Albert saw himself walking the muddy street of Jacksonville. His pockets bulged with the gold he had found. He was coming from the stables where he had been working as a blacksmith and was heading for the Chinaman's place. His head hung low and he was missing someone, but he didn't know who it was.

A sound caught his attention. A sign was squeaking in the breeze.

Squeak!

A silence followed until another squeak came as the breeze moved the sign again.

Squeak!

He looked to the sign and his heart jumped. It was the sign for the saloon spelled with that extra E but it said:

S A L O O N E, Mary Anne

with that extra E and the face of Mary Anne McAlister below the words.

All of a sudden, the sign made a SQUEAK! And it changed to:

S A L O O N, Mary Ann

With the face of Mary Ann Reynolds below the words.

That next morning, Albert told Mary Ann about the unsetting dream. "I woke in a cold sweat and still heard the squeaking so I got up and looked out the window. The large door to the smithy shed was half-open and making the squeaking sound. I went out and secured it, but I couldn't get back to sleep." He looked into her doe like eyes. "If I just knew where she was and what happened to her."

Mary Ann touched his arm and caressed it to calm him. "I understand. I wonder a lot 'bout her, too, and I think, Albert, someday I think we's goin' to know."

At the end of that first year, they felt like they had known each other for years, not just one year.

Soon, important events became building blocks to form a solid foundation in their relationship. In April of 1865, when Lee surrendered and the war ended, the whole town of Salem went out into the streets and celebrated. Though Albert and Mary Ann had nothing to do with the war, they relished the end as if they had had a hand in it. By the end of the year, Oregon ratified the Thirteenth Amendment to the U.S. Constitution and abolished slavery. Being together at this historic moment had deep meaning for them as well; Albert and Mary Ann hugged and clung to the other. "I never thought I would see this day. Albert, now all Negroes can feel how we do. They's free."

All of the Negroes in the Salem area wanted to celebrate together and they went to Mary Jane Holmes' place because she lived in a big house with Reuben Shipley.

"Uncle Albert and Mary Ann!" Mary Jane squealed. "Come in, come in."

Louis Southworth had already arrived and the music filled the house. A pig had been slaughtered and put out to cook in the back yard. They sang songs while the women cooked in the kitchen. Louis fiddled *Swanee River, Dixie Land* and *Home Sweet Home*; happiness and song filled the place.

One of the women commented, "Why look at Mary Ann and Mary Jane. They look like short and pudgy twins. They's got the same noses and are as black as night."

Mary Ann retorted, "We look the same, but I's'bout twenty years older." She grabbed Mary Jane and started twirling around the room with the music. Their skirts flew up and everyone laughed. "Louis play a dance tune while we dance! You thinks we's twins 'cuz I act young like Mary Jane. I's young at heart." She was.

One Saturday in 1866, after Albert and Mary Ann had been living together for almost two years, Robert Newell pulled up in a wagon piled high with furniture. He told them, "Rebecca and I have decided to stay up in Idaho and to sell everything here in Oregon. She is with child again and could not come, but she insisted that I bring some of my furniture to your house and Margaret's. Well, she said that you, Albert and Mary Ann, get first pick off the wagon ... on one condition."

Albert sensed something big and said, "Do you have some quote from the master of all quotes to prepare me for what this condition might be?"

"Ah, yes, Shakespeare. Hmmm, 'To be or not to be' straightforward. Let me think," Robert hesitated only a few seconds. "Yes, I have found one quite appropriate from Romeo and Juliet." His quick mind and tongue quoted:

Therefore love moderately; long love doth so;
Too swift arrives as tardy as too slow.

Robert whisked off his hat and made a bow with the sweep of his arm. "As you may surmise from that, Rebecca thinks the time has come for our furniture to be a wedding gift."

Albert let out a hearty guffaw and pulled Mary Ann close. "How did Rebecca know that Mary Ann and I decided to marry this fall?"

Later, while the group of friends sat around Margaret's table in her Salem place, Robert shared the details of his sales. He had sold all his remaining interests in Champoeg for $100 and his 230 acres for $3,000. "These are large losses, but Champoeg will never be what it was. And, it is obvious that Rebecca and I are going to stay in Lewiston. I like living up at Fort Lapwai, near my friends of the Nez Percé tribe.

"Did I ever tell you that *lapwai* means butterfly? Millions of butterflies migrate through the area. I love seeing them. Actually, I love hearing the words of my beloved Nez Percé people. The names of things in their language move me." Robert leaned closer with a twinkle in his eye and smiled, before he said, "Shakespeare comes to mind." And he made a quote that moved each of them:

What's in a name? that which we call a rose
by any other name would smell as sweet.

A silence spread through the room and enveloped the friends while they thought of their past times together. They realized without saying that Robert may never come visit again and that this might be the last quote he would give to them. Not one of the three had been without suffering and agony in their lives together. Margaret had the abuse from her husband and horrible divorces which left her quite poor. Albert still waited to understand how he was deprived of his marriage to Mary Anne. But Robert Newell seemed to have had more disappointments than the others.

Margaret broke the quiet with a question. She hoped the answer would tell them that Robert finally had been given the honor he deserved. She asked, "Have you been made the Indian Agent like you wanted?"

With apparent pain in his face, he shook his head and said, "No, I haven't. And I do believe that I have prevented a muss among the relationship of the tribes and our government. You know I've been doing the job of the Indian Agent; I just have not been paid as such."

"They are such fools!" Margaret seethed.

And Margaret would repeat that comment again within the year.

One Thursday evening on September 18, 1866, Albert and Mary Ann were wed at the Methodist Episcopal Church, where they were members. It was a simple ceremony – the bride and groom, the minister, and the two witnesses who were Margaret and Louis.

September of 1866 had another important event: Oregon ratified the Fourteenth Amendment guaranteeing citizenship and equal protection of laws for all, including Negroes.

It was a time of quiet passing for both the wedding and the new amendment.

One day in late 1867, Margaret charged into Albert's shop exclaiming, "Lo and behold, Oregon repealed its ratification of the Fourteenth Amendment! They are such fools!"

Up on Albert's wall next to the newspaper with the two-inch-high announcement of Emancipation Proclamation was the front page of the newspaper about the Fourteenth Amendment.

Albert put down the forceps and hammer, "Don't worry, Margaret, what that repeal means is nothing. It will have no effect because a sufficient number of the other states ratified it."

She repeated her logic, "I know, but it makes the Oregon legislators look like the fools that they are."

When 1868 arrived, Albert and Margaret would learn what had happened in Robert Newell's life through a letter.

Margaret stopped by the blacksmith shop and said, "Mary Ann told me that I needed to come see you but she would not tell me what this is about. Has something happened?"

Albert washed his hands in a bucket of water and splashed his face before he suggested they go to the house to talk. "I had a visit from Joe Meek the other day. He came with a letter from Robert Newell. Let's sit with Mary Ann while I tell you the news. Robert wrote it on his way to Washington DC. He's going face to face to get that job he wants as the official Indian agent."

When they entered the house, Albert asked Mary Ann, "Where did I put the paper with Robert's letter?" Albert turned to Margaret to explain what he had done. "I wanted you to see it so I copied it word for word. I didn't think I could tell you everything in my own words and I didn't want to forget anything."

Mary Ann went into the bedroom and returned with the paper.

Margaret, unaware of the contents of the letter, commented, "Sitting on and looking at this furniture that they gave you makes one think that Robert and Rebecca are right here." She reached out her hand and took the paper.

Begun: March 1867
Finished and ready to send: May 1868

Dear Joe and any friends you share this with:

I am behind on sending you news about my life. This letter will bring you up to date on the news of my past year.

At my ripe old age of sixty-one, I am again a father. I gave the baby my name; Robert Newell Jr. was born on the 5th of May in the year of 1867. After being with Rebecca for more than twenty years, she bore me eleven children. But this one was her last child because she died two weeks later on May 19th. It was the day before her birthday. On May 20th she would have been 35 years old. Rebecca is buried at Lewiston in Idaho Territory. May the Lord have mercy on her soul.

This made me realize how short life can be. I decided I must go to Washington DC to talk directly with our leaders about the Indian situation. So, I left Lewiston I.T. at 7 o'clock in the morning on horseback. The weather was fine, but it was a lonesome day. I was alone and traveling with a heavy heart for leaving my family for such a long journey. My destination seemed so far away. I rode a good distance of forty miles that first day and arrived at The Dalles.

On March 31st, I boarded a steamer at The Dalles and arrived in Portland at eight in the evening. Inasmuch as the next leg of my trip did not depart until April 10th, I visited old friends and wrote letters. It is never easy to travel such distances and the steamer reached Astoria and was delayed by inclement weather. So, I wrote more letters. On Monday, April 13th, I boarded the steamer for San Francisco again. Cape Disappointment did not disappoint all my fears; we had much trouble crossing the bar into the Pacific. Most everyone was seasick. Not I.

I am traveling to Washington DC with a party of six: four Indian Chiefs who want to resolve the re-division of their lands and James O'Neil, who is the Indian agent from Lapwai. As you know, O'Neil holds the position I feel should be mine so the travels have been uncomfortable since he knows I want his position. Possibly I can make my case by being there in the capital. As the beaver said to the otter, we'll meet at the hatter shop.

In San Francisco, I boarded the steamer Montana and had a pleasant trip. By gum, aboard the ship, I bought the best cigars for only 2 bits per one hundred and a pineapple for 1 bit. I had eaten pineapple only once before. I arrived in New York City on May 14th. (Only a few days short of a year since I lost my wife.)

New York is truly a wonder. I stayed at the Metropolitan Hotel and attended the theatre – what a grand sight it was. This old mountain man has finally gotten a taste of city life. I am going to post this tomorrow. This letter is quite lengthy. You will have to wait to learn of my success or failure for the Indian lands.

Yours truly,
Doc Newell

"Oh, no!" Margaret looked up to the others and continued, "Rebecca is gone. That sweet young girl has died and surely gone to heaven. Eleven children! And she lost four as babies. Oh, I am sad that I will never see her again. Let's say a prayer for her even though a year has passed since she died." They sat with bowed heads for many minutes.

Concerning the affairs of the Indians, Robert Newell worked from May 27, 1868 until August 19 in negotiations with the government. The Indians who came with him sat at his side at all times. At one point, they petitioned to have Robert as their Indian agent and the senate duly confirmed him on July 22. By August, Newell gave bond to the government for $20,000 as Indian agent, they completed the treaty, and Robert was ready to go back home. He wrote in a letter:

> By gum, I'm tired of this place. My patience is nearly gone trying to work with the Indian Department. We get no accommodating there and every one is displeased who goes there on business. I'm making an overland trip home to Idaho soon. I'll get things done when home.

Back in Idaho, Robert Newell began his duties as Indian Agent in October of 1868. Nothing was easy, nevertheless he found materials to rebuild fences, repair the sawmill, and build a new school. An outbreak of smallpox closed the school for months and a drought caused the failure of the crops; neither the wheat nor oats were harvested and only a third of the corn and potatoes matured. The year was difficult enough, and then whisky arrived making things worse. He couldn't find the source of the spirits to squelch the drinking.

The end was coming.

At the close of the summer of 1869, there were changes in policies in Washington D.C. The War Department was placed in charge of Indian affairs and Newell lost his job.

Robert had married Mrs. Jane M. Ward only a few months before he lost his job. She was the last bright light in his life; his candle was burning low.

In November of 1869, Robert Newell had a heart attack and died.

Marion Hotel in Salem
Circa 1871
(between S. Commercial, State, and Ferry Streets)
Photographer: Unknown.

CHAPTER 17

1881

Kneeling in snow and ice to check for a strange sound under his wagon, Albert looked up to Mary Ann who huddled on the bench. They were at Salem's train station. She was wrapped in blankets with the reins draped across her lap. In her gloved hands, she held a broad, black umbrella against the falling snow. Large wet clumps fell. Simultaneously, staring into the others' eyes, their lips parted into smiles.

Albert said, "I think I just need to oil the suspension when we get back home." And then he pointed, "Oh, look, the stagecoach is coming."

White and bright, the landscape quietly accepted more snow, adding to the eighteen inches. Mary Ann began to shiver and pulled the blanket up and over her head. The worst of the storm was yet to come; temperatures would drop to negative degrees. It was to be a killer winter, creating havoc across the whole Northwest. Cattlemen would lose ninety percent of their herds through starvation because, in most places, three feet of snow, from January into March of 1881, covered and killed the bunchgrass. Many of the wild animals and birds, deprived of sustenance, would suffer the same fate as the cattle.

The stagecoach stopped in front of the train station and the passengers emptied out onto the platform that had been cleared of snow.

Peering across the distance between them, they saw Margaret. She extended her arm and waved.

Albert shouted, "We'll hurry over there to get you out of the snow."

Once the three stood together and hugged, Mary Ann blurted, "Oh, I's glad you're here. I can't wait." She broke off her sentence upon seeing Margaret so close, for she appeared differently than the last time. Margaret's head was in a bonnet tied beneath her chin, but white hair protruded down over her lined forehead, and a double chin of loose skin was folded over the hat strings. With the smile still on her lips, Margaret's chalky face formed a lacework of wrinkles and creases. Mary Ann leaned over to hug Margaret again and felt a dowager's hump caused by osteoporosis.

Margaret blurted, "Albert, your hair has gone gray, but Mary Ann, you look the same. You haven't aged in these eight years!"

"Maybe that's what you see, but I don't move so fast no more. And my eyes don't let me sew no more either. But I don't care 'bout all that. It so good to see you."

Albert added, "We were happy to get your letter that you were coming to visit."

"I came all the way from Seattle, where I live now. And in this snowstorm! This weather started in mid-December. I thought I could not come. Then the Chinook winds brought a warm spell and I left Seattle. Last night the temperatures dropped and the snow started again." They stared at each other for a moment or two before Margaret complained, "What a trick to pull on me. Mary Ann, you stayed young and I'm an old hag."

"Oh, Margaret, don't be angry. I'm so happy to be with you."

They hugged again and Margaret confessed, "I am glad to be with both of you, too. I have been very alone for a long time. Everyone should have someone who knows them as well as we know each other. Oh, the times we have had together." She seemed to drift off into one of those times before finishing. "I have missed you and have only had my memories to fill me. Let's go and get out of this cold!"

That said, Albert dropped her traveling bag into the wagon and climbed up to the bench where he extended a hand to pull the women up before he sat and flicked the reins; the horse lurched forward. The narrow wheels plodded easily through the deep snow.

Margaret exclaimed, "Let's go make more times to be remembered. Salem, here we come!"

"Margaret, we rented a room at the Marion Hotel for you 'cuz our house is full of youngins." Mary Ann stopped talking when she saw the look of surprise on Margaret's face. She knew what the misunderstanding was. "No, these aren't our youngins. We got two of Mary Jane's stepboys living wit' us. George is fourteen or so and his brother, James is 'bout twelve, I think. And we have a young man in his twenties who works in the blacksmith shop. He lives wit' us, too. He called Jack Grubb."

Margaret threw back her head and laughed, "Here I thought you were foolish and went and had little ones of your own. But tell me; why do you have Mary Jane's boys?"

Albert stated, "We'll talk about that while we eat. So you're not upset that you can't stay at our house? We just wanted you to be comfortable."

Margaret patted Albert's knee and said, "No, how could I be upset? I thank you for doing this. It was me who wrote and invited myself. Thank you for getting me from the stagecoach, and I am grateful that I will have a warm, dry place to sleep."

"And eat! Let's go to the hotel. I am quite hungry." Mary Ann insisted. "We don't eat out much. This is a treat for me."

Mary Ann handed the umbrella to Margaret to hold. "The umbrella is big enough to keep the snow off all three of us if the person in the middle holds it."

Mary Ann tucked the blanket around all their legs and settled close to Margaret.

The snowfall started to abate and scattered clouds shifted above to expose some small patches of blue. Downtown Salem was only a mile from the train station. The ride was a winter wonderland with all the bushes, trees, buildings, fences, and parked wagons outlined in puffy snow.

Albert asked, "How was your trip here?"

"I took a stagecoach from Seattle to Portland and then took another to Salem. I had to wait on a bench in a small station for three hours before the second stage came for me. I was so cold. I'm a bit short of money because I used all I had to come here. I didn't even have enough to buy something to eat. Like I said, I'm hungry, so when we get to the hotel, I want breakfast."

They turned onto Commercial Street. Early morning shoppers were out on the street, some rushing and others moseying along, all bundled in their warmest coats and hats. They passed one block where a line of several horse-drawn wagons had parked along the plank walkway and farmers were selling produce from their wagon beds. Margaret was amazed, "It's winter! How can they have produce to sell?"

"Oh, they have last year's apples, potatoes, sweet potatoes, herbs and stuff like that." The wagons held a lot of bulging burlap sacks.

When Margaret turned away from looking at the vegetables, she cried, "That bank! I know it! Somehow I thought everything would be so different that I would not recognize Salem." On Commercial and State's southeast corner was a beautiful building with dozens of twelve-foot-tall arched windows on two sides and with the same windows on the second floor. The sign stated:

LADD AND BUSH BANK – 1869
SALEM'S FIRST FINANCIAL INSTITUTION

Margaret was bubbling with excitement. "I see other buildings I know. And there in the distance is the church spire of the Methodist Church."

Mary Ann said, "Course it is. We was married there with you as our witness."

Margaret didn't seem to be listening. "Can we go where I had my storefront? Back in 1869 when they were building this bank, I razed my wooden store and built a brick one and I put a big window facing the street so I could show my dresses that I sewed."

Mary Ann blurted, "Yes, we know. We was here." Albert looked over Margaret's head at his wife. They exchanged sad looks.

They went only a block. Margaret pointed. "See, that's my place just north of the Starkey-McCully Building." The Starkey building stretched almost the whole block and went from address number 223 to 233 on Commercial Street. "See all the cast iron decorations on Starkey's? Asa McCully and John L. Starkey built this place in 1867 with money from the California gold rush. They wanted it to be a bit fancy and hired people in Portland to make the pineapple motif ironwork done in the upper corners. Oh, Albert, can we go around the block so I can see more?"

Albert relented to Margaret's excitement, "I'll go around a few blocks, but remember all of us are very hungry."

As they passed places that Margaret knew, she explained what they were. Since all three of them had lived in Salem when most of these buildings were built, Albert and Mary Ann knew most of details, but let Margaret talk and she explained, "That's the Holman Building, built in 1857. It was the legislative hall after the Capitol building had burned in 1855. Most of Oregon's laws were passed there."

They turned back onto State Street and Margaret pointed to the Smith and Wade Building, built in 1870, and the J.K. Gill Building from 1868 at 356 State Street. Margaret explained, "On the upper floors of the Gill Building was the first Presbyterian Church of Salem."

When they turned back onto Commercial Street, Margaret saw the Dearborn Building at 110 Commercial Street and said that it had taken two years to build it from 1868 to 1870.

As they turned to go to the hotel, they passed the Reed Opera House on Court and Liberty Streets. Margaret stated emphatically, "This is the Reed Opera House that was built in 1870. The third floor holds the Oregon Supreme Court and State Library, the second floor has a 1,500 seat auditorium, and you can see on the first floor are shops along the street. This is the end of the tour; I am too hungry to go on."

Albert and Mary Ann glanced at the other again and rolled their eyes.

Finally they arrived at the Marion Hotel. Albert and Mary Ann offered to help Margaret get down. Margaret stood with her cane in her hand and frowned, "Git! Just git away. When I can't move by myself, I plan just to stop and die. Until then, let me get down alone." Margaret pushed some hinged steps that flipped down and then she turned, gathered her skirt into her arms, and backed down out of the wagon. "There! I'm slow, but I can still take care of myself." Hobbling along with her cane, Margaret continued to give directions, "Right now, you come put my bag in the room."

"You are in room number five on the first floor," Albert explained. "You and Mary Ann go to the dining room. I'll check you in and meet you there."

"Now, Albert," Margaret scolded, "you're intelligent enough to know I need to go to the room after a long trip. Mary Ann can take the bag and come with me." They arrived at room number five, and Margaret pulled out the chamber pot from under the bed. "You can be on your way and give me some privacy now."

Opening the door to leave the room, Mary Ann shook her head and grinned. Back at the table in the dining room, the couple chatted about Margaret. "I think she is almost seventy years old, so we should expect to see some forgetfulness."

Albert agreed, "But you can't feel sorry for her; she still has all her spunk. Her sharp tongue is the same as always."

When Margaret arrived to the table, Albert said, "We took a room with two beds and hoped that you would allow Mary Ann to stay the first night with you. She has never stayed at a hotel. It would be quite a treat for her."

"Of course, of course. Albert, you are paying for the room, aren't you?" When he nodded, Margaret continued, "Then I cannot refuse."

A waiter came and took their order for breakfast.

"Oh, I must tell you why I wanted to come to Salem. You must have wondered." Margaret didn't wait for their response and continued, "I wanted to find my husband, Dr. Bailey. I wrote to Dr. Tolmie, who used to work at Fort Vancouver, to find my Willy, but I didn't wait for him to answer because I had written to you and wanted to come myself. If I can find Willy, I want to see and talk to him.

"Oh!" Albert hesitated and then explained, "I don't think there is an easy way to tell you all the things that have happened, but you need to know ...." He hesitated and emphasized, "You need to know the truth. So I'll tell you all the bad news quickly.

"Dr. Bailey died five years ago. In fact, Joe Meek and Doc have died as well. Do you remember the letter we read that told us that Rebecca died about ten years ago?" Mary Ann turned to glance at Margaret, who gazed ahead without visible emotion.

"I see," Margaret sighed. She took Mary Ann's hand, "No one lives on. We all get old and die." With her other hand, she clutched Albert's. "It's just you two and me."

Albert sat straighter and in a bright voice said, "But you're wrong; there are other friends. Mary Jane Holmes lives here in Salem. After you moved to Seattle, her fist husband, Reuben Shipley, came down with smallpox and died. She remarried a Mr. Drake and had a houseful again with his four children and her six. They lived in her spacious house where she lived with Reuben. Do you remember Reuben's home where she lived for years and years?"

Margaret frowned and then looked up, "I think I do. I would like to meet Mr. Drake."

Mary Ann kicked Albert under the table before she said, "This is confusing for you, I's sure. Mr. Drake died after they's married only a couple of months. With no father, the stepboys were too much for Mary Jane. Remember, we told you that two of the Drake boys live wit us."

"But you said that Mr. Drake had four boys. Where are the others?"

Albert shook his head. "We should not have started this history. The two older Drake boys died by the rope. The oldest was convicted of murder and hanged; the other was lynched in 1877 over an argument among gamblers."

"Lynched!" Margaret exclaimed, "Oregon has people who lynch? Did the authorities arrest the lynchers?"

Mary Ann looked to Albert with unspoken words. "No, they didn't." And then she insisted, "Please no more talk about this. This was years ago and we can do nothing 'bout it. Please, we have so much good news. No more sad news."

Their food arrived and Albert was surprised that Margaret acquiesced to Mary Ann's request. He said, "Louis Southworth married and I invited him and his wife to come tomorrow. Of course, I invited his fiddle to come with him, too."

Margaret rotated her bent upper body, as an old person does, to glance at Albert, "Oh, I shall enjoy seeing him. I hesitate to say that I will enjoy meeting his wife. Does she live?"

Albert let out a roar of laughter.

Mary Ann leaned closer to Margaret and giggled. "She does."

Albert contained his mirth to say, "Yes, you are the Margaret I know with your wry sense of humor. Let's eat for a while with no talk. I do have more to tell you though."

When Albert finished the last morsel on his plate, he pushed back his chair, appearing to get ready to talk.

Margaret held up her hands, "Me first. Not that I am admitting that I am old, but I am all tuckered out from the trip. I would like to nap by myself in room number five, if I may. We can get together later and then Mary Ann can spend the night with me. All right, now you can speak, Albert."

He chuckled, "Thank you, Mrs. Bailey." He grinned, "Don't reprimand me. It is your rule that I call you Mrs. Bailey in public."

"Well, I married a Mr. Crane in Seattle, but I refuse to discuss anything about him. Call me Mrs. Bailey. I feel like Mrs. Bailey here in Salem.

"I wanted to let you know that I wrote a letter to George Luther Boone and invited him and his wife to come see you, as well. I did not have an answer. I told him that we are having a grand get-together at my house tomorrow. I hope he makes it. He is still living on the Pacific Coast. Oh, and his wife still lives. Her name is Mourning Ann, in case you didn't know.

"We'll have a fine get-together tomorrow, eating and remembering our fun times. Mary Ann will love to hear all the stories about our adventures being told by you and the other guests. Too bad that Joe Meek can't join us to tell his tall tales and Doc to quote Shakespeare to us. But, if we tell their stories, it will be like they are here with us."

Mary Ann said, "We'll be goin' now so you can have a nap. Albert is goin' to buy some fixings for our celebration tomorrow. And I'm going home to start cookin' for it. We'll be back later. After you nap, would you come to our house and help me do some cookin'?"

"Of course."

In bed that night at the hotel, Mary Ann let her thoughts randomly review the day and she remembered something she wanted to ask. In the dark she whispered, "Margaret, are you awake?"

"I am now."

Mary Ann was glad the darkness made it impossible for Margaret to see because she smiled at the cantankerous old woman's terse reply and then asked, "Would you tell me about the other Mary Anne?"

"I'm an old woman and yet I remember we talked with you many times about her. Don't you remember?"

"Yes, I do," Mary Ann took a deep breath, "but I want to know her like I'd met her. No one really wanted to tell me about her. 'specially not Albert."

Margaret interrupted with the clicking of her tongue, "Tsk, tsk, tsk! Don't assume we didn't want to tell you anything. I can't say for the others, but for me, I didn't worry that you would be jealous or hurt or anything. It's just that I didn't want to dwell on Mary Anne because it hurts me to talk about her. I imagine the others think the same. She disappeared from one minute to the next and we didn't even notice anything."

"What do you mean?"

Irritated, Margaret led Mary Ann through some logic, "Now, if you had a little runaway girl come to you because she was being abused by the men in her family and then you didn't protect her, how would you feel? No need to answer. I'm just telling you why I didn't talk much about her in the past. Most of us felt guilty. We didn't protect her.

"Possibly Albert has different reasons not to talk much. He fell in love with this pretty and loveable girl. She sang like a meadowlark and loved him as deeply as he did her. Why would he want to say those things that might hurt you? Do you understand?"

"Oh, I do. I not asking why you didn't talk before. I jus' want to know her like I'd met her. Can't you tell me more?"

"No!" Margaret turned onto her side and faced the wall. Her voice was muffled but irritated as she asked, "May I sleep now?" A minute passed and, in a fervid voice filled with shame, she said, "Mary Ann, thanks for being here for me. I'm excited like a child about tomorrow. I am so happy knowing I will see all these people who were in my life. I will become sad if I talk about her. Please forgive me; I have become a harridan."

"I forgive you. Let's sleep."

The next morning Albert arrived in the wagon and knocked at room number five. Through the door he said, "Are you ready for church?" He didn't wait for a response. "I'll wait in the lobby."

On the short drive over to the Methodist Episcopal Church, Margaret commented, "The snow looks like it is here to stay. I hope you have a nice warm house."

After church, they headed to the Bayless home. As he turned onto River Street, Albert said, "Look, a wagon. Someone has arrived. When they entered the house, it smelled of the baked beans and ham they had prepared for this day. Louis and his wife were there. Within a few minutes, Mary Jane arrived with her parents, Robin and Polly.

As the women started preparing the table, Louis got out his fiddle. "I'll start with the religious songs since it being Sunday. Now everybody sing."

He began with *Amazing Grace*.

Albert stopped in his tracks before peering over at Margaret who sat at the table pealing some hardboiled eggs. Their eyes locked as the room filled with singing voices. For Margaret and Albert the song became one clear singular voice singing from their memories – Mary Anne's voice in the Nez Percé tent so many years ago. Neither of them moved until the song ended. They glanced at the other again with melancholy eyes. Finally they smiled and continued their tasks.

All of a sudden, the front door burst open and an old George Luther Boone rushed in with his arms full; he carried a crate. His wife followed with a basket over the crook of her arm. He shouted, "You didn't start without us, did you?"

Margaret called out, "Close that door! Now come give me a hug and introduce me to your bride. How could you have married so many years ago and not have introduced me?"

George Luther put the crate on the floor and stood to remove his coat. "I brought canned salmon. Enough for today and enough for all of you to take some home. Scowloads of salmon are taken right in front of our house in Yaquina Bay. We get them canned. Bears come into our front yard and head to the water to get salmon. So I get a couple of bear to eat each year, too. But I didn't bring any bear today."

Mourning Ann placed the basket on the table and said in a soft voice, "These are some of our apples from the last harvest."

George Luther burst with pride when he said, "I put the first orchard in Yaquina Bay with a grafted apple twig. Have over a thousand bushels every year. And you won't find a worm in any of them. Why, I pay anyone a dollar apiece for any worm that can be found."

The room filled with laughter as plates were filled with food. And the afternoon progressed with conversations that had been waiting for years to be said to their friends.

After a couple of hours, people had stopped going back to fill their plates and Mary Ann stood to start gathering dirty dishes.

Margaret still was seated at the table. As she reached to her waistband where she usually tucked a handkerchief, she said, "Oh, I forgot my hanky."

Mary Ann now had a stack of dirty dishes and turned to Albert.

"Please get one of my hankies for her. I keep them in the top left drawer. Reach way in the back."

The two Drake boys were arguing about something or other and Albert told them to calm down before he left the room for the bedroom. The boys stopped only for the moment; once Albert was out of sight, they started bickering again.

Mary Ann called out to Albert, "Pick a nice one." And she faced Margaret to say, "I keep my hankies until they is ragged 'cuz they work jus' as good."

Most everyone sat around the table except Louis, who had started playing the fiddle again and the Holmeses who had eaten while sitting on the sofa. Albert had pushed it close to the table to have everyone in the same room.

A minute passed.

Mary Ann came to get more dirty dishes. She glanced to the open bedroom door. Albert was taking too long.

George Luther was bragging about his place again. "We have climbing yellow roses that bloom all year round. And there is tall pampas grass with plumes that sway in the sea breezes. Why, we found this man who trims our young fir trees into fanciful shapes with sheep shears; he made one look like a bear standing on his rear legs."

Their bedroom was next to the room where everyone sat and Mary Ann called out again, "Can't ya find 'em?" She was pouring more coffee into Margaret's cup when Albert appeared in the bedroom doorway. He stood with his hands in front of him. His left hand had a handkerchief hanging from it, but he clutched something in his right hand. He stood there not moving with a baffled look on his face.

One by one, people noticed something was wrong. Margaret looked up at Albert and froze with her coffee cup raised. She didn't drink. She knew him well enough to know he was upset.

Mary Ann saw Margaret's face and turned to look at Albert. She placed the hot coffee pot onto the table and nervously wiped her hands on her apron before asking, "What's wrong?"

Now the two boys stopped their bickering and looked to the doorway.

When all heads turned, George Luther stopped his banter.

The room was bright with the sunlight and the reflecting snow lit it more. The room was silent except for a crow complaining from the tall tree in the yard and a dog barking in the distance. Finally Albert moved. He took a hesitant step toward the table and then another. He was blinking more than usual.

Before he spoke, he swallowed and everyone could hear. In a soft voice that quivered, he said, "I reached all the way into the back of the drawer and felt something hard. I grabbed it and pulled out this box covered with handkerchiefs." He placed the box in the middle of the table and collapsed into his chair.

As the box touched the table and his hand was pulled away, exposing it, Margaret gasped and put her hands to her heart. "Lord in heaven!"

Mary Ann repeated her question, "What's wrong?"

No one answered.

Of the twelve people in the room, seven had been at the Newell's house the night that Mary Anne had disappeared. Those seven people knew what they saw.

The tinderbox!

It was Mary Anne's tinderbox from her Grandpappy. Everyone could see M c A L I S T E R punched across the tin top.

Margaret looked pale and stuttered, trying to find the words to begin to understand. "How? Why? Where did you ...?"

Albert was at a loss of understanding as well. He looked to his wife and finally found a question to ask. In a quivering and quiet voice, he asked, "How did this get into your handkerchief drawer?"

Mary Ann opened her mouth to speak and blinked. She didn't know what the fuss was all about. She asked a third time, "What's wrong?"

Margaret put down her coffee cup. She saw fear mixed with confusion in the face of Mary Ann. "Of course, you don't even know what this is, do you, Mary Ann." It was a statement, not a question. "Last night, you asked me to tell you about Mary Anne. You don't know that this is Mary Anne's tinderbox given to her by her beloved grandfather. Obviously, no one even told you that her full name was Mary Anne McAlister, or you would have known whose this was."

Mary Ann made a gulp. "No!" The dirty plate in her hand fell onto the table and it appeared that she was going to topple.

Albert wrapped his arms around her. He helped her to a chair and gently asked, "How did you get this tinderbox? I am so confused. How is it possible that you have this tinderbox?"

Now Mary Ann had tears in her eyes. Albert gave her the handkerchief that he had fetched. She blew her nose and started to sob, "Oh my goodness. I met Mary Anne." She looked up to her husband and repeated the revelation. "I met Mary Anne! Yes, I met her, but didn't know it. I didn't learn her name." She leaned over to her husband and put her head on his shoulder as she sobbed.

Margaret stood with her cane, hobbled over to Mary Ann, and caressed her hair. "Calm down. It seems you hold the secret that we all want to know. Take your time. In the meantime, I'm going for another handkerchief." Tap, tap, tap went the cane as she went to the bedroom. She said aloud but to herself, "Top left hand drawer."

Everyone waited. Even those who had never met Mary Anne knew the story of her disappearance. Even the two Drake boys.

In a weak voice, Mary Ann said, "Albert, I don't know how to start."

"Why not start a little before the day you met her. Make it a story, you know, like ones that are in the books I read to you."

Mary Ann nodded and dabbed her eyes. After she blew her nose again, she started. "All of you know that my husband and two girls died in a fire. So I needed to start a new life and came with my two boys on a wagon train arriving here in Oregon back in sixty-four. I met Mary Anne on that trip.

"Now, I don't know where we were exactly. After we left Missouri, we traveled for weeks or maybe even a month or two, it was before we got to mountains. We camped one evening and I saw a cabin in the distance. Me and another lady decided to walk to the cabin and see if someone lived there.

"It was out in the middle of nowhere. The land was all dry and flat. When we approached the cabin, it was still daylight. I remember there was one tree in the yard, but only sagebrush growing everywhere else. When we were closer, I saw two bodies on the ground. The other lady ran back to get help. I went on and found a white man dead and a dying woman. He was on his side, kind of curled with his arms sprawling this way and that. She was on her back and it was hard to tell if she was a Negro. She had curly hair, but not kinky like mine. Her skin was beautiful; I think I've heard people call that kind of skin, almond-colored. Mostly, I remember that she was pretty.

"He had been shot in the face and chest. A knife was on the ground near his hand. She was stabbed somewhere in the front. Her dress was so bloody I couldn't tell where she was stabbed. I got on my knees close to her because she saw me and was talking. I couldn't hear her until I got my face close to hers. She was clutching something on her chest. Her hands was all bloody, but I could see she held a gun. Finally she moved her other hand and held out this tinderbox. She said, 'Take it.' So, I took it. Then she asked, 'Oregon?' I told her we were going to Oregon and she smiled. She had such a pretty smile."

Tears were streaming down Albert's face. Margaret held one of her hands in a fist to her mouth.

Mary Ann's voice was soft and everyone sat transfixed, not wanting to move and cause a noise. She continued, "She started saying something that I did not understand. It sounded like she said, 'For Beagle,' and I asked her again. She repeated, 'For Beagle,' again and again." Mary Ann blew her nose. Her tears continued flowing. "Then she died."

The silence continued. No one had assimilated the story enough to comment.

Mary Ann wiped her eyes and turned to her husband. "Remember, Albert, I asked you if you knew a family called Beagle?"

He shook his head, "No, I don't remember."

"You told me to ask Joe Meek who knew so many people. He didn't know them either. Who is Beagle?"

Margaret looked to Albert. "I can see you don't understand. You don't know what it means."

Albert shook his head again, "No, I don't. Why did she say that?"

Margaret face brightened and she leaned forward with a grin. "She didn't say the word *Beagle*. She said, 'For Big Al,' to you, Mary Ann."

Albert dropped his head into his hands, "Yes, that makes sense. She used to call me *Big Al*." He turned to face the people in the room to clarify why she used that name. "Joe Meek named me *Big Al* on our trip to Celilo

Falls." Albert reached out and pulled Mary Ann to him. He stood with her in his arms. "You have ended this mystery. You have ended the pain I have felt for years." He kissed her forehead and rocked with her in his arms. "Do you realize what you have given me? I had feared that I would die not knowing what happened to Mary Anne."

His short, little wife cocked her head back and looked up at him. She nodded.

He said to everyone, "I used to think that I made my own destiny. Ha! I have lived for seventeen years with the woman who had the answer to this mystery. I took no action on my own to solve it. If Margaret had not needed to blow her nose, I would never have learned the answer to where Mary Anne went."

Everyone laughed except Margaret. She asked, "So what are you saying?"

Boldly, Albert proclaimed, "The unbeknownst holds a power over us. We can only control our own destiny through knowledge. We must seek knowledge."

George Luther spoke up, "To quote Doc Newell 'All's well that ends well.'"

Margaret shook her head, "Not Robert Newell, Shakespeare said that."

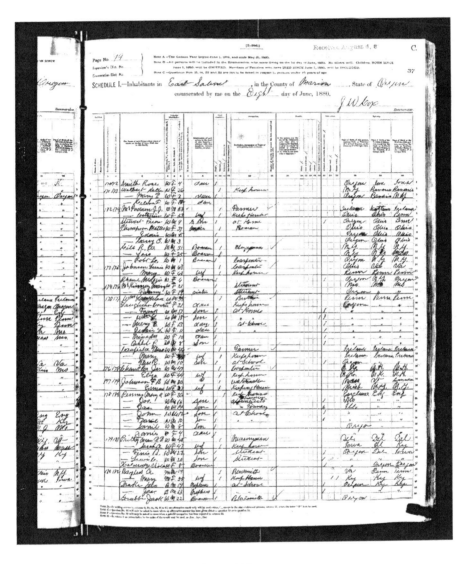

Page of the census of the United States from 1880
Albert Bayless and people living in his home are the last entries on the page.

EPILOGUE

Beaver Coins: The dies that were supposed to be flung off a rock at Willamette Falls, were later found (date unknown) by D. P. Thompson when cleaning out some rubbish in an old building that had been used by the Campbell and Smith Company in Oregon City. They were taken to a vault of the Secretary of State of Oregon and remain there as highly prized possessions of the state. The rolling mill was thought to have been taken south to the Umpqua region, but remains unaccounted for. Only a few of the original Beaver Coins are known to exist; they are mostly in private collections.

A letter from August 4, 1865 to the Honorable Samuel E. May, Secretary of State of Oregon was written by J.G. Campbell who stated that he was sending the dies made by W.H. Rector and Hamilton Campbell to the Secretary. However, "If you do not see proper to so dispose of the dies, please return them to me by a safe hand."

Albert Bayless: He lived in Salem for forty years with his wife Mary Ann. They both died in April of 1907 at the age of 84 and within one week of the other. Albert died first and friends said that Mary Ann died from grief. As shown in the 1880 census, two of Mary Jane Holmes' stepchildren (George and James Drake by her second marriage) lived in the Bayless home, although they were listed erroneously as nephews. Also, a white boy named Jack Grubb, whom they raised, was listed in the census as a boarder; Albert had taught him to be a blacksmith.

Joe Meek: After 1852, he was not elected again for U.S. marshal or other positions in the government. Joe's generosity toward others continued; immigrants who arrived without food, shelter, or means to obtain sustenance were welcomed at Joe and Virginia Meek's home. It has been written that no one was ever turned away. In 1855, he volunteered for duty in the Indian Wars; after a confrontation with a new colonel when he fired his rifle in camp, he requested to be discharged from the army and retired to his farm in the Tualatin Plains. This was a time of quiet in his life when the children and settlers called him *Uncle Joe*. The only excitement recorded in his remaining years were the arguments with local preachers in his neighborhood.

Margaret: Little is known after her divorce from Waddle, but she opened her Salem home to care for some girls because the 1870 census showed Martha Hyatt (20 years old) and Nelly Wilson (5 years old) living with her. Nothing is known of her time in Seattle from the time when she married Mr. Crane until her death in 1882.

Louis Southworth: In 1869, he lived in Buena Vista, opened a blacksmith shop, married, and learned to read and write with the help of the principal of Buena Vista Academy.

The two Chief Josephs: In 1871, Young Chief Joseph (1840-1904) succeeded his father, who was then called, Old Chief Joseph (1785-1871). Before the elder Joseph died he counseled his son with these words:

> My son, my body is returning to my mother earth, and my spirit is going very soon to see the Great Spirit Chief. When I am gone, think of your country. You are the chief of these people. They look to you to guide them. Always remember that your father never sold his country. You must stop your ears whenever you are asked to sign a treaty selling your home. A few years more and white men will be all around you. They have their eyes on this land. My son, never forget my dying words. This country holds your father's body. Never sell the bones of your father and your mother.

Young Joseph, whose real name was *Heinmot Tooyalakekt* (pronounced: Hin-mah Too-yah-lat-kekt*)* and means Thunder rolling down the mountains, commented: "I clasped my father's hand and promised to do as he asked. A man who would not defend his father's grave is worse than a wild beast."

The Nez Percé were forcibly removed from their ancestral lands in the Wallowa Valley in northeastern Oregon and told to live farther to the northeast in a significantly reduced reservation in Idaho Territory. Young Chief Joseph resisted through 1877 in what became known as the Nez Percé War. The skill and manner of their fight produced widespread recognition and admiration not only among their military adversaries but also among the American public. At one point, Young Chief Joseph led his people to find asylum with Chief Sitting Bull of the Sioux. He never relinquished his principles against the removal and is renowned as a humanitarian and peacemaker to this day.

In 1926, Oregon voters finally repealed the constitution's exclusion clause for Negroes.

Celilo Falls
Circa 1950

Native Americans fishing from wooden structures that they built.

In 1957, Celilo Falls disappeared beneath the waters from the damming of the Columbia River at The Dalles Dam.

Author's Note

For support and editing along the way, I would like to thank and commend two extraordinary people: Dave Picray who has a keen eye and mind – along with experiences from skinning bears to measuring gold – that allows him to find errors like no one else; and Joy Fargo who knows grammar and the English language backwards and forwards.

A special word of thanks goes to the historical societies for answering my many questions and for providing facts and materials: Benton County Historical Society, Clackamas Family History Society Inc., Marion County Historical Society, New York Historical Society, and Oregon Historical Society in Portland.

These are the main books and papers that I used to develop the history and views of Oregon: George Guy Delamarter, *The Career of Robert Newell* (1951); Caroline Dobbs, *Men of Champoeg* (1993); John A. Hussey, *Champoeg: A Place of Transition – A Disputed History* (1967); James W. Loewen, *Lies My Teacher Told Me (1995);* Sheridan McCarthy and Stanton Nelson, *Perseverance* (2011); R. Gregory Nokes, *Breaking Chains: Slavery on Trial in the Oregon Territory* (2013); Francis Parkman, Jr., *The Oregon Trail* (1849); Roscoe Sheller, *Ben Snipes-Northwest Cattle King* (1957); T. Elmer Strevey, *The Oregon Mint;* Lee Sturdivant and Tim Blakley, *Medicinal Herbs in the Garden, Field & Marketplace (1999);* Harvey Elmer Tobie, *No Man Like Joe: The Life and Times of Joseph L. Meek* (1949); Frances Fuller Victor, *The River of the West (1869);* Tricia Martineau Wagner, *African American Women of the Old West (2007);* Howard Zinn, *A People's History of the United States 1492-Present (1999);* and Margaret Jewett Bailey, *The Grains or Passages in the Life of Ruth Rover, with Occasional Pictures of Oregon, Natural and Moral* (1854) that was republished with copyright by Oregon State University Press and with editing by Evelyn Leasher and Robert J. Frank (1986).